Acclaim for Suzanne Adair

Deadly Occupation
"Thick with intrigue and subplots to keep readers guessing."
—Caroline Clemmons, author of the "Kincaids" series

Regulated for Murder
"Best of 2011" from Suspense Magazine:

"This is mystery writing at its best."
—Great Historicals

A Hostage to Heritage
winner of the Indie Book of the Day Award:

"Suzanne Adair is on top of her game with this one."
—Jim Chambers, Amazon Hall of Fame Top 10 Reviewer

Books by Suzanne Adair

Michael Stoddard American Revolution Mysteries
Deadly Occupation
Regulated for Murder
A Hostage to Heritage
Killer Debt

Mysteries of the American Revolution
Paper Woman
The Blacksmith's Daughter
Camp Follower

A Hostage to Heritage

Suzanne Adair

Suzanne Adair

A Michael Stoddard American Revolution Mystery

Acknowledgements

I receive help from some wonderful and unique people while conducting research for novels and editing my manuscripts. Here are a few who assisted me with *A Hostage to Heritage*:

The 33rd Light Company of Foot, especially Ernie and Linda Stewart

Marg Baskin

Dr. Jerry C. Cashion

Robert M. Dunkerly

Mike Everette

Nolin and Neil Jones

Joseph Moseley

Lara Neilson

Jenny Toney Quinlan

John Robertson

Susan Schreyer

Lourdes Venard

Special thanks to Ava Barlow for cover photography; to Ava Barlow and Jenny Toney Quinlan for cover design; and to Karen Phillips for interior design.

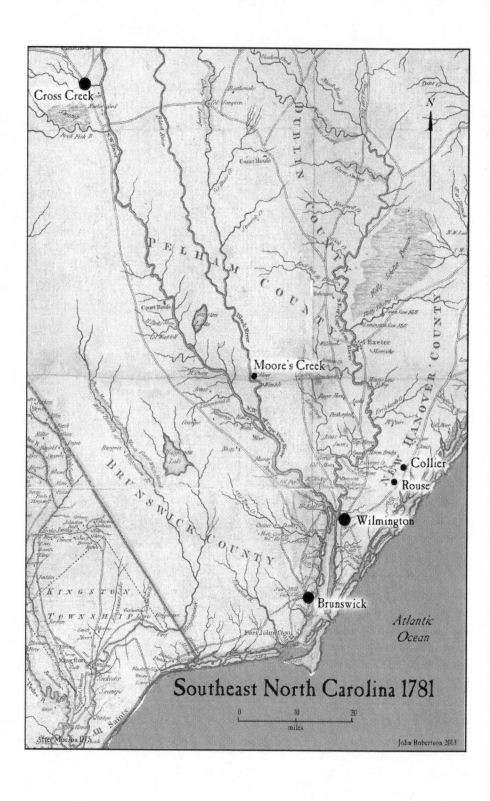

Cross Creek

DUBLIN COUNTY

N

PELHAM COUNTY

Moore's Creek

NEW HANOVER COUNTY

Collier

Rouse

Wilmington

BRUNSWICK COUNTY

Brunswick

Atlantic
Ocean

KINGSTON
TOWNSHIP

Southeast North Carolina 1781

0   10   20
miles

After Mouzon 1775

John Robertson 2013

Few men have virtue to withstand the highest bidder.
~George Washington

Chapter One

BY THE TIME the road to Cabbage Inlet had straightened out to a sand-and-shell ribbon south of Wilmington, patriot "Devil Bill" Jones and his accomplice, Captain James Love, had widened their lead over the five mounted men from the Eighty-Second Regiment. Lieutenant Michael Stoddard cantered his mare around the final crook in the road, spotted his quarry picking up speed one-eighth mile ahead, and twisted in the saddle. "We have 'em, lads!"

A brisk March breeze briny with Atlantic Ocean whipped the words from his mouth. He waved his patrol of four redcoats onward and kicked Cleopatra into a gallop, two loaded pistols in the saddle holster before him.

Cleopatra gained on the rebels' horses while the thunder of support behind Michael diminished. Low on the mare's neck, his breath paced to hers, he saw Love swivel in the saddle for a look behind. The rebel's gaze snagged on him, and his eyes bugged. In the whistle of wind, Michael heard his shout of warning to Jones. The fugitives' horses put on a burst of speed.

Michael steered Cleopatra around a perilous section of loose sand on the road. Somewhere behind, he heard a soldier curse as his mount stumbled in the sand, what Love and his cohorts called "sand shuffling." Michael grimaced but maintained his mare's gallop. For several weeks, Jones and Love had made it their sport to ride pell-mell through the streets of Wilmington and discharge their carbines at soldiers and sentries of the Eighty-Second Regiment—even at civilians who got in their way. Michael closed the distance between himself and the outlaws.

Pistol in hand, Jones contorted in his saddle to fire toward Michael. The ball went wide, into salt marsh studded with longleaf pines, but Cleopatra flinched at the noise. Michael steadied her and pressed her to keep galloping, despite the fact that he no longer heard the thunder of his team's support.

On their raids through town, Jones and Love had moved so quickly that no one had been able to pursue them. This time, Michael and his four men had been returning from a trip when Jones and Love paid their respects. The regiment might never have another opportunity to chase the rascals on horseback, so Michael stayed on the criminals, less than fifty feet ahead. He could taste their apprehension, flung back to him on the salty afternoon air.

When he was but thirty feet behind his quarry, their horses jumped a small patch of treacherous sand. Cleopatra followed suit. Jones squirmed around for a second pistol shot. Michael heard the ball whine through air near his right ear and thwack off the trunk of a pine tree. Cleopatra's stride faltered. Michael put his heel to her to encourage her forward, cocked one of his pistols, sighted, and, despite the odds, squeezed the trigger.

Jones cried out and clutched his upper right arm, fouling the rhythm of his gallop. His horse startled, almost stumbled. At a command from Love, the men veered off south into a sea of wind-beaten marsh grass, where a man could lose his life and that of his mount in a moment to the suck of sand. Michael galloped past their departure point by more than sixty feet. When he'd brought the heaving Cleopatra about, the criminals had split up. Jones was riding due south, and Love was headed southeast, both on terrain they knew as well as their own palms.

God damn it. Although the rebels were probably out of range, Michael snatched the other pistol from its holster, took aim, and fired at Love. Both rebels rode on. Michael seized his breath and bellowed into the pistol's report, "Whoresons!" He jammed the pistol, stinking of sulfur, back in the holster. Then he yanked off his hat, raked a sweaty sprawl of dark hair off his brow, and shoved the hat back on his head.

While he paced Cleopatra back and forth on the road and glowered after the escaped rebels, one of his soldiers trotted into view, he and his horse winded. A quarter minute later, another private caught up with them and shook his head at the fugitives, mere specks amidst pines and wavy marsh grass. "Sorry, sir. They were just too fast for us. And their horses know how to run in the sand."

The other man said, "Jackson's and Stallings's mounts went down back there, sir. I sure hope we don't have to shoot the beasts."

The Eighty-Second had few horses. Another grimace pulled at Michael's face before he composed his expression. "I gave Mr. Jones a kiss of the pistol ball. Maybe those scoundrels will think twice about resuming their sport in Wilmington."

Tension eased from the privates' faces. "Yes, sir," they said in unison.

"We've done what we can this afternoon, lads. Let's see to those horses." After a final glare southward, Michael patted Cleopatra's neck and headed her toward town, his shoulders straight to project confidence he didn't feel.

Two escaped rebels. Two injured horses. Major James Henry Craig wasn't going to like the news his lead investigator brought back to Wilmington.

***

Twenty minutes later a sentry bumped out on a broad-backed workhorse in search of Michael. Major Craig had demanded Lieutenant Stoddard's presence at his headquarters. Immediately.

Leaving the two mounted infantrymen and two unhorsed soldiers walking their lamed geldings, Michael trotted on ahead, the sentry clomping along after. He didn't push Cleopatra after her run, allowing her instead to enjoy one of the most temperate spring afternoons North Carolina offered. From the sound of it, ill humor had already found his commanding officer over the business of Jones and Love, so he saw no point in hastening to the inevitable ear blistering.

He dismounted before the house on Market Street where Major Craig's headquarters was located, secured Cleopatra at the post, and checked a watch drawn from his waistcoat pocket. Ten minutes to four. Craig had said, "Immediately." Michael replaced the watch, straightened his scarlet coat, and swatted road dust from sleeves and breeches. Not much he could do about three days' stubble on his face that moment.

Twelve men, two runner boys, and a gossipy goodwife named Alice Farrell had queued up the walkway and front steps, waiting their turn to speak with the Eighty-Second's commander. As Michael strode for the steps, they spotted him. Jabber silenced. Most expressions adopted the guise of a neutral mask. The crowd of supplicants parted for Michael as if he were Moses at the shore of the Red Sea. At the top of the steps, the provost marshal's guard shoved the door open with a squeak of hinges.

Had Major Craig somehow already received word about the escape of Jones and Love and the incapacitation of the horses? Michael's parched tongue skidded over his lips. Grit crunched beneath the soles of his riding boots during his trudge up the steps to the porch. He wiped his boot soles at the threshold.

The guard jerked his head toward the dark maw of the house interior. "Private Spry arrived just before you did, sir."

Michael frowned at the guard, then at the inside of the house. Why had his assistant investigator also been summoned? This didn't bode well. Muscles in his stomach twisted.

After removing his hat, he entered the house and eased out a pent-up breath. One of the study's double wooden doors was open. Inside, his commander stood at the north window, one hand on his hip, gazing out toward a pen packed with rebel prisoners. At a small table near where Craig usually sat, his adjutant scratched out a letter to the major's dictation, the quill-to-ink motion a blur.

Creaky floorboards announced Michael's entrance. His tall eighteen-year-old assistant from Nova Scotia, Nick Spry, stood at ease, away from the doors. Spry nodded once to Michael before resuming his attention on Craig. Michael stepped one pace toward him and held a salute for Major Craig, hat in his left hand.

Mid-sentence, Craig glanced over his shoulder. He squashed his lips together at the sight of Michael. Then the short, stocky commander of the Eighty-Second snatched the top paper off a pile on the table and, while traversing the study to Michael, completed his sentence about a desperate need for bandages. Michael's salute acknowledged, Craig thrust the paper at him, and motioned Spry to join Michael. Then he resumed his stance at the window.

His next sentence of dictation was a request for willow bark and other medicines to reduce fever and inflammation in hundreds of wounded soldiers. Paper in hand, Michael blinked at his commander in puzzlement. From the context, he presumed the recipient of Craig's dictated letter to be Lieutenant Colonel Nisbet Balfour, in Charles Town. Balfour had been generous with such supplies before. But the season for malaria and yellow fever wasn't yet upon them. When he'd left Wilmington three days earlier, only two men were lodged in the infirmary. How did two multiply to hundreds?

Aware of Spry at his elbow, he righted the paper. It was a letter dated exactly one month earlier, 21 February 1781, from the town of Hillsborough, North Carolina. The salutation was to Major Craig. The correspondent was Lord Cornwallis. And despite the clement temperature of the room, a glacier slid down Michael's spine to his feet and froze them to his stockings inside his boots.

In the letter, the Commander in Chief of the Crown's Southern army urgently requested provisions that Major Craig had agreed to provide in January and send on to Cross Creek, eighty miles to the northwest of Wilmington. Cornwallis was still following a plan from January, still dependent on having stores available in Cross Creek for his army. But Cornwallis would never get those supplies.

Rebel interference had prevented Major Craig from establishing the requisite supply depot in Cross Creek. Thus he'd sent Michael to the Hillsborough area as a dispatch runner to find Cornwallis and tell him so. And in the life-threatening peril that had ensued for Michael in Hillsborough, he'd been unable to deliver Craig's warning directly to Cornwallis.

That was, he hadn't delivered it *personally*. He'd transferred the message. The glacier vaporized. Michael crushed the letter in his fist.

Fairfax, that son of a dog! He'd shirked his duty. He hadn't delivered the message!

If it was the last thing that Michael did, he determined to find the dragoon and kill him. Oh, he'd already tried to kill that monster, but he hadn't planned it well. *Next* time—

"Mr. Stoddard, I received Lord Cornwallis's letter in this afternoon's post."

Michael jerked his attention back to Major Craig. Shock rolled over him. He'd been so absorbed in the letter's implications that he hadn't noticed the exit of Craig's adjutant. He, Spry, and Craig were alone, the study doors shut.

"And I find it as disturbing as you do, judging from your expression." Craig sat behind his table and gestured Michael to a chair opposite him. "Sit. We've much to discuss and, as usual, little time."

Michael rolled his shoulders back, smoothed out the letter, and passed it to Spry. As he seated himself, the major shifted his torso to present a profile like that of a Roman senator. With one hand, Craig massaged his jaw, as if he'd been dealt a blow. Then he clasped both hands in his lap. "The letter is a duplicate. Communications have been intercepted prolifically. I presume that his lordship never received the message you relayed in Hillsborough through Lieutenant Fairfax."

Damn Fairfax to hell. Michael unclenched his jaw but kept his voice even. "Reasonable presumption, sir." Instinct had warned him that Fairfax might be arrogant and self-serving enough to not bother with delivering the warning to Cornwallis. Even Spry had expressed doubts that Fairfax would convey the message. But at the time Michael had had no choice but to trust the other officer.

Failure scoured the inside of his gut, gripped the muscles of his abdomen. When he tried to settle against the chair's ladder-back, each vertebra of his spine scraped wood. He should have employed greater effort to make contact with Cornwallis last month.

Craig glanced his way. "Relax, Mr. Stoddard. Several senior officers have assured me of Mr. Fairfax's competence, courage, and dedication. Considering the intensity of combat action endured by the Seventeenth Light Dragoons, I must conclude that Mr. Fairfax was killed in action before he could deliver your message."

Michael started. Behind him, a soft sort of cough-choke sound issued from Spry.

Killed in action? Why, Michael had never considered that. Fairfax had emerged unscathed from so many battles and skirmishes that the cynic in Michael presumed him immortal.

Killed in action. Realizing that his jaw had dropped open, Michael shut his mouth. Knots in his stomach loosened. Surely this was too good to be true. He struggled to keep hope from his face. His cheek twitched with restraint.

Craig processed his expression before resuming his contemplation of the west wall of the study. "You were acquainted with him personally. My condolences."

Michael bowed his head and said what Craig expected to hear. "Thank you, sir."

Killed in action. A shudder of liberation wended through him. The Fates had smiled upon him. And upon Spry, too. His assistant must be squirming to contain his elation. The monster was dead.

But perhaps he'd jumped to conclusions. Craig did have more to tell him. Michael looked up.

The major pushed out a sigh. "Unless I hear otherwise, I shall operate on the assumption that Lord Cornwallis has no knowledge of the infeasibility of Cross Creek as a depot. Should he retreat there for provisions, he will find none. Thus the only refuge he currently has in North Carolina is here, in Wilmington. We must be prepared to accommodate his army for such a turn of events."

"Sir." Michael found his voice at last. And he understood the entreaty to Charles Town for medical supplies.

Craig must want him to courier that letter directly to Balfour. He detested running dispatches, one of the most dangerous jobs in the army. But this would be his penance for failing the mission in Hillsborough. He sat forward and awaited the order.

"The nautical supply line to Charles Town won't adequately provision his lordship's army, should he march here. Therefore, on the morrow, I shall head north with fifty men to supervise the drive of a herd of cattle to Wilmington. I expect to be gone no longer than three weeks."

Michael wiggled a finger in one ear, certain he'd misunderstood. "Cattle, sir?"

Craig assumed his original position facing his subordinate, the corners of his mouth pinched. He steepled fingers on the table and lowered his voice. "Cattle. *And* at least one rebel leader. Word has reached me of where I might find Cornelius Harnett."

"Ah." Muscles in Michael's shoulders relaxed. Harnett had been an aggravation to the Crown as chairman of Wilmington's Sons of Liberty and a member of the Continental Congress. Should circumstances require that Lord Cornwallis retreat to Wilmington, Harnett as Craig's prisoner would mitigate the testiness of his lordship.

"I shall take Captain Gordon and his dragoons with me." The major pressed the palms of his hands on the table. "I heard that you and your patrol gave chase to Captain James Love and William Jones an hour ago." He leaned forward. "How did you fare?"

Thank the gods Craig didn't appear to have heard about the lamed horses. Nine years in the Army had taught Michael to emphasize victories first, no matter how small. "I shot Jones in the right arm."

The major's head drew back, and a smile twisted his lips. "Did you, now? Good show, Mr. Stoddard. Where is Jones? In the pen?"

"No, sir. He and Love escaped into the marsh south of the Cabbage Inlet Road."

Craig's smile dissolved, and he slapped the surface of the table with his palm. "Blast!" He pushed back in his chair. "Jones and Love are a menace to the community, galloping through town, shooting at people. They planned to assassinate me several evenings ago, when I rode out with dragoons.

"Therefore, while I'm gone, Mr. Stoddard, I expect you and Spry to rid Wilmington of the pestilence of 'Devil Bill' Jones and Captain Love. Surely you comprehend how eager I am to see this matter resolved satisfactorily." Craig's gaze upon Michael sharpened like a hot spear of sunlight through a hand lens. His voice lowered. "Are my intentions clear?"

The commander of the Eighty-Second hadn't mentioned the overcrowded jail or pen for the two rebels, or even the belly of a prison ship. He'd used the word "rid." To Craig, Jones and Love were barely worth a noose or a musket ball. He wanted them exterminated like the varmints they were. Spring cleaning, in preparation for Cornwallis's visit.

Michael tracked a momentary drumming, a whisper almost, of Craig's fingertips among papers. What turmoil Jones and Love could inflict upon a Wilmington four times as crowded, its population bloated by Cornwallis's army. Craig wouldn't tolerate Michael's failure to neutralize the rebels. "I understand, sir."

Major Craig drew a breath. "Very good. I'm placing the resources of the Eighty-Second at your disposal for this task. Questions?"

Michael was fully aware that not only did Craig expect him to exterminate Jones and Love, but he also expected a halcyon Wilmington upon his return. All burglars, thieves, drunkards, murderers, and malefactors tidily contained in the pen. Michael's military career was indeed on the line with this assignment. Spry's, too. "None, sir."

"Excellent. You and Spry are dismissed."

***

On the front porch, out of the way of Major Craig's visitors and the marshal's guard, Michael checked his watch again. Only a quarter hour had elapsed since his arrival. He squinted in the westering sunlight. After his assistant had taken up a position beside him, he said softly, "So, Spry, what do you think of Major Craig's opinion that our good friend was killed in action?"

In his peripheral vision, he marked the way Spry drew himself to his full six-foot height, the motion swift and taut, his blond hair a splash of sunlight. Michael's gaze swept across the front yard and out into the street. Five weeks had passed since they'd escaped becoming Fairfax's sport, but neither he nor Spry had completely dropped his guard. A man's bones never forgot a monster's promise.

Spry's tone emerged low, even. "Shakespeare has words for every occasion, sir. For example, ''Tis a consummation devoutly to be wished.' That's from Hamlet's soliloquy."

Michael eyed his assistant and restrained black humor from informing his lips. In five weeks, Spry had learned about tactful communication without overt insubordination. "Act three, scene one."

Spry's gaze met his. "A bit of official confirmation would surely be balm for the soul, sir."

"Agreed, but don't hold your breath for it. Remember, this is the Army." Michael swept his hand outward, to encompass Wilmington. "And we've two cockroaches to corral and squash. Let's have at it."

Chapter Two

THE PREVIOUS WEEK, Major Craig had sent patrols to the homes of Jones and Love. Even before those soldiers returned empty-handed, Michael had known the move was futile. Outlaws always accrued deluded sympathizers who could warn them to flee their residences.

Thus Michael decided to work on the premise that the rogues had patronized local businesses prior to the Eighty-Second's arrival. After he returned Cleopatra to the garrison's stable for grooming, he and Spry paid a call to the overcrowded jail, to an incarcerated gunsmith whom Michael had arrested in early February for contracting with a band of rebel religious fanatics to repair smuggled weapons.

Guards brought the grimy, bearded gunsmith to Michael in the jailer's office, out of earshot of other inmates. Michael informed him that he was scheduled for transfer to the belly of a prison ship anchored just off the coast, to liberate room in the jail for more inmates. As Michael had hoped, the news bowed the gunsmith's shoulders and sent him trembling.

Of course, Michael could delay the transfer a few weeks should the gunsmith provide him with a viable lead to where he and Spry might find a storage facility for weapons he'd delivered to William Jones or James Love.

Minutes later, with the gunsmith locked back in his cell, the two soldiers bustled for the garrison. The location of the barn the gunsmith had named was less than an hour away by horseback. Daylight was waning.

On fresh horses, they galloped south from Wilmington just after four thirty with five armed, mounted infantrymen. Marsh grass to the side of the sand-and-shell road fluttered at their passage, and sea salt tainted the air. From the gunsmith's directions, the patrol found the barn without difficulty. Split, weathered boards bereft of paint gave it a dilapidated, unoccupied appearance. Nevertheless, the soldiers backed off to take cover while dismounting. Each man used shrubs or pines to shield himself as he approached.

No one was about. A search of the interior turned up several worn flints and damp cartridges in the moldy straw on the ground, one tattered haversack used by mice for a home, and a liberal layer of dust over everything. Michael collected the flints and cartridges and shoved them in the haversack. He added a torn, smeared note found by one of the men. It read "...me belongeth vengeance, and recompense...shall slide in due time; for the day of...is at hand, and the things that shall...make haste. Deuteronomy 32:35."

Rebel religion. But no rebel weapons. No Devil Bill. And no Captain Love. Damn.

Six weeks in jail had dated the gunsmith's information. The barn wasn't even worth the effort of surveillance. Exhausted from having spent a day in the saddle, and disappointed at the dead lead, Michael shoved the haversack into his saddlebag and eased his patrol back to Wilmington.

By the time men had been dismissed and horses returned to grooms, full night enveloped the town. Michael and his assistant strode from the stable onto Market Street and headed toward the Cape Fear River, the private carrying Michael's pack from his trip.

They'd walked less than a minute when Michael's stomach moaned. He hadn't sat down to a good meal in three days. A fine thing it was that the Welsh housekeeper where he and Spry were billeted was an excellent cook. The thought of eating one of her suppers eased the sting of not nabbing Jones and Love. "You know, I just might eat the kitchen if Enid doesn't have supper prepared."

"It's still early, sir. She may not have it ready. You can always take the edge off at White's." Spry's grin was audible. "Watch me win my first game in a backgammon tournament that starts tonight."

"A tournament, eh?" Michael smiled. Spry's opponents didn't know it yet, but they were doomed. Observing the competition at White's Tavern on Front Street, water hole of choice for most of the King's men in Wilmington, might make for worthy entertainment while he enjoyed a glass of claret.

"By the bye, sir." One corner of Spry's lips cocked. "Guess who arrived home from Hillsborough the day you left for Brunswick?"

The image of Kate Duncan, owner of White's Tavern, breezed through Michael's thoughts. In particular, he recalled the way her gaze had caressed him at the top of the stairs in her aunt's house his second night in Hillsborough. His smile enlarged to a grin.

"And she brought that feisty aunt of hers, the one who thinks ever so much of you. Sir."

At the thought of encountering both widows again after all they'd been through in Hillsborough, the empty cave of Michael's stomach felt as though five-dozen frantic moths had been trapped inside it. His smile wilted. "Er, perhaps I shall pass on the tavern tonight, Spry."

"Eh? You won't come to White's, sir?"

The moths in Michael's gut took flight all at once, seeking an exit. "No."

The two reached the intersection of Market Street and Second Street. Michael turned onto Second Street and continued walking. After a moment, Spry caught up with him. "But sir, Mrs. White has been nagging me about when you're coming in. And she insists that *I* call her 'Aunt Rachel,' too. Keeps referring to you as a 'hero.'"

Michael's stomach emitted a high-pitched yowl. He slapped a sweaty palm against the racket, then faked a huge yawn. "This 'hero' has been in a saddle all day and wants a clean shirt, Enid's cooking, and a solid night's sleep." He sniffed the air. Unless he was mistaken, that was the aroma of Enid's pork roast. "Just the combination to help me awaken on the morrow with additional strategies for tracking down Jones and Love."

"Ah. You've something else in mind, sir?"

"Of course I do, lad," Michael lied, his faith placed in a solid night's sleep. They stopped walking in front of the residence of the Widow Helen Chiswell, a brick two-story house where they lodged, and Michael faced his assistant. "I forgot to ask earlier. Did you solve the mystery of the missing pig while I was gone?"

"Hardly a mystery, sir. More a case of mistaken identity. Neighbor number two's pig did resemble neighbor number one's pig. Difficult to tell them apart, in fact. But we sorted it out, yes, sir. Returned both pigs to their proper pens. The men shook hands and promised to not bloody each other's noses again. Neither wished to spend a day in the town pen with human swine."

Michael chuckled and clapped his assistant's shoulder. "Good work."

Spry tilted his head a little to one side and sniffed the air, too. "You might be in luck, sir. That smells like Enid's roast."

"It does, indeed. Hand over my pack, run along to White's, and trounce your opponents at backgammon. Give my highest regards to Mrs. Duncan and Mrs. White."

"Yes, sir."

Pack in hand, Michael strolled through the side yard for the kitchen. The moths in his gut settled, vanished. Lamplight spilled from the study window and illuminated a patch of lawn at his feet. Although he didn't glance in, he knew Mrs. Chiswell sat at her desk in the study writing letters.

He emerged in the back yard, where the chimney on the kitchen building pumped out an invitation to sample Enid's roasted pork and root vegetables. Several lamps lit the kitchen interior, and the door was open to the mild spring night. Michael smelled nutmeg and cinnamon competing with pork.

As soon as he entered the kitchen, he spotted the baked tart on the table and sallied straight for it, dropping his pack beside a chair. Enid was nowhere to be seen. She'd never notice one little chunk of crust gone. He'd had plenty of practice at it. He flexed his fingers over the tart.

"Ah, it's you, Mr. Stoddard! You're back in time for supper."

Michael's arm muscles jerked with guilt and annoyance. He lowered his hand to his side and turned to greet the dark-haired woman in her late forties who'd huffed into the kitchen.

With a crash, Enid dropped an empty bucket trailing carrot scrapings to the floor beside the door, then she straightened. Her smile failed to reach her coal-black eyes. She glanced from the tart to him. "Heh. For a moment there, I thought you were Spry. Such a time I've had, keeping his fingers out of my baked sweets while you were gone to Brunswick." Her up-and-down stare scoured him. "Of course, I know *you* wouldn't do such a dishonorable thing

as picking at an old woman's apple tart. You're an officer and a gentleman."
She sniffed in his direction. "But gentleman or no, I'm running you out of my
kitchen until you've washed up proper. Otherwise, you'll make supper stink of
sweaty horses."

"I missed you, too, Enid."

The Welshwoman hiked a thumb over her shoulder, toward the door. "Out,
you. Behind the stable. Give me that pack of yours. I shall bring you warm water, soap, and a towel. And your kit and spare uniform."

Twenty minutes later, no longer in danger of stinking up supper, and minus
the barbarian beard stubble, he peeked through the study's open doorway near
the stairs. Seated at the desk, a slender woman with honey-colored hair was
bent over a letter. Her quill rasped on paper.

Every day since her return several weeks earlier from the South Carolina
hinterlands, Helen Chiswell had spent hours writing letters. She reminded
Michael of a prisoner, exhausting her final days on the earth by soliciting the
help of everyone she knew in commuting a death sentence.

During his one glimpse of her in the camp of the British Legion at the end of
December, she'd been vivacious, almost playful. Later he'd learned that on the
seventeenth of January, she'd been near the Battle of the Cowpens. Somewhere
between camp and battle, she'd earned Lieutenant Fairfax's hatred—yet she'd
evaded being tortured to death by him.

Curiosity gnawed at Michael. Escape from Fairfax was no simple feat, as
he and Spry had discovered near Hillsborough. Despite the conclusion Major
Craig had drawn, Michael wondered whether his nemesis was really dead. And
he itched to learn how Mrs. Chiswell had gotten away from him in January.

The back door squeaked open. Michael raised his hand to rap on the frame
of the study door. Enid's whisper behind him stayed his hand: "Mistress has
already dined. Come. The pork roast is warm."

Up-close, the aroma from her tray seduced Michael, convinced him to defer
until later his questions for Mrs. Chiswell. In the dining room, he sat at one
end of the table illuminated by golden candlelight and contained the watering
of his mouth while Enid uncovered his heaped plate and poured wine in a goblet. Yes indeed, far better fare than trail rations on the Brunswick Road.

The housekeeper hovered near his elbow. He shoveled in several mouthfuls
before saying, "Excellent, as usual." After a nod for the door, he cut more pork.
"Mrs. Chiswell writes a good many letters."

"Indeed, sir. She's a journalist."

He swallowed a bite. "With whom does she correspond?"

Enid's gaze veered away, the gesture of a servant guarding her mistress.
"Oh, I wouldn't know. Now, what's this I hear about you being a hero? You
risked your life to save the lives of Mrs. Duncan and her aunt, Mrs. White,
while you were in Hillsborough."

Michael swigged wine. The housekeeper was just as competent at dodging
questions about Mrs. Chiswell as she was at sniffing out and spreading gossip.
Fortunately he'd other means of learning what kept the lady of the house so
occupied.

By now, there was no point in ordering "Aunt" Rachel White to stop gab-
bing. If Enid had heard the story, it meant the whole town knew it. "It was all

in the line of duty."

"Duty? Bah." Candlelight captured a spark in Enid's eyes, like the flash of sunlight in a falcon's stare. "*Mrs. Duncan.*" She cackled. "I've had a certain feeling all along about you two!"

He too had a feeling about Kate and himself, but it was far more ambiguous than what Enid imagined. Confusing, and—oh, gods, why couldn't Kate have waited another month to return to Wilmington, so he could get his head in order over her? And she'd brought that nosy, perspicacious aunt of hers.

The moths in his stomach became grenadiers. He buried them in rutabagas and turnips. He didn't have time for the ambiguity, the confusion.

If he gave Enid no fuel, she'd eventually leave him alone. He swallowed the final mouthful of vegetables. "Who in town shod those fast horses of William Jones and James Love?"

"Eh?" Her eyebrows bunched up with the change of subject, as if he'd spun her around four or five times and expected her to walk a straight line. "Aye, I heard you'd given chase to Devil Bill and Captain Love. High time you ran those jackals to ground, sir. The tobacconist's wife, Alice Farrell, and I were talking about that menace just yesterday. We never know when it's safe to walk to Market. Those scoundrels almost ran over the vicar and old Mrs. Page this afternoon, so I'm pleased to hear that—"

"The name of a farrier, Enid. Or perhaps a blacksmith. Who might have shod their horses?"

"Talk with Hiram Duke or Ralph Gibson on Front Street." Enid's brows lowered, and her bottom lip pushed upward. "Mr. Duke's wife and the woman who cleans Mr. Gibson's house complain that both men drink too much. And Gibson is a poor loser at gambling. You men. Cannot resist a card table or a cockfight, can you? And where's Spry? The lad never fails to show up by six for supper. Like the hounds my uncle owned in Aberystwyth. He could tell the time each night from those hounds' empty bellies."

Michael wondered how much money would change hands that night on account of Spry's performance at the tavern, how many "poor losers" would totter home drunk from the tavern. "This evening, Spry's engaged in the Battle of Backgammon at White's."

"You reckon I should keep food out for him?"

"Is the stockade full of rebels?" He shoveled in another mouthful.

"Ah. Right. It looks as though you'll be wanting some of that apple tart in a minute. I certainly don't mind putting more meat on your bones. But you never answered my question earlier. You've been back in town for three weeks, and why is it that this afternoon is the first I hear of this hero business?"

His head cocked toward a one-shoulder shrug. He kept chewing.

She stabbed a forefinger at him. "You're too modest, Mr. Stoddard. That's why you're still a lieutenant, you know. You have to strut like a peacock to advance in the army."

If that were all it took to advance, he'd be a colonel by now. Enid wasn't shutting up. He redirected his concentration to the activity of sawing off bite-sized hunks of roast and savoring the taste of each bite. The housekeeper's voice became a drone.

She tapped his shoulder. "I said, did you know that Mrs. White has moved here from Hillsborough? This morning, she, Mrs. Farrell, and I were speculating that you need to be at least a captain before you marry."

"Enough of this." Michael set his knife on the table and, in a sudden movement, swiveled in his chair to face Enid with what he hoped was a cold expression. She took a step back from him, chin drawn in. "The prattle of women's gossip distracts me from my work. And I would eat my meal in peace."

She closed her mouth. Her sly eyes evaluated his expression. Then, the line of her lips pressed into shrewdness, she tossed her head and sashayed from the dining room, tray at her hip.

Busybody. Michael mopped a wayward turnip wedge through gravy on his plate. It flipped onto the table. He retrieved the turnip piece with his fingers, popped it into his mouth, wiped his hands on a napkin, and paced to the window with his wine goblet. Duke and Gibson, farriers on Front Street. A reasonable place to resume his search for two rebel mongrels. As for Enid's comment about Gibson being a poor loser, he'd never met a man yet who lost gracefully at gambling.

If the lead of the farriers failed to bear fruit, he'd consult the register in Major Craig's office. The commander of the Eighty-Second kept a list of civilians who fled Wilmington in January, when the regiment occupied town. The register also listed those who'd remained and, by suspicious actions or words, merited monitoring.

"Here you are, sir." Crockery clacked behind him: Enid replacing his plate with a smaller one containing a wedge of apple tart the size of a bear's paw. He downed the remainder of his wine and resumed his seat at the table.

She dropped an eight-inch deep stack of letters bound by twine on the table about a foot from his plate. He gaped at the letters. "Is all that *my* correspondence? When—"

"Mistress says the letters arrived this morning. From the size of it, I'd say you've been missing correspondence for awhile."

He gathered the packet to him like he would an old friend. The last time he'd heard from his family or his benefactors had been October. No, September. "At least six months." He'd almost given up hope that he'd hear from them again. Jubilation hummed in his blood. What had his sister, Miriam, and his nephews been up to for the past half-year?

Michael flashed Enid a quick smile and thanked her. She left, and he consumed all but a few crumbs of the apple tart, after which he pushed back from the table and seized the packet. Then he climbed the stairs, a candle in holder lighting his way. In his room, he lit a lamp and spread the pile of letters on his bed, dividing it into stacks from his family, his friends, other officers, and benefactors.

The most recent letter from his sister was dated 28 December 1780. He shoved his travel pack off the small table, sat, and opened Miriam's letter to the ambient glow of lamplight.

My dearest Brother,

I hoped the Pain would diminish with Time. But in each of my Sons, I see his Face, and it reminds me that he will know no more Grandchildren...

A huge hole ripped in Michael's heart, as if a five-pound ball had blasted out of Miriam's letter and rent the fabric of his life. Of all the things he'd lost in crossing the Atlantic almost a decade earlier— "Ye gods, no," he whispered, his eyes smarting, and he skimmed the letter to confirm news that soldiers dreaded receiving. His father was dead, sometime late in autumn. No doubt Miriam's previous letters would provide background. But that moment, his vision swimming, he pressed his sister's letter to his heart, bowed his head, and surrendered.

Chapter Three

IN EACH OF Miriam's letters, she chided Michael to settle down with a good woman and carry on the honorable family name. But in the three letters written after their father's death, her playfulness transitioned to a sober plea that was unlike Miriam. It inspired him to dream that night that he'd sired three hundred little bastards in America, every one of them with a grubby palm extended for money from Papa. Michael jerked himself awake and rolled to a sitting position, then lit a candle and checked his watch. Four o'clock. A lance of fire shot down his spine from the crick in his neck and pummeled his lower back. He grunted and crammed the knuckles of one hand into the sore spot.

Sleep wouldn't find him again that night. He dressed, eased his bedroom door open, and listened. Spry was lodged out back in the old servants' quarters. In the house, Enid and Mrs. Chiswell were still asleep. Good. Shoes in one hand, candle in the other, he tiptoed downstairs in stocking feet. He avoided squeaky areas in the third, fifth, and tenth steps that might disclose his stealth.

In the study he lit two lamps. The floor was cold, so he slid on his shoes, then surveyed the room. That Mrs. Chiswell had suffered a long-term cash flow problem was obvious. Her house contained little furniture, no costly silver or china, and few paintings. Not for the first time, he wondered whether creditors harassed her.

The previous month in Hillsborough, Fairfax had informed him that Mrs. Chiswell was a rebel spy. After she'd returned to Wilmington, Michael had sneaked into the study two separate mornings before anyone else was awake and read her letters.

Most were business exchanges with a land agent and an attorney in Boston. She was following up on a claim of property there. He'd felt like a scoundrel while reading a personal letter, its salutation, "My dearest Jonathan." Fairfax had insisted that Helen Chiswell's lover, Jonathan Quill, who lived several hours south of Wilmington, was also a spy.

But in no letter he'd read had Michael seen indication of the use of invisible ink or ciphered messages to warn rebels. Spies? Bah.

In the predawn that morning, he routed out letters she'd received in the past few days, tucked in one of the desk's slots, unfolded and clustered together. Among her most recently received correspondence, he found letters from both the land agent and attorney. Nothing threatening there. To the contrary, Mrs. Chiswell's inquiries about the property had borne fruit, as the land agent had issued an invitation for her to visit Boston and offered the hospitality of his own home. Although Michael was uncertain as to its importance, he committed to memory the agent's name and direction.

He also found a new letter from Jonathan Quill, received in the past day or so. In it, Quill mentioned that he'd return to Wilmington before the second week of April. From the context of the letter, it appeared that Quill planned to travel to Boston with Mrs. Chiswell.

Sometime in the next few weeks, Jonathan Quill would return to the house on Second Street. Excellent. Three weeks earlier, he'd stayed beneath Mrs. Chiswell's roof but one night before departing for his home near Brunswick. Michael wanted another opportunity to observe him.

His eyes widened on the postscript at the very bottom of Quill's letter. *Tell Lieut. Stoddard about the note.* Michael turned the paper over. The backside was blank. Tell Stoddard about *what* note? A note about a creditor who threatened her? He warmed the page near a lamp's flame, but no invisible lettering appeared on either side.

Curious and frustrated, he lifted the bottom letter to the light and read the correspondent's name: David St. James. Michael's heart skipped a beat. He knew that Mrs. Chiswell had ties to the St. James family. The patriarch, Will St. James, was a rebel printer almost as notorious as the fifty-six signers of the Declaration. However, David St. James, whom Michael had met the previous summer in Alton, Georgia, didn't share his father's political fervor.

But when Michael scanned the one-paragraph letter, he read of David St. James's impending arrival in Wilmington, too, before the second week of April. St. James's last words before his closing raised the little hairs all over Michael's neck. *Confide in Stoddard.*

Michael placed St. James's letter facedown on the pile of letters he'd already examined and began a systematic, neat inspection of nooks and crannies in the desk. He pulled out paper, ink, quills, and sealing wax so he could search for anything that Mrs. Chiswell might have hidden. The lady was clearly planning an escape from the Wilmington area. Her weeks of frantic letter writing to the agent and attorney in Boston took on new significance. Perhaps it was no mere creditor who menaced her. Perhaps it was an assassin.

Both Quill and St. James had advised her to unburden herself on him.

Lieutenant Stoddard to the rescue. Hero. Bah. Not if he could help it would he remain in the dark about her dealings.

Were Quill and St. James arriving to protect her? In particular, Michael wondered about David St. James. Wilmington wasn't the safest place for a St. James that moment, even if he was a neutral.

No additional information was forthcoming. Michael returned all writing implements exactly the way he'd found them and slid Mrs. Chiswell's recently received letters into the slot where she'd filed them. Then he extracted the letters she'd written the previous day but not yet posted. Using his dagger, he was able to loosen the wax seal on two without compromising the paper.

The first was a query to a transportation agent in Boston about booking passage to Britain for herself, Mr. Quill, and two unnamed servants. In his head, Michael assembled the logical progression of Mrs. Chiswell's plan. From Boston, she'd sail back to England. Would she return to America? Had Enid been apprised of the plan? What would happen to the house in Wilmington?

The second letter, to a land agent based in New Berne, told him that Mrs. Chiswell had set a price that would sell the house on Second Street as quickly as possible.

Escape, escape, escape.

Despite the encouragement of two friends, she hadn't divulged details to Michael about whomever she was escaping from and why. Was she being overly cautious, not a trusting sort? Or had she concluded that full details of her predicament could land her in greater trouble than what she faced with the mysterious creditor?

The clock on the mantle in the parlor announced the arrival of four thirty. Michael's gaze swept the room. Somewhere in that study, surely Mrs. Chiswell had left a clue identifying her dangerous creditor. Bookshelves and the desk could hold numerous secret compartments. If he'd another quarter hour to search—ah, but he didn't have such time. Enid would be rising soon. He'd no desire to be caught snooping.

Annoyed by his failure to get to the bottom of Mrs. Chiswell's flurry of letter writing, he removed his shoes for the sneak back upstairs and extinguished the lamps. Reading her letters had proved a convenient deferment of the task of acknowledging his father's death. He now had letters of his own to write. Alas, too many of them.

***

"No, sir, he hasn't had breakfast yet. See for yourself." Enid waved the coffee pot toward the dining room window. "That man of yours is helping Molly hang laundry again." She refilled Michael's cup. "If you ask me, the Morrises ought to be paying *him* as their laundress."

Seven thirty. Not of a mood to appreciate his assistant's burgeoning romance, Michael jammed his watch back in his waistcoat pocket. "Obviously he isn't hungry. No need to feed him this morning." Enid slid a plate of fried eggs and bacon to the table before him. He waved it away, pushed back from the table, chair legs squawking on the floor, and stood. "Keep mine warm. I shan't be long."

He stumped from the dining room for the back door, head foggy despite two cups of coffee. There was too much work to be done that day. He yanked open the back door. From the step, he barked "Spry!" to the Morrises' back yard.

In the act of pegging a stocking to the clothesline, Spry rotated his head toward Mrs. Chiswell's yard. Molly, who'd lifted another wet stocking from the clothesbasket, squealed, flung the stocking onto Spry's shoulder, and bustled for Michael. "Mr. Stoddard! Good morning! How are you today?"

Michael blinked at her. There was enough daylight for him to see her grin, generous and grasping. Had he fallen asleep on his feet and missed a conversation that explained why his assistant's sweetheart abandoned him to the laundry?

Spry picked the stocking off his shoulder, pitched it into the basket, and trailed after the blonde laundress. From his frown, he'd missed the same conversation.

Michael backed toward the door. The crick in his neck pulled at him. He winced and kneaded it. "Business, Spry."

"Yes, sir."

"Did you sleep on your neck wrong?" Molly gathered her petticoat in one hand, hopped the knee-high hedge separating the yards, and bore down on Michael with all the determination of a soldier who'd fixed his bayonet on the battlefield. "I can help." She flexed her fingers. "Give me ten minutes."

"I don't have ten minutes." He groped behind him and located the door handle.

"Five minutes. I'm good with my hands. Ask Nick. And why shouldn't I want to help? You're the Hero of Wilmington."

Blast Rachel White, Alice Farrell, and Enid Jones for marooning him on a very tall pedestal. He yanked open the door, put a two-inch-thick plank of oak between himself and his devotee, and left her on the back step.

In the dining room, he found Enid feather-dusting the already dust-free frame on the window that provided the best view of the Morrises' back yard and clothesline. He uncovered his plate and dispatched three fried eggs, six slices of bacon, and two slices of buttered toast. While Michael finished breakfast, Spry appeared in the doorway and stood at attention. Enid sallied from the dining room with Michael's empty plate. Michael pushed back from the table and rose, acknowledging Spry's salute.

The ceiling creaked. Both Michael and his assistant glanced upward; Mrs. Chiswell had awakened and was moving about in her bedroom. Michael motioned Spry to his side and pitched his voice low. "I believe the lady of the house is being harassed by a dangerous creditor to the extent that she's listed the house with an agent and made plans to sail to Britain."

Spry's shoulders stiffened, and his eyebrows rocketed up his forehead. "Good gods!"

"Creditors can be unscrupulous, ruthless, savage. Keep your wits about you. In the next few weeks, we're also due for a visit from Jonathan Quill and David St. James."

"She told you all this, sir?"

"No." Michael held his assistant's gaze and saw his eyes narrow with judiciousness. "But I intend to have a private audience with her soon enough, get to the bottom of it. I want you present."

"Yes, sir. You think she's a spy?"

"I doubt it. But I question whether we're safe in this house, so I must have an accounting from her. Of course, that isn't the business Major Craig charged us to transact." Michael rechecked his watch. "The farriers on Front Street may have shod the horses of Jones and Love. Let's pay them a visit after morning parade, shall we?"

***

In a shady stable that stank of brackish water, horse sweat, and dung, a dark-haired, stocky man had tucked a bay gelding's left forelimb, bent at the fetlock, between his leather-aproned thighs. He didn't see Michael and Spry at first. His attention was directed over his shoulder, away from the entrance. "Why is it that Rouse always expects me to drop whatever I'm doing and—heigh there, hold him steady, boy!" The farrier snapped out his words. Grumbling, he jerked his head downward and continued leveling the horse's hoof with a metal rasp. The faint odor of dry hoof mingled with the other smells.

Michael shifted to his left and craned his neck for a better look at the farrier's attendant, who held the gelding by its halter. He glimpsed a boy of about thirteen years with lank blond hair, dirty trousers patched at both knees, and feet enclosed by moccasins. At the same time, the lad spotted the two soldiers and jumped, startling the horse.

The farrier's head shot up, and he snarled, "Are you half-witted, boy? You want the horse to trample me?"

The lad concealed himself behind the horse. "Look to your visitors, Mr. Gibson!" His voice was that of a boy on the cusp of becoming a young man.

The farrier set the horse's limb down, twisted about, and straightened to regard his visitors, his expression cautious and composed, pockets of fatigue sagging his eyes. His gaze flicked back and forth between the soldiers and came to rest on Michael. "We're unable to help you fellows this moment. We've a surfeit of work through at least Tuesday the twenty-seventh."

Michael noted the way the farrier's fingers flexed about the foot-long rasp in his hand. "We came here for information. You're Mr. Gibson?" The farrier nodded once. "When was the last time you worked with a horse ridden by William Jones or James Love?"

Muscles around Gibson's lips twitched. Then his brows rose, and he jerked out a smile that fell short of his eyes. "What, those scoundrels? I haven't seen them since before you lads marched into town back in January. After them, are you? That's good news." His brows lowered, like those of an accountant processing a huge sum. "I wasn't the man who worked with their horses back in January. They'd only let one farrier in town touch them."

"And who might that be?"

"Mr. Duke." Gibson's smile enlarged. He snapped his fingers. "You know, I believe I heard him say a few weeks ago that Captain Love had contracted him to shoe his horse."

A fortuitous break for the Eighty-Second. Michael leaned forward. "Where may we find Mr. Duke?"

"Right here. Only he won't be in today because he engaged in a bit of jollification last night." Gibson's eyes sparkled.

"Where does he live?"

"Fourth Street West. Second house from the end." Gibson chuckled.

The farrier's humor set Michael's instincts buzzing. "You're amused, Mr. Gibson. Why?"

"Oh, I wish I could be a fly on the wall when you lads roast him about Jones and Love. It'll serve him right. That drunkard is to blame for my work being backed up." Gibson smacked the rasp into the palm of his hand.

It took a certain class of slug to relish the prospect of a coworker falling under the suspicion of redcoats for seditious activity. Michael hoped the Eighty-Second wouldn't need the services of Ralph Gibson in the future. He tilted his head a second for another peep at the wretch concealing himself behind the gelding and spied more ragged sleeve of hunting shirt. Gibson's apprentice? "Thank you, Mr. Gibson. Good day."

Michael and Spry located the residence of Hiram Duke on Fourth Street, just inside town limits. Competing for size with the house was a chicken coop out back. Chicken feathers swirled in the weed-and-dirt track with the men's passage. A rooster announced their arrival.

An exhausted brunette in her late twenties responded to their knock, a baby on her hip and a little girl clinging to her petticoat. In the room just beyond, an infant wailed. Michael allayed the alarm he saw widening the woman's eyes by telling her that the regiment needed to contract with a farrier and had been recommended to Duke. She relaxed and responded that she hadn't seen her husband since the previous morning—but it wasn't unusual for him to carouse for a few days after one of his prize cocks won a fight, spend money he'd made gambling. After she provided a description of her husband and the names of several establishments where he might be found, she implored them to bring him home safely.

Rounding up a drunken husband. Not unlike solving the mystery of the missing pig. Huzzah. A rooster crowed the departure of Michael and Spry.

Around two that afternoon they picked up Hiram Duke's trail of lavish expenditure from the previous evening and tracked his busy Wednesday night of tavern-hopping and two-dozen tankards of ale. At five that evening, the proprietress of a bawdyhouse assured the soldiers that Duke had just settled down to business upstairs with two of her ladies, but they could wait for him in the parlor. She seated Michael and Spry and served wine. Shortly after the parade of strumpets clothed in perfume and rouge began, Michael dragged his assistant out the door. They wouldn't find Duke while occupying themselves in the bordello. And Michael was sure it wasn't what Major Craig had in mind when he'd put the resources of the Eighty-Second at their disposal.

Surveillance of clientele outside the bawdyhouse revealed the identities of so many randy soldiers and wandering husbands that Michael was astounded the entire regiment and town hadn't been poxed. In about two hours, a fellow who, by torchlight, fit the description of Hiram Duke staggered out. He blew kisses to two doxies in the doorway, then sailor-gaited his way up Front Street. Michael and Spry followed the man with the unkempt, brown hair.

He wove over to Chestnut Street, zigzagged onto Second, then Princess, then Third. On Third Street West, he strode up to a house with darkened windows and banged on the door several times. Out at the street, Michael heard a man inside asking the drunk to identify himself. The drunk thrust back his chest and swaggered on the porch. "My name's Duke, and I live here."

"Uh oh," muttered Spry. "This may become foul."

The man in the house cracked open an upstairs window, denied that the drunken farrier lived there, and told him to leave. Duke pounded on the door some more. "Elizabeth? What are you doing in there with another man? Come on, Elizabeth, let me in."

"Be gone, you sot, or I shall empty the chamberpot on you!"

Michael prodded Spry's shoulder. "Time to keep the peace." He bustled up the walkway, his assistant beside him.

They caught Duke just before he tottered off the front porch and gripped him around both arms. The homeowner's dry tone floated down to them. "Hah! Who says there's never a redcoat around when you need one?" The window slid shut.

Duke looked back and forth between his captors. "Taking me to jail? But what have I done?"

They walked him out to the street and toward his house. Michael said, "Hiram Duke, right? Elizabeth's looking for you."

"That's my honey—say, how'd you know my name? Do I know you?"

"Got some horses that need shoeing, Mr. Duke. We're looking for a farrier."

"I'm a farrier." He tried to stick out his chest again but lost his balance.

Michael got a better grip on him. "When was the last time you worked on a horse of William Jones or James Love?"

Duke squinted at him. "Those boys are outlaws. I haven't heard from them since January."

"But Captain Love spoke with you recently about shoeing his horse."

"He did? No. Haven't talked with him since January."

"Damn!" Spry whispered.

Michael's empty belly felt as if it had filled with molten pewter. He took several deep breaths to shove down the swell of anger and made sure his voice emerged calm. "I'm curious, Mr. Duke. You've spent the last two days carousing. Where did you come by so much money?"

"Oh." Duke laughed. "Two nights ago, my rooster tore the shit out of Ralph Gibson's rooster. He paid up. Didn't like it, but he paid in full. Time for me to celebrate!"

Michael and Spry delivered the farrier home to his wife, who looked less than pleased with his condition. Then they plodded to the dirt track and back to central Wilmington in the dark. "Gibson, that snake." Spry's teeth sounded clenched. "Led us on a wild goose chase all day. He's laughing at us right now."

"No doubt, and I'm sorry to say Enid warned me last night that he was a poor loser at gambling."

"Let's arrest the bugger. He lied to us, sir."

The fire in Michael's stomach cooled. Ralph Gibson had attempted to manipulate soldiers of His Majesty into the instrument by which he settled a score, just as others across the colonies had used the tactic to "settle" feuds throughout the war. Maybe the farrier *was* laughing at pulling the wool over the eyes of redcoats that moment—but the outcome of the misadventure could have been much worse than a wasted Thursday. "Jail and the pen are full of men who've done far worse than lie to the Eighty-Second."

"But, sir—"

"Back off it, Spry. That's your pride talking. Remember, we're looking for Jones and Love, not a farrier with an ax to grind for his coworker. But don't fret. We'll find out where Gibson lives, keep an eye on him. If he's a snake worth staking, we'll nab him." He sighed. "And may we have better luck finding Jones and Love on the morrow."

Chapter Four

DURING THE ENSUING week, Michael and Spry followed four leads gleaned from Major Craig's register to ground without receiving a single break in their efforts to track down Jones and Love. Checking two of the leads necessitated their riding from Wilmington overnight with patrols to investigate allegations of rebel alliances in adjacent counties. That Craig remained absent with his own patrol hardly comforted Michael. On March the twenty-ninth, just before he and Spry rode out for an overnight search in Brunswick County, he heard a rumor that the armies of Lord Cornwallis and General Nathanael Greene had encountered each other somewhere in North Carolina's midsection.

Mid-afternoon on Friday the thirtieth, Michael and his men had just trotted their tired horses back into Wilmington when, one block over, Jones and Love thundered past on horseback. Carbines discharged. Devil Bill's triumphant *Yee-haaw!* shrieked through Michael's gut.

Michael snarled, kicked Cleopatra in the sides, and hollered, "After them!" The redcoats gave chase. Again, Jones and Love outstripped them. Michael called off pursuit south of town, before any of the regiment's horses succumbed to sand shuffling. The outlaws dwindled to specks in the wavy grass, and a sea breeze flung their glee back at the patrol. Michael slammed the pommel of his saddle with his fist.

He, Spry, and the men walked their mounts back to the garrison's stables. As soon as they dismounted, a message boy found Michael and thrust a sealed note at him from the surgeon, Clayton. Michael opened the note. While his patrol had been chasing Jones and Love south of town, another patrol from the Eighty-Second had brought to the infirmary the bodies of three bandits killed during a raid, north of town, upon the entourage of a peer of the realm.

A peer of the realm? Bloody hell! Major Craig was due back to Wilmington any day. Michael shoved the note at Spry, silently praising the discretion of

Clayton at keeping the incident quiet.

Spry looked up from the note to Michael. Michael's imagination produced a clear image of himself entombed in inventory and Spry digging latrines. Then the two of them stripped their packs from their horses. After Michael paid the messenger boy a penny to deliver the packs to Mrs. Chiswell's house, he and Spry jogged for the infirmary.

The other end of the regiment's stables had been converted into an infirmary with examining rooms, all possessing the ambiance of horse stalls. Above the door, Clayton had mounted a bell. It emitted a merry tinkle for the soldiers' entrance, like what Michael would have expected in the shop of the town confectioner or baker, except the infirmary didn't smell half as appealing. The surgeon's voice floated to them from a back room: "That you, Mr. Stoddard? I shall be right out. Andrews, either you cease squirming, or I shall have a couple of orderlies hold you down. That boil must be lanced."

Michael whispered to Spry, "Andrews?" Spry winced and pointed to his right buttock.

Rough break for Private Andrews, a boil on the bum. And Clayton would take his time with the needle, so Michael peered into the nearest stall. Three canvas-covered forms were stretched out on the dirt floor. The next stall over was empty. He crooked his forefinger for Spry to follow. The two of them tiptoed in. A few stalls down, Andrews's muffled moans added to the atmosphere.

Michael squatted and drew the cover down halfway on the first body. Breath jammed in his throat. A blond-haired boy no older than thirteen years lay supine, his skin already dusky with death, the blackened hole from a ball through his right forehead. Michael started, then blinked several times. Was the dead boy Ralph Gibson's apprentice? He wore the patch-kneed trousers and ragged hunting shirt that Michael remembered. "Spry, do you recognize him?"

"Sir." Spry scuffed closer. "He looks like the lad who was handling that farrier's horse last week."

"He does, indeed." Michael twitched the canvas over the corpse and moved to the next still form, noting its length, similar to that of the blond boy. Even with that knowledge, his hand trembled when he dragged down the canvas and found another dead youth, hair as dark as his own, engaged with him in a glazy, half-lidded stare. A musket or pistol ball in the heart had downed him. His hair, like that of the blond boy, was lank, filthy, probably lice-infested.

"Damn," muttered Spry. "What are these boys doing dead? I thought we were supposed to be looking at dead bandits, sir. *Men.*"

Michael, mute, covered the second body and moved on to the third, a grizzled man in his late fifties or early sixties with greasy hair. Someone had shot him through the chest, too. He peered closer at the fellow's threadbare, light brown hunting shirt. No sign of ejected powder around the hole the ball had made. The man hadn't been shot at very close quarters.

Voice soft, almost choked, Spry said, "Did someone murder a grandfather out hunting with his grandsons?"

"Good question." For if these weren't the bandits from the raid on the peer's entourage, where were the dead bandits? Who were these people, and who had shot them? And if these were the three killed in the raid, what in hell were boys doing mixed up in an ambush? When Michael was their age, he'd been sweeping out the mews for a kind, old nobleman, taking care of Lord Crump's falcons.

Michael's gaze traveled to the dead man's dusky fingers and thumb. Dirty, torn nails. He felt for calluses and found them. Not a merchant, probably not an artisan or peddler. A backwoodsman, or a small-plot farmer. A man near poverty.

Aware that Spry studied him, he shifted back to the boys. They also bore calluses on their hands. He covered all the corpses, stood to ease the cramping from muscles too long in the saddle, and backed to the stall's entrance, arms crossed. In his peripheral vision, Andrews stumped past their stall in a flash of red coat and a grunt of pain.

Michael waited until he heard the tinkle of the bell, indicating Andrews's exit, before he returned his attention to Spry. "Look at their feet and tell me something about these people."

Spry knelt and uncovered the lower quarter of the bodies. Both boys wore patched moccasins. The man wore battered shoes with soles worn through in several places. Spry sat back on his heels. "Backwoodsmen, I'd guess, sir. If that's indeed Gibson's apprentice, the farrier wasn't paying him much. Poor as dirt, like the other two. The man's left shoe is worn down more heavily. He dragged that leg. Injury, perhaps, or an arthritic hip."

"Good work. A chat with Mr. Gibson is in order."

"Yes, sir." Spry replaced the canvas and pushed to his feet.

The surgeon loomed in the doorway, a fresh spray of blood across his apron, and nodded at Michael. "Good afternoon, Mr. Stoddard."

"Afternoon. Are we alone?"

"My orderlies will return in about five minutes."

"I appreciate your discretion in this affair."

The surgeon shrugged. "Sorry I wasn't available to introduce you and Spry to yon trio of bandits. I see you've already made their acquaintance."

Michael's stomach felt heavy, as if loaded with sand. He jerked his head once toward the bodies. "Clayton, over there are two dead boys. They don't even have their first whiskers. Are you certain they're bandits?"

"No. I'm only certain that those are the three bodies brought in by the patrol and labeled bandits by them. And I know what you're thinking, sir. That someone swapped bodies, maybe. That boys cannot commit such vile deeds." He jammed both fists on his hips and spread his feet, like a pugilist ready for a challenge. "Don't tell me lads that age cannot wield a pistol or knife. Just last week I stitched up a soldier who got into it with an eleven-year-old wharf rat. You've seen how crazy those rebels are. Put a knife in a rebel boy's hand, and he'll spit a soldier, quick as he'll spit a chicken."

All this Michael knew, yet he had the feeling he'd stepped into a cavern so huge the ceiling wasn't visible. "What have you heard about this incident?"

"A peer of the realm was traveling from New Berne to Wilmington with her entourage this afternoon. The entourage was ambushed by no fewer than two-dozen masked bandits." Clayton jutted his chin at the bodies. "Those three were among the raiding party. The lady's ten-year-old son was abducted."

Michael recoiled. "Her son was abducted?" Christ Jesus! Never mind tracking down Jones and Love. If Michael failed to rescue a ten-year-old son of a noblewoman, *he'd* be the one digging latrines—or possibly cashiered out of the Army. Either way, the entrails of his military career would be spattered all over the *London Chronicle*.

What in God's name was a woman of the peerage doing traipsing down the coastline with a son so young? "Did the bandits abduct anyone else of her party? Was her husband in the entourage? Was anyone injured or killed? Who among the lady's party shot these three?"

"I don't know, sir. You must ask them yourself. I didn't meet any of them." Reaching into his pocket, Clayton stepped out of the doorway and into the stall, where he handed Michael a folded square of paper. "Men from the patrol informed me that you'll find the lady and her household lodged at the direction scripted there. She should be able to convey specific details of the incident and assist your investigation. Lady Wynndon is her name—or maybe Wynndon is the boy's surname. I'm not certain."

"So no one in Lady Wynndon's party was injured?"

"If they were, they didn't send for me to tend them."

Michael unfolded the paper long enough to glance at the written direction before tucking it into his waistcoat pocket. He returned his scrutiny to the shrouded bodies again and rubbed his jaw a moment. The stubble of two days scraped his hand. He probably looked like a beggar. What a splendid first impression he'd make upon the noblewoman and members of her household a few minutes hence.

Wynndon. He frowned. Faint memory eddied, suspicion that he'd heard the name before. Mentioned, perhaps, in connection with Parliament?

He corralled his thoughts back to the dead bandits. "When will the cabinet-maker dress them for burial?"

"I've already sent for him." Clayton had relaxed his shoulders.

"Hold off another hour. Spry and I will speak with the lady and her party. I'll send the men who shot the bandits here, have them positively identify the bodies. All possessions you remove from the corpses—*everything*—you must save for me so I can examine them, as well as any other possessions you've already removed. Daggers, purses, and haversacks. I shall return to inspect them before evening. And do continue your part at keeping this matter out of the civilian gossip stream."

Clayton nodded. "As you wish, sir. So long as those bodies are out of here quickly. If my guess is correct, I'll need the space soon enough. And at that point, the weight of civilian gossip will be irrelevant."

His comment got Michael's attention. He eyed the surgeon. "How do you mean?"

"Did you not hear the news, sir? Lord Cornwallis and General Greene battled on the fifteenth between Hillsborough and Salem. Some obscure court-house. Gifford. No, I believe the name was *Guilford* Courthouse. The Crown triumphed, but nevertheless—" Clayton shook his head. "I'm guessing that sooner or later, his lordship will be paying Wilmington a visit, bringing with him more wounded men than this infirmary can handle." The surgeon studied the three dead bandits. "If I were you, I'd make a happy ending for those nobles before Lord Cornwallis arrives."

***

Hair stood up on the back of Michael's neck. Cornwallis's army was coming to Wilmington. Clayton's "happy ending" entreaty was an understatement. He walked faster.

Spry sounded out-of-breath from the pace of their stride down Market Street. "But sir, if Lord Cornwallis was victorious, surely he'd have captured Greene's baggage and made use of the supplies. There would be no point in his coming to Wilmington."

The private had never been in a large field battle. He didn't comprehend the factors that could diminish a victory, render it but a marginally better outcome than defeat. "Not necessarily, Spry."

They arrived at the farrier shop on Front Street in time to watch an amiable Hiram Duke accept payment from a merchant and pass the reins of the fellow's mare to him. In the rear of the stable, Michael glimpsed two dark-haired lads shoveling horse dung and spreading straw. He saw no sign of Gibson or the blond boy who'd been helping him the previous week.

With the merchant's departure, Duke transferred his attention to Michael and Spry, no memory of having dealt with them in his expression, but a smile for them nonetheless as he brushed off his apron. "Afternoon, fellows. My name's Duke. How may I help you? Shoeing, perhaps?" His mousy brown hair was pulled back neatly with a ribbon.

"Lieutenant Stoddard. My assistant, Spry. There's a lad who works for you, Mr. Duke. He's about thirteen, blond hair, skinny. I've a question for him."

Although Duke kept smiling, his brows crimped down an inch. "Blond boy? Thirteen?" He shook his head. "We haven't hired a lad fitting that description. Are you certain you have the correct business?"

Michael had presumed the boy to be their apprentice. But another glance at the lads in the stable revealed the discrepancy. Both looked reasonably clean and well fed, unlike the boy he and Spry had seen the previous Thursday or the dead boy in the infirmary. If he hadn't been an apprentice, Gibson must have been acquainted with him in some other capacity.

Duke awaited his response. Michael said, "Well, perhaps we've erred. Where is Mr. Gibson this afternoon?" And what was the surname Gibson had used that morning before he'd become aware that they were watching him? Ross? No, it had been Rouse.

"Ralph took today off. Had some errands to run."

Errands to run. "When will he return?"

"On the morrow, first thing." Duke's smile faded. His gaze darted between them. "He isn't in trouble, is he?"

Michael stretched his lips into a wide smile and shook his head. "Not at all. Thank you for your time."

When he turned to leave, Duke hustled to his side. "Shall I give him a message?"

Michael waved away the offer. "Don't bother. I shall catch up with him eventually."

As soon as they walked out of earshot, Spry chuckled. "Hah! He was so pickled the other night that he doesn't even recognize us. Probably took him a whole day to sober up. Are we headed to Gibson's house now?"

Michael grunted. "No. Step lively. The noblewoman is staying on Second Street, five houses down from where we're quartered."

"Sir. I noticed that you de-emphasized our visit to Duke because you didn't want him telling Gibson we'd stopped by to speak with him. But I take it we shall return on the morrow for Gibson?"

"Yes. If he hears we're anxious to speak with him, he may arrange to run other errands." Crushed shells crunched with each stride Michael took. "Do you know anyone in town or the regiment named Rouse?"

"Rouse? No, sir. Where did you hear the name?"

"Last Thursday, before he knew we'd arrived, Gibson commented to that boy about someone inconveniencing him. I believe he used the name Rouse. It may not be salient to the investigation, but nonetheless, keep it in mind."

They turned the corner onto Market Street. Spry said, "I have to admit, sir. It pains me to see boys the ages of my cousins and brother dead like that."

Spry would have been sickened to see what bore arms against soldiers of the King on battlefields in 1777. Eleven- and twelve-year-olds in uniform coats too big for them, bearing muskets longer than they were tall. The previous year, the Congress had put out a recruitment call for eighty-eight infantry regiments. Children had responded. Their fathers were dead. "'He is a tried and valiant soldier.'"

Spry's tone tightened. "Octavian to Anthony, *The Tragedy of Julius Caesar.* Do you suppose there were other boys in the raiding party, sir?"

"Another good question. I certainly hope not. Those in the best position to answer the question are men from the lady's entourage who directly engaged the rebels. But if we ask that information of the retainers while she's present, it will elevate her anxiety over her son. So while I'm obtaining her detailed testimony, you must question her men where she cannot hear you."

"Sir."

"Get their summaries of the incident. We'll interview the men more thoroughly later. Take whoever made the killing shots to the infirmary. Confirm that those three corpses were, indeed, their targets. Find out whether the three bandits were armed and what happened to their weapons. And make sure neither Clayton nor the cabinetmaker accidentally tosses out any of the bandits' property. I shall meet you at the infirmary."

"Sir." Spry checked the angle of the sun. "When will we investigate the site of the abduction?"

"On the morrow, first thing. I doubt we've enough daylight left us today."

They halted before a handsome, two-story brick house, wild sprawls of tulips and daffodils in beds out front. Then the soldiers headed up the short walkway and stepped onto the porch. Curtains in the window beside the front door jiggled. Before Michael's hand lifted halfway for the brass doorknocker, the door swished open.

A middle-aged man, of medium stature like Michael, raked a dark-eyed gaze over Michael's uniform, lodging upon each dust-laden crease, and pausing on the film of grime that dulled Michael's boots. Every hair of his powdered wig lay in place. His hunter-green velvet coat and waistcoat would have cost Michael three months' pay.

He skewered Michael with a stare. His nostrils twitched. "Were *you* sent by the regiment?"

His accent marked him as gentleman from Yorkshire. Michael's deep memory acknowledged something about him as familiar. Judging from his erect carriage, he was ex-military, probably a veteran of the old French War. And he served as a reminder of why Michael had had no trouble keeping his distance from certain officers. Michael was glad the pompous turd didn't know that he'd been born the son of a stonemason, at one point the falcon boy for Lord Crump.

He gave the fellow a good view of the stubble on his chin. "Lieutenant Stoddard, lead investigator for the Eighty-Second Regiment of Foot. My assistant, Spry. I'm here to question your lady on the abduction of her son. The name I was given was Lady Wynndon."

The older man never regarded Spry and stood his ground in the entrance. "Lady Faisleigh is her correct title. What took you so long to get here?"

In Michael's opinion, the question didn't merit response. "Is Lady Faisleigh in residence? If not, direct me with all haste to where I may find her. A child's life is at stake. Stop wasting my time."

The corners of the bewigged man's mouth dragged down an inch. "You're from Yorkshire. *Common* Yorkshire." His dark eyes iced. "I shall see if my lady is ready to speak with you." He stepped aside and jerked the door wide. "For God's sake, wipe your boots. The parlor is immediately on the right. You may *stand* in there and await her ladyship's favor."

Michael scuffed his boots once on the mat and strode into the foyer. The bewigged man signaled a brunette lady's maid poised at the bottom of the staircase. She darted upstairs in a flash of striped petticoat, the heels of her fine, leather shoes tapping the polished, dark oak of each step.

Constructed of the same wood as the staircase, the doors to the parlor were thrown open, but Michael waited to enter with his assistant. Smiling with his huge, white teeth at the man in the wig, Spry took extra seconds to wipe his shoes ten or twelve times. When he finally entered the house, he passed within three inches of the man, emphasizing their height differential.

A faint scent, sweet and spice, wafted down the stairway. Michael's deep memory recognized it, too, yet he couldn't place its identity. Puzzled, he tilted his nose toward the stairs for a better sniff.

Faisleigh. That sounded even more familiar than Wynndon.

The wig interposed himself between Michael and the bottom of the stairs with a hiss. "You missed the entrance to the parlor." He pointed, his left arm and hand rigid.

In the parlor, portraits in gilt frames decorated the walls. Two overstuffed couches adorned with embroidered pillows and heavy walnut chairs padded with velvet offered appealing places to sit. An oriental rug softened the wood of the floor.

Amidst the opulence, Michael paced, of a sudden unable to focus or speculate on whether a Wilmington merchant had vacated his home to accommodate the entourage, or the entourage was using an unoccupied house listed with a land agent. That sweet, spicy scent had tracked him into the parlor, fingering and fondling him. His head flooded with memories of sweeping out Lord Crump's mews, caring for the peregrines when he was sixteen years old, the year before his uncle Solomon and Lord Crump had purchased his ensign's commission and sent him into the Army.

Through the opened parlor doors, he heard women's voices in descent from the second floor. Memory mated the maddening scent with one of the voices and the peer title. Lady Faisleigh.

His gut knotted, punched the breath from him.

No. It wasn't possible. The odds of such a meeting happening again were astronomical.

The confusion spun a web around his logic and cushioned his perception with a cotton-like unreality, slowed time until all he could hear was the struggle of his heartbeat as he faced the parlor entrance. The bewigged man's voice penetrated the thud of Michael's heartbeat to announce the arrival of Lady Faisleigh.

Still blonde and gorgeous, Lydia glided into the parlor in a rustle of burgundy-colored silk. She was seven years his senior and now thirty-three years old, yet she looked little changed from the succulent creature who had seduced him the summers of his fifteenth and sixteenth years.

Memory served Michael with a picture of Lydia as he'd last seen her in June 1770: curls tangled with straw, sweat rolling between her breasts, her arms extended for him. *Come here, my pet.*

And in the parlor on Second Street, on March thirtieth in 1781, Lydia's blue-eyed gaze bounced back and forth between Michael and his assistant. The rims of her eyes were red from tears. Her hands pressed together, as if in prayer. She exhibited no sign that she recognized Michael. "I thank God investigators have come. You must rescue my son."

Chapter Five

MICHAEL STODDARD THE infantry officer and criminal investigator dammed up the tidal wave of babble surging from the boy who'd never gotten any answers, although he suspected he'd hear plenty from him later. Like a marionette soldier on strings, he bowed his head. "Lieutenant Stoddard, at your service." He extended a hand toward Spry. "And my assistant, Spry."

Lydia paced, not sparing them a glance. "Lieutenant, will you and your assistant be able to rescue Wynndon? Whatever shall we do?"

Michael rolled back his shoulders to shred the daze over his perceptions and planted his stare on the lady's maid with the striped petticoat, who stood fidgeting in the doorway alongside a brown-haired slip of a housemaid and the bewigged fellow. The lady's maid, in her twenties, glanced at him, her mouth taut and eyes haunted. With one sharp toss of his head, he motioned her to go to Lydia. "The first thing you must do, Lady Faisleigh, is calm down enough to answer questions about the incident this afternoon. Please have a seat." He gestured to the smaller of the couches.

It appeared that Lydia didn't remember a pimply-faced boy in the mews, ever randy at her command. Through numbness in his head, he wondered whether that bothered him.

She allowed the maid to guide her to the couch. While she seated herself, the maid hovering nearby, the man in the wig interposed himself between Michael and Lydia. "I was in the carriage with them and can answer any questions you have of my lady."

Without altering the angle of his body, Michael bored his stare into the man. "No, you cannot, for the simple reason that you have admitted you're also a witness to the boy's abduction. A witness remembers best his own experience, not that of others." Imitating the man's rigid arm and hand posture from moments earlier, Michael pointed to a chair near the door. "Sit."

The scowl that rippled the other man's face revealed incisors. He remained standing, lifted his chin, and glared.

Spry took one step forward. Without diverting scrutiny off the older man, Michael shifted his extended hand, palm outward, to signal a halt to his assistant's progress. "Regardless of your position in this lady's household, you've no jurisdiction in Wilmington." He lowered his arm. "Now sit and allow me to do my work."

"Mr. de Manning, do sit, as the investigator has asked." Her back straight, Lydia rubbed the side of her neck and seemed to be calmer. "I know you're worried about Wynndon, too, but we must each cooperate to the utmost of our ability." She turned a helpful, hopeful smile on Michael. Again, there was no sign of recognition from her.

Well, why on earth should she recognize him? He was five inches taller than he'd been at sixteen. His voice had deepened further, his chest had broadened, and the pimples were gone. Unshaven and reeking of travel, he resembled a swarthy, gypsy horse thief from the Yorkshire moors. Who expected a mews sweeper to turn up as an officer in His Majesty's Army, on the other side of the Atlantic?

And he realized he didn't want to be recognized. Recognition would layer more bewilderment upon the churning mess in his soul. For all her voluptuousness, for all the hours of pleasure she'd guided him through—pleasure no red-blooded youth would have rejected—none of Michael's memories of her tasted sweet or hallowed. He'd never been able to figure out why that was so.

De Manning stumped to the indicated chair and stood beside it, chest out, shoulders back, chin level. The only thing missing was the red coat with braid.

Lydia continued to direct the radiance of the sun upon Michael with her smile. "Forgive my boy's tutor, Lieutenant. He and Wynndon have been so close all these years." The luster faded from her smile, and when she slanted a look at the other man, she sighed, her tone solid with exasperation. "And I wager he didn't introduce himself properly when he answered the door."

"Captain de Manning, retired." De Manning clicked his heels.

"Charmed to make your acquaintance, sir. Now have a seat."

Although the chair cushion appeared comfortable enough, de Manning perched himself upon it as if it were the bare, rough planks of a jakes in July, flies buzzing about his dropped breeches, and his business transacting with difficulty. Michael knew that de Manning had been one very fortunate retired junior officer to land the position of tutor in the household of a noble. After a war was over, the job market flooded with former ensigns, lieutenants, and captains. Most wound up working for a pittance to help stretch their meager pensions. He also suspected that de Manning detested being ordered around by an officer more junior than his rank at retirement, a man young enough to be his son.

In all likelihood, de Manning the soldier had supplied at least one of the three killing shots on the bandits.

Michael's hands were quivering with the shock of the past few minutes. He clasped them behind his back, low. To allow himself a few seconds to order his thoughts, he paced toward the window, his path supplying a visual separation between Lydia and her son's tutor.

Lydia tracked him with her gaze. Not just with anticipation of some sort of rescue plan, but with curiosity. The curiosity unnerved him.

He paced back to Spry, braced his boots apart, and planted hands on his hips. "My lady, state the name of the son who was abducted."

She pushed forward to the edge of the couch, hands in her lap, right cupped in left. "Geoffrey, Lord Wynndon. Upon the death of his father, he will become the seventeenth Earl of Faisleigh, master of Ridleygate Hall and twelve other properties." Expression smooth and lips soft, Lydia held his gaze.

The falcon boy in Michael's head chortled that he knew just where Ridleygate Hall was. Michael pounded him back into silence and breathed through his nostrils. "I've been told that Lord Wynndon is ten years old. Is that correct?"

"More or less. He'll be ten in a few weeks."

"Describe him."

"Not quite to my shoulder in height. Slender. Dark-haired and dark-eyed, like his father." Her lips pinched ever so slightly at the end of the sentence, and her gaze flicked to the right.

What was this? Was she lying about the boy's description, or withholding a physical detail? Maybe he'd been born with a defect like a clubbed foot, and she was embarrassed to mention it. "What distinguishing physical characteristics has he, such as freckles or heavy smallpox scars?"

"None." Her chin tilted up a bit, as if she dared him to prove otherwise.

"Have you a likeness of Lord Wynndon?"

She angled onto one hip to gain access to the pocket of her petticoat, deepening her cleavage in the process. Michael averted his attention until peripheral vision informed him that Lydia had righted herself and extended a miniature to him. "Painted in December, by an artist of the Royal Academy just a few weeks before our departure to America."

He captured the ribbon in one hand and held the ivory portrait in the palm of his other. The image of a dark-haired boy with a slender face peered back at him, his eyes alert and inquisitive. Faint recognition stirred in Michael. Yes, the boy had Lydia's generous lips.

With a pivot, he handed the miniature to Spry. The private perused the image, then returned the portrait to him. Michael closed his hand about the ivory. "My lady, may I keep the portrait overnight?"

She stopped herself from shaking her head. Then she looked away from him with a fresh shimmer of tears. Her voice emerged husky. "It's the only likeness I have of him, Lieutenant."

"I promise to return it to you on the morrow." With the slow nod of her head, he tucked the portrait into one of his two waistcoat pockets. "Has Lord Wynndon ever been to America before this visit?"

"No," she whispered.

"Describe his attire today."

She sniffled. "Dark blue velvet coat and matching breeches, embroidered waistcoat, silver buttons. White silk stockings and linen shirt. Black shoes, silver buckles."

Michael regarded the tutor. "Has she provided a fitting description, sir?"

De Manning nodded, curt. "He was also wearing his gray wool cloak."

"Very good. What else can you contribute to Lord Wynndon's description, sir?"

"He's an intelligent, healthy young man, Lieutenant. Quite interested in military matters."

Not surprising, considering the background of his tutor. Michael returned his focus to Lydia, who was watching him again, the tears gone. "Aside from your housemaid, what other children were in your party?"

She opened her mouth to respond, but de Manning's voice vaulted across the parlor. "My lady has no other children."

Now, that was interesting. Not quite the question he'd asked Lydia. He turned on de Manning, found the fellow's lips weighed down in frown again and the veins bulging in his neck. Was the tutor defending her or impeding her response? "I didn't direct my query to you, Mr. de Manning. Either you contain yourself and respond only when I require it of you, or I shall insist that you wait outside the parlor."

De Manning sealed his lips and crossed his arms high over his chest. His eyes became pebbles of obsidian.

Michael studied Lydia. She swallowed, swept her forefinger once beneath a slender choker that he'd first assumed was of pearls, but upon second look appeared to be made of small alabaster or ivory beads. "There are no other children in the entourage."

"Mr. de Manning mentioned that you traveled in a carriage. Large and easily marked for attack by a group of bandits. Who are the people traveling with you?"

"Two coachmen, one groom, six outriders, my lady's maid, my housemaid, my son's tutor. And Wynndon."

"Was anyone from your party injured in the attack?" She shook her head, no. "I take it that your lady's maid, your housemaid, your son, and Mr. de Manning rode inside the carriage with you?"

"Yes."

"Who from your party used firearms to defend you during the attack this afternoon?"

Her gaze dipped to her hands a few seconds. "I believe all the men did so. It was dreadfully noisy."

Michael threw a glance of question at Spry, who nodded to confirm the plan they'd discussed earlier for questioning witnesses. When Michael resumed contemplating Lydia, she'd focused on the rug between the two of them, and one of her thumbs caressed the opposite palm. He softened his tone. "In a moment, I shall have Spry question all the men from your entourage out in the stable while I obtain specific details from you. But first, summarize for us the moments leading up to your son's abduction and how he came to leave the carriage."

She placed her hands, palms down, upon her thighs and continued monitoring the floor. "We'd crossed a large area of loose sand in the road. The head coachman cracked his whip for the team to pick up speed. One of the outriders shouted a warning. The bandits must have been waiting there, using the sand as a trap, because—" Her voice wavered, and she firmed it. "A musket discharged in the distance. Then I heard a number of men's voices, united and raised in a charge upon the carriage from all sides."

She fell silent, searching for her next words. Without moving his head, Michael shifted his gaze for an assessment of the captain, expecting more of the bulldog expression and posture. Instead, de Manning had lowered his arms, in mirror of Lydia's posture, parted his lips, and leaned toward her. A crease appeared between his eyebrows, as if he were in pain.

What now—was the tutor in love with her? In disbelief, Michael shot a look at Lydia. Her body, angled away from de Manning, revealed the other half of the story. She was either oblivious to his affection or ignoring it.

Knowing what he knew of Lydia, he guessed the latter. That made for one very frustrated tutor. By her admission, de Manning had been in the household a number of years, perhaps as long as a decade. A decade was a long time to be frustrated over Lydia. Michael knew. He'd spent his final two years in England and his first couple of years in America walking the perimeter of the same cell. He grudged out some empathy for the retired captain.

At that moment, memory tossed a nugget to Michael from his sixteenth year: his recollection of seeing the tutor in Lord Crump's parlor, among an audience of gentlemen who listened to Lydia ensorcel the harpsichord. His pulse quickened for a second or two. He hoped de Manning didn't recognize him.

Lydia cleared her throat. "The carriage halted. The bandits were upon my men with much fist-fighting and exchange of fire. One scoundrel tried to force his way in the window of the carriage. The lower half of his face was concealed with a kerchief." She fluttered her hand in the direction of her lady's maid. "Dorinda punched him in the face and stabbed his hand several times with embroidery scissors until he finally dropped, screaming, off the carriage. An old man with greasy hair yanked open the door." Lydia hugged herself, rubbed her upper arms. "Mr. de Manning kicked him in the chest and out the door. Then he shot him with his pistol while the man lay upon the ground."

Michael's instincts about de Manning shooting a bandit had been correct.

"Two more masked bandits rushed into the carriage and knocked the wind from Mr. de Manning. While he lay gasping upon his seat, they dragged my son from my arms. And—and—" Lydia rocked herself and worked her mouth. No words emerged.

Michael spotted the quiver in her lower lip. He'd seen her wield it with intention in the past—not just for him, but for numerous men. His gaze flitted over her self-embrace and downcast eyes. This time, her distress appeared genuine. He said into the taut silence of the room, "Thank you, my lady. That will do for now."

Across the parlor, de Manning appeared to have fixated on the quivering lip. He'd clasped hands in his lap, fingers interlaced, and slumped his shoulders. "Mr. de Manning, did your party's outriders not give chase on the bandits?" The tutor continued to focus on Lydia, as if he hadn't heard Michael. Michael raised the volume of his voice. "Halloo, Mr. de Manning, I asked you whether your outriders chased the bandits."

"Yes." De Manning's voice seemed distant. "Of course. Our horses had difficulty in the sand off the main road. Unlike the bandits' horses. Our men were forced to return."

"What did the bandits make off with besides the boy?"

"A valise of clothing."

De Manning was smitten with his mistress. While he was in the presence of a dewy-eyed Lydia, Michael doubted the man's ability to render an accurate recounting of the abduction. Furthermore, there was nothing to be gained in insisting that Lydia sit through the tutor's description of her son's kidnapping. He pivoted to Spry. "Question Mr. de Manning and the other men outside." Travel dust rose in his throat, and he coughed. The inside of his mouth felt like parchment. "What you and I discussed on the way here."

"Sir." Spry strode to the tutor's side. "This way, Mr. de Manning."

The captain's shoulders stiffened, and he sprang to his feet, inches from Spry. "I'm not going anywhere, Private."

De Manning's chin stabbed the air between them. Spry stood his ground.

Irritation spasmed Michael's gut and clipped his tone. "Mr. de Manning, go with my assistant, or I shall—"

"We know nothing of your service record, *Lieutenant*." Red-faced, the captain whirled on Michael. "You're a jump-up! What success have you at solving crimes, eh? Why, I doubt you've been in the Army above two years. What's the date on your commission?"

Michael steadied his breathing. Let de Manning be the one to lose control. "September thirtieth, 1777." Right after Brandywine, Ensign Stoddard's promotion had come through. Michael would never forget the date. Alas, his uncle and Lord Crump were financially unable to help him advance further in the Army.

As biting as a bayonet, his command stabbed through the air in the parlor. "Now either you attend my assistant and cooperate fully in this investigation henceforth, or I shall declare you an obstruction to the investigation and have you arrested."

"For God's sake, Mr. de Manning!" The pitch of Lydia's voice leapt half an octave. "What do you think to gain by remaining here? Do you imagine you must defend my honor from an appointed criminal investigator, an officer of the King? Is it not apparent that the lieutenant is a gentleman who is trying to help me? Go with his assistant investigator. Tell him what you know."

Not once did she turn her face to regard de Manning. She'd dismissed him. Michael had been in his shoes before. A most unpleasant experience. Almost, he felt sorry enough for the tutor to buy him a drink later. Almost.

Chapter Six

DE MANNING'S SHOULDERS drooped. No one spoke while he and Spry left the parlor. The little housemaid rushed after them to close the parlor doors. Then she turned her back on the doors and clasped her hands before her.

Michael's scrutiny hopped from her to Dorinda, who'd been so handy with the embroidery scissors. She'd swiveled to watch de Manning's exit, her lips parted. Aware of Michael's scrutiny, she straightened, dropped her gaze to her hands, also clasped, and composed her expression.

"Bravo, Lieutenant. I've never witnessed anyone decimate Nigel de Manning in quite such a fashion." Lydia leaned back with one arm stretched across the couch.

Michael said to her, "My intention is to 'decimate' no one. This has been an experience of great horror for all of you." He coughed at the dusty tickle in his throat. "I've a few additional questions of a background nature. Then my assistant and I shall leave you for the night."

One of Lydia's dark gold eyebrows crooked upward, echoed a second later by the corner of her mouth. "You've such a disarmingly honest face. Has anyone ever told you that?"

The tips of Michael's ears heated. Plenty of people remarked on his honest face. On numerous occasions, he'd relied upon it. That moment, however, his honest face wasn't helping him. It was intriguing Lydia. And she was playing the Game of Favorites, one of the nobility's beloved galliards. Stoddard *versus* de Manning.

Michael wasn't going to play. A boy's life depended on him. What he desired most that moment was to find Geoffrey, Lord Wynndon so the boy, his mother, and their entourage could depart Wilmington, continue on their way to wherever they'd been headed. Another cough found him, and his eyes watered. "You realize that when there's an abduction, there's usually a demand for ransom. Expect it in the next day or so. When it comes, or if you receive any communication from the bandits, contact Spry or me at the home of the Widow Chiswell, five houses down on Second Street."

She nodded.

"What is your ultimate destination?"

"Charles Town."

He cleared his throat. "With whom are you staying in Charles Town?"

"Would you care for tea, Lieutenant? It will help with that cough." Without waiting for his response, she snapped her fingers at the housemaid. "Felicia, tea for the Lieutenant and me."

"Yes, my lady." The girl curtsied and hurried out.

"I don't have time for—"

"Sit, Lieutenant." Lydia stroked a cushion beside her.

Michael blotted sweaty palms on his breeches. "I've been in the saddle all day. I-I prefer to stand." He winced at the stammer. "Charles Town is your destination. With whom will you visit?"

"My sister."

Her *sister*? Was Lydia joking? On a lark to visit her sister. She'd endangered the lives of a number of people and diverted resources of the Eighty-Second. How like the nobility. "My lady, this isn't a favorable time for traveling to visit your sister." Michael heard the cynical bite in his voice and softened his tone. "You should be with your husband. Where is he?"

Lydia redirected her gaze past Michael's left shoulder to the far wall and twitched her fingers once upon the top of the backrest. Her hand stilled a few seconds, as if she were making a decision. Then she stood. "Dorinda, tea is taking too long. Go to the kitchen. Assist Felicia."

Dorinda stirred, her gaze wandering between Michael and her mistress, her brows bunching inward. "But Felicia just left, my lady, and if I leave, you'll be alone with—"

"With an officer and a gentleman for a few minutes. I want my tea, and the lieutenant is thirsty after a long day in the saddle. Go. And close the parlor doors upon your exit."

"Yes, my lady." Dorinda dropped a curtsy slower than Felicia's. Then she slipped from the parlor.

As soon as the doors clicked shut, Lydia swept to the portion of the parlor farthest from the doors and motioned Michael to join her. When he'd done so, she said in a low tone, "Our entire married life, Faisleigh has been at war with his younger brother. John envies my husband's estate and title and seat in the House of Lords. Of late, his behavior has become unpredictable, frightening."

Again, Lydia hugged herself. "My husband plans to join us in Charles Town, in June. From there, we shall continue to St. Augustine, in East Florida, and a new home for young Wynndon and me. Although my husband has never confirmed it, I'm certain that he's moving my son and me there to save our lives."

Michael swallowed, his throat as dry as rocks in a desert. Her husband, a member of Parliament, had considered a land in the throes of colonial insurrection safer than his family seat in England? "Do enlighten me as to the root of your husband's rivalry with his brother."

She stroked her throat once. "My husband's father, Henry, possessed some well-substantiated claims that he'd descended from King Henry the Second."

Michael refrained from rolling his eyes. Amazing the number of nobles and commoners alike who made the claim. If all were true, King Henry would have spent his thirty-five-year reign in a constant state of futtering.

"So when Henry sired four boys, he naturally named them after Henry the Second's legitimate male children who survived to adulthood. Henry, Richard, my husband, Geoffrey, Lord Faisleigh, and John. Henry and Richard Wynndon died before age twenty, leaving no children. John Wynndon led the wastrel's life from early on, frittering away his inheritance." She hugged herself again.

Proximity enabled Michael to discern that the beads of her choker were, in fact, intricately carved ivory roses. King Henry the Second. White roses. The House of York?

Another memory swirled into his consciousness, whispered of the white rose's connection to something else. His thoughts reached for the connection. The mist shredded and tucked back into the depths of his mind, leaving a vague uneasiness behind.

Lydia murmured, "John and his wife have two sons. His wife is with child again. But my husband and I have only our son. Faisleigh has sired no children upon his three mistresses. If something happens to our son, the family fortune defaults to John and his heirs. John will blow through the estate before any of his children inherit it. He'll bring disgrace upon the title in Parliament."

"Do you and Lord Faisleigh suspect John Wynndon of foul dealings?"

"We do. There have been several—" She massaged the back of her neck. "Several suspicious accidents. Most recently in late November. An axle on a carriage in which my son was riding cracked. It might have been tampered with." Her voice trembled. "Fortunately he wasn't injured, but—but—" The tremble dissolved into a sob, and she groped her pockets. "Oh, where is my handkerchief?"

Michael passed her his handkerchief, which was fortunately clean. Then he walked away. Behind him, Lydia wept in soft gasps.

When her sobs had lessened, he faced her again. She dabbed her eyes and nose with the handkerchief. "Until my son reaches the age of majority and claims his position in the House of Lords, my husband holds all that power for him. Should anything happen to my dear husband, God forbid, I would become Wynndon's protector and guardian. It isn't an inconsequential amount of power, especially when combined with that from my own title."

Michael recalled that Lydia was a baroness in her own right. And if both Faisleigh and his son were dead, as well as the powerful, influential Lydia, John would inherit the title and fortune, uncontested. God's Teeth. Even were it not imperative for Michael to find Lord Wynndon so he could protect his own career, his personal code of honor would have bound him to try his hardest to rescue the boy.

But something bothered him about the internal logic of the abduction itself. "How long did your passage to America take?"

"Seven weeks."

From Lydia's comment about Lord Wynndon's portrait, Michael knew they'd departed England in late December or early January. "You and Lord Wynndon arrived in which American port late-February?"

"Boston."

"Then I presume that you booked passage on a ship that carried your party to a port north of Wilmington? New Berne, perhaps?"

"No." Lydia wrung the handkerchief. "With this—this insurrection, I learned that it would be more than a month before passage became available for all of us to depart together from Boston on a ship. I had no desire to split up my party, and after I'd been in Boston a week, I received communication that John's spies might be looking for us there. So I decided to take the King's Highway south."

Which made her vulnerable to highwaymen. Michael curbed exasperation before it leaked into his tone. "Who in your immediate household was privy in advance to Lord Faisleigh's plans to send you to America?"

"No one."

If John the wastrel brother were responsible for organizing his nephew's abduction, someone on American soil must have been in his employ well before Lydia and Lord Wynndon arrived. After mother and son set foot in Boston, there would have been no time to plot or confirm strategy with a schemer back in Yorkshire. Michael frowned.

Lydia's eyes widened. She pressed his handkerchief to her mouth a few seconds and whispered, "Yes. You, too, suspect that John has agents here, in America."

"Unless this crime is what it appears on the surface, a simple abduction for ransom. For the time, do not discuss this event with any townsfolk, and instruct your household to do the same."

"Very well." The knock on the parlor door fetched a gasp from Lydia. "Tea," she said, low, then elevated her voice. "Come in."

Dorinda and Felicia entered bearing trays with a teapot, cups, and saucers and proceeded to arrange the service on a side table. Much as Michael desired tea, he knew this was his opportunity to exit with grace. "I appreciate the invitation, my lady, but I cannot stay. I've evidence to examine, informants to interview, and my assistant to consult." He backed several steps from her and bowed from the waist.

"But—"

"Spry and I will stay in contact." Now, that was a splendid idea. His assistant could act as go-between as much as possible. "I appreciate your trust in us. Good evening, Lady Faisleigh."

Lydia leaned forward, her lips parted. He spun about before she could speak and spotted a flustered Dorinda scurrying ahead of him to let him out the front door. Not until he stood on the porch, a solid door shut between himself and Lydia, did he relax his shoulders and gulp in a full breath.

On the walkway, he heard his exhalation rattle, the tortured lungful of a man who'd seen a phantasm from his past. He righted his gait to that of an investigator with too few hours in his day and headed back to the infirmary.

***

Michael turned onto Market Street and almost collided with brunette, buxom Alice Farrell. She beamed her broadest smile from beneath her straw hat. "Look who we have here! The Hero of Wilmington."

His gaze tracked to her companion. His stomach sank. "Aunt" Rachel White favored him with her tight-lipped smile of certainty. "Well, well, well."

Thoughts of Lydia, her son, and Lord Cornwallis splintered apart. Aggravation exited in a noisy rush from Michael's nostrils. The women stood between him and the infirmary. There was nothing for it but to act the busy officer that he was. Shoulders thrown back, chest out, he gave the women a formal nod of greeting and stepped past them.

Mrs. Farrell bounded in front, causing him to halt to avoid bumping into her. Her dark eyes widened with mock reprobation. "Fie on you for rushing off in such haste. Haven't you heard the excellent news?"

How she, burdened by panniers and petticoats, had moved more speedily than a man in breeches Michael didn't understand. "Ah. News so excellent must mean you've talked the Almighty into adding eight more hours to my day, so I can complete today's duties." He sidestepped.

Mrs. White blocked him, her visage stern. Iron-gray hair peeked from beneath her lace-trimmed mobcap.

"Such a sense of humor!" Mrs. Farrell batted dark eyelashes at him. "No, gallant knight. The Wilmington ladies are rescheduling the festivity for which you're the guest of honor. Remember? All we needed was Major Craig's approval on our new date."

The weapons smuggling operation from which Michael had arrested the jailed gunsmith had been fronted by the infamous Church of Mary and Martha of Bethany, also known as the Bethanys. In January, Michael had led the mission in which he and his men captured and imprisoned the corrupt preacher and half the scoundrels in the congregation. It earned him the guest of honor position at the dinner and dance the Wilmington ladies were so determined to organize and carry out. Michael's stomach knotted. Maybe he had an ulcer starting. "Best of luck with that, madam. Major Craig is out of town."

"We received his approval on the new date just before he left."

Damn. "Excuse me, ladies. I've an appointment in the infirmary."

Mrs. White stood at full height, barely an inch shorter than he. "I've been in town the better part of two weeks, Michael, and not once during that time have you visited us."

Mrs. Farrell blinked at him, then at Mrs. White. "When did you two come to be on such close terms?" Her smile gleamed with teeth.

Tight-lipped certainty reappeared on Rachel White's mouth. "Kate, Michael, and I had quite an adventure in Hillsborough last month, didn't we, Michael?" She winked at Mrs. Farrell. "Such modesty after saving my life and Kate's."

"Yes, yes, of course you'd be on close terms after that ordeal." Mrs. Farrell's cheeks pinked. She licked her lips, sucked in a huge breath, and let it out with a tremor of delight. "*C'est magnifique!*"

Under different circumstances, Michael might have enjoyed watching the swell of her bosom when she breathed like that. This time, he pinned his gaze to Rachel White's face. "Good day, madam."

"*Aunt Rachel.* You've been remiss. I insist that you stop by White's Tavern.

In fact, I approve your visit. You're an excellent influence upon Kate."

Mrs. Farrell pressed hands to her cheeks. "Of course he's an excellent influence. He's a hero. It would be a lucky thing for poor Kate to have a hero for a *friend*."

Michael's neck and ears smoldered.

"Luck can be made." Aunt Rachel hadn't taken her gaze off Michael. "You know how much Kate will appreciate your visit." She stepped back, allowing him to pass.

"Divine! You've made him blush, Mrs. White." Mrs. Farrell crossed her arms. "Well. What's so important in the infirmary that you must rush off without polite conversation?"

"Dead criminals. Good day, ladies." He touched the brim of his hat and swept past without waiting for them to respond.

Chapter Seven

BY WANING DAYLIGHT in the infirmary, Spry spilled the contents of a haversack on the surgeon's scrubbed, bloodstained table. He caught a withered apple before it escaped onto the floor and piled it with the rest of the items. "Inventory of the dark-haired lad's haversack, sir. One apple. One tinderbox. One wooden bowl. One horn spoon. One hunk of bread." He knocked the bread against the table. It rapped like a wood block. "Hard enough to cause bodily damage, if used as a weapon." He held up mold-speckled cheese. "And one chunk of yellow cheese, well on the way to its eternal reward." He shoveled everything back in the haversack. "Much like what the other boy was carrying."

Michael, at the opposite end of the table, flipped through pages of a tattered Psalter with greasy, scratched covers, a book of the size to fit in a man's waistcoat pocket. As the surgeon's orderlies were within hearing, he'd reminded Spry to keep his voice down while discussing details presented by Lydia and her party. He said, low, "Did the dark-haired boy also have a Psalter, like this?"

"No Psalter for him, sir. But he carried a tomahawk."

"Both boys had daggers. And cartridge boxes. Reasonable enough to assume that they had muskets or rifles, although our men didn't recover them."

"Scooped up by cohorts during their retreat, sir."

Michael nodded and, with a grimace, downed the remainder of the coffee he'd half-begged off Clayton. True, it had taken the edge off his thirst. However, each swallow of the surgeon's black sludge smeared the inside of Michael's mouth with the flavors of tar and fish, Wilmington's ubiquitous odors. The coffee also tasted of bone saw. Michael didn't want to know how Clayton had managed *that*.

Tea would have tasted far more pleasant. But he'd had to set a precedent with Lydia. No social occasions.

She'd ogled him. Was he so very certain that she hadn't recognized him?

No. He'd no time to ponder that. He set the cup on a side table and continued thumbing the book. The Psalter included the Book of Proverbs. His gaze snagged on an underlined verse. He read it aloud. "'Train up a child in the way he should go: and when he is old, he will not depart from it.' Proverbs twenty-two six."

"Not a good portent, sir, considering the context."

"Agreed." Michael lowered his voice. "How many boys did Mr. de Manning spot?"

"He claims he saw no boys."

"He was inside the carriage during the incident, yes? He saw only men from the raiding party. How about the coachman and footman, then?"

"They counted at least ten boys, sir. Several may have been escaped slaves."

"Holy Christ!" Michael muttered. "That means half the bloody raiding party was made of boys. Let's hope we aren't observing a trend in the tactics of North Carolina's rebels." He propped elbows on the table and flipped to the front interior pages of the palm-sized book. With sloppy penmanship, someone had scrawled a name. "Looks like this book may have belonged to one Rephael Whistler." He and Spry cocked eyebrows at each other and broke into a few whistled bars of song to commemorate the word "whistler." Then they snorted with dark humor. "So is Rephael Whistler the name of our deceased blond boy, or did the lad inherit Whistler's Psalter?"

With a wrinkled nose, Spry shoved the dark-haired boy's patched breeches and shirt off to the side. "All three of these people surely inherited their clothing from numerous relatives. I doubt even the town beggars would want it now, handed down and patched so. Looks more appropriate for ragpaper."

Michael straightened. "Find any money among the second lad's belongings?"

"No money on any of them, sir. Poor as dirt. If the old man had a haversack, the guards didn't bring it in with his body."

No ciphers on any of them, either. The two soldiers had checked the usual places in clothing for hidden messages, such as shoes and waistcoat linings. Because rebels sometimes got clever and hid ciphers in hollow buttons, Michael and his assistant had pried apart all the buttons on the bandits' clothing. To no avail.

"They're like cockroaches, sir. We stamp out a few, only to have thrice as many take their place. Where have they nested, so we can squash them all?"

Nothing in their possession yielded an obvious clue about where the two boys and the man had come from. Michael tapped the Psalter on the table a few seconds and allowed his logic and imagination to play together. "Care to guess how many lads in the plunder party had their parents' permission to embark upon a career of highway robbery?"

Spry's tone became glib. "Why, all of them, sir. Robin Hood makes a glorious hero. A valise of clothing would be welcome in any poor family."

"Robin Hood. Is that what they're about?" Michael tapped the Psalter again. "And now they're presented with an opportunity to collect ransom for Lord Wynndon so they can feed poor families?"

Spry shrugged. "A reasonable presumption."

"Or is Lord Wynndon a recruit, albeit forcibly?"

Spry stared at his commander, then shuddered. "Ye gods, I hadn't thought of that, sir. If so, surely the boy will resist."

"A ten-year-old?" The vision of a lad with the same hair and eye color as Michael unfolded in his head. He imagined him huddled, sobbing, on the ground and an adult man seizing the child by the hair, then slapping his cheek, leaving a red handprint on the pale flesh. Michael winced and paced, the Psalter in his hand. "He won't resist for long. And maybe they'll still collect a ransom for him."

His assistant said in a quiet voice, "Sir, maybe there's another explanation for the number of boys in that party of bandits. We've gone through six years of fighting with the rebels. So much fighting for so long—the rebels aren't any better off than we are. Some families in North Carolina can get no supplies. They're starving. What if these highwaymen prey upon them, make promises that any starving lad who joins their ranks could eat his fill after each raid? A boy might run away from home into such a snare."

Spry had figured a great deal out, even though he hadn't seen the gaunt, hungry children in uniform across the battlegrounds at Brandywine. Each time Johnny had gone for a soldier, he might have left behind gaunt, hungry women: mothers, grandmothers, sisters, and cousins. Maybe sweethearts. When Johnny ran away, did the womenfolk weep? Or did his departure mean there was one less mouth to feed?

Michael stopped pacing and pondered the Psalter again. Had the boy who'd carried the book left a family behind, people who might know more about the highwaymen? If so, how could he find them?

The logical first step would be to ask someone who had lived in Wilmington for a number of years, someone who was familiar with the residents. He expelled a slow sigh of inevitability at the "someone" who came to mind. She'd give him her opinion on avoiding her for almost two weeks. But he couldn't hide from her forever.

Ah, what the hell. White's *was* the best tavern in town.

He shoved the Psalter into his other waistcoat pocket. "Not much more to be gained here. I believe we've reached the point in this investigation where we need assistance from a woman."

"Sir!" Spry clicked his heels. His teeth gleamed in the gloom. "Are recommendations in order?"

Although Spry had never said so, he thought his commander lived a dull life of work, work, work. Although Michael had never said so, he agreed with his assistant. For some ungodly reason, some asinine, self-imposed scourging, it had been at least a year since he'd last frolicked with a woman. Spry's ribbing rankled. "Pack up the rebels' property and bring it with us. We'll drop it at the house, then talk more in White's Tavern."

"Ah. That tavern. *That* woman." Spry seized the tote bags, his grin wider. "Right away, sir!"

***

At White's on Front Street, windows open to the spring night allowed laughter and bergamot-scented pipe smoke to waft out to the street, along with lazy fiddle melody. Friday evening at five o'clock: more than twenty horses hitched to the post out front meant business was ripping along well. A huge burst of laughter from the inside of the two-story wooden building implied that business was the best it had ever been.

As soon as Spry tugged the door open, the moths returned to Michael's stomach. Why should he feel so jumpy about seeing Kate again? She was a sensible woman. Surely she'd rationalized the rush of emotion they'd shown each other in Hillsborough as the result of a life-or-death situation. And she'd recognized that there was no romance: that her aunt, who wanted to see her widowed niece married off, was matchmaking. Surely.

He doffed his hat and entered, and Spry followed him. Smells of beer, men's bodies, and roast beef greeted Michael, along with grins and waves from a number of patrons and all six busty barmaids. Like warriors invoking an honored chieftain's name before battle, men at a long backgammon table thumped the table with their fists and chanted Spry's name for about ten seconds. Several scooted aside to make room on a bench. Spry puffed out his chest and smirked.

Ah, the backgammon challenge. Michael had forgotten to ask Spry how he was faring. From the looks of Spry's supporters, he was faring well indeed. Michael caught his assistant's eye. "Business first."

"Sir." Spry pointed at one of the backgammon players. "Finley, be a good boy and don't run away. Soon enough, I shall be over to trounce you."

The other man hooted. "Sure, and then you'll wake up!" Men, including Spry, roared.

Kate's brother, Kevin Marsh, a lanky blond man in his early twenties and nearly Spry's height, waved Michael over to a table at the rear of the tavern where he usually sat. While Kevin shooed patrons from the table, Michael forged ahead, the moths in his stomach converting to mockingbirds. Even before the patrons had fully vacated the table, Kevin, shirtsleeves rolled to his elbows, was wiping the surface down with a corner of his apron.

While Michael was *en route*, three barmaids altered their trajectory so they could bump into him. "Love you," whispered one. "Marry me," said the second. "Hero," murmured the third and pinched his buttock. Bemused, aware that a fourth barmaid approached him with a leer that signaled far more mischief, Michael scurried ahead. Surely she wouldn't be so brazen as to squeeze his arse while he was in the company of her supervisor. What in blazes had gotten into Marsh's wenches, anyway?

Michael gained the table with no further propositions. "Evening, Mr. Marsh." He extended his hand.

"Kevin. Call me Kevin." The blond man wrung his hand a couple seconds, his smile so broad it narrowed his blue eyes to slits. His gaze measured stubble on Michael's face. "Haven't seen you in two weeks. Heard you were traveling."

Kate's brother wanted to be on a first-name basis with him, too. And he looked ecstatic, not sensible. The mockingbirds in Michael's gut were swooping. He mumbled something about business for the Eighty-Second.

"Good to have you back. You certainly do move around these days." Kevin glanced at Spry, who'd sauntered to the table, and added in one breathless stream, "Hullo, Spry. You fellows having the usual? My sister's in the kitchen.

I'll hop out there and let her know you're here. Won't be but a moment."

Kevin hustled for the back door. Michael was certain he saw him skip once.

"Well, there's a happy fellow." Spry, another member of the fraternity of happy fellows, turned an expression of humor and expectation upon his commander.

The mockingbirds transformed into a flock of hawks with razor-sharp talons. Michael's palms felt clammy again. He hoped to God that Spry didn't notice his jitters. He set his hat on the table, leaned against the nearest wall, and crossed arms over his chest, noting with satisfaction that Spry remained standing, arms at his sides, hat tucked under one arm.

Appropriate postures for the situation. The caste distinction in the military adamantly discouraged jollification between officers and men. Even so, Captain Nigel de Manning, entrenched in convention, would die of apoplexy if he saw Lieutenant Stoddard and his assistant investigator proximate in a tavern.

And discussion of the tutor was an excellent segue into talk about the investigation. "You questioned Captain de Manning, the coachmen, and the outriders about the incident. What did they have to say, Spry?"

"Sir. Their testimonies of the attack dovetail with the account provided by Lady Faisleigh. Mr. de Manning was the only one of them who was in the carriage at the time." Spry gnawed his lip a few seconds. "The two bandits who made off with the boy stunned Mr. de Manning momentarily inside the carriage. He thinks he remembers one of them trying to pull Dorinda from the carriage, too. As Mr. de Manning opines that Dorinda had cast herself as a shield across her mistress and the boy, it would make sense for bandits to remove Dorinda so they could grab the boy."

Michael grunted. "Dorinda's a brave woman. And what did you think of Captain de Manning?"

The private had shifted his gaze to watch a fellow juggle half a dozen pewter spoons on the other side of the tavern. By candlelight and lamplight, the spoons had become a gleaming silver circle. "I think he's in love with Lady Faisleigh. Sick in love, sir. I hope I never lose my head over a woman in such a way."

Years earlier, Michael had pronounced himself immune to lovesickness, but he'd seen enough of what it did to others. "Do you think he's irrational?"

"Possibly. He's terrified she's going to replace him. When I questioned him this afternoon, almost every sentence from his mouth was an endorsement for his indispensability to her and the household."

Michael felt another pang of pity for de Manning. The juggler missed a spoon, unbalanced himself trying to catch it, and lost the others in a clatter on the floor. "She doesn't return the sentiment."

"No, sir." Spry rotated his head to study Michael. "I rather think she fancies you."

A chill screwed its way up Michael's neck. Was he so certain that Lydia hadn't recognized him? Spry wasn't smiling. He didn't find the situation amusing. Michael decided to level with his assistant about portions of his predicament. "I received the same impression. Disconcerting, and a nuisance."

"Why, sir? She's a beautiful woman. She's suffering."

"She's a crime victim and witness."

"But she's from Yorkshire, as you are. Sir."

"That makes no difference. The more personally an investigator becomes involved with victims and witnesses, the more difficult it is to call upon his logical mind."

"Ah." Spry broke eye contact, frowned, and nodded.

"Lady Faisleigh invited me for tea this afternoon. I declined. I hope she responds appropriately henceforth. Otherwise, delivering updates on the abduction might become awkward."

"I could easily convey messages, sir."

Some of the talons in Michael's stomach released. "Yes, Spry, I had that in mind." He caught his lip with his upper front teeth a moment. "After you and de Manning left the parlor, Lady Faisleigh sent both maids to the kitchen. It left her alone with me. She told me that Lord Faisleigh's younger brother, John Wynndon, is greedy for the estate. She thinks he's scheming against them. Of course, John Wynndon is on the other side of the Atlantic, but he could easily have an agent planted in Lady Faisleigh's party. When someone is the victim of a crime such as abduction or murder, the culprit is often a member of the household."

Spry snapped his fingers. "It's de Manning."

Michael chuckled. "Very well. Postulate on a motive for Mr. de Manning to have a hand in Lord Wynndon's abduction."

Spry grinned. "Money. Sir."

Michael decided to let his assistant hammer out the logic. "How so?"

"He retired a junior officer, sir, and his pension isn't large enough to support him. John the rascal brother offers to pay de Manning a handsome settlement if he'd get rid of the boy in America."

"But surely Lady Faisleigh already pays de Manning a handsome salary. The fellow isn't poor. And if he's sick in love with her, what would make him jump into John's camp, especially if it brought grief to the object of his love? Wouldn't she dismiss him after the boy was gone, having no further need for a tutor? Thus our suspect has effectively shot himself in the foot."

The younger man stared off into space a moment. The fingers of one hand drummed his thigh. "Sir. What if Mr. de Manning, not Lord Faisleigh, is really the boy's father?"

Michael stared, hard, at his assistant. Lydia *had* mentioned her husband's inability to sire children upon his mistresses. And de Manning had been part of the household for many years. Had Spry latched onto something? "An interesting twist." He relaxed neck and shoulders. "Worthy of Machiavelli."

"Machiavelli, eh?" The private rubbed his palms in anticipation. "Many thanks for the recommendation. I shall track down his works."

Nick Spry and *The Prince*: Michael wondered whether the world was ready for such a combination. He pulled out the ivory likeness of Lord Wynndon and studied it. Was that de Manning's face? Recognition stirred in him again—or was it his mind tricking him? He rotated the portrait to Spry. "So we're looking at a young Nigel de Manning when we gaze on this portrait?"

His assistant pondered it a few seconds and nodded. "Perhaps, sir. There's something familiar in his eyes, I think."

Michael pocketed the portrait. "There's also great power in suggestion, Spry."

"Sir, you mentioned Lady Faisleigh's fears of her brother-in-law. Suppose John has suspected all along that the boy isn't a Wynndon? Now his enemy is in America. He can leave foul business to his agents there while pouncing upon the family fortune and title at home."

"But if de Manning is in love with Lady Faisleigh, you haven't explained how he remains in her circle after he disposes of their child."

"Yes, sir. De Manning would point out that Lady Faisleigh and her husband still need an heir, and de Manning himself has successfully sired upon her a healthy child. They can try for another healthy child. That gets de Manning back in her bed."

"Ah. Not money, then, but *lust*." Michael chuckled with black humor. For the moment, Spry's story hung together. Lydia was no fool, but if de Manning acted upon the motivations that Spry suggested, it might be the only way the tutor could manipulate her. "From what you've observed, you believe he's brainsick in love with her. You're suggesting that his connection with her is the paramount relationship of his life, to be preserved at all costs. That any offspring he produces with her are expendable. Correct?"

Spry met Michael's gaze. "Yes, sir."

"You've described a man who would kill his own son to continue to have access to the boy's mother. Hmm. That would make Captain de Manning a dangerous, ruthless scoundrel. In conjecture."

"Yes, sir."

Michael nodded once, an abrupt motion. "Men are demons sometimes. I won't rule out de Manning embodying such motivations. He's a clever fellow. However, we must still interview members of Lady Faisleigh's household, one at a time. We'll start on the morrow. We need a guide to the site where the abduction and robbery occurred. Fetch the head coachman at seven-thirty."

"Sir."

"And we mustn't lose sight of the boy in all this. If de Manning played a role in his abduction, the tutor's our link to recovering him."

"Yes, sir. But I wonder—if there were no witnesses in the parlor to contest what Lady Faisleigh told you, can you be certain that anything she said during that time is true?"

"No. All we know for certain is that Lord Wynndon was forcibly removed from the carriage by what appeared to be bandits."

Spry glanced toward the back door. "Sir, I'm curious to hear how you believe the lady who owns this fine establishment can help us track down those bandits."

Michael had already spotted the approach of that lady in his peripheral vision. Because he could delay the inevitable no longer, he turned to face a petite blonde in her mid-twenties who bore a tray with three tankards and a wine glass. Her smile, easy with friendship, dissolved all the claws in Michael's gut. Only then did he become aware of effortless warmth inhabiting his chest and the airy laughter of his heartbeat, and that somehow both had encouraged his lips to explore a type of smile that encompassed new territory.

Spry bowed. Chagrined that he'd needed a reminder, Michael bowed, too. When he straightened, Kate Duncan had slid the tray onto the table, shifted closer to him, and was favoring him with a sparkle in her eyes to rival sunlight upon indigo water of the deep Atlantic. His tongue pasted itself to the roof of his mouth. Fiddle music and conversation buzz in the tavern faded away.

He finally worked his tongue loose. "Good evening." Good evening? Was that all he could say to her? Ye gods, what was wrong with him? He sounded like a half-wit. Probably looked like one, too, with his idiot's grin and dusty clothing.

She laughed. "Good evening, indeed." She turned her head. "And greetings, Spry. I presume you know Finley at the table over yonder boasts of overturning your latest victory."

More big teeth. "And it'll rain eels and orange mice tonight, too."

"I'm so glad to hear it." Her smile grew sharp as a razor worked on a strop. "Who knew backgammon could be such a barbaric activity? And speaking of barbarians—" She allowed her sentence to trail off, and she slanted a glance at Michael.

He recognized the game as soon as her smirk took shape and produced a scowl. "Now, that's low. Can you believe it, Spry? All in one afternoon, a man rides back from Brunswick, chases two rebel scoundrels out of town, and comes to the aid of a visitor—and here he's labeled a barbarian, just for looking a little untidy. I can get no respect."

"Perhaps you can get no respect, but you *can* get a free sample of a refreshing drink Aunt and I are developing for the summer." Kate placed a tankard on the table before Michael. "And you, too, assistant investigator."

Michael peered into his tankard. "Where's my claret?"

Spry picked up his tankard of experimental potable and swirled the contents around, his lips twisted to one side. "Looks like water with torn up leaves in it."

"That might explain why it's free, Spry." Tankard in hand, Michael sniffed at the liquid. Mint in there somewhere.

"What's the matter with you men?" Kate propped one fist on her hip and wagged the other forefinger at them. "I do believe you're more afraid of this beverage than you are of battle. Drink up. Tell me what you think."

Still thirsty, Michael knocked back part of the room-temperature drink, a tea made with honey and mint plus at least one other herb. It quenched his thirst. Not bad for a summer drink. A pity they couldn't keep it cold. He downed the remainder, including the leaves, then fished for flecks of mint from his teeth with his tongue. "Needs whiskey."

"Plenty of whiskey," said Spry. But he licked his lips.

"Bah, you two are incorrigible. What is it with men and whiskey, eh? There are more drinks in heaven and earth than are dreamt of in the taverns of your minds."

Spry squinted at Michael. "Hamlet, sir?"

He shrugged. "Act one, scene five."

Kate jutted her chin at Michael. "Of course, Horatio. And Aunt and I hope whiskey will be deemed optional for this beverage." She retrieved the empty tankards, placed them on the tray, and set the drinks they'd ordered before them. When they paid, she pocketed their coin then shifted her gaze from Spry to Michael. "Well. Spry isn't running off to beat Finley at backgammon. That tells me you two have business to conduct. I shall check back with you later. Enjoy your drinks." She grabbed her tray and turned to leave.

Michael clutched her upper arm. Before she'd dropped the mask of business in place, he'd seen the quick push of her lower lip, the downcast glance. "Stay a moment. We need your help."

Tankards clattered when she thumped the tray down on the table. Unsmiling, she looked him in the eye. "It's been six and a half weeks since I last saw you. Should I be surprised that you visited today only because you need my help? Apparently not." She directed her gaze to her upper arm, where he still grasped her.

He uncurled his fingers and released her, exasperation escaping him with a sigh. What the devil? He'd just said something wrong to her again. He was forever saying something gauche around women, particularly Kate. Damned if he understood the fairer sex. "I meant no disrespect."

"Of course you didn't." The sparkle left her eyes, and her shoulders sagged. "Obviously you've another investigation at hand. I shall help you if I can. Only, do hurry. Cook is short one of her lads today, and I've been helping in the kitchen."

For the first time, Michael noticed the strands of her hair escaped from a plain cotton mobcap, hair darkened to the color of honey by sweat. A smudged apron covered a faded, checked polonaise gown. Her slender waistline looked just as appealing in the shabbier gown as it looked in her usual fine attire, but he'd never before seen her in a state approaching dishevelment. How intriguing. Barbarian, even.

His tongue tried to paste itself to the roof of his mouth again, but he coughed it loose. "Er, where might I find the family of Rephael Whistler?"

Kate's eyes widened. Then her head jerked to the side, and she gazed past Spry, over the heads of patrons. "The Whistler family lived up the northeast road, near the taverns of Collier and Rouse."

Michael felt his eyes bulge. In his peripheral vision, he saw Spry's jaw dangle. "*Rouse?*" That was the name Gibson had mentioned to the blond lad! He glanced where she'd directed her attention but saw only the usual assortment of smiling, drinking civilians mingled with smiling, drinking soldiers. When he returned his attention to Kate, she dodged his gaze and angled her body so she could more easily look elsewhere. "Who is Rouse, Kate?"

"Alexander Rouse. Busy tavern owner." She flashed him a dry smile. "Doesn't care for King George."

A rebel doing business with Ralph Gibson. A rebel possibly connected with Lord Wynndon's abduction through that blond boy. He wondered whether the tavern was near the abduction site. "How far up the northeast road is Rouse's Tavern?"

"Eight miles or so."

"You said the Whistlers lived up the northeast road. Past tense. Where are they now?"

Her voice became hurried, low. "Years ago, lightning struck the house. It burned to the ground. The father was killed. The mother was left with a brood of children."

"Sad," said Spry. "Where are they now?"

Kate shrugged. "I don't know. I don't care. They're rebel scum. I'd rather not discuss them." She inched away from the table, toward the back door.

Talking about the Whistlers made Kate nervous, even hostile. Michael exchanged a raised eyebrow with Spry. He leaned toward Kate. "What were the ages of the children then?"

"I don't recall exactly."

"Have any of the children blond hair?"

"I don't know. And I don't care." Kate smashed her lips together.

Spry stirred. "Sir, in the morning, we'll be riding out that way."

"True. Should we find the family, though, I doubt the Widow Whistler will talk to the King's Men." He flicked his gaze back to Kate. "Perhaps she'd talk with the Widow Duncan."

Kate scowled and crossed her arms high over her chest. "I assure you she won't speak with *me*."

Spry reached for his beer, then stopped himself. "It isn't a safe trip for Mrs. Duncan, sir. Nor are we guaranteed to find Mrs. Whistler."

Spry was right on both points. Michael returned his scrutiny to Kate.

Her upper lip curled. "It sounds as though the Whistlers are in trouble with the law." Her lips spread into a cold smile.

Her hostility slapped at Michael. He steeled himself from backing a step from her. "Not necessarily. But they might be able to help me find someone who's in trouble." He measured her smile. "You don't care for the Whistlers. Why not?"

"I already told you. They're rebel scum."

He felt his eyebrows climb his forehead. "Kate, you've no qualms sitting down to coffee with the Wilmington ladies, some of whom are most definitely not the King's Friends. Come, now. What is it between you and the Whistlers?"

The smile faded. She lifted her chin. "It has nothing to do with your investigation. It's personal."

Personal. The fare Michael bought with his "honest face" had gotten him as far as he could with Kate Duncan on the issue. He wasn't sure her enmity with the Whistlers impacted the investigation. Thus he'd no rationale to pursue it. But damned if he wasn't curious over what had gotten Kate's back up.

One corner of her mouth crooked. "Spry will waste away if you don't let him have his beer and backgammon soon. And tonight's the final night of the competition."

How did Kate come to be so interested in backgammon, of a sudden? Then Michael felt like Wilmington's biggest blockhead. All her peculiar fidgeting, even the acerbic attitude—Kate must be trying to get rid of Spry so she could have a few moments to talk alone with *him*. Michael laughed. "Ah. Very well, Spry, we're done for now." He swept one hand through air, in the direction of the backgammon table. "Off to the front line you go."

"Sir? Er, yes, sir!" Spry grinned, confiscated his tankard, and swaggered for the other table.

Michael swiveled to Kate. She'd uncrossed her arms, and her expression had softened. They gazed at each other several seconds, sighed at the same time, then laughed at the absurdity of sighing together. He felt his tongue stick to the roof of his mouth again and blurted, "How—how have you been? What happened—you know, in Hillsborough, with your aunt selling her house?" He pulled out a chair for her. "Will you sit with me a few minutes?"

She rolled her head and darted a glance to the right. "Oh, I cannot. I'm—we're too busy back in the kitchen." She scratched her neck where loose hair brushed it. "But—but might I have some help moving a fifty-pound bag of rice from the storage shed to the kitchen?"

"Certainly." He waved toward the backgammon table. "Let me fetch Spry before—"

"No, don't bother. Spry needs all his concentration to beat the breeches off Finley and two other fellows." She hefted the tray and tilted her chin to him. "I plan on keeping him well-supplied with beer tonight." She whispered, "I wagered good money on Spry as champion."

Michael's jaw dropped. "You—" He caught himself, glanced around, and lowered the volume of his voice. "You wagered money on my assistant?" He gaped at Kate, feeling as dazed as a bumpkin mired in the spell of a sorceress. A woman who gambled. What would his mother and sister say? What would his father have said? He swallowed at tightness in his throat.

"Of course. I only bet on horses that are running, and surely you agree that he shows rather well." She sashayed for the back door, her voice trailing. "Come along."

If Spry lost, he might not be allowed in White's again for awhile. Michael scooped up his hat and wine glass, cast a look at the backgammon table, and muttered, "Good luck, lad," before following Kate.

Chapter Eight

LONG SHADOWS HERALDING dusk awaited him beyond the tavern's back door, encouraging return of the jabber of thoughts when he was mulling over an investigation. As usual in the early stages, all the pieces he'd been handed appeared to have come from different puzzles.

What on earth was Lydia doing in Wilmington—*Lydia*, of all people? Fate thumbed its nose at him. That it had thrown her in his path again seemed more the stuff of his fancies during his first year in the Army, rather than the reality that had faced him an hour earlier in a house on Second Street.

Of course she hadn't recognized him in the parlor. He hoped she'd never recognize him. Although she never failed to make an appearance in his dreams two or three times per year, it was always upon the backdrop of war horror. Over the years, he'd assimilated the impression that Lydia was at home among the King's collection of reptiles in Parliament. Watching de Manning grant her possession of his soul substantiated that impression.

Michael wanted no part of her world of deceit and tainted love. That moment, as earlier, his greatest desire was to find a boy who had, by now, likely endured rough handling from his captors, a boy who was among other boys not much older than he was, boys who were generating terror and confusion in him. Find him, yes, and return him to his mother so they and their party could leave Wilmington.

He thought of Spry's revulsion over the idea of forcible recruits for the bandits. It was one thing for highwaymen to seduce others into a life of banditry with false claims of wealth and full bellies. But if the robbers recruited via abduction—ah, a pity such scoundrels could only be executed once.

As to the robbery and abduction, Michael did wonder how John Wynndon, on the other side of the Atlantic, might have schemed everything. If he'd done so, he possessed an incredible amount of cunning. There were Lydia's household members to question, particularly Dorinda, Felicia, and, in more depth, Captain de Manning. Surely one of them would know something to further the investigation.

He caught up with Kate behind the kitchen building, where she handed over the empty tankards to a couple of boys who were washing dishes in wooden tubs foamy with soap. Nibbling on a final piece of mint leaf he'd worked from between his teeth, Michael didn't question when she snatched his hat and full glass of claret away, set them and the tray just inside a kitchen redolent of roast beef, and emerged with a ring of keys. No man could juggle a fifty-pound sack of rice and a full glass of claret with success.

At the rear of the tavern property, while Kate unlocked the door of a shed, he realized he hadn't been more specific with her and asked who Rephael Whistler was. Was he a Psalm-quoting highwayman? A boy who had lost his way in life, then ultimately his life? A man whose Psalter had fallen into the hands of others?

The shed door groaned open. "In here, Michael." Kate hooked the padlock and key ring on a nail just inside and moved from the doorway.

He entered the shed, dim inside with the approach of night. Did Ralph Gibson or Alexander Rouse know Rephael Whistler?

And what was he looking for again in the shed? Oh, yes, a fifty-pound sack of rice.

"See, on those shelves along the back?" Kate stepped into the doorway.

The shed smelled like a grain bin. He made for the shelves and sacks stored on them. Behind him, light dimmed further. He bent, poked at the sacks. "This looks like flour, not rice." Did Gibson or Rouse have enough money to supply boy bandits with Psalters?

"Try the shelves to your right." Kate's voice softened. "You know, I never thanked you for saving my life and that of Aunt Rachel. You're a hero, Michael."

Hero. Oh, not *that* again. It must have been Aunt Rachel and Alice Farrell, hard at work spreading gossip and proclaiming him a hero across town, that influenced the barmaids' sudden fascination with him. He pivoted ninety degrees to the sacks on the other set of shelves. "All in the line of duty." The door had swung halfway closed, and Kate stood less than two feet from him. "Don't you store rice in a barrel, Kate? This isn't rice in these sacks." He straightened and swiveled to her, arms spread.

"Of course it isn't rice, silly goose," she whispered. Her arms glided around his neck. "It's gratitude." She brushed his lips with hers: soft, warm, and tasting of cinnamon and honey. Then she drew back her head a few inches and studied his reaction.

The thump of his heartbeat in his ears encompassed the only sound he heard at first. His mouth flooded with saliva. He gulped. His watch ticked, a whisper, within his waistcoat. Just outside the shed, two or three birds produced nocturnes, and farther away, one of the boys washing tankards called to the other.

Kate's arms were warm. The last remnants of daylight gleamed in her eyes and on the full curves of her lips. He slid one hand to her waist. Her body nestled inward, to his. With his other hand, he cupped her cheek. She sighed and closed her eyes.

First with his thumb, then with his forefinger, he followed the shape of her lips. Like a painter layering a rich hue upon a canvas, he traced the lines over and over, fascinated, engrossed. She chased his fingers with her lips. He held her chin still, tilted up to him, and captured her upper lip between his. Again, he tasted cinnamon and honey—and salt, like tears. He pressed his forehead to hers. Their pulses aligned. Her exhale brushed his cheek. Far away, in another world, birds continued their nocturnes.

The taste of her lingered in his mouth. His hand strayed from her cheek to her shoulder, guided her to him so he could savor the arcs and corners, the soft and firm, of both lips. She moved with him, her body rising to greet his.

Even when her lips first parted and invited him to taste deeper, he didn't hurry. Kisses were Act One. An entire decade of his life, he'd rushed through that act, each time with the hearty encouragement of the woman he was kissing.

Kate didn't want Act Three in a grain shed. Despite what she'd implied to him in Hillsborough, he wasn't even sure she wanted Act Three. So he stayed with the kiss and let her guide him down into the slippery cinnamon and honey of her mouth. He didn't expect the salty tears that rolled, slow, down her cheeks, like thunder behind a distant mountain, and almost pulled back to ask her what was wrong. But she seized his head and pressed him to her.

Starlight and the scent of the heavens swept over him. He felt lightheaded, buoyed away from Earth into the glow of a million stars, a man lying in a vast, grassy field on a summer night and surrounded by the majesty of the Milky Way. All around him seemed luminous and open and deep, like the face of the divine. It embraced him and moved through him without beginning or end.

What must have been a good while later, he realized that night had gathered in the shed. The birds had grown silent, although his watch kept ticking, soldier in the waistcoat marking the march of time. Kate's breath rested against his neck, her breasts pressed his chest, and her hips snuggled, warm and certain, to his.

Never before had he lost track of time during a kiss. But that hadn't been a kiss. What on earth had it been? A flutter dove back into to his stomach. Like a man who'd buttoned himself into a new set of clothing without a mirror at hand, he wondered how Kate had felt about the kiss that was far more than a kiss, why she'd wept over it. He'd never made a woman cry before.

He slid his hands from around her waist, and she lifted her head with a tiny plaintive noise. He brushed her cheek with his thumb. Still damp. "Tears?" he murmured. He didn't sound like Lieutenant Michael Stoddard. He sounded like another man. Someone who didn't wear a uniform.

"It's nothing."

Why did women always say that? She tried to pull him back to her, but he caught her hands before him and kissed them. He couldn't see his watch, but surely in the length of time they'd been embracing, a colony of ants could have hefted a five-hundred-pound sack of rice to the kitchen. "See here. Your brother will soon send out a search party." He laughed softly. "Then he'll clean his dueling pistols, and—"

"Kevin doesn't have dueling pistols. Nor does he need them." Her voice grew clear, firm, as if she'd straightened her shoulders. "I've managed my honor good and well all these years."

And she'd sure blindsided him with balderdash about a fifty-pound sack of rice. "Indisputably. I appreciate this clever routine you've worked out. Trap a man in the grain shed, when there aren't many witnesses about, then have your way with him."

"Oh, you." She gave his chest a playful shove.

He wanted to ask her whether she'd enjoyed the kiss, but in his head, the words sounded lame, timid. Never had he kissed a woman like *that*. It was the difference between seeing a watercolor of a rose in bloom and burying his nose in a real blossom while grasping it by the stem. Thorns and all, yes. As if impaled on thorns, his heart ached for another kiss from her, another touch of the heavens. He wasn't sure where he went when he kissed her, but he wanted to return, and he wanted her with him.

Irritatingly, his groin berated him for a fool. He resorted to banter. "I shall be glad to oblige you again, when the need for heavy lifting grows just as pressing."

She laughed. "Shall I schedule it for each evening, then?"

He caught his breath and smiled, huge. Ah hah! She *had* enjoyed it. "I shan't argue. But as a criminal investigator, I must advise you that doing so establishes a pattern by which your wiles are soon evident to others. Thus may your honor become compromised."

"Compromised. Oh, no. What do you recommend, Investigator?"

The jollification in his breeches gave a leap of joy at being consulted and barged ahead of wisdom. "The poets would agree that honor is problematic, best dispensed with as soon as possible. I recommend that I share your bed. With the speed at which gossip travels in this town, the worst of the compromising will have passed by six o'clock the following morning. And after I share your bed night after night, you won't be plagued by this issue of honor again." One at a time, he kissed her hands. "I guarantee you'll never regret the hours well spent."

She chuckled, and the sliver of light from the half-closed door revealed the shine of her teeth. "No doubt." Then the smile vanished into night, and he received the impression of her shoulders drooping.

"Kate?" He released one of her hands so he could tilt her face up to his, stroke her cheek with his fingertips. Then he caressed her lips with his again before exploring the contour of her chin. She shivered. He whispered into her throat, "Yes?"

"I-I-I shall think about it."

Think? His eyes crossed for a second or two. What on earth was there to think about? He trailed his tongue to the hollow of her throat and coasted his free hand over her petticoat, in quest of the rounded underside of her buttock.

She intercepted the wanderer and placed it with his other hand, like two hands clasped in prayer before him. Expelling a ragged breath, she backed a step for the door and released his hands.

It sure looked as though "yes" wasn't forthcoming. Michael lowered his hands to his sides and dragged blood back into his brain. The tears. This must be about the tears. But what were the tears about? *Nothing*, she'd said. No. He was missing something. He seized upon the first explanation his reasoning provided and did his best to pitch a conciliatory tone. "If this has to do with your husband, he's been dead awhile. At least five years. And it sounds as though he wasn't very good at helping you celebrate life, even while he was alive."

"You don't understand."

He spread his arms again. "How right you are." And with each passing second, he understood less and less. Such as why he could suddenly taste the bitter blackness that filled the holes cored out of his soul in Hillsborough.

"Michael, I might need to discuss it with you first."

He bit his lip to stop himself from uttering an unsavory oath, and because he knew she couldn't see him do it in the dark. That moment, standing a foot away from a lovely woman who'd kissed him like—like nothing he could describe, he tasted her and the bitterness, and he named the holes in his soul. Loneliness. His soul was moth-eaten by it.

"I wish I had time to discuss it now. But I—uh, Cook, she was expecting my help with the roast beef."

The dispirited merrymaker in his breeches was the least of his concerns that moment. He wondered that he'd never picked up on such loneliness in her voice before then. Perhaps this time he heard it because he couldn't see her face, wasn't misled by an imperious toss of her head, or shoulders thrown back, or that Ice Widow gaze of rebuff that she'd mastered. But loneliness burdened the posture of her voice like a set of full buckets on a pole across a person's shoulders.

Her plans for the night didn't include him. A gentleman didn't argue a lady's choice, even if it was for roast beef. He cleared his throat. "Well, then, I shall fetch my claret and hat from the kitchen and be on my way." He walked past her and exited the shed.

While he waited for her to padlock the shed closed, he gazed south. In the sky, Orion the Belted Hunter chased indigo twilight. At Orion's heels, the hounds shimmered blue-white amidst the glow of the Milky Way. And the luminous stream taunted Michael from where it hung in the sky, pathway to a paradise that the gods had rolled up away from Earth, like a big carpet.

Chapter Nine

MICHAEL'S REAPPEARANCE IN the tavern caused all six barmaids to circle him like a pack of wolves. In the brief time it took him to learn that Spry had stomped the tar out of Finley at backgammon and was closing on victory over another challenger, Michael received no fewer than three propositions from each wench, not counting the creative ways in which his buttocks were fondled. Having satisfied himself that Spry was earning a decent rate of return on Kate's investment, Michael beat a retreat from the tavern, his arse feeling like a loaf of bread that too many goodwives had tested for freshness at the baker's shop.

He slunk back to the kitchen at Mrs. Chiswell's house. Enid clucked over him for his begrimed and famished state. Inside half an hour, he was clean-shaven and devouring half a roasted chicken.

When the housekeeper returned to the dining room with coffee, he asked her, "What do you know of a fellow named Rephael Whistler?"

"Rephael Whistler?" She balanced the empty tray on her hip. "I've not heard that name for several years. He was a wheelwright who lived northeast up the New Berne Road, near Topsail Inlet, with his son and his son's family. About five years ago, their house was struck by lightning and burned. Sad day. Mr. Whistler and his son died in the fire."

The dead blond boy had been of an age to be Whistler's grandson. "What happened to the mother and children? Where are they now?"

"I believe they're still living up there off the New Berne Road somewhere."

"Did the widow remarry?"

Enid shook her head. "I don't believe so, sir."

What the housekeeper told him tallied with what Kate had reported. He realized he should have fought off the barmaids and stayed at White's longer, asked patrons about the Whistler family. The Whistler clan and that blond lad

were the only solid leads he had in the abduction of the future seventeenth
Earl of Faisleigh. "Who in Wilmington can provide me with information on
the family?"

"Hmm." Enid's brows lowered, and her bottom lip pushed upward.

"You said Whistler was a wheelwright. So perhaps the wainwright on
Front Street." He snapped his fingers near his jaw. "But I cannot remember
his name."

"Mr. Smedes. And yes, Mr. Whistler repaired wheels for him. Now let me
see to your dessert."

Michael flashed Enid a quick smile and thanked her. Smedes. Yes, that was
it. Had he seen Mr. Smedes's name in Major Craig's register, too? Surely not.
Smedes had volunteered his services the first week of the Eighty-Second's arrival and cooperated during the occupation.

After Enid left the dining room with his empty plate and wine goblet, he
sipped coffee. Despite his efforts to douse the line of inquiry in his head, he
kept pondering whether the connection between Kate and the Whistlers was
salient to the investigation. *Personal*, she'd said. Bloody hell. Where did an
investigator draw the line?

That kiss. Not only had it blurred the line between personal and professional for him, but it had already assumed the quality of a dream, half-imagined, a
reflection in a pond rather than reality. From Kate's skittish behavior after she
locked the storage shed, he expected to find on their next encounter that she'd
retreated into Ice Widow propriety, and there would be no more kisses. The
confusion she projected snarled his logic.

Were Jones and Love mixed up in that tangle of boys and banditry? To what
extent were Gibson and Rouse involved? Was the dead blond boy Whistler's
grandson? Where was Geoffrey, Lord Wynndon?

Someone pounded the front door several times. Michael sprang to his feet,
coffee cup clattering the saucer. What now—news of the boy's abductors? Enid
was likely out in the kitchen still and hadn't heard the visitor. After flinging his
napkin to the table, he seized a candle in holder and strode for the door.

In the foyer, he almost collided with Helen Chiswell, who'd rushed from the
study. Clenched in her right hand was a half-cocked pistol, its barrel tilted up—
loaded, he presumed. Reflex stormed his muscles. He gripped her wrist and
held it steady, tilting the pistol away from both of them. His heart whammed
his ribcage a couple times. "Whoa!"

She expelled a breath. "Release me."

He lifted the candle aloft and stared at her, found her pupils contracted.
"Madam," he whispered, "where do you presume you're going with that pistol?"

She cocked her chin and glanced at the door. Her stare returned to challenge his, and she matched his low tone. "I'm not fond of night visitors who
pound upon my door."

A pulse hammered in the hollow of her throat, belying confidence in her
posture. Obviously she had a history of receiving rude, menacing visitors after
dark. He thought of the letters he'd read in her study and the conjectures he'd
drawn from them. "And whom do you expect to welcome with this pistol?"

Mrs. Chiswell darted a look to the right and tilted her chin higher.
"A creditor."

A creditor. His gaze swept over her lower lip. All healed now. If he hadn't seen the faded remnants of a split lip there three weeks earlier, he'd have guessed a great deal more of the ordeal she'd endured at the Cowpens. "And hogs have wings."

She sealed her lips and scowled.

"You've no need to defend yourself tonight." Michael jerked his head once for the door. "That call is for me. Business." At least he hoped so. He gave a brief squeeze to the pistol wrist. "You well know I've the authority to confiscate all firearms in this house. I shan't take the pistol if you unload it immediately and secure it. Agreed?"

For several heartbeats, she defied him with her stare. Then her eyelids fluttered once, and she lowered her gaze, chin, and shoulders.

Tension drained from her arm. He freed her wrist and watched her release the pistol from the half-cocked position. He said, "On the morrow, you and I will discuss your 'creditor.'"

She retreated to the study, her teal-colored polonaise gown whispering. A faint scent trailed in the air behind her, essence of a waterfall cascading into a clear, jade-green pool. The scent was unique to Helen Chiswell. It reminded him of sketches another officer had shown him years earlier: lotus and orchid flowers, a tiger crouched at the edge of a stream, and tooth-like mountains that seemed to separate earth and sky.

He flushed the woman's emotion from his lungs with an exhalation. He hoped she'd comply with his order and not mistake Spry, Enid, or himself for her "creditor" in the night.

At the door, he set the candle on a nearby table to straighten his coat. When he opened the door, glow from the candle held aloft spilled across the front step and ignited in the dark eyes of Nigel de Manning, his stance a military attention minus the salute. Michael squared his shoulders and jutted his chin. "Mr. de Manning. How may I be of service?"

The tutor's nostrils twitched. "I've information for you, *Mister* Stoddard."

Michael's free fist balled. He relaxed it. "My coffee grows cold. Unless your information pertains to the investigation, you may deliver it on the morrow."

De Manning's gaze flicked to the interior of the house. He backed to the walkway. "Out here."

Michael returned the candle to the table, stepped into the night, and drew the door shut. On the porch, he braced his feet apart. A blanket of raw air tucked around him. "What is it?"

The tutor's smile rent the pale oval of his face with a slash of darkness. "I queried around the regiment for information of your service record."

Michael knew what was in his service record, and he snorted. "Disappointed, de Manning?"

"Hardly. I know when you arrived in America, and I know that someone else funded the purchase of both your commissions. It confirms what I suspected earlier. You're common stock, Stoddard, a Yorkshire peasant flaunting an epaulet."

Michael's gut simmered. "In what way does this pertain to the investigation?"

The volume on de Manning's voice rose. "Now that I think of it, you're worse than a peasant. You don't talk like honest Yorkshire stock. Nine years you've been in America." He shook his fist at Michael. "You sound and act like an American. You aren't English. You're *American!*"

The unexpected angle of his attack slapped at Michael, and he felt his head jerk an inch. Was it true? Cold fingered his throat and compressed his vocal cords.

"Do the American pigs like you, Stoddard? I wager you eat and drink with American pigs, like that loutish man of yours, Spry. Do you *think* the way they do, espouse their causes?" De Manning laughed, short and sour. "Had you been born a gentleman, you'd have retained your roots."

Only one of them was a gentleman that moment. Michael counted to five and sucked in a deep breath frosty with the spring night. Another deep breath. He un-balled his fists so he wouldn't gratify his impulses and reduce the number of gentlemen in Mrs. Chiswell's front yard to zero. And he listened.

For a minute, the tutor created an avalanche of words, as if he were frantic to fill the night with sound, desperate to convince himself of Michael's unsuitability for the investigation. Spry's comment from earlier, in White's Tavern, sprang to Michael's memory: *He's terrified she's going to replace him.*

De Manning was terrified, all right. Was he really afraid of being replaced, as Spry had said?

"Even I've performed an investigation. Childs' play." De Manning's forefinger jabbed air less than six inches from Michael's chest. "At your first mistake on this investigation, I shall take over."

Michael unclenched his fists again and pitched his tone soft. "Stay out of my way, or I shall have you thrown in irons."

De Manning's voice whipped the air. "Find Wynndon alive and unhurt, or I shall have you kicked out of the Army."

Christ Jesus, the man was irrational. And he was bloated on his own self-importance. "This isn't about Lord Wynndon. This is about *you.*"

The tutor flung up his hands. "Of course it's about Wynndon! He's my s—" His eyebrows lowered. He clapped his mouth shut and glared at Michael.

Whoa! Had Spry's conjecture been correct? Michael leaned toward the tutor and said, "Finish your sentence, Mr. de Manning."

"He's my *student.*"

"He's your *son*, isn't he? And he's the only reason that Lady Faisleigh continues to employ you."

"Damn you!" The whites of the tutor's eyes shone.

"Naturally, a pig with an epaulet wouldn't be expected to understand such pressure on a gentleman, the desperate chances he'd take to remain in the company of a lady who doesn't return his affections."

"Desperate chances? You dare imply that I had something to do with the monstrous deeds of this afternoon?"

"Thank you for broaching the subject. Let's talk about it. How much did John Wynndon pay you to lose the boy in America?"

"*What?* God damn you to hell! John will never purchase me."

"But he's tried to do so."

"I refuse to dignify your insult by answering. I'd give my life for Wynndon."

"Lord Wynndon? Or Lady Faisleigh?"

A hiss rushed from between de Manning's lips. "Stay away from her, pig."

He sucked in air, and his teeth flashed once. "She's fascinated with you. Only God knows why."

Still playing the Game of Favorites, was she? Or was it more than that? Michael shoved back a nudge of premonition. "Obviously this is about you and Lady Faisleigh. That young boy is incidental. But his life is imperiled somewhere out there." He swept his hand northward without breaking eye contact. "And at least a pig with an epaulet knows his duty to King and country, his *moral* duty."

De Manning thrust out his chest. "Were you a man, I'd demand that my honor be repaired!"

Michael twisted about and yanked open the door, surprising both Enid and Mrs. Chiswell just on the other side in the posture of listening. Their foreheads furrowed. They stole deeper into the foyer. He stomped inside, spun about, and addressed de Manning, one hand gripping the door handle. "And now the pig with the epaulet shall finish his coffee." He slammed the door.

Back in the dining room, he fumbled his napkin onto his lap, belted down coffee, then gnashed at a slice of tart that should have been delicious. But he was too angry to enjoy it.

May as well admit it. At times he did think like an American. He'd found doing so requisite to success as an investigator, even to remaining alive.

Had the Nidderdale Valley truly faded from his tongue? He wondered what his family would think, could they hear him speak. Of all the things he'd lost in crossing the Atlantic almost a decade earlier, he never dreamed that the voice identifying him as a Yorkshireman would be one of them.

He glowered up at Enid, who'd stood in silence nearby for several minutes, tray on her hip. She beamed at him. "I know just why you're sulking. Don't you pay that rude fellow any mind, sir. Yorkshire's still on your tongue, good and strong. I knew you were from Yorkshire first time I heard you speak. And by the bye, there was another fellow in town who might have answered your queries about Mr. Whistler."

Michael felt his glower dissolve, the tension in his jaw dissipate. "*Was*? Tell me more."

"He fled in January with the rebel Committee of Safety. No one's seen him in town since."

Ah. *That* was more like it. "What's his name?"

"Mr. Travis. He was Mr. Smedes's business partner."

Travis. Yes. *That* was a name Michael had seen in Major Craig's register, in a reference about Mr. Smedes. But he couldn't recall what had been noted about Travis in the register. He'd look it up on the morrow. "Tell me more about Mr. Travis."

"He was trained to make fine carriages." Enid snorted. "To be sure, we've little need of that in Wilmington, so he helped Mr. Smedes repair wagons and gigs. I shall fetch my coffee pot, warm up that coffee for you, sir." She headed for the door.

The gnat of curiosity returned to buzz Michael's brain. "Enid, one moment." He wiped his mouth with the napkin and swiveled in the chair to regard her where she stood facing him in the doorway, tray propped on her hip. "You know a good bit about Wilmington and its residents."

"Oh, yes, sir. Lived here with Mrs. Chiswell for more than a decade."

"Is there a reason for Mrs. Duncan to dislike the Whistlers?"

Enid's eyes bugged. Then she cawed out a short laugh. "I should say so!" She pressed a fingertip to the side of her nose and squinted one eye at him. "Eve Whistler was Daniel Duncan's mistress." After a glance behind her, toward the study, Enid lowered her free hand to her other hip and dropped her voice. "Those two were making merry well before Jed Whistler wed Miss Eve. They carried on, even after Duncan married Miss Kate." A sneer rippled Enid's mouth. Her head wagged. "Need I say that it was obvious before a year was over that Duncan married into the Marsh family for the tavern?"

Michael sank back in his chair. He'd never heard anything stellar about Daniel Duncan. The man's finest accomplishment appeared to have been getting himself killed in service to the King under Donald McDonald at Moore's Creek Bridge back in 1776.

Enid again sneaked a look behind her, then shuffled a few steps into the dining room toward Michael. "Miss Eve's eldest boy is thirteen years old. He's the spawn of Duncan."

Now *that* would rankle any childless widow, watching the get of her dead husband and his mistress grow into a strapping lad. More so if the widow had suffered a miscarriage while married, as Michael suspected Kate had from information she'd almost spilled to him in Hillsborough.

He caught his breath a second. Thirteen years old, Enid said. "Has he blond hair?"

"Yes."

Michael suspected that he'd met a very dead son of Daniel Duncan in the infirmary that afternoon. "What's his name?"

"Zeke, I believe."

He wondered whether Zeke's mother, Eve Whistler, would talk with him if he returned the Psalter. Probably not. Kate had said the Whistlers were rebels. But it was worth a try. "What does the widow Whistler look like?"

"Medium brown hair, same height as Mrs. Duncan, but skinny, and about five years older." Enid licked her lips. "Mr. White, the fellow who built the tavern that Mrs. Duncan now owns? Uncle to Mrs. Duncan and her brother, you know. He and Mr. Whistler smuggled whiskey about the Southern colonies beneath the noses of many a royal governor. Scooted right by the taxes, they did." Enid's eyes sparkled. "At one point in the area between the Rouse and Collier taverns, Whistler had so many stills you could hardly throw a stone without hitting one. He and his lads always knew when revenue men were looking for them." She switched the tray to the other hip. "They never got caught. They'd move the stills."

"And I suppose Mrs. Duncan and her brother helped with the family business."

"Oh, yes, sir."

"When did they become loyalists?"

Enid frowned. "Loyalists? I wouldn't call them loyalists, sir. They're practical, rather than political."

Michael sat up straight. "Are you saying that Mrs. Duncan is a rebel?"

"You know how it is. Mrs. Chiswell, you, and I were born across the ocean. His Majesty ain't perfect, but we know he's still the King. Mrs. Duncan's an

American. So's her brother and her aunt. It's business."

Come to think of it, Michael never had heard Kate profess passionate loyalty to the King. Not that such an omission necessarily conferred the cast of treason upon her, as it might for a King's man with a narrower notion of human capacity. Rather, it brought to mind Kate's peculiar evasion of his questions earlier in the tavern about the Whistlers. "What of the Widow Whistler? Is she a rebel?"

"Again, sir, it's business. The families of Whistler and White sold whiskey to him whose coin was good. They didn't distinguish politically."

If Eve Whistler was another neutral, why had Kate labeled her "rebel scum?" His thoughts skipped back to Zeke Whistler, son of Daniel Duncan and his mistress. Then the obvious answer smacked him like a board torn loose from a barn in a windstorm. Michael's shoulders tensed, and it was all he could do to keep from swearing aloud and hammering the surface of the table with his fist.

Enid's brows folded down, and her eyes peered into the past. "Ah, me and my big mouth. From your questions, I must have made you doubt Mrs. Duncan's character. She's a good lady, truly, but she hasn't a happy past. Turned her head a time or two for ne'er-do-wells."

Mrs. Chiswell's firm voice emerged from the study. "Enid, come here."

The housekeeper leaned toward Michael. "Have a look at Mr. Duncan's grave in the churchyard."

"Enid!" Mrs. Chiswell's tone snapped like a pennant in the breeze. Enid bobbed Michael a curtsy, and her shoes rapped the wood floor as she exited the dining room.

Michael brushed aside the housekeeper's cryptic final remark, braced elbows on the table, and propped his forehead on the heels of his hands. How could he have been such a buffoon? Kate had deliberately misrepresented her rival in attempt to triumph in her personal feud. *Personal,* she'd said. Ralph Gibson had done the same.

Kate's special twist on the contract was a signature both alluring and unforgettable. How close he'd come to signing with her.

Chapter Ten

THE PARLOR CLOCK announced seven thirty Saturday morning, on the final day of March. Seated at the dining table, Michael blinked into his coffee cup. The evil of dreams. An army of boys wearing crowns of white roses had abducted his father last night. Michael swigged the remainder of the coffee and forced his focus off the vagaries of his sleeping mind and back onto what his assistant, standing near his left elbow, was saying. "...surprised to see Ames and three outriders, each enjoying a pint and watching me win the tournament."

Ames was Lydia's head coachman, and—wait a moment. Spry had *won* the backgammon tournament. Michael felt sarcasm stretch his lips. That meant at least one man on the face of the earth knew how to please Kate Duncan. He cocked an eyebrow up at that man. "Congratulations."

"Thank you, sir. I chatted with Lady Faisleigh's men afterward. Ames agreed to guide us to the scene of the abduction. Two outriders are willing to come along. They'll be here by eight o'clock, ready to leave with us."

Splendid. Overnight, Michael had decided that after he and Spry examined the terrain around the scene of the abduction, they would seek out Eve Whistler among the residents who lived at least eight miles to the northeast, between the Rouse and Collier houses. Considering that homesteaders of those parts were, at best, neutral, inclusion of civilians in the party might help two redcoats to be perceived as less threatening. And maybe Widow Whistler wouldn't respond to their presence in the area by vanishing.

"Good work, Spry. See to it that the men understand they'll be following my orders."

"Sir."

In a quieter tone, Michael summarized for Spry what Enid had told him about the whiskey smuggling connection between the Whites and Whistlers, including the name of Zeke Whistler, but omitting the background of his parentage. He also told him about the incident with Mrs. Chiswell and the pistol. Then someone knocked at the front door—not de Manning's pounding, but a light rap.

Spry said, "Enid's probably in the kitchen, sir. I shall answer the door."

Michael followed him as far as the study doorway, where he peered in at Mrs. Chiswell. Seated at her desk, her torso rotated to allow her to face the study door, Mrs. Chiswell flattened her lips together at the sight of him. Then, quill in hand, she swiveled back to the letter she'd been writing.

His teeth clamped. He must confront her before they rode out that morning. Otherwise, she'd continue the evasion and possibly put them all in danger.

Spry stepped aside from the opened door to reveal Lydia's lady's maid, Dorinda, at the front door, a fine wool shawl draping her shoulders and pinched closed with one hand, the other hand clasping her petticoat. Michael moved forward where she could see him. She curtsied like a member of the *haute ton* offering her favor to a dance partner, reinforcing Michael's fragmentary first impression of Dorinda. Daughter of a prosperous merchant, or perhaps gently born. Older sister had received the dowry. "How may I help you this morning, Dorinda?"

She extended the handkerchief to him that Lydia had borrowed in the parlor the day before, pressed neatly and, from what he could tell, washed. Lydia's sweet, spicy scent leapt out and tackled him. She must have drenched the handkerchief with her perfume. Michael resisted grimacing and held it down at his side. He'd have to fetch another handkerchief from his room before they left. "Thank you."

Dorinda's smile almost overcame the bags of sleeplessness beneath her eyes. "My lady invites you to join her for breakfast."

"Has Lady Faisleigh received communication from the bandits, then?"

A quiver in Dorinda's lower lip dissolved her humor. "Oh, no, sir, we've heard nothing at all."

The quick smile that Michael forced cramped his face. "Thank Lady Faisleigh for her gracious invitation. Regrettably, I must decline. My assistant and I are riding out shortly to resume investigation into the abduction."

Dorinda's head tilted an inch. "So Ames has informed my lady. She wishes to hear what progress you've made on the investigation first."

"Very little progress overnight. Tell her that."

"She wishes to hear it from your own lips, sir. She told me so. And she's set a generous table."

Lydia expected him to attend her. She'd expected it in Lord Crump's mews, too. Fortunately he had a different employer, now. He nodded once, curt. "I've already dined this morning."

"Coffee, then." The sparkle returned to Dorinda's eyes. "Gentlemen find my lady most excellent company, sir!"

And now Dorinda was selling her mistress's merits, pushing Lydia on him. Michael studied the maid in silence, ire bumping about in his gut. "Mr. de Manning and I don't see eye-to-eye on this investigation."

"Nigel—Mr. de Manning is overwrought, concerned for the young master. Please overlook his defensiveness. Besides, he likely won't be there for breakfast. He stepped out to take some exercise."

Nigel. Dorinda was sticking up for him, too. Was she sweet on the tutor?

She broke eye contact. "Forgive me. I spoke out of line."

"Oh, I don't believe so. Sentiments are important in any investigation, especially in establishing motives."

The sparkle in her eyes doused. Her smile vanished. "Here, now, sir, let us not speak of such things. My lady is prepared to pay you a visit, if need be. Shall we say ten o'clock this morning?"

Perseverant, both of them. "At ten this morning, my man and I will likely still be out investigating." Michael took a step toward her, into her intimate space. She backed down onto the first step. "Does Mr. de Manning confide in you, Dorinda?"

Her cheeks colored. "Seldom. No. No, actually he does not."

From her blush, the tutor confided in her more often than "seldom." "When have you seen John Wynndon speaking with Mr. de Manning?"

Her gaze darted right. "I shall inform my lady that you're indisposed this morning." She jerked through a curtsy, seized a fistful of petticoat, and swept down the front walkway for the street.

Michael's eyebrow lifted, and he called after her: "I shall send Spry as soon as I've news to report."

Had Nigel de Manning sold his own flesh and blood to an enemy? If so, Michael would uncover proof of it and see the cur hanged. And Dorinda wasn't merely supportive of de Manning. She was protective of him. His accomplice, perhaps? That, too, bore investigation. What a charming household.

Inside the house, he closed the door and tossed the perfume-soaked handkerchief on the nearby table, yielding at last to his need for a grimace. Spry sniffed and fanned the air. Michael nodded toward the study and lowered his voice. "Let's get to the bottom of this creditor business."

With his assistant following, Michael walked to the study and rapped on the doorframe, waiting only long enough for Helen Chiswell to look up from her letter before he entered the study. Spry shut the three of them in and remained at the closed door, ready to deter any disruption from the dutiful Enid.

Eyes wide on Michael, Mrs. Chiswell dropped her quill. He snagged one of two ladder-back chairs and continued toward her. She hunched her shoulders and drew back in her chair, both hands palm outward. Before she could rise to her feet, he planted the captured chair closer than propriety dictated for an acquaintance, in the space where a lover or family member might sit, and took a seat.

She raked letter, quill, and ink to her. Her shoulders straightened. She jutted her chin and held his gaze, blue eyes frosty. "What is the meaning of this intrusion?"

He propped an elbow on the area of the desk that she'd vacated and angled toward her. Daylight allowed him to discern the faint purple circles beneath her eyes. "We're here to discuss your creditor."

She glanced at Spry. "Why?" Her word swatted the air.

"Most people don't greet creditors with a loaded pistol, even if they might dream of doing so. From where I'm sitting, this 'creditor' looks more like an assassin. I'd rather that Spry, Enid, and I not intercept your pistol ball meant for that assassin. You tell me about him. Now."

Her gaze didn't waver from Michael, eyes like blue pebbles. Her tone plunged low. "So I tell you the details, and as an officer of the law, you think in absolutes and arrest me. No, thank you."

He matched her tone. "You and I have lived under the same roof for three weeks. Do you really believe that *I* think in absolutes?"

She seared him with her stare. Then she swiveled to the letter and busied herself by covering it with a blotting page, wiping off the quill, and corking the inkbottle. In an even tone, she said, "I tried to kill a man."

"Your 'creditor.'" She nodded without resuming eye contact. "When? Where?"

For a long moment, he thought she wouldn't answer. A muscle twitched in her cheek. "January seventeenth, the battle at the Cowpens in South Carolina."

Christ almighty. She must have been caught up in combat. Since she'd traveled to the backcountry with Tarleton's army, she hadn't been fighting on the victorious side.

"I was mad with terror and hunger and lack of sleep. And—" She gulped. "And the thought of what he planned to do with me." A hollow-eyed crone more than three decades older than Helen Chiswell beseeched Michael with glistening eyes.

He flinched, understanding. Too often, he awakened sweating and shaken from dreams that were pieced together from the severed limbs of battle. His gaze swept over her healed lower lip and the exhaustion beneath her eyes, and he sat back from the desk, gave her space. "Madam, you'd be hard-pressed to find any magistrate who would classify such a gesture of self-defense as premeditated murder."

"In a civilian court, you'd probably be correct." She twisted to grope her right hand beneath the writing surface of the desk, near her knee. After a couple of jerking motions, she withdrew a folded note from its hiding place and transferred it to her left hand. She focused on something out the window, took several steadying breaths, kept her voice low. "After I arrived home in Wilmington, I relaxed and slept better. I told myself that I'd seriously injured him.

"But two weeks ago, I received this." The note quivered in her hand, as if a feral beast trapped in the folds of paper fought to free itself. With a noisy exhalation, she pressed the note on the desk before Michael. Still gazing outward, she wound her fingers in her petticoat and grew quiet.

He retrieved and opened the note, dated 26 February, from the town of Hillsborough:

> *Divine Sister, Sibyl of the Gods, we decamp today. I trust your return journey to Wilmington was pleasant. I look forward to our Reunion: soon enough, darling.*

Hillsborough on February twenty-sixth. That had been Cornwallis's army decamping.

The hand that scrawled the message was masculine and audacious, the signature simply the letter "D." But every hair on Michael's neck and arms stood out. He flung the note to the desk and scooted his chair back a couple inches. "Bloody hell!" he muttered. A hundred little black spiders of evil had crawled across the paper seeking him in eldritch intimacy.

Too well, he was acquainted with that intimacy.

He clasped Mrs. Chiswell's shoulder and forced her gaze to him. "You stabbed Lieutenant Dunstan Fairfax at the Cowpens. Where? Arm? Leg?"

"In the right thigh." Her breath hoarsened.

He released her shoulder, looked back at his grim-faced assistant, and shoved out a sigh. "Alas, it wasn't as severe a wound as it must have appeared. Spry and I can assure you that he was both mobile and lethal when we encountered him on February thirteenth, near Hillsborough. Were you his prisoner at the Cowpens?"

Her face paled. "Yes." Her gaze jerked away and sought the window again. "He used me to bait and capture two spies. Then he forced me to—to listen while he tortured both men to death."

Spry swore.

Horror slid down Michael's backbone. Mrs. Chiswell was the only living witness to Fairfax's full immersion in his private game. From her fear and Fairfax's pursuit of her, she must have heard enough to provide damning, career-wrecking testimony against him.

Well she knew her fate if he were still alive, and he found her again. Fleeing Wilmington wouldn't be adequate to ensure her survival. She'd have to put the Atlantic Ocean between herself and the monster. If he were still alive.

"Those two men had tried to kill me, but—but—" Her words careened onward, ran together. "I never would have wished *that* kind of death on anyone. He tortured them for sport, Mr. Stoddard. Some nights they follow me into my dreams, screaming for their lives."

She yanked her head around, faced him again. "So I stabbed Fairfax to escape. He knows I'm here in Wilmington. I must leave."

Michael contemplated the note several seconds, then studied her. "What would you say if I told you that from information Major Craig received, he has formed the conclusion that Fairfax perished in combat?"

"Perished in combat?" She threw back her head and laughed, short. "No, oh no. That's far too easy." She pressed fingertips to her brow, eyes downcast, before meeting his gaze again, unsmiling. "Do *you* think Fairfax is dead?"

To the contrary, Michael could almost feel Fairfax's pulse running counter to his own, as if his nemesis had wedged a parasitic splinter of himself through Michael's ribcage, lodged it beside his heart, and was trying to disrupt the rhythm of his heartbeat. He voiced what intuition had been whispering to him for more than a week. "No. I do not."

"Then you see why I must flee."

What hell. "I do." He swallowed, hard. "Assume that he knows where you're going. Don't stay more than a week. Move on from there, far away."

"Yes, across the Atlantic. Britain."

"Even farther than that, if you can."

"Yes, if I can."

The pieces still baffled Michael. Fairfax had written the note to Mrs. Chiswell thirteen days after he tried to kill Michael and Spry, thirteen days after Michael had conveyed Major Craig's message to him. Had Cornwallis received the information that Michael relayed to Fairfax, the general wouldn't have written the letter that Michael read in Craig's office ten days earlier.

So where the devil *was* Fairfax? Why hadn't he delivered Michael's message to Cornwallis?

Mrs. Chiswell spread the palm of one hand upon the desk surface, near the note. Her voice again steadied. "I know why you rode to the Legion camp in December, why you met with Lieutenant Neville."

Adam Neville: ranger, scout, and double spy. Mrs. Chiswell couldn't possibly know what had been behind Michael's collusion with Neville. Yet she spoke with conviction. His palms grew clammy.

She nodded, as if the two of them had come to an agreement. "You must rid us of Fairfax, Mr. Stoddard. If Lieutenant Neville won't help you complete the task, find others who will."

He opened his mouth to protest, but no sound emerged, as if someone had grabbed him by the throat. What she spoke of doing, murdering an officer of His Majesty, was treason. If he responded on the topic, he, too, would be talking treason.

It was one matter to discuss with Spry the killing of Fairfax. Spry had fought at his side in Hillsborough. Like Michael, he'd been on the receiving end of Fairfax's torture. But Michael really didn't know Mrs. Chiswell and dared not trust her. And her suggestion of enlisting others for the undertaking was absurd.

He shut his mouth. How he wished he could ask how she knew that he'd run those dispatches in December with the intent of killing Fairfax. But he mustn't incriminate himself by pursuing the topic. It was his responsibility to divert conversation far afield from the subject of killing Fairfax.

Fortunately, he had more questions for her. He sat forward. "Why did

Fairfax address you with the terms 'divine sister' and 'sibyl of the gods?'"

The muscle in her cheek twitched a second time. "I used to be the society page writer for a magazine here in town. For my publisher's story about Colonel Tarleton and the Legion, I posed as Fairfax's sister in the backcountry to have access to the Legion. Due to a series of coincidences that happened during the march to the Cowpens, Fairfax believes I possess the ability to envision the future when encouraged by a combination of wine and laudanum."

Her earlier words returned to his memory: *I was mad with terror and hunger and lack of sleep...and the thought of what he planned to do with me.* Fairfax believed he'd found his own personal seer. Not by accident had he baptized her with knowledge of his pastime. He hadn't intended for her to escape. He planned to intoxicate her, exploit her presumed skill to accelerate his appointment to Parliament, then kill her when he'd exhausted her.

That son of a poxed whore. Michael clamped his jaw. His gaze swept over Mrs. Chiswell's face, and his gut smoldered. The eerie light in Fairfax's eyes when he'd spoken of her near Hillsborough made a great deal more sense now. "Why does Fairfax think you're a spy for the rebels?"

Her eyes widened. "Do you not know? For a decade, I was David St. James's mistress. David's father was deeply involved with rebels in Alton, near Augusta, Georgia, and last summer he—"

"I know what happened last summer in Alton. And in Havana. I also know David St. James isn't a rebel, like his father. But Fairfax is of a mind that the entire St. James family is comprised of rebels, as well as many of their associates. Is that why he claims your current lover, Jonathan Quill, is a spy?"

She shook her head. "Fairfax flattered himself that—" Her lower lip jutted upward, and she glanced toward the desk. "That Jonathan was competition."

The peculiar intimacy that Fairfax had used in the note seemed to substantiate her belief. But Michael felt certain that Fairfax would never enter intimacy with anyone for longer than necessary. The place of a woman in his world was either to serve immediate needs or advance long-term schemes.

"Competition" for Fairfax meant anyone or anything that stood in the way of his attaining a goal. Back in January, Helen Chiswell and Jonathan Quill had stymied him near the Cowpens, prevented his using her. Then they'd escaped him. *That* had earned his enmity. Of course he'd labeled them spies.

And in that instant, Michael realized that he and Spry hadn't truly escaped Fairfax near Hillsborough. Fairfax had let them go. He'd also let Michael's accomplice in December, the ranger Adam Neville, go. If Fairfax were, indeed, still alive, he had long-term plans for all of them.

Slickness returned to his palms.

Helen Chiswell leaned toward him, hands in her lap. "Listen to me, Mr. Stoddard. Perhaps you thought in December to catch Fairfax unaware at the Legion camp and slip a dagger between his ribs. Perhaps you've since realized that making an attempt on his life by yourself was foolish and reasoned that if you have help from your man, Spry, the two of you will succeed.

"But you'll never kill Fairfax that way." Her voice grew raspy, and her face lost color again. "He guards himself too well. He's a master at evading suspicion. And he's been murdering and manipulating for years. In England, when he was a boy, he framed household servants for crimes they didn't commit and got them dismissed, for sport. Just before he joined the Army, he murdered his stepfather, the man who'd raised him and purchased his commissions. For sport."

Michael gaped. He'd known that Fairfax and Mrs. Chiswell were natives of Wiltshire, but he'd never imagined that they might have been acquainted in England. "Are you repeating rumors?"

"Not at all. His stepfather was Lord Ratchingham of Redthorne Manor. I was personally acquainted with Lord Ratchingham and his second wife, Fairfax's mother."

Awe and revulsion spiraled through Michael. He wasn't certain which revelation shocked him more: learning that Mrs. Chiswell had been involved with Fairfax's household years earlier, or hearing the depth of Fairfax's depravity in his youth. "Before you leave town, I would hear more of these stories, and the details."

She nodded. "Surely you've realized that Lieutenant Neville is one of the disaffected. You may not be able to rely on him to help you in ridding the earth of Fairfax."

She'd returned to the topic of treason. He swiped his palms on his breeches.

"Even if you recruit Neville," she said, "he's just one man. You need a team—no, you need an *army* to combat Fairfax."

Michael wedged his forefinger beneath his shirt at the neck stock, suddenly too tight and chafing his skin. "Madam, I never said anything about combating or killing Fairfax."

"Don't make the mistake of believing that you and Spry alone can bring him down."

What gibberish was this? Did she find Spry and him lacking in skill or valor? Fairfax wasn't invulnerable. She didn't know that they could easily have killed him in February. Two well-placed pistol balls from Michael and his assistant at close range would have sent the monster to his Maker in short time. If the circumstance repeated itself, Michael would most certainly seize the opportunity.

That moment, however, he incriminated himself by remaining in her company while she talked of murder. In one smooth movement, he pushed himself to his feet and pivoted to stand behind the chair and face her, arms at his sides. "I appreciate your time and trust, madam. My man and I must be off to investigate a crime committed yesterday."

Mrs. Chiswell's lower lip trembled. "You're a good man, Mr. Stoddard. The world truly isn't black and white for you. But do think on what I've said. Recruit an army. Don't overlook opportunities to build your army. Otherwise, Fairfax will back you into a corner and force you to make decisions you may regret." She stared through him, and her eyes glazed. "He knows whether to offer a carrot or a stick. You'll do his bidding."

She blinked. The glaze vanished, but the smudges beneath her eyes remained. "Is it true what Enid has heard in market, that Lord Cornwallis and General Greene battled on the fifteenth?"

"Yes."

"Should you hear news that his lordship marches to Wilmington, I would deeply appreciate your notifying me at least two days before his arrival."

Mrs. Chiswell, focused on planning her escape, was already nervous enough, so Michael saw no reason to point out Fairfax's knack at securing detached assignments that allowed him great liberty to travel. If Fairfax were determined to hunt down his "sibyl of the gods," he wouldn't wait on Cornwallis's itinerary. *Soon enough, darling* might be that day, or the morrow. Michael and Spry must maintain extra vigilance.

Michael bowed. "I shall give you as much notice as I can. You have my word."

Chapter Eleven

THE CONVERSATION WITH Mrs. Chiswell rankled Michael while he made a final check of his fusil and cartridge box and awaited Spry's return from the stables with their horses. Not that he found the lady's suggestion of assembling an army ludicrous. He knew the value of posses in ferreting out criminals. Fairfax was indisputably a criminal.

But Fairfax didn't need ferreting out. Michael and Spry had come close to extinguishing him near Hillsborough. They didn't need an army to get close again. All they needed was a little luck.

Michael gave Enid more Yorkshire-bound letters to post that day, along with postage money. At seven fifty-eight, Spry returned with the mare, Cleopatra, and the gelding he occasionally rode. Then Ames the head coachman and two outriders rode up on well-groomed, well-rested horses.

All three men were older than Michael. The eldest of them, Ames had a few threads of silver in the brown hair at his temples. As with de Manning, Michael found Ames vaguely familiar. The coachman must been a retainer in Lydia's entourage when she'd visited Lord Crump. Michael hoped Ames never recognized him, either.

Lydia's men dismounted before Michael with their fowlers and bowed: three strong, competent horsemen, prepared to obey his commands in service to their lady. Although Michael might disdain quirks of the nobility, he acknowledged the value of servants who knew their place. They were much like disciplined men of rank and file.

The party of five set off toward Market Street in the cool clear morning, Michael in the lead. Ames fell in beside him, per Michael's instructions. In a few blocks, they trotted the horses past the Anglican Church and graveyard.

The night before, Enid had recommended a visit to the final resting place of Daniel Duncan, but that was low on Michael's list of priorities that morning. He had three members of Lydia's household all to himself, several hours to find out what they knew, and the certainty that casual conversation would gain him much information.

A sentry at the New Berne Road saluted Michael and waved the party onward, northeast. "From what part of Yorkshire do you hail, Ames?" Michael held his breath that Ames wasn't from the village of Pateley Bridge.

The coachman perked up. "Oh, Kettlesing, sir."

Michael eased out a sigh of relief. Kettlesing was a few miles south of Pateley. "Ah. I'm a Scarborough man myself, but I've visited Kettlesing. What's Yorkshire like now? I've been stationed in America for more than nine years. Some days I think I'm forgetting home."

Ames waxed eloquent about stone quarries, lead mines, and linen production. The packed dirt-and-shell street beneath their horses' hooves transitioned to a highway of sand and crushed shell, and the outermost buildings of Wilmington vanished behind a bend in the road. Stillness and solitude closed about. Crows and buzzards circled, perused the arid, salt-scented landscape of wiregrass and prickly pear, broken by an occasional copse of pines, live oaks, or mulberry trees, but seldom by a breeze. Isolation made the New Berne Road a highwayman's hunting ground.

Michael kept one eye on their surroundings, pleased to glimpse Spry also monitoring the landscape with his casual alertness. After a little prodding, Ames shifted from talk of Yorkshire to talk of his employer. For the next half hour, Michael heard about what went on beneath the roof of Ridleygate Hall, occasional comments from the outriders corroborating Ames's observations.

Lydia was intensely devoted to her husband and son, to the point where her fidelity to her husband was beyond reproach. As Michael suspected, Nigel de Manning hankered after Lydia. And Dorinda, fourth daughter of a carriage maker with patrons among the wealthy of Yorkshire and New England, was sweet on de Manning.

Lord Wynndon, far from being a spoiled brat, was intelligent, discerning, and affable. He'd already exhibited a predisposition toward applying deductive reasoning and seemed driven by a desire to see justice done. Ames opined that the lad might make an excellent magistrate when he grew up.

John Wynndon lived five miles down the road from Ridleygate Hall. Once a month or so, he visited and brought with him two over-rambunctious, ever-hungry sons, a worn-out wife who complained of a migraine headache, and greasy servants who had to be watched lest they pinch valuables. While at the manor, John spent most of his time in his brother's company, although he'd been spotted conversing with Lydia. Neither the head coachman nor the outriders had seen de Manning speak with John longer than an exchange of greetings. And John and his brother always seemed congenial in each other's company, not at all the "war" of which Lydia had spoken.

When the nobility stepped out of line, servants were the first to point fingers and the last to cease gossiping. Lydia's servants offered nothing incriminatory about her. Nothing.

Irritation gnawed at Michael. De Manning had been incensed at his suggestion that John was trying to buy him. Dorinda had been upset at his suggestion that John was trying to buy de Manning. Ames and the outriders hadn't given him much cause to interrogate de Manning on suspicion of conspiracy with John Wynndon. What if John and de Manning weren't colluding?

To further frustrate Michael, the head coachman and the outriders seemed content with their employment. On the surface, domestic life in the household of Faisleigh seemed bloody good. Too good to be true, whispered Michael's instincts. De Manning was tormented. His misery must be affecting Dorinda. Michael refused to believe that Lord Wynndon's abduction was random.

Around nine o'clock, they approached a two-story wooden building in need of paint. In the back yard, a kitchen, stable, jakes, and other outbuildings needed paint even worse. A lone, red mulberry tree nearly forty feet high stood sentinel in the arid landscape off the west side of the road. Other than a few shoats grunting and nosing about in the spindly grass of the yard, nothing moved. A thorny, leggy rose vine twisted up a trellis nailed to the side of the building, its occupant one wilted rose faded to pink. Two well-worn hitching posts and a salt-battered sign out front informed the party that they'd come to the tavern owned by Alexander Rouse.

On Michael's command, the men slowed their horses to a walk, so each of them might observe the tavern *en route* to the abduction site, which Lydia's men had agreed was a couple miles farther northeast. During his instructions to the men back in Wilmington, Michael hadn't elaborated on the tenuous link between the Whistlers and the Whites. He'd just told the men to keep their eyes open, for they were entering what had been "still country." Rebels may have run out Royal Governor Josiah Martin in 1775. Rebel preachers may have shut down gambling, horse racing, and theater productions while a Committee of Safety governed Wilmington. But whiskey hadn't become unfashionable.

As they passed the front door of the tavern, it squealed open, and a thin woman wearing a grimy apron lugged a bucket out. At the sight of them, she hunched her shoulders and bowed her head, her facial features concealed in her mobcap. With a grunt, she heaved filthy water from the bucket out into the sand. Then she pivoted, hastened back inside banging the empty bucket, and slammed shut the door. The entire event took less than ten seconds.

The men kept riding. When they'd picked their speed back up to a trot and were out of earshot of the house, an outrider laughed, short. "What a dump! Judging from those hitching posts, Rouse must receive his share of business, but faith, where do the patrons come from? Holes in the sand?"

The other outrider laughed at his suggestion. "Sure, but no amount of whiskey would make that old woman dazzle me onto the sand with her."

"She might have a daughter more to your liking."

"True. Now there's a lovely thought."

"Of course, they both might be better at picking our pockets."

Old woman. Michael wondered how old she'd actually been. A stop at Rouse's Tavern on the way back was in order.

Seven minutes later, Ames announced that they'd arrived at the abduction site. Michael pulled back on Cleopatra's reins. "Dismount, everyone."

Pine barren peppered with live oaks surrounded them, offering enough shade to conceal men and horses. Just to the north, the sand of the road was loose and deep, full of dune-like wheel ruts. Silence beat upon the five men afoot, firearms in hand.

Lydia's men stood in the road and gazed about them, expressions solemn. Michael didn't disturb them while they explored the abduction in memory. Instead, he motioned Spry to him and said, low, "The woman at Rouse's Tavern. How old was she? Enid's age, perhaps?"

Spry's attention sailed past him into the distance, and he frowned. "Hard to say, sir. Probably not. Younger, I'd wager. But I wouldn't swear to it. I couldn't really see her face."

"What makes you think she might have been younger?"

Spry's frown deepened. "She—" He kneaded his cheek. "For just a second, when I first spotted her, she wasn't hunched over like an old woman. My impression was that she was younger, sir. She was quick to change her posture. Limber. If you'd blinked, I daresay you missed the change. You only saw an old woman."

"Yes. I'd guess that she's practiced that transformation a good bit." Memory offered him the fragment of a folk tale, something about a shape-shifting faery maiden on the moors. His grandfather had told him the story. Hah. Grandfather Andrew Stoddard. Not for several years had he thought of the old man. And that odd, soft trill that crept into his speech during rare moments. Michael frowned. Interesting how his grandfather would catch himself—not unlike the woman at the tavern, who'd revealed her age to them for a few seconds—and transform the trill into cadences of Yorkshire-speak.

Spry's big teeth reappeared. He threw back his shoulders. "Surely we're imagining this, sir. No woman wants to look older than her years."

Humor curled Michael's lip and emerged in a snort. "How fortunate I am to have an assistant who's such an expert on what women want."

Spry's grin wilted, and he studied his commander. "Sir? What woman wishes to look older?"

Michael held his gaze. "A woman who doesn't wish to be recognized." He nodded over Spry's shoulder, where Lydia's men had dispensed with their paralysis and begun strutting around and discussing the abduction. "Let's see what these fellows have to say."

Over the next half hour, undisturbed by any travelers on the road, Michael encouraged the coachman and outriders to recall, singly and together, the abduction of Lord Wynndon. Some twenty to twenty-four bandits, they insisted, had descended on the carriage. At least half were boys, some riding double on horses, three boys of African descent. Many were younger by several years than the two lads who'd been shot. No one stated the obvious, that the youngest boys were Lord Wynndon's age.

Ames found the flattened area in the grass where the grizzled man had landed after de Manning had thrown him from the carriage, blood rusty-dark on the sand. And that was where Spry found a haversack almost buried in sand, missed by soldiers the previous day because it blended with the sand and bleached wiregrass. He handed it to Michael, and Michael opened it.

Three strips of dried venison. One dented tin mug. One petrified crust of bread. Extra flints for a musket. And a folded piece of paper upon which had been scripted a Bible verse:

> *To me belongeth vengeance, and recompense; their foot shall slide in due time; for the day of their calamity is at hand, and the things that shall come upon them make haste. Deuteronomy 32:35*

Ice pricked Michael's backbone. He'd read part of that exact verse ten days earlier, on a scrap of paper found while his patrol searched the abandoned barn south of town where rebels had stored smuggled weapons. Rebels had trafficked the weapons in January, before the Eighty-Second's arrival. Michael's investigative activities disrupted their ring and their church.

He'd stored that scrap of paper in his room on Second Street. He should compare handwriting. But at that point, connecting the Bethanys with Lord Wynndon's abduction made sense. Their wily new preacher may have schemed the deed. Not good news. No, not at all.

He turned the note over. Finding no other verbiage, he passed it to his assistant. Spry read it and looked up at him. "The Reverend Paul Greene's work, sir?"

"Possibly." Michael circulated the note among Lydia's men.

Ames pointed to it with a scowl. "Those are mighty ominous words that someone's quoted."

Michael retrieved the paper, folded it, and tucked it into his waistcoat pocket. "This note may have originated with a local church that bears no excess of goodwill for those loyal to His Majesty."

"God bless the young master! Do you mean he was kidnapped by *fanatics,* Lieutenant?"

"Well, we don't know for sure whether—"

"Rebels! Where is this bloody church?" Ames shook his fowler once. "I shall visit on the morrow, Sunday. Let 'em hear the hymn I have to sing."

The other two added their sentiments to that of Ames. Michael elevated his voice. "We burned the physical church in early February after imprisoning about half the congregation."

An outrider grinned. "Good show!"

"However, intelligencers inform us that the rest of them still meet, changing the location every Sunday to avoid being found. And as much as I'd enjoy throwing those fanatics in the pen for abducting the boy, the note is but circumstantial evidence. It includes no salutation, you see." Around Michael, men's shoulders hunched. "Suppose the old man shot by Mr. de Manning never met a church member. Suppose he found the paper lying in the street at market one day. And we assume he could read what was on it."

He hated collapsing the hope that had sparked to the eyes of Lydia's men, but he couldn't allow them to proceed where they wanted to go. "The preacher of this congregation is skilled with propaganda. He waits for mistakes from the regiment so he can pounce on those mistakes, inflate them, use them to steer public sentiment in favor of him and his church. Suppose we accuse him of taking the boy, and we're wrong. What then?"

Ames hung his head. "He'd make *us* look like the criminals."

"Exactly. Never hand rebels such a victory." Michael brushed his gaze back over Lydia's men. "I know how it is. You want a solution now, simple and swift." He shook his head. "It won't come simple or swift. So you keep your eyes open."

He swept his arm with the haversack in a horizontal arc that indicated the site. "A crime was done here yesterday afternoon. I doubt those dogs were too careful. They left things behind, things neither you nor the Eighty-Second's soldiers found." He lifted the old man's haversack briefly. "Odds are there's more to find than this haversack."

He focused his attention on the head coachman. "You mentioned that they rode west with the boy."

"Yes, sir."

"Then we shall search west afoot. Ames, you stand guard at the horses just off the road, in the cover of the nearest trees." Michael regarded those trees. "And the rest of us will spend some time looking around."

"Are we tracking the bandits, then?" said an outrider.

"No. Their trail's too cold. They could easily be in Onslow or Duplin County by now. Perhaps even farther away. And the sand off the road becomes too loose to allow easy tracking. What we'll look for, close to the road, is something that shouldn't be here but is, or something that's missing." The brows on all three of Lydia's men lowered, and their heads drew back. "Yes, that's a vague instruction, but that's the way I do it. Further questions?"

The men were silent. Already, Spry was contemplating trees to the west.

"Good." Michael returned to Cleopatra, hooked the haversack to the saddle, and checked his watch. "Going on nine thirty. Plenty of sunlight this morning, and the shade isn't dense. Let's give it fifteen minutes in, then turn around and come back to the road. Don't rush to cover a great deal of ground. Just look. See what you can find."

Ames hitched the horses together and guided them into the foliage. Michael, Spry, and the outriders fanned out from the churned area of the road and began canvassing the pine barren. They found the ground loaded with hoof prints made within a day, likely by the escaping bandits, men of Lydia's entourage, and the Eighty-Second's patrol. About thirty feet from the road, one of Lydia's men found a trampled hat, and Spry found a dagger, testament to the highway-men's haste. Another twenty feet beyond that, Spry found a handkerchief. If they'd wanted to track the bandits, they'd certainly been supplied with a clear trail of broken branches, torn grass, and hoof prints at the outset.

A quarter hour elapsed. Michael signaled them to return and reminded them to maintain vigilance. Shortly after, when he was backtracking along a trail of fresh hoof prints, a ray of sunlight flashed on something metallic in pine needles ahead of him. He made his way to it, scooped the object off the ground, and stared, dumbfounded, at a two-inch diameter brooch of gold and silver in his palm, styled after the white rose of York. It was the type of brooch that held a cloak pinned closed at the wearer's shoulder.

According to de Manning, Lord Wynndon had been wearing a gray wool cloak when he was abducted. The brooch was too far into the pine barren to have been lost by a traveler on the road. It must have come from the boy's cloak. Michael pivoted to scan his surroundings, up and down, but he saw no cloak. He examined the brooch closer and detected no torn fabric, as he might have expected if the brooch had been ripped off. The bandits who'd abducted Lydia's son wouldn't have torn off such a brooch and discarded it. They were poor. They'd have sold it.

That left Michael to draw the startling conclusion that Lord Wynndon, not quite ten years old, had possessed enough presence of mind minutes after he'd been dragged from his mother's arms to remove and discard his distinctive brooch without also losing his cloak. Done to assist his pursuers in finding him?

Michael turned the white rose of York over and over slowly in his fingers. Its unique image sank into his brain, stirred his learned folklore and history about, and eddied to the surface of conscious thought a more portentous pos-sibility. Had the boy discarded the brooch to keep his captors from finding it on him, identifying him with the symbol?

White rose of York, red rose of Lancaster. Henry the Second's descendents squabbling in a bloody civil war that culminated on a battlefield in 1485. But that made no sense. Why should a conflict three centuries in the past resurrect as a threat now? Michael was missing something.

The suspicion that Lydia had lied or told him partial truths about the fam-ily's connection to King Henry prodded him. He stood a moment longer in the pine barren, trying to sort out why she'd lie, what she had to gain by not telling him the full truth. Then, bemused, he wrapped the brooch in his handkerchief, wedged it into his already-stuffed waistcoat pocket, and continued his search back to the road.

Chapter Twelve

LYDIA'S MEN CONFIRMED the brooch as Lord Wynndon's and the design as the white rose of York. They also advanced the conclusion that the boy had dropped it in a desperate attempt to let his rescuers know the direction his kidnappers had taken him. Espousing Lord Wynndon's cleverness heartened them so much that Michael refrained from steering speculation down darker paths. However, he caught Spry's eye for a second and conveyed with a cocked eyebrow and twist of the head that they needed to talk further, alone.

Nothing else had been found of the bandits or their captive. Michael checked his watch, called off the search, and headed them back south at a trot. During the party's approach to Alexander Rouse's tavern, Michael noticed thin curls of smoke wafting from the kitchen chimney. The chimney hadn't been smoking when they'd come through an hour earlier. Closer, he spotted sheets and men's shirts hanging on a clothesline behind the house. The clothesline hadn't been occupied earlier. He halted the party and ordered them to dismount.

They hitched their horses to the post nearer the spindly, faded rose. Michael and Spry mounted the steps. The front door didn't budge when Michael tried the latch, probably barred on the inside. No one answered when he knocked, and neither he nor Spry saw anyone inside among the tables and benches. Leaving Lydia's men with the horses, Michael and his assistant walked around to the back, firearms in hand, keeping to the shadows on the north side of the building.

Michael peeked around the side of the house. The woman they'd seen earlier plopped a half-full laundry basket into the wiregrass at the far end of the clothesline, her back to them, and stretched. From her flexibility, she wasn't much older than Kate Duncan. And from what Michael could tell, she matched the description Enid had provided of Eve Whistler. She pulled a wet shirt from the basket and pegged it to the clothesline. The wall of laundry, dangling and white and still in the morning air, swallowed the woman and grew longer.

With his head, Michael motioned Spry to follow him into the back yard. As he left the cover of the house, he tried not to think about how well the scarlet of his coat stood out against all that white laundry. The woman side-stepped in his direction and pegged one of the sheets more securely, not seeing him, a frown tugging down the corners of her mouth.

When Michael was only about twenty feet from her, a blond boy about ten years old burst laughing from the stable, followed by two blonde girls, both younger. The boy's breath snagged in a gasp when he caught sight of the two soldiers. The girls scrambled back into the stable, but he squealed an alarm, ran at the woman, and grabbed for her waist. His momentum nearly knocked her off her feet.

"Mama! Soldiers!" The boy stabbed his forefinger in the direction of Michael and Spry.

She staggered, then righted herself. When she saw the two men, she yanked the boy behind her and faced them, countenance drained of color. "G-g-go away! We haven't any m-m-money. We've done nothing wrong. Leave us b-b-be!"

Michael halted his approach, Spry beside him. Never taking his gaze off mother and son, Michael handed his fusil to his assistant and held up empty hands a moment. "I'm not here to harm you. I need to speak with Mrs. Whistler. Are you Mrs. Whistler?"

Her arm on the boy tensed a moment, and her lips pressed together, trembling. Her gaze darted to the right for half a second. "Don't know anyone n-n-named Whistler. G-g-go away."

Michael wondered whether she stuttered when she wasn't terrified. Certainly she must be the Widow Whistler. But although she was no older than her early thirties, the ravage of poverty had stolen her youthful attractiveness, replaced it with hollow cheeks, a thin frame, and gaunt eyes. She and that exhausted rose climbing the front porch trellis bore more than a few features in common. No wonder she'd been able to "transform" into an old woman so easily.

And she wasn't giving him access to Widow Whistler. He gauged her a moment longer, then pitched calm into his voice. "A mother and her son became separated yesterday afternoon." Without taking his gaze off the woman, he waved in a vague, northward direction. "It happened a few miles up the road."

He spied the boy peeking out from behind his mother's petticoat. "The boy is about his age." The lad dove back behind his mother. "I'd like to find him, return him to his family." Michael studied the woman's face again and realized he wasn't reaching her. Damnation. He'd have to spin fiction.

He glanced toward the stable. No sign of the girls. He walked two steps closer to mother and son. "The distraught mother lay awake weeping all night." He doubted Lydia had done anything of the sort. She'd spent the night calculating a variety of other issues, such as the effect of drenching his handkerchief in her perfume before returning it to him. Nevertheless he slumped his shoulders, spread his palms, and tucked his chin an inch. "And she hasn't been able to eat since it happened. You have a boy who's the same age. I'm sure you can imagine how horrendously she's suffering. Tell me, have you seen a dark-haired, dark-eyed lad, a stranger to these parts, in the last day?"

Her "No" emerged clipped, as if invisible fingers had closed about her throat to prevent her testifying more. Again, she glanced to the right. Her hands crossed above her heart, and her fingers shook. Then she swallowed and repositioned her clasped hands above her grimy apron.

A little chill shimmied down Michael's neck stock. Either she'd seen Lydia's son, or she'd heard talk of him, but someone had intimidated her into silence. He closed the distance between them a few more feet. "All right. I know this tavern gets a good deal of business. I'm thinking that some travelers may come through here with the boy. I've a likeness of him. May I show it to you?" She didn't shake her head in negation or run away, so he reached calmly into his waistcoat pocket and withdrew the miniature portrait. He held it out to her by the ribbon and walked a little closer. "Here he is. Might you verify that you haven't seen him?"

Her gaze shot to the picture, flicked to Michael's face, fixed on the portrait, then lowered. One hand still on her son, she backed from Michael. "I h-h-haven't seen him. G-g-go away, please. Men will come."

Of course men would come. Michael wondered which men. He'd seen the spark of recognition in her eyes when she looked at the portrait. Without a doubt, Lord Wynndon had been at the Rouse house last night in the presence of his captors.

He replaced the miniature in his pocket. "My name is Lieutenant Stoddard. If you see the boy, please send me word of it at the home of Mrs. Chiswell on Second Street in town."

The woman bowed her head and refused eye contact. Michael recognized the posture. Exasperation tinged with desperation gripped his gut. She was too afraid to be seen at the home of a loyalist. He realized then that if he wanted her help, he'd have to extend his trust well beyond where he was comfortable. "Here's a better idea. You know Mrs. William Hooper, don't you? She lives on Third Street." He waited a few seconds, dropped his tone to just above a whisper. "Her husband signed the Declaration of Independence."

The woman's gaze sprang up to meet his, then dove for the ground again. Michael continued. "If you see the boy, go to Mrs. Hooper. Ask her to deliver a message to me." Unsmiling, the woman lifted her head and cocked an eyebrow at him, as if she thought him a lunatic. Why should a redcoat and a wife of a Signer align themselves? "Mrs. Hooper will get word to me." Yes, he'd have to pay a very diplomatic visit to Anne Hooper that day, make certain that of all the redcoats of the Eighty-Second, she—part-captive, part-resident in Wilmington—still had the least negative opinion of Lieutenant Stoddard.

Michael patted the waistcoat pocket that held the portrait, the gesture calculated to project nervousness. In the act, he felt the Psalter and worked it out for one more gambit. "Thank you for your time. Oh, yes, I found this yesterday. It's an old Psalter with the name Rephael Whistler written inside. Take a look."

Wide-eyed, the boy gasped, "Mama!"

Teeth gritted, she shoved him back behind her, then jammed her gaze at the ground, blinking away a shimmer of tears. "T-t-told you. Don't know Whistler."

The lump in her throat was audible. Michael maintained his soothing tone. "Ah. My apologies. Townsfolk informed me that a wheelwright named Rephael

Whistler lived up this way with his family, but he perished in a fire a few years ago, along with other family members." He shrugged and put the Psalter away, watching how her gaze snaked up to follow its disappearance into his waistcoat. "I assumed that you were his wife, but you've already denied knowing the Whistlers.

"Should you encounter any surviving members of the family, tell them that I shall be glad to return their property." Michael tipped his hat to her. "Again, thank you for your time. Good day." He pivoted and strode briskly back the way he'd come, Spry at his heels.

***

Southbound in Cleopatra's saddle, Michael spotted a cluster of pines set well back from the road and only about two hundred yards from the Rouse house. He said nothing to the rest of his party about what a good surveillance spot the pines made. He didn't even swivel around to check whether the boy was watching their party. He knew the boy was there. Poverty-stricken Eve Whistler, worried to leanness over the disappearance of her eldest child, intimidated into keeping her mouth shut by someone who possibly threatened her with eviction, unnerved by the appearance of the cultured but captive Lord Wynndon last night in the ramshackle tavern, had sent her next eldest boy to the edge of the property to make sure the redcoats were, indeed, gone.

Eve Whistler didn't want any more trouble in a life that had gone horribly wrong for her.

Michael knew he couldn't depend on her swallowing the bait of the Psalter. Even dropping the name of Anne Hooper may not have been enough to induce her cooperation. So after his group rounded the next bend in the road, and he knew they were out of sight of the tavern, he halted them again and told them his plans for surveillance of the house from the shade of the pines, just for half an hour. *Men will come,* she'd said. Michael wanted to see who went in and out of Alexander Rouse's tavern.

They dismounted. Michael walked to the bend in the road, crouched, and peered around. Five hundred yards distant, he spotted the blond boy slumped against the south side of the house, watching the road. No sign of the girls. Michael returned to his group and waited five minutes before taking another look around the bend. The boy, still at his post, kicked at something in the sandy dirt, then leaned over, picked up what was likely a small rock, and pitched it eastbound. Michael smiled and withdrew. Most ten-year-olds found more interesting things to do than stand sentry over a road. And sure enough, after Michael had waited another five minutes, he saw that the boy was gone.

He and the other men muffled the horses' tackle, walked their mounts single-file back around the bend, and assumed position in the cluster of pines. From the post, they could observe the front, back, and south side of the tavern. Between the pines and the house, the coverage was mostly tall grass.

Michael, Spry, and Lydia's men watched. Nothing moved at the house except in the back yard, where the woman was still hanging laundry. A quarter hour passed. Lydia's men fidgeted. Attentions wandered elsewhere.

Twenty minutes after they took up their post, hooves rumbled on the road. At a gallop, eleven civilian men on horseback rode up from the south, their rugged attire suggestive of clothing worn by backwoodsmen, farmers, and militiamen. Lydia's men ceased their woolgathering and trained their attention on the riders, who reined back at the house, dismounted, and hitched their horses to the posts.

Carrying firearms, the eleven strutted around back. "Sandy Rouse, you louse, where are you, lad?" bellowed a tall, raw-boned fellow in his twenties. He laughed at his own play on words.

Michael grinned in recognition and said, low, "Well, now, that's a lovely sight."

Spry snorted. "What luck. We've finally found one of his rat holes."

Just louder than a whisper, Ames said behind Michael, "Who are they?"

Michael glanced at him. "That big fellow is Captain James Love. He and his partner, Bill Jones, make it their sport to gallop through town shooting their rifles. Several weeks ago, they'd planned to assassinate Major Craig but lost their nerve at the last moment. Major Craig wants both of them dead."

Ames hefted his fowler. "The lads and I will be glad to assist you in that."

Michael kept his voice at a murmur. "Those men outnumber us, two to one. And Jones isn't with them. These scoundrels know how to vanish into the marshes. If we kill Love this morning, Jones will become more cautious, make it more difficult for us to rout him out."

He nudged the tip of Ames's fowler down. "But now that the Fates have revealed to us one of their water holes, I shall have this place watched and send scouts to track Jones and Love, find out where they're hiding. Then we'll be in position to eliminate the entire nest of rats at once."

Love had located the woman hanging laundry and was questioning her, the volume of his voice lowered. Michael presumed he asked her about the location of Alexander Rouse, his query when he arrived. The language of her body—shaken head, spread hands palms upward, a jerky shrug—told Michael that she was unsure of Rouse's whereabouts. Love tipped his hat at her, spun about, and waved his men to follow him back to the horses.

Each man in Michael's party held his horse still and quiet with one hand, his loaded firearm ready in his other hand. Each held his breath while Love and his men mounted their horses. Love's party galloped north on the New Berne Road. The beat of hooves in the sand faded. The five men concealed in the pines released sighs.

Their party had, indeed, been blessed with good fortune. The rebels hadn't so much as glanced in their direction. Michael realized that had he not decided to stop and perform surveillance on the house, his party and Love's might have bumped into each other on the road in a very messy altercation.

Spry said, "The woman didn't tell them about us."

Michael smiled at his assistant. "And how do you know that?"

"The way they walked when they left. Loose, arrogant, confident. If they'd just heard about soldiers nosing around the tavern, asking questions, they'd have run back to the horses, held their muskets ready for firing instead of at their sides."

Michael nodded. "You're correct. She didn't tell them. I suspect that if she'd done so, they'd have caused her even more grief." He turned to the house and stiffened, breath hung in his throat. Arms crossed low, the woman stood at the south border of the property staring at the pine trees, right at them.

One by one, the men with Michael followed his gaze, then held still. One of the outriders muttered, "God's foot. She knew we were here the entire time."

Ames shifted. "Why didn't she betray us?"

Michael remembered the tears in her eyes when she saw the Psalter. His throat relaxed. "Because we have something that Eve Whistler wants." And it had been to his advantage to supply her with no details about how the Psalter had come to be in his possession, for it would make her life even more miserable when she received it. He took a deep breath, let it out, and patted Cleopatra's neck. "All right, lads. Back to Wilmington. No telling when Rouse or Love will return."

Chapter Thirteen

DURING THE RIDE back to Wilmington, Lydia's men grew quiet. Perhaps they pondered events from the morning. The lull in conversation allowed Michael to pursue his own thoughts.

Too much had happened for him to send Spry to Lydia with an update. He'd visit her himself. Besides, he planned to question her about the brooch and probe into her story about her wicked brother-in-law, John Wynndon. Huge pieces of the puzzle felt as though they came from another game.

Lord Wynndon's captors had flaunted him around the Rouse house last night. Where were they hiding him today? Hoping to shed new light on the boy's location, Michael analyzed all the information he'd collected. But it failed to reveal a detail he'd overlooked, a clue to where the boy might be held.

So in his head, he stepped back and approached the investigation from a new angle. Both Kate and Kevin possessed excellent business acumen. Commerce at White's Tavern was robust. Yet when Michael considered the garnets and pearls he'd seen on Kate, and the fashionable gowns she wore, he suspected that tavern business alone didn't account for their income. Did brother and sister continue to uphold the whiskey trade started during the previous generation?

If they concealed the production and distribution of whiskey, they'd dodged taxes for a number of years. Legally they had accounting and fines to deal with, or a jail sentence. Seldom would such charges stick, however. As long as the insurrection continued, local government instability would favor the persistence of such businesses, prevent accurate records from being produced.

Michael wasn't foolish enough to lose sleep at night, burning with a desire to arrest every colonist who dodged paying taxes on a trade. There were hundreds of those businesses in the Cape Fear. People would offer leads with glee, keep him running around like a decapitated chicken, divert him from resolving far more important crimes.

But *if* Kate and Kevin were involved in production and distribution of whiskey, and they were in partnership with Rephael Whistler's successor, whomever that might be, Michael's greater concern was whether that representative might have inside knowledge of the abduction of Lord Wynndon. Enid had said, *At one point in the area between the Rouse and Collier houses, Whistler had so many stills you could hardly throw a stone without hitting one.* For all he knew, stills might have been there that morning between the Rouse and Collier houses, their locations disguised. He hadn't detected them. Concealing an abducted boy from Major Craig's investigator might be an easy task for someone who'd concealed whiskey production equipment from revenue assessors for more than a decade.

How was Michael to learn from Kate what she knew about hiding places for those stills? Could he encourage her to share the information, perhaps? His appeal to her carnal nature hadn't generated in her the enthusiasm so abundant in tavern wenches and laundresses. He squirmed in the saddle. Something told him that Kate responded to incentives far less tangible. Incentives with which he had little experience.

Close to noon at the perimeter of Wilmington, a sentry saluted Michael and welcomed the men back to town. The party continued south on Market Street, where they passed the Anglican churchyard again. The vicar, who stood just outside the opened doors of the church building, was conversing with a private. Memory replayed for Michael Enid's suggestion from the night before: *Have a look at Mr. Duncan's grave in the churchyard.* Michael drew back on the reins and, from the saddle, stared hard at the rows of tombstones.

At Ames's query, he instructed Lydia's men to go on without him. Then Michael dismounted and handed Cleopatra's reins and his fusil to Spry. "I've a brief bit of sniffing around to do here. After you return the horses to the regiment, meet me at Mrs. Chiswell's house. Lady Faisleigh is lying to all of us, even to her own retainers."

Spry nodded. "It's about that brooch you found, isn't it, sir?"

"Yes. It means something to her other than the symbol of Yorkshire. And I think her son may have rid himself of it so his captors wouldn't find it on him."

Spry grimaced, as if he'd whiffed a dead animal. "You believe this affair is a good deal larger than John Wynndon hiring random bandits to kidnap his nephew. That he's somehow commissioned Paul Greene and the Bethanys for the abduction. Is that it, sir?"

"I don't know, Spry. If that's it, how do we explain the boy bandits, Ralph Gibson, and the white rose of York? And we need to follow up on those wainwrights Enid mentioned. Smedes and Travis."

"Yes, sir." Spry eyed him. "You realize we might also speak with Mrs. Duncan and Mr. Marsh. Depending on how involved they were with the whiskey business and all those fellows who hid the stills, they might recall some places suitable for hiding a boy."

Michael grinned up at his assistant. "Exactly what I had in mind. So meet me back at Mrs. Chiswell's, and we'll decide the direction of our next inquiries." He patted the gelding's rump. "On your way."

Spry saluted him, then trotted the horses down the street.

Michael faced the churchyard. Time for him to investigate a piece of Kate's background. Maybe he'd learn what constituted an incentive for her.

He wandered the nearest row of gravestones, searching for that of Daniel Duncan. The vicar and the private stepped aside to allow the exit of two more privates who carried between them one of the pews and scuttled it, huffing and puffing, down the steps toward the street.

The vicar clasped his hands above his belly. "My son, I'm certain our Heavenly Father doesn't mind the temporary removal of a few pews to create room for the storage of ammunition. But when will you bring back the pews?"

Michael couldn't make out the response of the private, whose back was to him, but the vicar's jaw hung slack, and his eyes widened. Then he threw up his hands. "Fence posts? *Fence posts?* But—but where is my congregation to sit?"

Michael moved on to the fourth row of tombstones. If Lord Cornwallis came to Wilmington with his army, the vicar would have far more to concern him than ammunition stored in the sanctuary, pews converted into fence posts, and a congregation that had to stand for the service.

Moments later, he found the grave of Kate's husband. The tombstone had some sort of design carved into it, worn by five years of sun, thunderstorms, and ice. In the process of kneeling beside the tombstone to get a better look, he realized he'd stepped on another grave. No, not just one other grave. He sprang up and backed off, surprise hammering his chest a few heartbeats. Daniel Duncan hadn't been laid to rest alone in the plot. Beside him were four infant-sized graves.

The logician in his head performed calculations. Kate had married at the age of sixteen or seventeen. By the time she buried her husband when she was twenty-one, some four years later, she must have already buried at least three of those infants.

Apparently, she was unable to bring healthy children into the world. Perhaps that had convinced her to not share her bed with any man.

A husband with a heart would have modified the expression of his physical love to give her some relief and respect. Judging from the number of infant graves, however, Duncan had remained on task, determined to produce offspring. Michael recalled Enid's comment from the night before—*Duncan married into the Marsh family for the tavern*—and tallied cryptic, negative comments he'd heard about Duncan from Kate, Kevin, and Aunt Rachel since February. It rather looked as though Duncan's plan had been to inherit the tavern after killing Kate in childbirth.

Michael clenched his fists and squeezed his eyes shut briefly, resisting the urge to spit on Daniel Duncan's grave.

Every time Kate saw Eve Whistler's oldest child, Zeke, she must feel— Michael studied the little graves. What *did* Kate feel when she saw Zeke Whistler, rumored to be the son of Daniel Duncan and Eve Whistler? Michael realized he wasn't sure, except that it must include equal portions of worthlessness, self-loathing, anger, and disillusionment.

He squatted at the foot of Duncan's grave and glared at his name on the tombstone. "You're a rat, Duncan. Bum fodder. You deserve to be in that hole. What you don't deserve is to be counted a hero by the King's Friends. Or by the Scotsmen with whom you marched to Moore's Creek Bridge."

Disheartened Highland Scots, they'd been. Forced to surrender three decades earlier, swear allegiance to King George the Second after their attempt to bring Bonnie Prince Charlie to the British throne collapsed in 1745. Michael's pensive gaze focused on the tombstone, found and traced a familiar pattern, faint lines of a symbol he'd seen his entire life in Yorkshire. A symbol he'd recognized again just two hours earlier in a pine barren north of Rouse's Tavern.

Ice drove up his spine. "Damn!" he whispered.

He bolted to his feet, clawed at his waistcoat pocket, and brought forth Lord Wynndon's brooch for confirmation. Then, in a convulsive motion, he closed his fist over the brooch, feeling the pin stab his palm as he pumped his fist once at the sky. Damn it all to hell!

At the pine barren, he'd been trawling history too far in the past. The white rose of York had been used as a symbol far more recently than the civil war three centuries past. It was the symbol of the Jacobites: men and women who had struggled for decades to restore the Stuarts to the thrones of England, Scotland, and Ireland. "The Fifteen" and "the Forty-Five"—rebellions in 1715 and 1745—had pitted a number of Scottish clans against each other and killed thousands of men. The Hanoverian court had issued Writs of Attainder for treason against those who had sided with the Stuarts.

How Daniel Duncan, an American sentimental over a movement he couldn't possibly understand, had been allowed to march for King George the Third with crusty old Donald MacDonald, a Scot who'd eschewed his Stuart prince though it must have broken his heart, Michael didn't know. But Duncan had had plenty of company in his idealism that cold February morning in 1776. He *still* had plenty of company. Some of them had money. And peerage.

Michael stood a moment longer at the foot of the grave while his mind sped through conjectures. Might Lydia be enmeshed in a revitalized Jacobite movement, one to overthrow King George the Third? Had she lied to him about the "war" between her husband and his brother? What was her true reason for fleeing Britain with her son? Were they pursued by men with the financial reserves to hire fanatical, weapons-trafficking rebels who engaged in abduction and murder?

No one would be demanding a ransom if that picture were accurate. The future seventeenth Earl of Faisleigh might already be dead. King George the Third held no greater love for Jacobites than his predecessor did.

If Michael didn't act, Major Craig might ride to Wilmington straight into another Jacobite fray. So might Lord Cornwallis and his wagons of wounded soldiers. Lives of Wilmington residents would be imperiled. Michael thrust the brooch back in his pocket and strode from the churchyard to find Lydia.

***

At the residence on Second Street where Lydia was housed, an outrider who hadn't traveled with them that morning answered the door. "My lady isn't here, Lieutenant. She left about an hour ago and awaits you in Mrs. Chiswell's parlor."

Michael thanked the man and strode for Mrs. Chiswell's house. Enid must have been watching for him at a front window. When he'd traversed the side yard and emerged out back to wash travel grime off face and hands, she exited the back door, on target for the kitchen. "I won't be but a moment bringing you some warm water, sir."

Looking more presentable than he had at his last meeting with Lydia, he entered the house from the back door a few minutes later. The opened doors of the parlor permitted him to hear a discussion between Lydia and Mrs. Chiswell on Plato's *Republic*. He hung back to absorb it, amazed at the unconventional education both women had received.

It wasn't the first time he'd heard women in America pursuing discussion of unconventional topics such as philosophers. Kate tackled those topics, too. Well, and why shouldn't the ladies do so? Women in England seldom discussed philosophy, science, and politics. He'd often found their talk dull.

He entered the parlor and bowed. The buzz of conversation ceased. Dorinda and Felicia, standing near him at the door, avoided his gaze. De Manning smirked at him from his position of sentinel at the end of the couch nearest Lydia, feet braced apart, arms crossed high on his chest. Lydia pursed her lips at Michael, that look of disapproval he'd seen directed at men too many times on Lord Crump's estate.

Alas, no Spry. Michael was outnumbered again.

Mrs. Chiswell set her coffee cup into its saucer on a table, the clink of earthenware piercing in the silence of the parlor. "Ah, good, you're here, Mr. Stoddard. Do speak with Lady Faisleigh. I believe she's quite concerned about your investigation." She rose from her chair and tilted her head to Lydia. "May Enid bring you more coffee?"

A smile breezed over Lydia's lips, never touching her eyes before it vanished, and she waved her palm in an arc. "No, thank you, Mrs. Chiswell. I do appreciate your hospitality. How refreshing to find an English gentlewoman's grace in an American parlor."

Mrs. Chiswell curtsied and glided for the door. When she passed Michael, she rolled her eyes, a message only he received.

He closed the doors behind her and faced the people in the room again. Lydia sashayed to him, her lips compressed, her eyes frozen sapphires. Today's gown was satin the indigo hue of the Atlantic Ocean, and it was trimmed with velvet and tiny pearls around the bodice. When she breathed, the pearls swelled like waves. He focused on her face. "Good afternoon, Lady Faisleigh. Have you received any communication from the bandits?"

"No. Nothing." She took a stance two feet from him, almost beneath his nose, and cocked her head to scrutinize him. "You invited three of my men to ride with you all morning, Lieutenant. That's a long time to have my men at your disposal. I expect to hear that it paid off. Where is my son?"

Without shifting his head, Michael glanced at de Manning. Teeth punctured the tutor's smirk, and his shoulders were relaxed. Michael's palms grew damp.

A game of cricket had been set up in the parlor. He was the ball. De Manning was the mallet.

He yanked his attention to Lydia and focused on her eyes. Cold, cold. "I appreciate the loan of your men, my lady. I'm relieved to inform you that, with their help, we made progress on the investigation and have gained valuable leads toward locating Lord Wynndon."

Her nostrils widened a moment. She laughed, an acrid sound. "I must say, I've heard less skillful evasion from veteran statesmen in the House of Commons. You don't know where Wynndon is, do you?"

He waited several heartbeats to respond. Although he didn't dart another look at de Manning, he could feel the tutor's gloat across the room. Still frozen in Lydia's gaze, Michael said to her, "I'm prepared to update you right now."

Her teeth flashed. "Excellent. Let's hear it, then."

"I request a private audience with you. Based on this morning's findings, I have questions of you that are of a sensitive, familial nature."

She maintained his gaze, but her eyebrows contracted in the middle, and her smile vanished, as if he'd thrown a half-dozen more balls into the cricket game, and all the balls now looked identical. De Manning grunted. "My lady, aren't you going to tell him?"

She dragged her tongue across her lower lip. "Mr. de Manning interviewed townsfolk this morning and found out that Wynndon was here in Wilmington last night."

Michael blinked. How could that be? The boy had been at Rouse's Tavern last night, he was certain of it. He shifted his scrutiny to the tutor and frowned. "Where was he here in Wilmington?"

"On the Market Street wharf." De Manning's smile drained away, and his complexion turned waxy. "I spoke with two men who saw a boy fitting Wynndon's description being loaded into a rowboat at the Market Street boat slip about ten at night." His voice hoarsened, shook. "He was bound and gagged."

What was this? Bound and gagged at the wharf? Michael's head snapped back. The boy couldn't have been two places at once. His gaze skittered between Lydia and de Manning. The inhuman seething in her eyes blasted him, and his stomach ached as if de Manning had punched it. He wiped sweaty palms on his breeches and forced his tone to stand firm. "I've evidence that Lord Wynndon was elsewhere last night."

Lydia leaned into the space he'd relinquished. "You do? What evidence? Where do you believe he was?"

Now that Michael thought about it, he wasn't sure how much of what he'd acquired that morning was actual evidence, and how much was a hunch. He sealed his lips against the pressure to declare himself. The previous summer, he'd learned the repercussions of generating an official statement before he was ready.

But de Manning had handed him a new crime. He must find out what had happened on the wharf. He pivoted from Lydia and took a couple steps toward de Manning, trying to settle the spin in his logic. "You said you spoke with two men who witnessed the act of a boy, bound and gagged, being loaded into a boat. Why did they not rescue the boy or report the incident to the night watch?"

"Both were into their cups, outnumbered by the other party, and felt the men of the night watch wouldn't believe them."

Drunkards as witnesses. Michael let his breath out slowly. Although it wasn't implausible that a sot could supply reliable testimony, the fact that both witnesses were drunk did chew a bite out of the story's credibility. "So this morning, they showed you where the incident occurred?"

"Yes."

How much detail could a *sober* man pick out on the wharf after dark? The incident must be restaged somehow so Michael could determine what the men had actually been capable of seeing at ten o'clock in the night. "I presume the witnesses supplied you with contact information, and you can track them down for additional questioning?"

"One did, of course. A direction on Front Street. But I'm satisfied with his testimony and don't believe he needs further questioning."

"As I'm the investigator here, I shall be the judge of that. Give me the contact information."

De Manning snorted. "Dig up your own evidence, Mr. Investigator."

Michael felt his eyebrows climb his forehead. "You're withholding evidence in a criminal investigation, Mr. de Manning. That's grounds for arrest."

"You're bluffing. A bluff is all you have."

Michael turned back to Lydia, found her eyes sparkling, her forefinger caressing her lower lip. His gut clenched again. Stoddard versus de Manning, Round Two. He kept his expression stone, his voice firm, low. "I'm expecting my assistant's arrival presently. Unless you wish Mr. de Manning to be arrested for withholding evidence, you will order him to release the witness's contact information to me immediately. If he does not do so, I shall arrest him and have Spry conduct him to an outdoor pen holding dozens of rebels."

Lydia lowered her hand to her hip and sent a smile oozing over her face. Michael repressed a shudder at the eerie familiarity of it. She swiveled, tilted her chin to de Manning and showed him the waves of pearls. "La. He's going to arrest you. What do you think of that?"

De Manning puffed out his chest, took a step forward, and murmured, "He's bluffing." Color suffused his cheeks. Lydia was his princess, he was her knight, and Michael was an oaf.

Michael's throat parched, and little hairs stood out all over his neck and arms. Lydia wove a net of intimacy about de Manning, him, and her. It was like watching a black widow spider court two mates, two meals. He tensed muscles in his legs to stop himself from bolting for the doors of the parlor and abandoning the entire web.

Lydia shifted an angelically luminous blue-eyed gaze between Michael and de Manning. "I don't think he's bluffing." Her voice was husky. "And I'd rather my son's tutor not be in such a deplorable pen at the time when he's returned safely to me. So don't be a fool. Give Mr. Stoddard the information."

"But—"

"Do it!" In one second, her voice transformed to a whip.

De Manning jerked, spanked by her tone. Vibrancy drained from his face. He hung his head to fish a folded piece of paper from his waistcoat pocket, then extended it to Michael with a flick of his arm.

Michael crossed the parlor and retrieved it, his nod curt. "Thank you."

I will ruin you, de Manning's eyes said.

Michael angled away from him, thumbed the paper open, and stared at the name of the drunkard who'd seen Lord Wynndon loaded into a rowboat the previous night: Paul Greene.

What the hell? Paul Greene wouldn't dare return to Wilmington while the Eighty-Second occupied the town.

Would he?

Michael wondered what he'd find at the location on Front Street, if it even existed. He waved the piece of paper at the tutor. "Did you visit this direction supplied by the witness?"

"No. I'd no need of it."

A mistake on de Manning's part. "Describe the two men."

"Greene was about thirty years old, I'd say. Lean but muscular build, just under six feet in height, well-dressed, and wearing a wig. The other fellow was roughly the same age, shorter, balding brown hair, not quite so well-dressed."

"Did Greene have a broken nose?"

De Manning gazed past Michael, his scowl softening while he searched his memory. "I believe his nose was crooked." He refocused on Michael, slicing him with a stare. "Stop procrastinating, Stoddard, and answer my lady's questions. Where do you think Wynndon was last night? What is your evidence?"

Michael swept his gaze over the people in the parlor, turned his back on de Manning, and walked toward Lydia, the folded paper in his hand. One of those two men might have been Paul Greene. However, sneaking into town was extremely risky for Greene, considering the outstanding warrants posted for his arrest since early February. Giving his name as a witness to seeing a boy being smuggled into a boat was suicidal. Michael saw no good reason for Greene to stick out his neck in such a way.

But if de Manning's witness wasn't Greene, why would someone have used his name?

He tried to stuff the paper in a waistcoat pocket, but his pockets were full of evidence, evidence he was reluctant to share. He felt pity and horror for Lydia's son, a boy without a childhood, whose value was derived from his position on a political chessboard. And he felt curiously cautious for Eve Whistler, whom he found it impossible to imagine in the role of the villainess in Kate Duncan's unhappy marriage. He would share evidence on his terms only. "My lady, I requested a private audience with you. Do you grant it? I doubt you want your household hearing what I've found."

She measured him with her gaze, now flat, devoid of heat or chill. Without breaking eye contact, she flicked her hand at the doors. "All three of you, wait for me outside in Mrs. Chiswell's garden. I'm certain this won't take long."

No one moved, so Michael strode around her to the doors and opened them. Waiting just outside in the foyer, likely where he'd overheard all the sparring, was Spry. Michael let out a breath of relief and crooked his forefinger to motion his assistant into the parlor with him. Lydia was skilled at lying. Michael wanted Spry present when he revealed the larger political picture. Besides, he suspected that she'd behave herself better with Spry in the room.

Dorinda and Felicia passed Spry in their exit, and Michael handed his assistant the paper from de Manning. "Here's a little something for us to discuss later."

"Yes, sir." Spry stepped to one side of the parlor doors and unfolded the paper.

Michael had no time to gauge his reaction to the scripted message. De Manning hadn't budged from his post near the sofa, and Lydia was glaring at the tutor, her chin hiked. In the interest of removing the fuse from another round of sparring, Michael advanced to Lydia's side and regarded the tutor with what he hoped was an impassive expression.

De Manning scowled at Lydia's disapproval and stumped out. Michael followed him and, from the parlor entrance, watched him plod for the back door. He waited until de Manning had banged the back door closed before he shut himself into the parlor with Spry and Lydia.

Chapter Fourteen

AS SOON AS the latch for the parlor doors clicked shut, Lydia bustled over. "Where is my son's portrait? Return it immediately!"

Bloody nobility. His back to Lydia, Michael contemplated the wood grain of the parlor doors and counted to five to douse the burn developing in the pit of his belly. Then he strolled past her into the parlor while retrieving the portrait from his pocket.

She stalked him. He offered the miniature to her. She snatched it from his outstretched palm, pressed it to her heart, and shoved it in her pocket. "Nigel de Manning spent the morning uncovering compelling evidence that my son was spirited out of Wilmington by water last night." She tossed her head. "How did you spend *your* morning? Let us not waste any more time. What evidence have you?"

Her haughtiness battered him, fanned the flames in his gut. He'd watched her control people on Lord Crump's estate, and she had de Manning choking in his own marionette strings. Michael was damned if he'd let her control him, too. For a long moment, he held her stare and made no attempt to respond. Then he took one step toward her, noting with satisfaction that she retreated one step. "I agree that we should waste no more time. Do you truly want us to find your son?"

Her dark golden brows dipped. She flung up her hands. "Is my distress not apparent? Of course I want you to find Wynndon. Cease patronizing me this way and answer my questions."

"Certainly, if from this point onward you agree to stop lying to us."

"Lying to you?" Her eyes widened. "I haven't lied to you. How dare you accuse me of lying?"

He pulled the brooch from his pocket and unwrapped it. "This morning, your men impressed upon me what a clever boy Lord Wynndon is. At the site of the abduction, he left this behind." He tossed her the brooch, and she caught it clumsily. "Your men are certain he left it for us to find, so we'd know the direction his captors had taken. But I suspect the boy got rid of it to avoid having it found on his person. He knew better than to let that symbol identify him to his captors."

Her nostrils flared. "You dare imply that the white rose of York is nefarious. I find your implication insulting." She held up the brooch. "There's nothing ominous about it. The conflict between the houses of York and Lancaster was settled hundreds of years ago. So much for your theory."

His gut clenched. He glanced back at his assistant before gesturing to her. "Look there, Spry. Scarcely a minute has gone by, and already she's lying to us. Descent from Henry the Second isn't the issue here. That's the white rose of the Jacobites."

Lydia's jaw dangled. Behind Michael, Spry sucked in a breath of astonishment. Then Lydia's eyes narrowed, and she snarled. She shoved the brooch in her other pocket and turned her back on them.

The gods only knew who was listening outside the parlor doors, so Michael kept his voice low. "You didn't flee England to escape John Wynndon. You fled to avoid being implicated in some harebrained scheme to overthrow the King, didn't you?" She kept her back to him. The fire in his belly ramped up. "And you know who abducted your son."

"No. I don't know."

Michael spat out an oath, strode over, and faced her. "The safety of Wilmington's citizens is our responsibility. My assistant and I will have naught to do with Jacobites. Who abducted your son?"

"I told you, I don't know!"

He didn't temper the cynicism pouring into his voice. "Then I shall presume your husband belongs to a secret organization that's backing a new Stuart claim. They've been betrayed, and the King's men are picking off the membership. Your husband sent you and the boy to America. Assassins followed. They overtook you ten miles north of Wilmington and abducted Lord Wynndon. Brave soldier, he dropped the brooch. Because he did so, he may still be alive. But eventually they'll find out who he is and what he knows. Then will they come to Wilmington for you?"

"It isn't like that at all."

"Oh, of course not. And at this point, you cannot supply a logical reason why I should continue to divert the resources of the Eighty-Second Regiment toward assisting enemies of the King. Or why I shouldn't arrest every one of you this moment."

He thought he saw a flash of genuine panic in her eyes before she lowered her gaze to the rug. "Please." Her voice wobbled a bit. "Wynndon and I aren't enemies of the King. And we aren't Jacobites, either."

"Out with it. Where lies your loyalty?"

Still regarding the floor, she licked her lips. "It's true that my great-grandfather, grandfather, and father were Blackhalls who supported the Jacobites financially and militarily in the Fifteen and the Forty-Five. Yes, there's a new succession movement afoot. And yes, in October, Jacobites came to me for support. 'For old times,' they said." Lips softened, eyes wide, she captured his gaze and whispered, "But I refused them."

"Who is chasing you, then?"

She paced, massaging the side of her neck. "In early December, my husband's intelligencers informed him that Jacobites might have been planning to abduct our son or me for ransom. It became another reason for him to secretly send us away.

"We've estates in Charles Town and St. Augustine. Faisleigh's plan was for us to wait out the movement, which appeared to lack coherence. Ill-coordinated political efforts often dissipate. Witness the number of times that the Prince made additional attempts on the throne after the Forty-Five. But if you suspect Jacobites and not my husband's brother, that means those desperate men have found us. Now they've taken my son."

Michael left her still pacing and walked toward Spry, who was white-faced and wide-eyed at the depth of the dung pile they'd fallen into. Michael whipped back around to Lydia. "You realize you might have chosen a less conspicuous design for the boy's brooch."

With a jerk, she stopped pacing and dug her fists into the panniers at her hips. "I'm proud of my York ancestry. Are you not proud of yours?"

He raised a forefinger to her. "So help me God, if you're lying again—"

"I've spoken the truth." Her eyes blazed. "I swear it!"

He parted the curtain on the front window and peered out, ordering his thoughts, not really seeing the traffic on Second Street. "Why did you lie to me yesterday?"

"No one wants to hear talk of the Jacobites. You know that."

"So you spun balderdash about your brother-in-law, John, and falsely accused him."

"It's hardly a falsehood." Michael, who'd allowed his weight to press the window frame, heard the sulk in her voice. "John wants Ridleygate Hall and my husband's other properties."

"Of course he does. Any younger brother who's spent his inheritance would be a fool not to want more." Michael detached himself from the window and faced her. "But I question whether John is stooping to abduction and murder to get more. According to your men, he has neither the intelligence nor the money to do so."

"John is neither stupid nor lacking in resources, Lieutenant. Don't dismiss my concerns about him."

In Michael's head, he relegated John Wynndon to an outer ring of suspects while he circled the couch toward Lydia. "Plotting an abduction across the Atlantic Ocean requires intelligence and money. If you are, indeed, telling me the truth, the Jacobites hounding you have both. And if your departure from England truly was kept secret, they must have an agent planted within your party. Someone is coordinating and directing their efforts on this side of the Atlantic."

"An agent." Smugness tightened her lips. "You think Mr. de Manning is that agent. Dorinda told me so this morning. You'll have difficulty convincing me that he's a traitor."

"Really? What's his background? Scottish? Catholic?"

She scowled. "That matters not. He adores Wynndon."

"He adores you more. The man has motive aplenty for ridding himself of the boy. Your son is his greatest rival for your affections. Perhaps all he needs to push him over the edge is a monetary promise from Jacobite blood kin."

Her eyebrows bounced up. "Hah!" She paced to the far wall of the parlor, then back, stopping within five feet from Michael. "I'm afraid we shall agree on neither Mr. de Manning's guilt nor my brother-in-law's innocence. But you've evidence, you say. Evidence that Wynndon wasn't in a rowboat at ten last night. I would hear this evidence now."

Michael glanced at Spry, who'd recovered his color but was frowning. "We identified one of the bandits who was killed during the attack on your carriage. His kinfolk live eight miles northeast of town. One of them recognized Lord Wynndon's portrait this morning. Although the woman declined to comment further, I've strong reason to believe she saw your son up there last night, in a tavern with his captors."

"In a tavern?" The syllables wiggled with fastidiousness. Her upper lip curled, and one of her eyebrows cocked. "What an education my son is receiving."

Education, indeed. The Rouse house was a far cry from Ridleygate Hall. While Michael hoped the boy was still unharmed, he found himself haughty over Lydia's discomfort. "Welcome to Frontier America, my lady."

"Bah. What are your plans for the tavern and the witness?"

"Surveillance for the tavern. While we watched from a point of concealment, a local scoundrel who'd recently schemed to assassinate Major Craig arrived at the tavern with his fellows. It would please Major Craig to no end if we tracked down the vermin and exterminated him."

She leaned toward him. "Ah. You think he was one of the bandits who attacked my carriage."

"No." Michael heard more sarcasm seep into his voice. "For the simple reason that I was chasing him and his partner on horseback miles south of town while your carriage was being attacked."

"Oh." Some of the harsh lines faded from her face, and her gaze smoothed over him from head to toe. She drew back and studied him, intent.

Michael received the impression that Lydia was listening to him—truly listening—for the first time. Far from pleasing him, the realization rifted his concentration until he found the thread of the conversation again. "But I wager the scoundrel has plenty of traffic with the bandits who attacked your carriage. As for the witness, I've supplied her with a safe way to notify me when she sees Lord Wynndon again. And I've a few more leads to follow that may yield the location of places where the abductors are holding him."

"Good." She clasped her hands, fingers interlaced, before her. "What did you think of the evidence that Mr. de Manning produced?"

"I found it puzzling. Spry and I shall investigate the Market Street wharf as well as the Front Street direction the man provided for Mr. de Manning."

"You recognized his name. I saw it in your expression when you read the note. Who is he?"

"He leads a radical Protestant congregation whose members are fond of washing each other's feet and smuggling weapons for rebels. For no rational reason would he show his face in Wilmington while the Eighty-Second occupies town."

"Footwashing?" Her neck elongated. "My, my. London papers don't report that side of Frontier America. Have you been to one of their—er—ceremonies?"

It would have taken too much time for Michael to explain that the one evening he'd done so, the Bethanys had deliberately omitted the footwashing element. Besides, he was ready to terminate the conversation so he and Spry could be about their work. So he just smiled.

Her gaze again swiped the length of him. "Well. I daresay even an investigator from Bow Street encounters less diversity in his work. But it does sound as though you and your man have a busy afternoon ahead of you, so carry on. I find your evidence curiously nebulous, not at all solid."

"Evidence is seldom solid at the beginning of an investigation. The pieces that seem the most absolute often turn out to be false leads."

She held his gaze, blinked back a sudden shimmer of tears, and stilled a quiver in her lower lip. "Is that your way of saying that I shouldn't expect you to find Wynndon today?" she whispered. When Michael didn't respond, she sighed, hard. "But it isn't unreasonable for me to expect you and Spry to turn *something* up this afternoon."

"I make no guarantees, my lady."

***

He and Spry escorted Lydia from the parlor and out the back door to the garden. The household departed. Enid emerged from the kitchen. "Busy day, eh? Here's something for your empty haversacks." That "something" turned out to be bread, cheese, and apples. The men thanked her and strode for Market Street and the wharf, their haversacks laden.

"That was an excellent conjecture you made yesterday about de Manning as Lord Wynndon's father, Spry." Michael reached for bread. "It may be accurate."

Spry grunted, then swallowed a bite of apple. "Christ's wounds, Jacobites. Do you think Lady Faisleigh was telling the truth this time?"

Michael gulped down a mouthful of bread. He'd be a fool if he believed that everything Lydia told him was the truth. One corner of his mouth crooked, and he cocked an eyebrow.

Spry nodded. "I doubted it, too, sir. Do you plan to arrest them for treason?"

"Not right away. She may actually be telling the truth about not supporting the Jacobites. But if Jacobites kidnapped the boy for ransom, why hasn't she received a demand for money yet? And I suspect there's still some information she's withholding from us. Perhaps it's a confession about Lord Wynndon's parentage. Have you pieced together why we're visiting the wharf next?"

"Sir. This morning, a man calling himself Paul Greene apparently told Captain de Manning that he'd seen a boy resembling Lord Wynndon being loaded into a rowboat at the wharf last night."

"Correct."

"Greene is too smart for that, sir. If he actually set foot in town last night or this morning, I'll eat a backgammon board."

No one at White's would be including Spry in a backgammon tournament for awhile. Michael grinned at him. "I agree that it's unlikely Greene was in town. So we must wonder who and why." They passed the commerce of Front Street, and Spry's silence made Michael realize that his assistant was studying him. "Yes? What else?"

"It's rather obvious, sir. Lady Faisleigh has her cap set for you."

Michael snorted. "Bloody nuisance." He rifled through his haversack for cheese.

"You're both from Yorkshire, sir. Do you know her? From Yorkshire, I mean."

Michael felt his shoulders tense, then made the muscles relax, made his eyebrows dip with what he hoped looked like candid puzzlement. Nick Spry was perceptive. Most of the time, Michael was glad for it. This time, he hoped Spry had missed the nuance. "Yorkshire's a big place, Spry. Why would you think that?" He bit off some of the cheese.

"This morning you told Ames you were from Scarborough after he said he was from Kettlesing, inland. I know you aren't from Scarborough, sir. Scarborough's on the coast, and you're from somewhere inland." Spry pitched his apple core to the side of the dirt street. "It sounded like you didn't want Ames figuring out where you—"

"As I said, Yorkshire covers a good bit of land." Michael waved his arm ahead, at the activity on the wharf. "And what we need to determine this moment is whether two drunkards could have kept themselves hidden here on this wharf while getting close enough to identify that what men were loading into a rowboat was a ten-year-old boy, bound and gagged. And that the boy looked like Lord Wynndon. All at ten o'clock at night." He stepped out of the way of a horse-drawn wagon of lumber and stopped walking. Spry joined him. "So. What do you think?"

They gazed about. On the wooden dock, piles of lumber and stacked barrels of pitch and turpentine created canyons through which sweaty-backed men unloaded and maneuvered crates from a shallow-draft, two-masted ship secured alongside the dock. The driver of the wagonload of lumber was chatting with a man who held what looked like a ship's manifest. A pig squealed from one of the crates mounded to one side of the activity. Chickens clucked from a crate in another canyon. Smells of tar manufacture, tobacco smoke, brackish water, and animal dung warred in the warm air, and feathers circulated on a flutter of breeze off the Cape Fear River.

"I think we need to test the plausibility of the story, sir." Spry swung his gaze from left to right. "And search the wharf. If the abductors came here with the boy, they'd have been hurrying to escape notice of the night watch. They may have dropped something."

"Right you are. You start over there with that ship, and I shall have a look at the boat slip."

Spry strolled closer to the ship, crouched behind a stack of lumber, and peered over it, then around it. Michael found the boat slip and tested his own concealment and visibility around barrels of tar. Then he tried optional points of observation farther back from the wharf.

His search of the ground and between piles and stacks of goods yielded a broken comb, one penny, a torn and grease-laden haversack, and miscellaneous animal byproducts. Nothing that appeared to have been dropped by men in a rush to offload a bound, gagged hostage into a rowboat.

When he and Spry met up closer to Front Street and off the road, Spry said, "You asked, sir, so here's what I think. De Manning's evidence is balderdash."

"I agree. With so many obstructions, it's difficult enough to pick out details here in the daylight. Imagine how night impacts the perceptions, plus the desire to keep one's presence a secret. And the men told de Manning that they'd been drinking last night."

Spry laughed. "Why didn't de Manning see how badly that story stank instead of championing it?" He snapped his fingers. "Oh, that's right. He's trying to please Lady Faisleigh with news of her son. Any news will do, I suppose."

"He's also trying to prove me incompetent. He wants desperately to give her news that looks more promising than whatever I provide her."

"Does that mean he fabricated that entire story, sir?"

"Difficult to say. If he did so, how would he have known to use Paul Greene's name, eh?" Michael held Spry's gaze and dragged out a smirk. "Unless he's the abductors' agent, of course."

Spry's eyebrows rose, and his teeth shone. "Hah! I'm sure Greene wouldn't mind seeing King George the Third deposed for a Stuart, sir. He and de Manning might have been in communication well in advance of the party's travel into this area." He clapped his hands once. "When do we arrest Mr. de Manning?" His expression sagged a little. "Ah, we don't really have proof yet, do we?"

"No, alas. *If* he's the abductors' agent and he's fabricated this story, he's shown his hand in several ways. But if he's innocent of conspiracy, we must find out who set him up with this story." Michael let his attention wander into the distance and felt his way carefully through the next level of thought. "If de Manning's innocent, perhaps he was used for dupery. Someone knew he'd report the story to Lady Faisleigh, and then—"

"And then *we* would hear about it."

They stared at each other two seconds before Michael said, "Let me see that direction on Front Street again." Spry had already reached in his waistcoat for the paper. Michael unfolded it, read the direction, and tucked the paper in his own pocket. "Right beside the farriers' shop. Someone wants us to have a look. Let's oblige them."

Chapter Fifteen

FROM WHAT MICHAEL could tell peering in through dusty windows, the tannery on Front Street beside Duke and Gibson's farrier shop was closed. According to Hiram Duke, who'd spotted them and moseyed over to chat, the merchant who owned the tannery building was visiting family in Pennsylvania. No one had been in the building for weeks.

Duke sent one of his apprentices to locate the merchant's business partner and bring a key for the front door of the tannery. Because he wasn't busy that moment, the farrier agreed to wait in the outer shop and keep an eye out for the business partner. Michael and his assistant entered the stable, where they found Gibson, who'd just finished shoeing a horse.

When he spotted their approach, Gibson sent the horse off with the other apprentice. Expression flat, he said, "Afternoon, fellows. You need work done on the Eighty-Second's horses, right? We can handle it first thing on Monday."

Michael noted that Gibson kept a grip on his hammer with his right hand. He also noted that the farrier sported a black eye, and the middle of his left hand was bandaged, leaving his fingers free. He pinned Gibson with a stare and flicked him a humorless smile. "So long as you don't lose more money at cockfights between now and then, eh, Mr. Gibson?"

Gibson's dark eyes glowered. "What do you want?"

"When was the last time you saw Zeke Whistler?"

The farrier started, and his unbruised eye widened for a second. "Who?" His lips twisted shut.

"Zeke Whistler was the blond boy who was helping you with a gelding on the morning of the twenty-second, when Spry and I came in."

"Never heard of him. You're mistaken. That boy's name was—uh—Albert."

"Albert. Of course. Where does Albert live?"

"I don't know. Somewhere out of town, to the north." Gibson's fingers flexed on the hammer.

"Near Rouse's Tavern? That was Alexander Rouse's gelding you were tending on the twenty-second."

"Rouse? No, no, it was Albert's father's plough horse."

Michael and his assistant glanced at each other. Both stepped closer to Gibson. "Plough horse? Didn't look like a plough horse to me. Was that a plough horse, Spry?"

"No, sir. That wasn't a plough horse."

"Do you think us blind, Mr. Gibson?"

The farrier scowled. His bruised eye twitched.

"Well, you must think us idiots, then, imagining we'd swallow the false witness you bore about Mr. Duke and arrest him. Maybe next time you won't gamble so much money on a cockfight. Or maybe there won't be a next time because you'll be locked up in the pen."

"Arrested? For what—lying? About a horse? Hell, you'd better arrest all the residents of Wilmington, then."

"No, not just for lying. For consorting with highwaymen *and* lying."

Gibson's fingers tensed on the hammer. "Highwaymen?"

"And if you don't drop that bloody hammer straight away, you're going to the pen regardless."

Gibson's gaze popped between the men several times. Sweat shone on his forehead. Then he allowed the hammer to slide from his hand. The dirt-and-straw floor dulled the thud.

Michael eased breath from his nostrils. He and Spry would have had a bruising struggle on their hands to bring Ralph Gibson down. Working with horses had made him a powerful man. "Thank you, Mr. Gibson. Let us not waste more of each other's time. When did you last see Zeke Whistler?"

Gibson's shoulders lowered, and he dodged Michael's gaze. "On the twenty-second, when he brought me his horse."

"That wasn't his horse. It was Alexander Rouse's horse. I overheard you discussing it with the boy. You've done work for Jones and Love, too. When was the last time you saw them?"

Gibson's gaze remained averted. "January."

Michael studied him without speaking. In the pause, Gibson darted a look his way before digging his gaze elsewhere. "That's quite an impressive black eye, Mr. Gibson. And I see that you hurt your hand. How did you come by those injuries?"

"Unruly horse early this morning," he muttered.

Michael knew all about the swelling and discoloration associated with black eyes. He'd acquired several in his youth and in battle. He'd also seen black eyes on fellow soldiers. Gibson had had his at least twenty-four hours. "Where were you yesterday between noon and four in the afternoon?"

The farrier's body jerked, as if he'd touched a door handle and received a shock after scuffing over carpet. His gaze, rocketing to Michael in the first second, swung right. "I was running errands."

Duke sallied in with a smile and clapped his hands once. "Hullo, fellows, the key to the tanner's shop has arrived. Shall I have the gentleman open the front door and air the place out for you?"

Gibson gnawed his lower lip at his partner's announcement, his gaze darting about even more, like a trapped mouse. Michael dragged his attention off him to the cheery Duke. "No, Mr. Duke. Wait for us outside the front door. We won't be but a moment longer here. And thank you."

"You're welcome. It's no trouble at all, sir." Duke left the stable humming.

Michael regarded Gibson, whose gaze slid to a window, shadowing his bruised eye. "Mr. Gibson, where did you go when you ran those errands yesterday afternoon?"

He shrugged. "Everywhere."

"Write a list of all the places comprising 'everywhere' between noon and four yesterday. Include the names of people who can verify that you were where you say you were."

"I cannot do it right now." Gibson hiked a thumb over his shoulder. "Got another horse waiting on me out back."

"Then find time to make the list. Spry and I will return for it later this afternoon."

Gibson's brows dove for the bridge of his nose. He opened his mouth, and Michael strode from the stable, Spry following. Best to not give the farrier the inch he needed for another mile of prevarication.

The tanner's business partner held up a ring of keys at the appearance of the soldiers and unlocked the door. He pushed it open and made to enter the shop ahead of the soldiers, but Michael held him back a moment by the upper arm. "Spry, look at that." He pointed to the wood floor of the entrance.

Someone had entered the shop recently, or so multiple sets of footprints in the dust revealed. The business partner's bewilderment looked genuine. He told them he knew of no one else who had a key to the padlock. Someone must have picked the lock.

Michael released the man's arm, instructed him to wait there at the front door, and, while still outside, studied five or six sets of footprints wandering over the dusty floor of the main room. Clumps of straw had been crushed underfoot. He wondered what the men had carried and why they'd needed straw.

Men? At least two sets of footprints looked smaller than the rest. From all the smearing, Michael couldn't be certain, but it appeared that the smaller prints had shorter strides associated with them. Made by children, most likely.

The footprints veered into the back room. Michael entered the main room and sent Spry into the back room. The place still retained the faint odors of dye and leather, and although all equipment had been moved out, an empty waste bin and a couple broken benches remained. Seconds after his assistant's footsteps halted across the wooden floor, his voice wandered out with a catch to it that suggested that Spry was restraining himself from laughing: "Er, Mr. Stoddard, you'd better have a look at this, sir." Michael strolled over and paused in the doorway of the back room.

In an otherwise-empty area, two human-sized, straw-stuffed dummies had been posed upright facing each other. One was garbed in the type of threadbare, black ecclesiastical robe that Michael had seen on Paul Greene back in January. Black paint had been used to create features of a scowling face on the figure's canvas head. Its right arm was lifted, bent at the elbow, and the digits of a gloved hand were positioned to convey an obscene finger gesture at the other figure—clearly a soldier of the Eighty-Second Regiment, from its red uniform coat.

Annoyance and alarm grated Michael's gut. How the hell had civilians gotten their hands on a soldier's coat for this prank? He walked in for a closer look.

That was when he realized that the redcoat wasn't just any redcoat. The dummy's head had been painted with crossed eyes and dark hair. A piece of carved wood affixed to the right shoulder suggested a lieutenant's epaulet. Out of reflex, Michael glanced at his own epaulet.

Spry stood beyond the figure of the preacher and regarded the ceiling. His mouth muscles twitched and tensed. Every bit of his concentration was devoted to suppressing laughter, preserving his commanding officer's dignity.

Yes, Michael was fortunate to have an assistant as perceptive as Nick Spry. The irritation in his stomach dissolved. He cocked his head and smiled at the crude likeness of himself. "Ye gods, lad, what have they done to you? The last time you looked in the mirror, you weren't cross-eyed."

Spry doubled over and roared. While he subsided into titters and wiped his eyes, Michael circled the duo of dummies, eying them up and down. And that was when he spotted the small folded note secured with string inside the preacher's gloved left palm.

His humor evaporated. He untied the note, brushed past Spry, and unfolded it at one of the rear windows. The quotation scripted at the top of the note was cited as coming from the seventy-eighth chapter of Psalms, verses fifty and fifty-one:

> *He made a way to his anger; he spared not their soul from death, but gave their life over to the pestilence; and smote all the first-born in Egypt.*

Below it was a message:

> *In a Basket, five hundred Pounds, to be delivered two Hours before Sunrise on the morrow, to the Base of the mulberry Tree at Alexander Rouse's Tavern. Else the First-born Lamb of Faisleigh shall be sacrificed.*

A dirk of ice embedded in Michael's skull and dragged down his spine. A verse from Isaiah 65:17 followed the instructions for delivery of the ransom:

> *For, behold, I create new heavens and a new earth.*

Michael examined the other side of the note but saw no additional communication, such as where Lord Wynndon would be delivered safely upon his captors' receipt of the money. More ice pinned his spine. If the beasts got their claws on five hundred pounds, Lydia would never see her son alive again. And the abductors would use the money to create their new heavens and earth.

The ransom note was unsigned. Michael fished in his pocket for the note given to de Manning that morning as well as the paper they'd found in the dead bandit's haversack. He compared the handwriting samples. They appeared identical. Unless he received evidence to the contrary, he'd assume that Lord Wynndon's abduction was the work of Paul Greene.

He spun about and planted all papers in Spry's waiting hands. Then he examined the dummies up close for clues and more instructions.

Greene had exploited a security breach in the Eighty-Second's defenses to steal a uniform of a man of rank and file. Michael must find out how he'd done it and seal the breach. Otherwise, Greene and his footwashing fiends would help themselves to more uniforms, impersonate soldiers of the King, and raise all manner of hell. Especially if Cornwallis came to town.

To be on the safe side, he'd place the tannery shop under surveillance for a few days. But he suspected that nothing would come of it. Greene was too clever to piss on the same ground twice.

Behind him, Spry said, low, "These handwriting samples look the same. So Greene abducted the boy? Damnation. Who has five hundred pounds to pay a ransom, sir?"

Michael ran his hand down Greene's robe, found a pocket, and turned it inside out. Nothing. He knelt and examined the ragged hemline. "Perhaps Lady Faisleigh is traveling with a portion of that amount."

He wondered why Greene had asked for five hundred pounds. What made him believe he might receive it? Or did the preacher intend to negotiate, use the figure as a starting point?

What countermoves would Michael's team have to make on the chessboard to avoid placing five hundred pounds in the hands of rebel scum two hours before sunrise Sunday morning? Greene, cocksure, had vaulted past the requisite step of proving that he had a live prisoner. Some of Michael's dread dissipated, and he rolled back his shoulders. The preacher expected money in the basket. Instead, he'd receive Michael's demand to see the boy, so he could ensure that Lydia's son was uninjured.

"Their threat to the boy if they don't get the amount is clear, sir. But they don't specify what will happen to him if they *do* get it."

"Exactly, which is one reason why they mustn't get the money." The black robe, Michael was certain, hid nothing, so he moved on for an examination of the Stoddard figure.

"Five hundred pounds. Bloody hell, what do they purport to do with so much, sir?"

"Read that second Scripture verse again."

Paper rustled behind him. "Oh, no. They're going to rebuild their footwashing church."

"That's my guess, too." Michael felt the crackle of folded paper in the left wrist cuff. "Ah, another love note from Saint Paul." He extracted the note and unfolded it, then felt his expression sour. "Here you are, Spry. Surely this message was meant for you." He handed over the note.

"'Burn in hell, sinner.' No thank you, sir. But the handwriting matches the other samples."

"I expect so. Greene's patronage is making a stationer quite happy somewhere. Yes, I suppose that's a vague lead we could follow, but we're drowning in more substantial leads. Check the other arm, will you? See if Greene hid anything in that sleeve."

They finished the search without finding further information and stepped back from the straw figures. Spry handed Michael all the papers, and Michael pocketed them. Then Michael crossed his arms over his chest. "I consider this shop a supplemental scene of the crime. These straw men are evidence, but they shall remain here for now. Let's make certain all windows are locked. I shall have that fellow out there loan us a duplicate key for a few days, until surveillance informs us that Greene and his men aren't coming back."

They tugged and pushed on the two windows in the room to ensure that they were latched. Hands clasped behind his back, low, Spry gazed outside at the sky. "Sir, if Greene is on good terms with people who hid stills and whiskey from revenue men, he may have access to plenty of places to hide the boy between the Rouse and Collier houses. Why would he need to bring him here, send him off in a boat at ten o'clock at night?"

"I doubt that Lord Wynndon was here last night. If he was being trotted around the tavern eight miles northeast of town, it implies that his captors were full of confidence over their theft and had found a place nearby to secure him. They wouldn't threaten their victory by bringing the boy to Wilmington." Michael ran his forefinger along the top rail of the window, examined the dust he'd picked up, and brushed it off on his breeches. "I also doubt that Greene was on the wharf, especially this morning. The price on his head is too high. He has henchmen who can set all this up and masquerade as him."

Spry rotated his scrutiny to Michael. "How could de Manning be such a fool, sir?"

"If he's part of Greene's scheme, he isn't a fool. He's misleading us. And if he's innocent, it's just as well that he didn't think beyond their deception and find his way in here." Michael extended a hand to the straw men. "No telling what he would have made of these fellows."

Spry turned about and leaned against the sill. "Where to next, sir? Lady Faisleigh?"

"Yes." Michael drummed his fingers on his jaw a moment. "We've received a ransom note. The stakes are now raised. Time for us to find out what else Lady Faisleigh may be withholding from us."

"How? If she'd intended for us to know, she'd have told us in Mrs. Chiswell's study, sir."

Michael sauntered a figure-eight pattern between the Greene and Stoddard dummies, inspecting them one more time. "She needs a reminder that we don't work for her. That we are, in fact, responsible for investigating all criminal activity in Wilmington."

"Ah. And we devote more attention to those investigations for which we have more information and cooperation from witnesses. Correct, sir?"

"Correct." Michael smiled. "Then we'll pay a visit to the wainwright, Mr. Smedes, to inquire about his dealings with Rephael Whistler as well as with his assistant, Mr. Travis. Give some thought to the men you know who are responsible enough for surveillance. By the time we've finished up at Mr. Smedes's shop, I want you to recommend at least eight."

"Yes, sir."

***

Ames admitted them to the parlor of the house where Lydia was lodged, sent Felicia upstairs to notify Lydia of their arrival, and exited the parlor. Spry took a stance over by the window, and Michael waited beside the doors. Multiple sets of footsteps in rapid descent on the stairs told him that Lydia had been sitting on the edge of a chair upstairs.

She entered the parlor almost out of breath seconds later, followed by Felicia and Dorinda. "Yes? You've news for me, Lieutenant?"

While the maids assumed position on either side of the doors, Michael poked his head out the doorway and scanned the foyer from left to right. No head coachman. And no tutor. "Where's Mr. de Manning?"

"At the wharf. He said he had more investigation to perform. What news do you bring me?"

More investigation? Bah. The tutor was spinning fiction, making himself look indispensable. Michael's gaze went from Lydia's gripped, white knuckles to her eyes. "We've received a ransom note. Sit. I'll show you."

She pressed her cheeks with her fingers. "Oh. A ransom note. Oh." She inhaled a deep breath, then let it out slowly. "Where? When? How?"

Michael swiveled his attention to Dorinda and waved her toward Lydia. While the maid seated her on the larger couch, he closed the doors. Then he fetched the note, unfolded it, and took it around to her.

She read it three times. Her brows dipped further with each successive reading before she handed the note back to him, scowling. "I understand the demand, but what is this about 'sacrifice?' Does it mean that they plan to kill my son?"

He secured the note in his waistcoat. "That's the implication, although surely such action defeats the advantage of having a hostage."

"Animals." She hugged herself and rubbed her upper arms, as if cold. "I can make no sense of the Biblical gibberish they use."

"We believe your son is the prisoner of the rebel preacher Paul Greene, of the Church of Mary and Martha of Bethany."

"Is this the footwashing lout you mentioned earlier?"

"Yes, and he's also a weapons smuggler. Early in February, we burned his church building to the ground and arrested about half the congregation. However, they multiply like fleas and have continued meeting in secret locations."

"Ugh. The London papers are full of stories about these barbarian Protestants. Baptists, Anabaptists, Presbyterians, and the like. A Bible in one hand, and a musket in the other." Again she rubbed her arms. "These bandits must lie in wait of carriages such as mine."

"Many do." He caught her gaze. "But as you and I discussed yesterday, I think Greene had a little help this time."

She shivered and looked away. "How did you come by the ransom note? Why wasn't it sent to me?"

Michael felt his way with care along the explanation. "We found it at the direction given to Mr. de Manning this morning."

She balled both fists on her thighs and leaned forward. "What? But he'd declined to visit the building because he felt he'd collected enough information from those men's testimony."

"Obviously he was mistaken. As for why the note wasn't sent directly to you—" Michael shrugged. "There's no love lost between Greene and me. He wanted to make certain that Major Craig's criminal investigator found the note. It's his way of thumbing his nose at me."

She sighed, repositioned hands in her lap, and sat back. Her gaze trailed over him. "What is your analysis of Mr. de Manning's story of the two men who contacted him?"

Michael took in the bland expressions of the maids. Lydia was convinced of the loyalty of de Manning and everyone else in her household. Twelve years earlier, Lord Crump had also been convinced of his servants' trustworthiness, until Michael, at the age of fourteen, had brought him evidence pointing toward embezzlement from his steward and gamekeeper.

That the stakes were now higher meant Michael's errors would yield more disastrous consequences. To find Lord Wynndon alive and unharmed, he must trust Lydia only marginally more than her individual household members. He resumed a position facing the door, between the fireplace and Lydia, where he could see the maids and Spry. "From this point onward, Lady Faisleigh, if you wish to learn my analyses of specific elements of this investigation, I shall comply only while in a private audience with you." Before she could protest, he added, "What are your thoughts on this ransom amount?"

Her gaze lost focus, and she shook her head. "Five hundred pounds." She groaned and dropped her face into her palms a moment. When she raised her head, her cheeks lacked color. "And I must pay it all tonight?"

"No. The truth is that we don't know whether your son is still alive and unharmed. You shouldn't pay a penny unless they can give you proof of that."

"So you intend to ask them to produce that proof first? But—but it appears that they'll kill him if I don't pay."

"Greene isn't stupid. At this stage, he's playing chess. Logically, you and I must see the boy alive and unhurt for his abductors to expect you to move forward in complying with their demands. Waiting for them to arrange such proof allows us to stall for a day, possibly longer. During that time, Spry and I will follow up on leads, and you can access your resources to make an estimation of how much you can actually pay."

She blinked at him. "Do you mean they aren't expecting the full five hundred pounds? But won't they kill Wynndon if I give them less?"

He scratched behind one ear while he deliberated. He didn't know Greene well enough to gauge whether he'd kill the boy if he received less than five hundred pounds. But he did know that Greene, unlike his church, was far from destitute.

One slow exhale later, he said to her, "I believe the best course is to establish communications with your son's captors. If it's impossible for you to meet the initial demand of five hundred pounds, well, nothing can change that. Greene must then consider whether it isn't wiser to accept what you *are* capable of paying."

She rubbed her palm with the thumb of her other hand. "And then they still might kill Wynndon."

"If it's their intention to kill him, they'll do it regardless of what you pay them. I'm afraid that's out of our control." He wondered whether her thumb was gouging a channel in her palm.

She pursed her lips. "What *is* in our control? I want you to cite in detail what you and Spry will do while you're waiting for them to produce proof of Wynndon's well-being."

He faced her straight on and allowed his arms to hang, loose and relaxed, at his sides. "Spry and I will perform surveillance and interview witnesses."

"That sounds altogether too vague." Her fists balled on her thighs again.

"It is vague."

She glowered. "Unacceptable. I want details. Now."

Her anxiety, along with renewed pressure to declare himself before he was ready, leapt the ten feet between them and battered at him. He held her gaze and expelled another long breath. "I shall be happy to provide you with more details in a private audience."

"Private audience. Private audience. Is finding my son a priority for you? I don't think so."

His jaw clenched. He relaxed it. "Are you still withholding information from us? I do think so."

She stood, eyes narrowed, chin hiked. "You're mocking me. I've told you everything you need to know. Why do you need to know more?"

The electric charge of her will groped for him. Irritation peppered his gut. What in hell was she guarding? "Understand that those investigations receiving our greatest attention are those for which we've been supplied the most information. Understand also that as Spry and I act as criminal investigators in service to His Majesty, we hesitate to commit ourselves in an investigation where details are withheld."

The lines around her mouth tensed. "Very well. I shall grant you a private audience now. Just you, Lieutenant."

"My assistant investigator remains in the room with me." Michael strode to the doors, yanked one open, and, one hand on the door, regarded Dorinda and Felicia, his shoulders rolled back and chin level. "Wait outside." They looked to Lydia, eyebrows hiked. She rose and faced Michael, fists balled. Before her lower lip pushed upward any farther, he injected a snap to his voice. "You two, cease dawdling. Your lady's time is valuable." He pointed to the foyer. "Out!"

Chapter Sixteen

DORINDA AND FELICIA scurried from the parlor. Michael made sure the doors latched shut before regarding Lydia.

Her eyes had become blue glaciers. "You will *not* order members of my household about."

His glare pinned to hers, he walked past Spry at the window around the couch to the fireplace, forcing her to compromise her unyielding stance to follow his movement. "I remind you who is the investigator here." His back to the empty grate, he moved in and stamped to the posture of attention.

Too close. She backed away half a step, the rigidity of her expression wavering. After another few seconds, her glare dissolved into a sulk. Her fists relaxed.

"Now, then." He softened his tone but not his bearing. "Earlier, you asked for my analysis of Mr. de Manning's story about the two men at the wharf. I find no evidence that your son was at the wharf last night. I maintain that he's being held eight or ten miles to the northeast." When she didn't respond, he added, "Thus either Mr. de Manning was duped by Greene's henchmen, or he's in Greene's employ, sent to provide misdirection and counterfeit clues, sent to encourage us to search somewhere other than northeast."

She stepped to the mantle, fingered wood on it, and matched his tone. "Wynndon might have been at both places last night."

"Certainly. However, the short time span makes it unlikely. Also, if his abductors wished to move him by water, they could have loaded him aboard a boat at any number of locations that are far safer for their operations. Wilmington is entirely too dangerous for them." He dropped the volume of his voice further and voiced his suspicions. "And you are withholding relevant information about your son from criminal investigators. If you expect us to help you, you must be forthcoming with that information."

He thought she'd continue to stall. But after several seconds, she swallowed and glanced at Spry before returning her gaze to the mantle. "It most certainly isn't for the ears of common soldiers."

"Spry is my assistant. He and I swear to keep your information confidential. Out with it."

She took a deep breath and swiveled her head to Michael. "My dear husband was unable to sire children upon me or his three mistresses. We refused to allow John to have the family fortune, just because he had heirs. So my husband and I decided that I must make a discreet arrangement with a man who was trustworthy enough to keep the secret."

"I see." Michael advanced the conjecture Spry had made the night before. "That man was Captain de Manning."

Lydia bowed her head.

That explained *everything*—why the captain longed for Lydia, why she dismissed his affections, why he was so close to the boy, why the boy's likeness in the portrait had seemed familiar to him and Spry. And why Michael's question of Lydia the day before had generated a sense of deception in her statement that her son had dark hair and dark eyes "like his father." Like *de Manning*, not like Faisleigh. Eleven years earlier, the captain had served his primary purpose as a stud. The only further use Lydia had for him was as a tutor for his son.

De Manning needed to rethink his lovesick attitude, realize his good fortune, and find a mistress or three to ease his loins. His offspring would be the seventeenth Earl of Faisleigh, set to inherit multiple properties, thousands of pounds, and a seat in the House of Lords. If de Manning played his game of one-and-thirty well, he'd be gifted with a lavish retirement, something few junior officers ever received.

Lydia's tone flattened. "My husband wanted another heir, just in case John should contrive a horrid extermination for Wynndon. But I lost sleep thinking about it, and—and I didn't have the nerve to dally in such an arrangement again."

Michael glanced at Spry, who wore a neutral expression. Then he walked past Lydia and expelled a breath fouled with the stench of the nobility's gambits. Lydia's conscience had apparently never been troubled enough to cause her to lose sleep over dallying two summers with a falcon boy. More than ever that moment, he wished to be anywhere except in her company.

Her voice softened, like the scent of a floral garden on a summer night. "Lieutenant, I can tell I've offended your sensibilities, but I hope you'll take pity on me and keep my confidence in this matter. Aside from Mr. de Manning, the only person to know the truth is my husband. You and your man now possess highly sensitive information."

Indeed. They could damage Lord Faisleigh with it. He faced her. "Does John Wynndon suspect this?"

Her fingers entwined atop her petticoat. "Yes, although he has no proof."

John was on the other side of the Atlantic and couldn't have physically taken part in the abduction. But he had a powerful motive to get rid of Lord Wynndon, the boy whom he suspected wasn't his blood kin but stood in the way of his inheriting a fortune. John was quite capable of scheming to kill the boy. Michael moved him back to his inner circle for suspects.

Lydia swallowed again. "You spoke of witnesses and surveillance. What witnesses will you interview? Where do you plan this surveillance?"

"There's a connection between the dead bandit we identified and some whiskey smugglers in business a decade ago to the northeast. I shall interview a wainwright who may have done business with a principal in the whiskey trade. Also the niece and nephew of another principal must be interviewed. They operate a tavern. All three may recall places to the northeast where whiskey and equipment were once concealed, places where a ten-year-old boy might be hidden now."

Lydia's lips pinched. She nodded, curt.

"And I shall place the vacant shop on Front Street under surveillance for a few days. I expect naught to come of it, for my suspicion is that it has served Greene's needs. The tavern eight miles northeast of town will be placed under surveillance, too. That's where I expect our efforts to bear fruit."

"Do you believe the woman there will help you?"

"Possibly. I do have something that she wants." Lydia faced him in curiosity, so he pulled out the Psalter.

She thumbed through the pages, then passed it back at him. "For all that these rebels profess to be Christians, they seem overly fond of the Old Testament, do they not?"

"Jesus preached forgiveness, love thy neighbor, render unto Caesar. Not popular themes for those with a musket in one hand."

She shuddered and looked away. "What beasts. My poor son."

"Give me an idea of your limitations for negotiation. How much money are you carrying with you?"

After a sharp glance at him, she diverted her gaze and murmured, "Five hundred pounds."

Michael felt his jaw dangle, then jammed his mouth shut. Spry mouthed the words *five hundred* at him, his eyebrows stretched nearly to his scalp. Michael leaned back to Lydia. "You've *five hundred pounds* with you?" Christ almighty! Paymasters for regiments might hold that much, but they were protected by armies. "Your son's abductors named for ransom the exact amount you stated. This is no coincidence. How did it happen that they demanded that precise amount?"

"I don't know." Again she hugged herself and rubbed her arms. "But obviously I cannot give Greene the entire five hundred."

"Who in your household knows how much money you're carrying?"

As if trying to escape, she rushed past him. He snagged her upper arm. The way she dodged his gaze confirmed his suspicions and shoveled fire into his gut. "De Manning? You told de *Manning*?" Of course! It was as clear as the sun in the sky. "He knows how much money you have. He provided Greene with the amount, and he told him when to expect your carriage on the highway. De Manning has betrayed you and your son. And now I shall arrest that cur—"

"No, don't, please!" She yanked herself free and backed from him a few steps. Like the previous afternoon, when he'd first seen her, she appeared flustered, unsure of herself. "We're overlooking something. He cannot have done this to us. Nigel adores Wynndon. There must be another explanation."

"Then I expect you to find that explanation."

"This makes no sense. I gave Nigel everything!"

"Everything?" Michael advanced on her one step, anger freezing the expression on his face. "Everything except your *love*. That's obvious every time he lays eyes upon you. And if he's sold out to an enemy for lack of love, he wouldn't be the first man in history to do so."

"*Love?*" Her upper lip lifted in a sneer. "Love is an illusion of the lower classes, a deception, a trap." She placed more distance between herself and Michael and paced back and forth. "Nigel knows better. Love has no place in the lives of the nobility. He cannot have betrayed us."

Michael stared, incredulous. "No place in the lives of...You don't love your husband, your son?"

She whipped her head about to glare at him while she paced. "I am completely devoted to both of them. I would give my life for them."

"That sounds like love to me."

"You confuse love with loyalty. Which is it that you would give Major Craig? And would you not give your life for him?"

Michael opened his mouth, but speech abandoned his throat at the sterility of the world she occupied. Like a vivid welt across his imagination, he envisioned Lydia torturing de Manning with his own thirst for an entire decade. If he'd sought the beds of other women as a substitute for hers, Lydia enjoyed the thought.

Then the realization clobbered him: why Lydia resisted the idea that de Manning could have sold out to an enemy. It would mean admitting that she no longer controlled him, that de Manning had snapped his own marionette strings, even if it meant hanging himself in the process.

Lydia did love. She loved *control* over the very breath and thoughts of others. Even at the age of sixteen, he'd recognized that on some level. It was why his memories of their encounters held not joy but gloom. Finally he understood why he'd been able to move beyond her after several years in the Army. Marionette strings, stretched across the Atlantic Ocean, became tenuous with time. Pity for de Manning speared Michael.

He caught his breath a second, then let it out. He'd met only one other person on the face of the earth who loved control over others as much as Lydia did: Lieutenant Dunstan Fairfax. Coupling with Lydia was like coupling with—

Nausea swirled in the acid bath of Michael's stomach. He *must* find Lord Wynndon so he and his mother could depart from Wilmington.

The door handle rattled, then the door burst open, and de Manning shouldered his way in a few steps, his face ashen, a bundle of gray wool beneath one arm. With Spry three strides ahead of him, Michael stalked around the couch. "Mr. de Manning, what is the meaning of this?" His jaw clenched over the ploys of Lydia and de Manning, balderdash that wasted his time and the Eighty-Second's resources and perpetuated the danger to Lord Wynndon.

Spry reached the tutor's side. "This is a private audience, sir. Step back out into the foyer." He gestured for the doors.

Behind Michael, the temperature of Lydia's tone approximated that of sleet. "How dare you interrupt us, Mr. de Manning."

The tutor never looked at Spry, or at Michael, who'd reached his assistant's side. "I've evidence, my lady." De Manning's voice trembled. "Evidence that I found at the wharf." Then he shook out the fabric and held it up between both hands.

A moan rose from Lydia. Her expression crumpled. "No—Wynndon's cloak!" She rushed forward to seize and enfold a fine, wool cloak. One side of it was dark and stiff with a spray of what looked like blood.

De Manning hung his head, arms empty.

Spry sucked in a breath of shock. The maids gasped from the doorway, then inched their way into the parlor agog, hands covering their mouths.

Michael started forward, then braked before he'd taken a step. His hands clenched at his sides. His teeth ground at the sight of all that blood on the cloak. Why in hell had Greene—

No, wait. That could be livestock or game animal blood. Come to think of it, the dramatic flair and gruesome suggestion of violence was more Greene's style than dicing up a hostage who might be the source of a spectacular ransom. Furthermore, if Greene did want to steer his adversary to search the wharf and not to the northeast, planting the boy's bloody cloak on the wharf was quite a coup.

De Manning's voice was thick, as if he'd been weeping. "My lady, we must search the wharf and along the river. There's no telling what those animals have done to him." Lydia moaned again.

The discovery of the cloak on the wharf bolstered de Manning's theories. He planned to run with it on the platform of his indispensability.

Michael shot his voice out. "My lady, do not presume that the blood on the cloak came from your son. And the cloak is evidence that my assistant and I must confiscate for the investigation." He took a step forward.

De Manning interposed himself and bared his teeth. "The cloak won't tell you two a thing. Neither of you is fit to bear the title of investigator. Searched the wharf earlier, did you? *I'm* the one who found the cloak." He shook his fist at Michael. "Now leave my lady alone."

Locked into a stare with the tutor, Michael felt a flutter of air on his cheek, signal that Spry had moved into place at his right hand. Blood hammered in Michael's ears. Feet apart, he leaned toward de Manning and threw his arms wide. "Go ahead. Swing your fist at me. You'll be served supper in the pen tonight."

"No, don't arrest him!" Lydia rushed forward, the cloak extended. "Here. You may examine it." Spry relieved her of the cloak, rolled it into a bundle, and set it on a chair near the window.

Michael hadn't taken his gaze off de Manning's red-rimmed eyes. "Thank you, my lady. I have questions of your son's tutor, pursuant to the evidence he's just found and information you disclosed to me a few minutes ago. Do take your maids and wait outside the parlor."

He heard her expel a breath. Silk-coated steel infused her voice. "Mr. de Manning, I order you to cooperate with him." She glided from Michael's peripheral vision. Behind him, she clucked the maids out into the foyer.

Michael nudged his chin up a little higher at de Manning, then backed away one step, giving himself room to pivot and strut to the doors. He looked like a rooster, and he didn't care. The day's liberal dose of pretentious nonsense and ulterior motives, the pressure placed on him to find the boy—all of it had compressed his temper. After making sure that the doors were latched, he faced de Manning again and squeezed his lips into a two-second smile.

Spry, rocked forward on the balls of his feet, remained close enough to the tutor to restrain him. De Manning's nostrils flared. "I hear that you think I'm an agent for Wynndon's abductors. You must also think that I'm an idiot."

Michael hefted two chairs from beside the door and wedged them in the center of the room facing each other, away from any furniture, but near de Manning. "Sit."

The tutor remained standing, his expression conveying his sentiments that Michael would soon find himself caught between a mare and a stallion in rut.

Michael locked into another stare with him and advanced to finger the facing of the tutor's coat. "Superb tailoring. And if you don't cooperate, by this time on the morrow, your coat will cover the back of some rebel wretch in the pen. You'll be lying unconscious in the dirt, the piss of six-dozen rebel wretches upon you. Sit."

De Manning perched at the edge of one chair, back straight, hands on his knees, chin level.

Michael mirrored his posture, except that he allowed the back of his chair to support his spine. Their knees were two feet apart. "Where did you find the boy's cloak?"

"On the Market Street wharf."

"Specifically where on the wharf?"

"Near the boat slip."

"I don't think so. Spry and I searched the Market Street wharf, including the area near the boat slip. We found no cloak."

A sneer snagged the tutor's lip toward his nose. "I'm not surprised you didn't find it, considering your inferior investigative abilities. The cloak was rolled up between a couple of trash bins."

"Was it, now?" Michael studied him up and down. "How do you suppose the cloak got to the wharf?"

"Obviously Lord Wynndon's abductors dropped it when they were loading him into the boat last night."

"A reasonable guess." Michael shrugged. "Who took the time to roll the cloak up afterward and place it between two trash bins? His abductors? Dockworkers? Passersby?"

The piercing surety in de Manning's eyes clouded. His sneer faded. "It could have been anyone."

"I doubt it. That's an expensive cloak. Had the boy's abductors noticed it falling off him, they'd have confiscated it, if only to keep it for themselves." Michael rubbed his chin a moment. "And the bloodstain wouldn't prevent a passerby from picking it up and absconding with it. If he were a decent fellow, he might show it to a soldier."

"I don't see where you're going with this."

"There's only one reason I can imagine for the cloak to have been rolled up and placed between two trash bins. It was planted there by someone who wanted us to believe that Lord Wynndon, wounded grievously, had been transported from Wilmington by water." Hands on his knees, Michael leaned closer to de Manning. "Either you've been duped by Lord Wynndon's abductors, or you're working with them. Which is it?"

De Manning's shoulders stiffened. He tilted his head to enable him to look down his nose at Michael.

Michael squeezed out his two-second smile again. "You claim you were an investigator. Do you realize how badly the story that those two men supposedly told you reeks?"

"However do you mean?" The tutor adopted a bored expression.

"When you tested their claims at the site, of course." De Manning's brows twitched. He frowned more but said nothing. Michael realized that if the tutor had been duped, he must have swallowed the whole story. "When Spry and I went to the wharf, we made an effort to duplicate their claims of hiding and observing. That wharf is so cluttered that even in broad daylight, we had difficulty seeing clearly to the boat slip from any nearby point of concealment. Night would decrease visibility further."

De Manning's stare bypassed Michael and focused on the wall near the doors. From his expression, he was a soldier again, captured by the enemy, undergoing interrogation.

Michael exhaled in growing annoyance. "If Lord Wynndon were wearing his cloak at the wharf last night, how could the witnesses tell he was bound?"

The tutor's gazed drifted, and his frown intensified. "I don't know."

"Did an abductor bring the rolled-up cloak along and deposit it between the trash bins? If so, that makes no sense, except if he planted it there." Michael snapped his fingers, recapturing de Manning's attention. "If Lord Wynndon were bound, hand and foot, his abductors must have been carrying him, but why did the witnesses not mention that?"

De Manning shook his head, like a small shiver.

"You see, Mr. de Manning, now that you're thinking about it, you realize that the little pieces don't fit. That's what happens when a story is false. As in a poorly sewn seam, a thread pokes out of a false story. You pick at the thread, and the whole story falls apart."

The tutor scowled, evading Michael's gaze again. Michael tapped his knee once. "Halloo. It's difficult for me to believe that an investigator would overlook such obvious inconsistencies. Lord Wynndon was never at the wharf last night." He narrowed his eyes. "But Spry and I found the ransom note this afternoon."

De Manning snapped his gaze to Michael. "You found a note? Where?"

"At the direction on Front Street that you provided. You know, the place you thought it unnecessary to visit because you believed the testimony of the two men."

For the first time, de Manning dipped his chin and diverted the aggression of his stare. After a few seconds, his gaze sought Michael's face again. "Who's behind the abduction, then? What does the scoundrel want?"

Michael scrutinized de Manning's face and posture, all the openness of a man awaiting, not concealing, information. "The note appears to have been written by Paul Greene."

"Paul Greene? But he was one of the witnesses who approached me this morning. Why would—?" Pressed forward, gaze on Michael, the tutor regarded him in silence, his expression a careful blandness as he processed the information. "Who is this Greene?" His tone thrust at Michael like a sword retrieved from a snow bank.

"The *Reverend* Paul Greene, of the Church of Mary and Martha of Bethany."

De Manning's brows dug a furrow above the bridge of his nose. "Why would a man of God abduct Wynndon?"

From de Manning's response, he'd never heard of the preacher or the Bethanys. "For the same reason that man of God would smuggle weapons and take up arms against the King."

The tutor's lips parted, and his brow smoothed. "Fanatics? Are you saying that fanatics have abducted the boy?" His gaze swept the closed doors behind Michael. "My God. I've read about them. There's no shortage of religious fanatics in America." He clasped hands before him and met Michael's gaze. "What do they want for ransom?"

De Manning looked sincere and innocent of the abduction. Not what Michael had expected. He must be a damned good liar, then. Michael sat back in his chair. "Money."

"Of course. How much money?"

"How much money is Lady Faisleigh carrying with her?"

The tutor's scrutiny darted to the impassive-faced Spry, then drifted back to Michael. He muttered, "Five hundred pounds."

Michael didn't take his gaze off de Manning. His tone low and dry, he said, "What a coincidence. That's the exact sum Greene has demanded."

Comprehension of the implications whipped through the tutor's expression. He regained his focus on Michael and steadied erratic breathing. "I did *not* communicate with Wynndon's abductor about that ransom amount."

"Then what did you communicate to him?"

"Nothing at all."

"How did he know to ask for five hundred, Mr. de Manning? Why not another amount?"

"I cannot imagine."

"Well, then, allow me to paint the portrait. You're in love with Lady Faisleigh. She's devoted to her husband and son, reluctant to return your affections. You decide to create a drama while she's in America with the boy, away from her husband. You contract with bandits to abduct Lord Wynndon. You tell the leader how much money Lady Faisleigh is carrying. After the abduction, they help you plant evidence. You single-handedly figure out where the boy is being held and rescue him. You're a hero. Lady Faisleigh is grateful. And the breadth of the Atlantic Ocean prevents her husband from recognizing the depth of her gratitude to you."

Chin lifted, de Manning glared at the double doors. "What a tale you've spun off circumstantial evidence. You'd be a fool to arrest me today with just that piece."

"Arrest you? You said it, not I. Do you expect me to arrest you?"

Pride radiated from de Manning's posture. Like a prisoner of war, he remained silent. If he did envision himself as Lydia's knight, Michael wouldn't get far on the tack he'd just used.

So there was the issue of the Jacobites. "Are you Scottish, sir?"

"My mother was a MacKenzie." De Manning's dark-eyed gaze flicked to

Michael. Then he unfolded his arms and scrutinized Michael's face. "Ye gods. You're a MacKenzie, too." His voice was part-groan, part-growl, an invocation to heaven that it not be so.

Michael felt his eyebrow hike. "I assure you I am not a MacKenzie, Mr. de Manning. In fact, I've no Scots blood at all."

"But I see it." De Manning let out a deep breath. "You looked familiar when you arrived here yesterday. I raked my memory all night." He laughed once, a harsh sound. "Kept imagining you as a stable drudge at the estate of a peer my lady enjoys visiting during the summers while Lord Faisleigh is in London. But a drudge wouldn't have the money for an officer's commission, would he?" De Manning leaned back in his chair for the first time, palms upon his thighs. His stare bored through Michael to a land thousands of miles away. He nodded. "Yes. You're a MacKenzie."

Michael maintained eye contact and kept his voice low. "You're mistaken. My family has been in Yorkshire for two centuries."

The tutor chuckled. "As has mine." Then, for a moment, his eyes glistened. "As have families of many who had no choice but to place the doings of the first half of this century behind them."

De Manning had been a youth during the Forty-Five. Perhaps he'd been at Culloden Moor, like Donald MacDonald, and watched the King's men bayonet a boulevard of blood through the ranks of Highland kinsmen. In subsequent days, he'd have surrendered to the dismay and disillusionment and grief that bore down upon those who'd lost a cause. Resigned to the rule of Hanover a decade later, he'd donned the King's scarlet and fought the French and Indians in America.

Perhaps de Manning did know duty, as Lydia had claimed. But he did not know joy.

The tutor blinked. A smirk peeled one corner of his lip away from his teeth. He tapped his thighs once. "So. *Cousin.* Are you going to arrest me?"

De Manning was crazy. Michael maintained an even tone. "I'm a Yorkshireman, sir. English. To my knowledge, you're no relation of mine."

The truth of Lord Wynndon's abduction wouldn't be found that afternoon by questioning an obsessed, embittered ex-soldier. Michael was wasting his time with de Manning. He pushed to his feet, signed for Spry to join him with the cloak, and walked to the doors. "We must be about this inquiry. I've no further questions for you at this time." He pulled the door open. "Thank you for following Lady Faisleigh's orders and cooperating."

Chapter Seventeen

THEY STORED LORD Wynndon's cloak in Michael's room at Mrs. Chiswell's house. Michael posted an updated warrant in six locations about town for Paul Greene's arrest. To the preacher's crimes of sedition, armed assault, unlawful assembly, and weapons trafficking, it added the charges of abduction, highway robbery, unlawful imprisonment, and extortion.

Then Michael exercised Major Craig's exhortation that he use the resources of the Eighty-Second by assigning men, hand-picked by Spry, to perform surveillance in shifts at Rouse's Tavern and the tannery on Front Street, starting that night at eight. Another patrol of privates would accompany Michael and Spry at two o'clock Sunday morning, when they headed out the New Berne Road. Along with the men observing the Rouse house, they'd watch for whoever came along predawn to collect five hundred pounds from beneath the mulberry tree. Except that instead of money, Paul Greene would find a note requesting a meeting on Sunday afternoon to assure Lydia and Michael of the boy's well-being.

At the wainwright's shop at the east end of Front Street, Michael and his assistant found stocky Mr. Smedes and his apprentices preparing to install a transom on a wagon frame. Off to the side were wheels in need of repair. Smedes told his lads to pause their work and ambled over to the soldiers, his smile cordial. "Afternoon, Mr. Stoddard." He blotted his brow with a handkerchief, none too clean. "How may I be of service?"

Michael jutted his chin at the wheels. "You've quite a backlog."

"Indeed." Smedes cranked his neck so he could roll his eyes heavenward. "I've a fellow who comes in from New Berne every six weeks or so to help me with wheels. I'm expecting him on Monday. Lost my wheelwrights about five years ago."

"Would that have been Mr. Whistler and his son?"

"Yes. Tragic, that fire."

"Indeed. What happened to the family?"

Smedes scratched the side of his face. "I think Sandy Rouse employs the widow for scullery and chambermaid duties. I hope you fellows in the Eighty-Second don't need wheel work for at least a week."

Michael shook his head. "Actually I'm curious about the interest that Mr. Whistler and Mr. White had in whiskey."

The congeniality froze on Smedes's face. "Whiskey, uh, I-I don't know anything about—"

"Let me be clear, Mr. Smedes." Michael maintained eye contact and lowered his voice to make sure the apprentices didn't eavesdrop. "I don't give a fig about arresting people who once helped Whistler and White evade paying taxes on their business. Nor am I interested in arresting people who are still in the business and evading taxes. And I've no plans to confiscate production equipment that's in use. I've far larger matters to concern me."

Smedes squinted and scraped his tongue across his upper lip. "What do you want with me?"

"You worked for Whistler and White—"

"Well, no, I—"

"You repaired wagons that hauled their whiskey. And you've hauled their whiskey."

Smedes tucked his head and crossed his arms.

"I've been in town long enough for you to know what kind of man I am. I give you my word that disrupting production and confiscating equipment are low on my list of tasks."

Smedes held his gaze a few heartbeats. "If that's so, what's your interest in this?"

"I'm trying to find an item that's been temporarily hidden with equipment and whiskey—something that has nothing to do with business operations. So I'm looking for places where equipment and whiskey are concealed. How can you help me?"

The wainwright's steady gaze measured him a few seconds longer. Then he twisted partway around to his apprentices. "Lads, I'll be just a few moments up in the front. Go over the perch again. Make sure it isn't cracked."

Michael and Spry followed Smedes to the front of the shop, cluttered with parts: linchpins and kingpins, swaybars, chains, a couple of gritty hubs, a splintered spoke, and canvas. Smedes shoved aside strips of leather on the dusty counter, brought forth a map from a shelf below, and unrolled it. After a glance over his shoulder, he darted his gaze between them. His voice dropped to a whisper. "Mind you, there's only one place I've ever loaded whiskey." He leaned an elbow on the map where it curled and tapped his forefinger to a spot about three miles west of the New Berne Road, equidistant from the Rouse and Collier houses. "It's an old barn."

On the map, Michael studied roads, homesteads, and creeks in the region where Smedes's forefinger had marked. "How do you access the barn with your wagon? I see no road."

"Northbound, just before you reach the Rouse house, here, there's a cart track bearing to the left." The wainwright's forefinger grazed another area on the map. "Not on most maps. Your eyes must be sharp to find it." Smedes straightened.

Michael watched the edge of the map curl, no longer restrained by Smedes's elbow. "When and at what time was your most recent pickup?"

"Last Sunday, the twenty-fifth. About one in the morning."

"Who assists you?"

"No one."

Risky. Smedes could have highwaymen lying in wait of him—unless the highwaymen were in on the whiskey business and knew the wainwright was their courier. "What did you see in the barn besides whiskey?"

"Three disassembled stills, ready to be relocated."

"Who met you there?"

"No one. No one's ever met me there. It's just me and the whiskey."

"Who pays you, then?"

Smedes scratched his collarbone beneath his shirt. "Cash is waiting for me in a sack Tuesday mornings on the doorstep here."

"Who owns the property where the barn is located?"

"Rouse, I believe."

"When, where, and to whom did you deliver that whiskey?"

Smedes moistened his lips with his tongue again, flicked his gaze between the men. "By two thirty Sunday morning. White's Tavern. Mrs. Duncan and Mr. Marsh."

In Michael's peripheral vision, Spry stiffened. Michael wondered why he felt no dejection at Smedes's confirmation of his suspicions. His expression remained impartial because of it, as if he'd no personal relationship with Kate Duncan and Kevin Marsh. But, of course, he did have a personal relationship with them. With Kate, in particular. And he wasn't sure how much farther the professional mask of investigator would stretch. "When does whiskey next become available to you in the barn?"

Tension hovered in Smedes's shoulders. He swallowed. "Mr. Stoddard, you said you weren't planning to apprehend people involved in this business."

"Correct. My interest is in *avoiding* them while I search for the item of importance. I'd be helped in that endeavor if I knew their schedule."

Smedes expelled a sigh. "Right." He looked to the counter long enough to roll the map and stash it below. "I'm due out there on the morrow, one in the morning, just like last Sunday."

"Same delivery arrangements as last Sunday?"

The wainwright nodded once.

Kate and her brother were turning a regular profit from sales of whiskey. And it was going to be a long night for Michael and his assistant. "Thank you, Mr. Smedes." He stepped out for the front door, then whipped back around. "I almost forgot. You had a partner named Travis?"

Smedes gaped, then shut his mouth and relaxed his shoulders. "Yes. Harley and I parted company in January, just before you lads marched into town."

"I heard he was trained in the production of coaches."

"That's correct. The quality of his work is excellent."

"Why the split, then? Not enough business?"

"Oh, we had the business. Probably not as much as he'd have liked, but—"

Smedes stared hard at Michael, then looked away, rolling his lips inward, as if to seal in words.

"Mr. Travis was a rebel," Michael said quietly. "He fled with the Committee of Safety."

"Yes." Smedes's gaze wandered anywhere in the shop except Michael and Spry. "And some of his ideas repulsed me." His tone tightened. "I think they'd repulse even rebels like Governor Nash and Mr. Harnett."

Harnett. Michael wondered whether Major Craig had located Cornelius Harnett yet. A chill crawled inside his neck stock. Craig expected him to have dealt with Jones and Love. How much time did they have before Craig or Cornwallis showed up in Wilmington?

"Harley's a fanatic," muttered Smedes. "Like that footwashing preacher."

Comparing anyone's fervency to that of Paul Greene wasn't a compliment. "When was the last time you communicated with Mr. Travis?"

"End of January." Chin up, Smedes met Michael's gaze. "Just before he fled town."

"Were you friends with him?"

"No."

"Who were his friends?"

"I don't see that it matters anymore. They're all gone from town, too. All except—" Smedes nodded his head in a vague, westward direction. "Except Gibson. And I'm not sure how much of a friend he was."

Michael gaped again, and he and Spry glanced at each other. He faced the wainwright full on. "Ralph Gibson, the farrier?"

"That's the man."

Michael inclined his head to the wainwright. "You've my gratitude, Mr. Smedes."

After leaving the shop, Michael and Spry hurried west on Front Street. The door to the farrier shop was unlocked, but no one answered their greeting. They passed through to the stables, and Michael turned a circle in the straw, his gaze encompassing the stable. "Mr. Gibson? Are you here, Mr. Gibson?"

One of two horses snorted from a stall. The door to the stall, not latched well, creaked open, permitting the men to see the horse nudge a bundle of cloth in the straw with his nose. The cloth moaned and shifted.

The soldiers rushed forward. Spry grabbed a halter from a peg beside the door, slipped inside, and slid the halter on the gelding. "Good boy. Yes. There's the good fellow. Come with me, eh?"

Michael waited until his assistant had led the gelding out of the stall before advancing on a semi-conscious Hiram Duke. He knelt beside the farrier. Duke attempted to roll onto his back, then pressed his head with one hand and groaned. Michael slid Duke's hand aside, probed the knot he felt through his hair, and grimaced.

A farrier as experienced as Duke shouldn't have placed himself in a position to be kicked by a horse—and in the head, for God's sake. "Easy. You've quite a bump there."

Duke mumbled, "Ralph. No. Where are you going with the till?"

Michael sucked in a breath and straightened his back. In the next stall, securing the gelding, Spry heard Duke and growled. "Gibson, that cur!"

"Mr. Gibson, here's them nails you was asking for—" One of the apprentices ambled into the stable, a small sack in his hand, and stopped short, jaw dangling. "Mr. Duke!"

Michael bolted to his feet. Shoulders flung back, he exited the stall. "Your master's taken a clout to head. He'll need your assistance." He eyed the sack in the young man's hand. "Mr. Gibson sent you for nails?"

"Y-y-yes, sir. From the blacksmith, sir."

"How long ago?"

The lad's Adam's apple bobbed in a gulp. "Fifteen, maybe twenty minutes ago."

"Where do you keep the till?"

The apprentice threw the sack of nails onto a shelf and spun about to advance to the farthest stall. As soon as he opened the door, he gasped and recoiled. "It's gone!" Eyes wide, he whirled on Michael, who had followed him there. "I didn't take the money, sir! Please, don't arrest me!" His voice cracked.

Michael shouldered his way past him. An open, foot-high door was imbedded in the lower rear wall of the stall. The recessed space it had concealed was empty. An open padlock lay in the straw nearby.

The apprentice pawed at Michael's upper arm. "I didn't take it, sir! Please, believe me!"

Gibson had sent the apprentice on a mindless errand to get him out of the way. Michael shrugged off the young man's clutch. "Burglary and assault have been done here. I'm certain you'd naught to do with either. We must be after the scoundrel who did this, and quickly. Don't touch anything in that stall. Tend your master, and tell the men of the regiment who respond to my summons everything you know." He pivoted from the apprentice. "Spry, to me!"

"Yes, sir!"

***

With a patrol of five armed and mounted infantrymen, Michael and Spry raced the setting sun northeast on the New Berne Road. To Michael, an old barn used to hide whiskey and production equipment sounded like an excellent place to hide a kidnapped heir. What he didn't yet know was whether Gibson's desperate need for money extended to a lunge for a five-hundred-pound ransom.

He slowed the horses' gallop to a trot when they neared Rouse's Tavern. Even so, eyes keen on the brush to the west, he almost missed the overgrown cart track that Smedes took for his whiskey runs. He diverted the patrol onto the track at a trot. The path ahead appeared churned to frenzy, as if by the passage of sixty-foot-long sand serpents. Marsh grass to either side of the path twitched in the horses' wake. The air was still, warm, and muggy, sour with a spring gone foul. Songbirds silenced at their passage. Crows jeered at them from the tops of pines.

A quarter hour in, from somewhere not far ahead, Michael and his men heard a shrill scream of denial from a woman or child, truncated by the echoing report of a firearm. The redcoats kicked their horses into a gallop. A minute later, they came upon a dilapidated, worm-eaten structure of two stories that fit the description of the barn where Smedes loaded his wagon with whiskey in the wee hours of Sunday mornings. No one besides the men of the Eighty-Second was in sight. A saddled horse was picketed out front.

Michael ordered the men to fan out, encircle the barn, use the pines for partial cover, and keep their eyes open for anyone fleeing the scene. With all his men in place, muskets aimed at the barn, his hanger loosened in its scabbard, he bellowed, "Gibson, it's Lieutenant Stoddard! You stole money. My men have you surrounded. You cannot escape. Come out peacefully, and hold your hands high, where we can see them!"

Not a sound issued from inside the barn. Nor did Michael see any movement. In the lull, a few songbirds attempted nocturnes, and his watch marked an unbearably loud minute. "Halloo, Gibson! Don't make us come in for you! Do you hear me, Gibson?"

The farrier didn't respond. The sun reached for the horizon. Michael listened to unnatural silence resonate from the barn. Evening's chill whispered through the pines and crawled beneath his neck stock. Despite the haste of his patrol, he sensed that Ralph Gibson had indeed eluded them.

Michael hissed a command for Spry and a soldier named Wigglesworth to enter the barn. He and two other soldiers covered their approach. Spry swung open the barn door and darted inside with the other private, their muskets ready. The ticking of Michael's watch shouted well beyond a minute. He fidgeted. The last thing he wanted was to be caught out there with his patrol at night, made vulnerable by darkness to rebels who prowled the area.

Spry reappeared in the doorway, expression grim. "Gibson's down, sir. We see no one else in the barn."

After ordering the four privates outside to remain on guard, Michael entered the barn. Just inside the doorway, while his eyes adjusted to the dimness, his nose picked out the familiar metallic stench. His gut knotted.

Private Wigglesworth opened the opposite barn door and stood beside it, allowing more daylight in. In the middle of the barn lay Gibson, splayed upon moldy, mucky straw, and shot in the head. His body twitched in its final denial.

The soldiers had heard a scream before the shot was fired. Michael's gaze swept the barn interior, then he strode past Gibson. At the other barn door, he breathed of late-afternoon air not tainted by violent death. The color of the arid landscape was fading with daylight. He saw no sign of anyone out there except for his soldiers on guard.

He spun about and returned to Gibson. A civilian pistol lay in the straw a couple feet away from the farrier, its barrel still warm. Michael handed it to his assistant, who stood nearby. Then, wishing he were elsewhere, he knelt beside Gibson's torso and assessed what remained of the man's head.

The pistol ball that had entered Gibson's left temple had made a much larger exit from the right side of his skull. His fingers on Gibson's bristly chin, Michael rotated the dead man's head for a better look at the entrance wound. Then he scooted back and examined the farrier's still-warm hands.

He waved Wigglesworth over to join them. "Someone thought to make this appear as suicide, but there's no powder on Gibson's hands. He was murdered. I presume his murderer has fled the scene and knows the terrain far better than we do."

He unwrapped the bandage on the farrier's left hand. The linen had concealed two inflamed puncture wounds on the top of Gibson's hand. Michael rotated the hand to Spry.

Spry cocked an eyebrow. "Embroidery scissors might easily have made those punctures, sir."

Dorinda, the warrior woman. "I was thinking the same." Michael positioned Gibson's left arm beside his body and searched him. In the farrier's waistcoat pocket, he found a key. With the key on the flat of his palm and a hunch what lock it fit, he rose. "Care to guess where this goes, Spry?"

"The till would seem the obvious choice, sir." Spry's gaze fixed on the key. His brow lowered.

"Obvious. Logical. Anything else?"

His assistant's gaze met his. "The padlock on the door to the tanner's shop."

Spry's astuteness plucked a brief smile from one corner of Michael's mouth. "Excellent. You shall have the honor of testing it when we return." He pocketed the key and craned his neck back for a glance at the decrepit loft. "However, we must use the next quarter hour to search the barn, inside and out, before daylight is lost to us. Gibson came here with money. Either his murderer took it, or it's been hidden here. And we heard someone cry out just before Gibson was shot. Someone other than Gibson's murderer may have been here with him. See what you can find."

"Yes, sir," said Spry. He tagged the other private on the shoulder and pointed to the loft. "No ladder. I shall give you a boost up."

"Do be a good fellow and break my fall if I crash through a rotten board, won't you, Spry?"

"Clean my boots, Wigglesworth."

Michael left the two privates to their work and banter and walked a slow, back-and-forth pattern across the dirt floor of the barn, his gaze probing the decomposing straw beneath him. To whom had Gibson brought the money, and why? Why had the recipient killed him?

At the wall, equidistant from the barn doors, he found a four-inch crust of brown bread. He sniffed at it. Rye, possibly oats, and molasses. The crust retained some elasticity, so the loaf had been baked in the past few days. It also retained a bite mark that looked smaller than the arc left by an adult's teeth.

He thrust the bread chunk in his haversack and squatted, squinting in the gathering gloom at the ground, picking at straw with care, revealing small, still pliable chunks of orange cheese. Amidst the orange, he spotted a glint of silver. Michael retrieved a shiny button from where it had been placed in the dirt, breadcrumbs, and cheese.

He weighed it in his palm. It was of the size to fasten the waistcoat of a man or boy. But no commoner's waistcoat had been graced with the button, for it was silver, not pewter or tin. He turned it over in his fingers, confirming that no fiber clung to the shaft. The button, like the white rose brooch, had been deliberately removed and left behind by its wearer. And no sign of violence marred the straw.

Even as frustration bit at Michael for having missed Lord Wynndon by less than five minutes, the warmth of admiration caught and buoyed him. He visualized the boy, hands freed from bonds long enough for him to eat bread and cheese, long enough for him to work loose the button from his waistcoat while his captor's attention was otherwise occupied. How many other boys not quite ten years old had the courage and presence of mind to leave clues behind? Very few.

The spot so radiated with his presence that Michael could almost hear his voice. He closed his fist over the silver button and stood. "Clever lad," he whispered. "Brave lad. I'm coming for you, and I shall find you. I swear it."

Chapter Eighteen

"DON'T LOCK UP yet, Mr. Smedes." The wainwright, in the act of applying key to padlock on the front door of his shop, jumped at the sound of Michael's voice from the street behind him. He twisted about, key clutched in his hand, his gape rabbit-hopping over the four redcoats on horseback in front of his shop. Michael dismounted. "I would have another word with you inside."

The key clanged to the floorboards of the porch. Smedes knelt and fumbled for it. Michael, his jaw tense, pivoted from the wainwright and handed his fusil to Spry, who'd also dismounted, and the reins of the horse he'd ridden to Private Wigglesworth, whose search of the barn's loft had turned up nothing but varmint turds and spiders. "Make certain the other three men returned safely with the body," he said, low, "and that the horse we found wasn't borrowed from the farriers' shop."

"Sir." Wigglesworth saluted from the saddle. The other private accepted the reins to Spry's mount. Then the two soldiers and four horses headed for Market Street.

Smedes opened the door and preceded them inside. Michael and Spry followed him and closed the door, jingling the little bells at the top. Spry propped Michael's fusil beside the door. An outpost of light bloomed in the dusk of the shop: the wainwright lighting a candle. He coughed once into his fist, then lowered both hands to his sides, chin level, gaze bypassing the soldiers, like a prisoner awaiting the gallows.

Michael squared off with him and pitched his voice soft. "About an hour ago, in that barn where you load whiskey, my men and I found Ralph Gibson murdered."

Smedes retreated one step and emitted a noise like a strangled cough. "M-m-my God!" He gawped at Michael.

"What do you know of it?"

"Not a thing." Smedes shuddered. "I'd naught to do with such devilry."

"Really? You told me where to find that barn. You also implied that your former partner Mr. Travis and Mr. Gibson had a level of acquaintance greater than casual.

"About two weeks ago, Mr. Gibson made a bet with his business partner, Mr. Duke, for a large sum, in expectation of winning. He lost. Before he left town this afternoon, Mr. Gibson assaulted Mr. Duke and left him unconscious so he could raid their business till."

Michael studied the effect of his news on Smedes. The wainwright's jaw hinged open and closed without speech. Ropy veins in his neck protruded. "So clearly Mr. Gibson was in dire need of money. Unfortunately what he took out to that barn this afternoon didn't satisfy whomever he met there."

Smedes wagged his head. "Believe me, Mr. Stoddard, I'm as horrified by this turn of events as you are. But it's no good questioning me further. I don't know what it's about."

"I think you *suspect*."

"No, I—"

"Blast!" Michael balled his fists to stop himself from lunging for the wainwright. "I already told you I don't give a damn about arresting people who skip paying taxes on a whiskey business. But when a whiskey business crosses over the line to assault, burglary, and murder, I *do* give a damn." He snarled at Smedes. "Now what in hell is this about?"

The wainwright backed against the counter. His gulp was audible. The whites of his eyes glowed. "I told Harley he was crazy in January. Insisted that I'd have naught to do with it."

"Harley Travis, your former partner? Why do you think he's crazy? And what is 'it'?"

"He's a devil. He's been trying to form a congregation the way Paul Greene has done. He envies Greene's success, you see. But his group isn't based on footwashing. He intends to train and deploy an elite army for the rebels' governor, Abner Nash." Smedes dropped his face in his hands and moaned. "I thought his plans would collapse by now. God almighty, forgive my silence all these weeks!"

"He's building an elite army?" Michael advanced and batted the wainwright's hands away. "What sort of army, Mr. Smedes?"

"Boys. An army of boys."

Spry slammed the wall with his fist.

"They join as young as the age of eight. Whistler's thirteen-year-old grandson, Zeke, is one of their lieutenants."

God *damn* it all to hell! Heart hammering in a flare of disbelief and horror, Michael spun away from Smedes to an ashen-faced Spry and yanked his assistant in close so he could whisper, "Go. Tear down and destroy all six of those updated warrants on Greene that we posted earlier." He released Spry.

"Sir!" Spry saluted, then sprinted for the door. It slammed shut behind him with such force that one of the bells fell off and clanged to the floor.

His countenance averted from Smedes, Michael squeezed his eyes shut briefly and indulged in about five seconds of self-flogging over the blunder of his own making, an error that could explode and destroy his career—and result in the murder of Lord Wynndon. Then he steadied his breathing, squared his shoulders, and whipped around to the wainwright, who was staring at the floor, wallowing in his own revulsion. Michael spat, "Where can I find Mr. Travis?"

"I don't know. I don't even suspect, Mr. Stoddard! He vanished into the wilderness to the north."

"Most men don't vanish completely. I wager that someone in town knows where to find him. Let's start with the role he has in the whiskey business. And he obviously has a role, so what is it?"

Smedes licked his lips. "With Whistler and White dead, Harley has taken over production."

"I see. You're transportation. Mrs. Duncan and Mr. Marsh are retail and distribution."

"Something like that. So perhaps Mrs. Duncan or Mr. Marsh knows where to find Harley."

Despondency surged through Michael: the same despondency that he'd buried earlier beneath a layer of iron detachment upon hearing confirmation of Kate and Kevin's involvement. He pounded it back again. "Describe Mr. Travis."

Smedes's attention wandered over him. "An inch or two taller than you are. Lean build, like you, but light brown hair. In his early thirties."

Alas, Travis was not the old man that de Manning had shot during the raid on Lydia's entourage the previous day. Travis may not even have been present in that raid. But the raid was surely where Gibson had earned his black eye and injured hand. Michael considered de Manning's description of Travis while they'd been in Mrs. Chiswell's study—for surely the tutor had been describing Travis. "You forgot the crooked nose," he said, without inflection.

Smedes squinted at him. "Oh. Yah. How did you know that, eh? He told me he broke it in England, during an accident, while he was working on a coach."

England. Michael studied Smedes. Candlelight flickered, giving the wainwright an insubstantial quality. "Mr. Travis learned his trade in England?" Smedes nodded. Hair stood up on Michael's neck. "Where in England?"

"I believe he said Yorkshire. I didn't ask further. The quality of his work speaks for itself."

Michael stared long and hard at Smedes. Was it significant that Harley Travis, engineer of an army of rebel boys, had been trained as a coach maker in Yorkshire? He grasped for the intuition that ghosted about his tired brain, but it kept eluding his reason, so he backed off it with a sigh. After all, he'd quipped to Spry earlier that Yorkshire was a big county.

But he didn't let it go completely. As he'd learned, the world could be capriciously small on the most damning of occasions.

His next thought stripped the moisture from his throat.

Travis was building an army of boys. At almost ten years old, Lydia's son was the ideal age for a recruit. Furthermore, he was intelligent, highly educated, and healthy. After Travis got his paws on Lydia's five hundred pounds, he wouldn't part with so splendid a recruit. No. Forcible indoctrination of the future Seventeenth Earl of Faisleigh into that army of young warriors would commence with earnestness.

Michael realized that he had Smedes nearly pinned against the counter, so he moved off and paced across the small outer shop, swinging both arms a few times. Travis had weaknesses. Michael would unearth them and capture that whoreson. "Mr. Smedes, aside from creating this army of boys, did Mr. Travis speak of other ambitions?"

"Ye gods, yes." Smedes rolled his eyes. "He's been a sick calf for a miss in England, daughter of his master. Years ago, just before Harley came to America, her father sent her to the household of a nobleman. To hear Harley talk, he'd been cut off from the love of his life. But from what he hinted to me, he'd followed her everywhere, left her flowers, written her poetry, made a pest of himself." Smedes grimaced. "After he moved here, he got his two brothers and a friend to send him regular reports on the girl. Obsessed, as I said. I wager he made clear his intention to impress and marry the girl, and Papa would have none of it."

Christ. The lunatic had dreams of building a dynasty. "Mr. Smedes, surely this army of boys isn't part of his plan to impress the young lady?" And if the Englishwoman were impressed by Travis's army, she was just as crazy as he.

The wainwright threw up his hands. "I don't know. I'd no reason to pry. Harley's work in this shop was outstanding. And frankly I didn't want to hear about his mad dreams, his plans for an army."

Travis must train and provision that "army." That meant meeting certain general needs. Food. Shelter. Possibly clothing. Michael thought back to what he and Spry had found in the tanner's shop on Front Street. "Speculate, Mr. Smedes. How might Mr. Travis obtain a uniform coat of the Eighty-Second?"

The wainwright emitted a weak laugh. "Oh. You'll never believe what he bragged to me just before he fled. He claimed he'd distract one of the regiment's laundresses and lift a red coat she was airing out, just so he could thumb his nose at the Eighty-Second after a few months."

Michael jammed his lips together to seal in a string of oaths. So that was how Travis had done it.

The wainwright read his expression. "God bless us, Mr. Stoddard. Has he been stealing the regiment's coats for those boys?"

Michael visualized an army of frenzied, screeching boy warriors in red coats too large for them descending on Wilmington, simultaneous with the arrivals of Lord Cornwallis and Major Craig. It didn't matter whether Travis had twenty boys in his army or a hundred. Such an event must never come to pass.

"I wouldn't count the effort as beneath him. Incidentally, I share your opinion of Mr. Travis's sanity." After walking to the counter, Michael leaned against it and regarded his fusil, propped upright beside the door. "Do you feel threatened by him, Mr. Smedes?" When the wainwright didn't respond, Michael glanced over to find him also leaning back against the counter, arms crossed, a wary watch upon the door. Michael lowered his voice. "Mr. Travis was here in town this morning. Did he visit you?"

The wainwright's nostrils widened. "No. I haven't seen him since he fled town in January."

"He returned this morning, disguised, to plant false evidence, throw off my tracking. He sees some of his plans coming to fruition. Seems reasonable that he might have found it worthwhile to stop by and brag." Michael allowed a few seconds to elapse, aware that Smedes had permitted himself to be suspended in the silence. "You do realize that you know enough to be dangerous to him."

"Yes." Smedes's voice was almost inaudible. "And I'm not the only one in that position."

Gooseflesh pricked Michael's arms. Kate and Kevin. He composed his tone to be level. "Precisely. I advise you to not ride out to pick up whiskey early on the morrow."

"Excellent advice, Mr. Stoddard." Smedes let out a sigh, as if divested of a huge load.

"However, I want you to arrive for delivery at White's Tavern as usual." Michael rotated his head to regard the wainwright.

"Without any merchandise?" Smedes frowned at him. "What would be the point of that?"

"Aside from my desire to avoid more murders, you mean? It's time to throttle the funding for Mr. Travis's army. The first step is to deprive him of his business partners." Michael kept his expression neutral. "Hence Spry and I shall stand in for the whiskey." With the delivery of Major Craig's criminal investigator and his assistant instead of a shipment of whiskey, the field would be obvious. Kate and her brother would know that they couldn't bluff.

Smedes's eyebrows shot up. His mouth contracted into a little "o."

"We shall meet you out front of your shop at two in the morning, sharp. Bring your wagon and a canvas to cover the whiskey." A peculiar, novel agony shivered through his soul. After this trick, he needn't concern himself with what constituted an incentive for Kate. She'd likely never trust him again. But he saw no way around it. "Say nothing of this to anyone."

"Very well, sir."

Someone rapped on the door. Michael and the wainwright tensed, eyed each other, then the door. Curtains had been drawn over the windows on either side, preventing the men from seeing out. "Expecting a visitor?" Michael evaluated Smedes, who pressed his lips together and shook his head. Michael snapped up his fusil and positioned himself so he could react quickly, if necessary. "Open the door, Mr. Smedes. I have you covered."

Smedes did as he asked. Outlined by the frame was one of the dragoons who'd ridden with Major Craig nearly two weeks earlier. Michael started, then braced the butt of his fusil on the toe of his boot.

In the next second, cold washed over him. Had Craig returned to Wilmington? Michael tried to swallow. On the third attempt, he succeeded.

"Ah, good, you're here, Mr. Stoddard." The dragoon saluted and stood at attention. "Spry told me where I could find you, sir."

Michael finally got his larynx unfrozen and motioned him over the threshold. "Rowe, isn't it?"

"Yes, sir." Rowe entered, and Smedes closed the three of them into the shop.

"May I presume Major Craig has returned to town?" said Michael.

"No, sir. He's still a few days out. I'm sent as courier to you."

Relief cascaded through Michael. He repressed an exhalation and set his fusil aside.

The dragoon groped in his waistcoat, withdrew a small, sealed note, and presented it to Michael. "Major Craig directed me to wait on your response, sir."

At the candle, Michael broke the seal and read Craig's message:

Picked up H's scent. Where are J and L?

From the terseness of the message, Michael knew that Cornelius Harnett's capture wouldn't be enough to put a jolly smile on Craig's lips. Rather, the commander of the Eighty-Second allocated space at the bottom of his note for Michael to indulge him with the mechanics of how he and Spry had obliterated crazy rebel men who'd terrorized Wilmington with their carbines and quick horses. Michael's only saving grace was that Craig didn't appear to have heard about crazy rebel boys who'd captured the son of a peer. If Michael had his way, Craig wouldn't hear about *that* until after the happy ending.

Much as he hated to declare himself on the Jones and Love investigation without standing on firmer ground, he knew that Rowe wouldn't leave without a response to Craig. Michael regarded the wainwright. "Kindly permit me the use of a quill, ink, and wax."

"Of course."

When Smedes brought the implements, Michael straightened the note, dipped the quill in ink, and wrote his own terse message: *Vermin sighted 8 mi NE of town. Surveillance established.* After waving the note to dry the ink, he folded and sealed it.

He handed it to the dragoon. "A safe journey to you. And give my regards to Major Craig."

Chapter Nineteen

SPRY CAUGHT UP with Michael as soon as Michael turned onto Market Street. A crescent moon rode high above them, and sunset painted the western sky salmon and turquoise. "Sir." The private sounded out of breath. "Did Rowe find you with a message from Major Craig?" He matched Michael's stride on a street busy with townsfolk and slaves returning from market or errands, or closing down businesses for the day.

"Yes. Thank you for directing him to Smedes's shop." He handed Spry his fusil, then lowered his voice. "Major Craig is now actively tracking Harnett and may be *en route* back to Wilmington within a day or so. That means we may have no more than four or five days to resolve the issues of Travis, and Jones and Love. Did you find all six of—"

"Yes, sir. All six warrants have been burned." Spry blew out a breath, the sheen of sweat on his forehead. "That was uncomfortably close. How did Travis hoodwink us so?"

Even with all six updated warrants against Paul Greene destroyed, Michael couldn't be certain that some of Greene's sympathizers hadn't reported the content to the preacher. "From Mr. Smedes's description, Travis has a broken nose, like Greene, and is close enough in age, build, and complexion. With a wig, heels to add a few inches height, and a fine suit, those who'd never met Greene might provide a description suggestive of the preacher."

"Sneaky rogue. He was setting up Greene, sir."

"And possibly duping Mr. de Manning." Michael grudged out that point, realizing how fond he'd grown in the past day of his desire to throw the tutor in the pen.

"Yes, sir. And using the Eighty-Second to eliminate his competition."

A popular theme lately. "Or using us to eliminate one who'd rebuffed him. I imagine that there are some people that even Greene rejects from his congregation."

Spry groaned. "Perish the thought. When will you post a warrant for Travis's arrest? He's quite busy on the wrong side of the law." He ticked items off on his fingers. "Sedition, armed assault, abduction, highway robbery, unlawful imprisonment, extortion."

"I won't post a warrant just yet. Travis went through a good bit of effort to frame his rival, Greene. Let's let him think that he may have succeeded, that we followed Gibson to that barn because Gibson spilled some information. Maybe Travis will let his guard down."

A gig rolled past, headed away from the river. Michael recognized the occupant and took off at a run after it. "Mrs. Hooper! I say, Mrs. Hooper, do wait!"

The gig pulled to the corner of Market and Second and halted. Michael caught up, followed by Spry. In the seat, Anne Hooper, wife of one of North Carolina's signers of the Declaration of Independence, kept hold of the reins, her shoulders angled forward, her face in three-quarters profile to him, and her straw hat hiding much of her features. Michael understood her opinion of him from her uplifted chin and tense lips. "Madam." He bowed. "Good evening."

"Lieutenant Stoddard." The fingers of her dainty hands, thinner than he remembered from two months before, played with the reins, then calmed.

He cast the day's outrageous dose of agitations aside to soften his tone and place a hand on the side of the gig not far from her elbow. "You're familiar with the Widow Whistler?" Mrs. Hooper nodded. "She may have need to contact me with an urgent message. She only felt comfortable with the idea if she could reach me through you."

Mrs. Hooper exhaled once, the sound a measure of her exasperation, and revealed more of her face to him. "And why should she do that, Mr. Stoddard? You're a King's man, and she's—"

"She's a rebel." He relaxed his brow. "You have young children. If the life of your child were threatened, might you eschew political boundaries in effort to save him?"

The muscles in Mrs. Hooper's small, plain face relaxed. Lips parted, she twisted her torso, permitting him to see most of her face, and the acknowledgement that glistened in her eyes.

She'd developed purplish circles beneath her eyes since the last time they'd spoken. That anxiety would deepen, he presumed, when she heard of the capture of Harnett, a friend of her husband's. Major Craig had allowed Mrs. Hooper to remain in Wilmington with her children and a few servants because they caused no trouble—but also because he'd seen no sign that they were communicating with rebel leaders, including William Hooper. But a woman might also eschew political boundaries to save her husband.

Michael removed his hand and stepped away from the gig. "Should the Widow Whistler come to you, please send word to me at Mrs. Chiswell's house."

Again she nodded. He thanked her. Blinking at the dampness in her eyes, she faced ahead, twitched the reins, and sent the horse into a trot.

Michael rolled back his shoulders and watched the gig drive away. From what he'd seen that morning, the burdens of Eve Whistler's life had almost crushed her. He'd no great faith that she would come through for Lord Wynndon. But Lieutenant Stoddard still held the dubious honor of being Anne Hooper's least-abhorred redcoat. Huzzah.

***

At the barracks, he reviewed a schedule of surveillance shifts with the men Spry had selected and saw the first team for the pine copse near Rouse's Tavern off around seven fifteen. With the thud of their horses' hooves fading in the street, he and his assistant walked back down to Front Street, accompanied by the first team picked for the tannery. There, Michael handed Spry the key from his pocket. Neither he nor his assistant was surprised when the key fit the padlock on the front door of the tannery. It confirmed how the shop had been accessed to set up the straw dummies.

Whether that meant the merchant who owned the shop, conveniently absent in Pennsylvania, should be added to Major Craig's register of suspicious persons, along with his business partner, remained to be seen. But that could wait a day or two. Spry relocked the shop, and he and Michael headed to the two-room, one-story wooden house on Fourth Street belonging to the late bachelor Ralph Gibson while the two privates they left behind on Front Street got comfortable and inconspicuous for tedious hours of surveillance upon the tannery.

Gibson had barred the back door of his house from the inside and padlocked the front door, but Michael found a window with a faulty latch. In no time, the two soldiers had crawled inside, lit four candles, and applied themselves to a search beneath the mattress, rugs, and chair cushions, inside pots, even within the pages of a Bible. The final crumbs of Enid's midday meal were long gone and Michael's gut was growling in protest when he discovered a loose stone above the mantle. He worked it free, and revealed a cavity. Light from Spry's candle shone on a small, flat package wrapped in oiled paper.

Michael extracted the package from the cavity and, on Gibson's table, spread open a well-thumbed map covering the area eight to twelve miles northeast off the New Berne Road, a total of about forty square miles. The map was studded with at least two-dozen tiny black circles of ink. He and Spry bent closer. The taverns of Rouse and Collier, identified as landmarks, weren't noted with black circles. However one circle matched the location of the barn where Smedes picked up whiskey and Gibson had been murdered.

The men straightened. Spry grinned at Michael. "Just like winning at one-and-thirty, sir."

Michael threw back his head and laughed. "There may very well be one-and-thirty locations marked here."

"Needle in a haystack." Spry's eyes narrowed. "Do you think all the locations are in use, sir?"

"No." Michael folded the map to fit in his haversack, as it was too big for a waistcoat pocket. "I suspect that in the five years since Whistler and White died, whiskey production has operated at reduced capacity." Over at the fireplace, he slid the oiled paper in the cavity, then wedged the stone in place. "Mr. Smedes told me that Travis has been in charge of production for five years. He's had to stretch himself between making whiskey, miles to the northeast, and repairing wagons in Wilmington."

Still facing the fireplace, Michael frowned at the loose stone. His instincts whispered to him that Travis's coach making in England was relevant, connected. He was certain he was overlooking a minute detail that would put it all in perspective. How frustrating that he couldn't quite pin that detail down.

Annoyed, he turned back to Spry. "Thus I don't think he could have managed both lines of work without cutting production and consolidating his resources, including active locations."

"Perhaps what he's been earning from the whiskey business isn't enough to support his army, sir. He needs more. What a boon Lady Faisleigh's five hundred pounds would be." It was Spry's turn to frown. "Who shot Gibson, sir? Do you think it was Travis?"

"Yes. Lord Wynndon was in the barn. I wager that Travis is keeping him close at hand."

"Gibson brought Travis money from the till on Front Street. I've been wondering why Travis shot him. Maybe Travis knew Gibson's cover had been compromised, and he'd picked us up as a tail."

"I suspect so, too."

"Then Travis won't be using that barn again, sir." Dry humor infiltrated Spry's tone. "That leaves us only thirty locations to search before he expects ransom money. Before he realizes that we're onto him." The private sighed. "All in just a few days, before Major Craig returns."

"We needn't search all thirty of those locations if we can strategically choose where to send men. We've a meeting at two in the morning with Mrs. Duncan and Mr. Marsh. I wager that they will assist us in the selection process." Michael blew out a candle on the mantle.

"But sir, whiskey has provided them a stream of revenue for a number of years. They may pretend they don't know any locations."

"They may, but not for long. Travis has made a large mistake. He's murdered a member of the team and allowed us to find the body. I doubt Mrs. Duncan or Mr. Marsh wants to be the next team member to anger him. Better to take their chances with the Eighty-Second.

"Besides, they've known Travis at least five years. Even if they know nothing of his 'elite army,' five years' acquaintance will have provided them with signs that Travis is irrational. And his murder of Gibson suggests that he's become more irrational."

"He's short on sleep, sir. Been guarding the boy constantly. Always looking over his shoulder. That would make any man crazy."

"No, it's more than that. According to Mr. Smedes, Travis learned his trade at coach making in Yorkshire and became so romantically obsessed over his master's daughter that his master sent her away, into the protection of a nobleman's household."

"Yorkshire, sir? Is that not an odd coincidence?"

"Yes." Michael clenched his teeth, made a fist with one hand, and punched his other palm with it. "The problem is that I don't know whether it's important or not."

Spry's expression grew long. "Well, I don't suppose we'll be welcome at White's Tavern after our two o'clock meeting, sir." He blew out the candle he'd been holding and set the holder on the table.

Dimness engulfed the room, and the stench of smoky wick wafted to Michael. He headed for the window where they'd made their entrance, his passage piercing the plume of smoke. "Granted, men enjoy their whiskey. We're assuming the good business at White's is due partially to whiskey sales from Travis's operation. But how much business at White's is actually due to sales from his operation, Spry? Have you noticed how much whiskey they sell at White's? I certainly haven't." One corner of his mouth crooked, he threw a glance over his shoulder at Spry, who was on his way over to the window. "I say we have a look." Michael's stomach groaned again, and he clapped his palm to it. "But not too long a look. Enid will have supper waiting."

***

Five tankards of beer. Two wines. Four ales. Michael nodded at the barmaid in White's Tavern as she passed, then redirected his attention on the next wench's tray. Near his ear, above the jollification from laughing men and sawing fiddles, Spry hollered, "Hah! There's a whiskey bottle for someone, sir."

"No, that's rum. And several more beers." The barmaid blew Michael a kiss. A third wench hustled past, two foamy pitchers of beer on her tray plus a tankard of— "Ye gods, Spry! There's another one of those things."

"Yes, sir. It's Mrs. Duncan's refreshing summer drink made of water and leaves."

"That makes seven of them we've seen in as many minutes." The barmaid mouthed "Hero" and winked at Michael in passing. The wenches seemed to contain themselves better when Spry stood at his side. Or maybe they were too busy fetching drinks and didn't have time to pinch him. "Surely those tankards have whiskey already added to the tea. Otherwise I fail to see the appeal."

"Quenches the thirst, sir. Freshens the breath. Eases a man's temperament and sobers him up for his wife."

One eyebrow cocked, Michael glanced at his assistant. So that had been Kate's motivation last night. He snorted, swiveled back around, and gazed across the packed, stuffy, smoky tavern straight into the dark eyes of Lieutenant Adam Neville, scout for Lord Cornwallis.

Michael stiffened. He and the ranger had played this game too many times. What was that Janus-faced son of a jackal doing in Wilmington this time?

The hair on Michael's neck rose. Cornwallis. Neville's business this time was about his lordship's army.

A smile whipped over Neville's mouth, as if he'd read Michael's thoughts. Locked in the stare with Michael, he rose, tossed a coin on the table, and jerked his head toward the exit. Then he snatched up his battered hat and picked his way toward the front door.

"Mrs. White closing from the port side, sir," said Spry.

"Let's go. Now." Without sparing a glance for Aunt Rachel, who was no doubt bringing their drinks, Michael made for the door.

"But our drinks, sir—yes, sir."

Michael departed the tavern with his assistant following and tracked the man in the battered hat the distance of several storefronts in the empty street before Neville stepped onto the porch of a business closed for the night and awaited them. They joined him on the porch and faced off. After Michael and Neville gave each other a quick head bow, Michael said, low, "My assistant, Spry. And this is Lieutenant Adam Neville."

Spry snapped to attention. "Mr. Neville." He saluted. Neville acknowledged it with a wave of his hand.

Spry had heard much about Adam Neville since January. While his assistant and the ranger scrutinized each other, Michael conducted his own quick inspection of Neville. Same hat. Same dusty hunting shirt, trousers, and boots. Same irritating smirk. Nothing about Neville had changed. "Why have you returned to Wilmington, Neville?"

Shadow clung to the ranger's lean face and black hair. In the ambient light, a gloat slid across his expression. "What tender regard you give a man who has survived the battle at Guilford Courthouse but sixteen days ago."

Michael felt no awe and little curiosity. "Without a scratch. I'm not surprised. You hop fences from camp to camp at opportune moments to save your skin." He braced fists on his hips.

Neville tilted his head and affected a sulk. "I shall have you know that I remained with the Crown forces the entire battle and fought my arse off for the King." His sulk melted back into the familiar smirk. "Little good it did. Hence the news I now bring to the Eighty-Second."

"Bah. We already know your 'news.' Lord Cornwallis triumphed." Michael swept one hand outward to indicate the street. "You've delivered your message. Leave Wilmington."

The ranger chuckled. "But you don't know how badly Lord Cornwallis triumphed, Stoddard. I was there. In my whole life, I've never seen fighting so desperate." Neville's smirk collapsed into a scowl. "There are victories, and there are abominations that are labeled victories to appease men across the ocean, men bedecked in politics, perfume, and silk." He shifted forward on the balls of his feet, a whip-slender obelisk of darkness leaning over Michael. "Lord Cornwallis turned the cannon on his own men."

Shock speared Michael, as if the length of a bayonet had punctured all the way through his belly. Fists at his sides, he tensed his abdomen. Near his right shoulder, he heard Spry suck in a breath and mutter, "No!"

The ranger pinned his focus on Michael. "At least one quarter of his lordship's army is dead or wounded from 'victory.' What's left has turned south and is limping toward Cross Creek. I estimate they'll arrive in Cross Creek by this time next week."

One side of Neville's mouth crooked. "Picture it. Wagon after wagon of bleeding, festering, dying redcoats. The men still marching or riding are in little better shape after winter and weeks of short rations. Gods, how they stink, too. And the unfortunate louts bringing up the rear of the train? General Nathanael Greene's best marksmen pick them off whenever they can."

Michael's shoulders slumped beneath the hammers of foreboding and guilt. Lord Cornwallis would find neither medical supplies nor food in Cross Creek. Lieutenant Stoddard had failed him last month in Hillsborough.

Now that the general had been backed into so dire a corner, what choice had he but to march his victory straight down the Cape Fear River? The pummeled, exhausted, "victorious" army would arrive in Wilmington within a week and a half.

"What will the redcoats do now, Stoddard? Give it up, or keep fighting? Either way, it matters not to me."

No witnesses on the street. On the porch, it was just Michael, Spry, and one arrogant double-spy. Good. Michael allowed a long-stymied burst of anger, white-hot and primitive, to fuel the slam of his right fist into Neville's stomach. The ranger folded, smirk wiped away by surprise and pain. Michael shoved his shoulders and hooked his heel with his toe. Neville sprawled to the porch.

Well aware of the ranger's reach and agility, Michael maintained his distance and breathed through the rage. Words spat from him. "Of course it doesn't matter to you. You're a worm, not a man."

Neville caught his breath, then chuckled again. "You throw a wicked punch, Stoddard. But it doesn't change a thing." He rolled up to one elbow. "Since the beginning of the year, the Crown has made error after error." He pushed to a sitting position and braced himself back on his hands. "Behold all the regulars you've lost between the Cowpens and here. You cannot recruit more. Like a lake in a drought, the King's great army is drying up in America."

"Name one reason why I shouldn't toss you in the pen with the rebels."

"Only one reason? It's seldom wise to kill the messenger." Neville grinned. "And I'm not a rebel. You know that."

"No, you aren't. You're a weak-minded worm. You fight for no clear cause and frustrate the efforts of all."

"No clear cause. You think so?"

"In fact, the pen sounds like the perfect place for you. Spry—"

"Very well, I shall redeem myself with another piece of news." Still lounged on the planks, Neville darted a look to Spry, the whites of his eyes glistening. "But you may not want him privy to this. It pertains to our mutual friend." He wrapped the word "friend" in antipathy.

At Neville's suggestion, Michael's pulse jumped rhythm for a few beats. He and Spry exchanged a glance. He returned his attention to Neville. "Whatever you have to say, say it in front of Spry. He's already sampled Fairfax's hospitality. And on your feet, unless you prefer to be stomped underfoot, like you deserve."

"As you wish." Neville grabbed his hat, heaved himself to his feet, and brushed off his clothing, looking not the slightest like a man who'd just been punched. His dark-eyed gaze impaled Michael, and his teeth flashed in the night. "So there I was, unhorsed in the thick of the fighting sixteen days ago. Easily within rifle shot of me, a group of dragoons from the Seventeenth Light, Fairfax among them, had engaged Continental dragoons. I saw my chance. I loaded my rifle, took aim on Fairfax, and shot. Down both he and his horse went, and the horse rolled over him." Neville laughed out at the night. It echoed up and down Front Street.

Michael realized he'd never heard the sound of Neville's humor. Something about it reminded him of the scrape of a cougar's claw on rock as it sprang for prey. Night's chill penetrated his uniform. His brain tried to wrap around information the ranger had fed him. He lowered his voice. "Don't lie to me, Neville."

"Why should I lie? I've slain a monster under the cover of battle, Stoddard. For months, I waited for that moment." He propped his hands on his hips. "Now. Do you still believe that I fight for no cause?"

"Did you see them remove Fairfax's body from the battlefield?"

"No."

"Did you see them bury him?"

"No."

"Did you see him in the wagons of the wounded?"

"No, I—"

"Then he isn't dead, you fool!"

Neville laughed again. "The horse rolled once more, then lay there, kicking, beside him. Fairfax wasn't moving at all, and he had blood on his face. The bastard's dead, I tell you!" He wiped his eyes. "And you, you sound like a wife, by God, denying the ultimate bad tidings."

"If you didn't see him die, how do you know he's dead?"

"The devil—how many men do you know who've survived having a horse squash them?" Neville jammed the hat on his head and scowled at Michael. "Hellfire! Would you wish the monster still alive, torturing people to death here and there, manipulating others out of rank and standing, sucking the life out of everyone he meets, like a spider? Maybe you envy me the deed and flog yourself for not being the one with the rifle, eh?"

Neville cranked up his shoulders. "Or maybe your luxurious life in Wilmington has made you forget why you wanted him dead. Well, not for one day while I was riding with that son of a jackal did I forget why he needed killing. That moment on the battlefield was all about me." He slapped his chest once with his open palm. "Me, making sure that that dung pile will never trap me and peel my skin, or strangle me, or cut me into pieces. Me, sleeping easier henceforth for one well-placed rifle shot. It so happens that my shot also saved your miserable hides, Lord Cornwallis's army, America, and Parliament from a hell-beast walking on two legs. Huzzah!" The ranger flung up his hands. "You and your pride be damned!"

"Neville, what would you do if you learned you hadn't killed him, that he was only dazed, that in the time you've been here in Wilmington strutting like a stupid rooster he'd gotten back in the saddle?"

Neville growled. "I'd kill him again. *You* understand, of course. Now I'm done talking with you. Going back to White's to finish my celebration. Get out of my way." His right hand jerked, a blur. In it a blade reflected intermittent lamplight on the street.

At his left side, Michael heard Spry's quick hiss of drawn breath, but his assistant remained in position. Michael also stayed still, his gaze locked with Neville's, although he relaxed his knees, just in case Neville escalated his aggression. He'd never seen the ranger cocky or spoiling for a fight like this before. Neville truly believed that he'd killed Fairfax. Perhaps Guilford Courthouse had unhinged him. "You've drawn a dagger on an officer of the law. Put it away, or we'll throw your arse in the pen."

The porch grew so quiet that he could again hear the whisper of his watch. It marked a good ten seconds of the ranger's glare. Then the dagger vanished with the same alacrity that it had appeared.

A silent stream of relief issued from Michael's nostrils. "Enjoy your celebration. See that you aren't involved in any altercations tonight." A snarl quivered his nose and hacked harsh edges into his voice. "Because Spry and I really want to arrest you." His lips peeled back from his gritted teeth. "And if you ever draw a weapon on me again, you jakes-hole, I shall put you in a place that makes the pen look like paradise."

Chapter Twenty

THE ENCOUNTER WITH Adam Neville left Michael stewing in a fury that diminished only in part during his stump back to Mrs. Chiswell's house accompanied by his assistant, who possessed the sagacity to keep his mouth shut so Michael could wrestle personal demons. Michael knew he wasn't the only person in America who wanted Fairfax dead. The dragoon officer had made numerous enemies. The odds that one of them would kill Fairfax were great. Thus Michael shouldn't have expected to be the one who succeeded.

But the fact that a double-spy scout in a ragged hunting shirt had done so galled him. It intersected with his self-recrimination over having failed to deliver Major Craig's message to Cornwallis. Some dark piece of his soul must have goaded him into believing that killing Fairfax could assuage his guilt over failing his mission to Hillsborough. Perhaps that was why Neville's news made him detest the ranger even more.

In the back yard of Mrs. Chiswell's house, Michael and his assistant washed hands and faces. Enid had kept fried fish warm for them. Spry headed to the kitchen. Michael headed for the dining room.

He dined alone. As the clock on the mantle struck eight, he pushed back from the table and made his way to the study, where he spotted Mrs. Chiswell engaged at her desk. He rapped on the doorframe. This time he waited for her to invite him in.

The chair he'd appropriated that morning had remained beside the desk. While Mrs. Chiswell set her quill aside and capped the inkbottle, he took a seat in the chair. His nose detected faint traces of Lydia's perfume. Annoyance jammed his teeth together. He imagined her flouncing into the house that afternoon during the time that he'd been questioning Smedes or galloping out to the barn. He doubted that her visit had been to provide information that would shed light on the investigation.

Mrs. Chiswell plucked a sealed note from one of the partitions in her desk. "Lady Faisleigh's maid brought this for you." She slid it to the edge of the desk closest to him. Then she sat back, hands in her lap, and waited.

"Thank you." Reluctant to transfer Lydia's scent to his waistcoat and shirt, he left the note on the desk and returned his attention to Mrs. Chiswell. "Lieutenant Adam Neville has arrived in town."

Her eyebrows arched. One hand flew briefly to the hollow of her throat. "He scouts for Lord Cornwallis. That must mean—"

"Yes. Expect Lord Cornwallis's army to begin arriving here in a little over a week."

"Gods." She gulped, her face pale. "I do appreciate the warning, Mr. Stoddard."

"Will you be able to leave before the army arrives?"

"I shan't be able to sell my house by then. But I shall post to Mr. Quill and expedite our departure plans." She let out a deep breath and hung her head a few seconds.

Michael watched her rub her palms in her lap, the motion of someone washing hands. "You're prudent to move on without waiting for your house to sell. Have you received communication from Fairfax since that 'sibyl of the gods' note?"

She shivered. "No."

"Neville relayed to me details of the battle. He boasted of shooting Fairfax off his horse."

Her head jerked up, nostrils widened, jaw dangling. After a moment, she closed her mouth. "Neville saw Fairfax buried, then?" she whispered. Her gaze searched his face, hungry.

Michael shook his head. "Nor did he see him among the wounded."

"Gah!" She pounded the top of the desk with her fist once. The inkbottle jiggled, and a bead of ink dropped from the quill to the letter she'd been writing. "Then we cannot assume that he's dead." Her voice thickened. "Well, can we?"

"No, we can assume nothing. Thus you're indeed wise to expedite plans to leave Wilmington." Blinking at a shimmer in her eyes, she swiveled to face night outside the window and pressed fingers to her lips a moment. Michael realized how wrenched she must feel. She'd lived in Wilmington for almost thirteen years, had friends and business associates among the residents, had watched the town prosper and expand, and had buried her husband in the churchyard.

When she seemed more composed, he said, low, "You spoke this morning of crimes that Fairfax committed for sport before coming to America. False witness and murder, I believe." She met his gaze and nodded. "I'm likely to be engaged in an investigation for the next few days and don't know when we shall have an uninterrupted moment again. If you will tell me of these incidents now, I will be grateful."

Without hesitation, Helen Chiswell nodded and closed away her writing implements for the night. Then she turned her chair to his.

***

Downstairs, the final soft chime for nine on the mantle clock faded. By lamplight, Michael stood over the desk in his bedroom, Spry at his side, and studied two scraps of paper. "I should have compared them before assigning Travis's crimes to Greene." He tapped first one, then the other, with his forefinger. "You see?"

"Yes, sir. The scrap of Scripture verse that you found in the barn from the gunsmith's direction clearly isn't written in the same handwriting as the other samples." Spry straightened and regarded his commander. "The warrant was posted for only a couple hours."

"It may have been enough time for Greene."

"I recovered and destroyed all six warrants. It'll be his word against ours."

Michael laughed, short. "Business as usual. We don't need to be handing Greene that kind of opportunity again. We must be more careful."

"Sir." Spry pointed to Lydia's note, still sealed, on the desk near the wall. "What's that?"

"Ah, blast. I'd forgotten about it." Michael snatched it up. "Too many things to ponder after Mrs. Chiswell's testimony."

"And what a testimony. Sheer devilry, sir." Spry shuddered. "Mr. Neville was right. Mr. Fairfax is a hell-beast. Torturing poor, dumb farm animals to death when he was twelve. Framing the butler for burglary when he was fifteen. Hanging his stepfather when he was eighteen. Ugh. Between you and Mrs. Chiswell, you know enough to wreck Mr. Fairfax's Army career and see him arrested for murder."

"Don't be so certain." Michael broke the seal on Lydia's message. "Nobility and commissioned officers protect their own with vehemence." He unfolded the paper. Lydia's scent advanced into his bedroom and claimed it. "Good gods." He coughed, swept to the window, and waved the paper outside to disperse some of the scent into the night.

Spry grinned. "Too bad the bandits didn't steal her perfume instead of some clothing. Sir."

"The deprivations of war." Michael pulled the note back in and read Lydia's script: *Lieutenant Stoddard, an issue of family business, hitherto not discussed, is germane to Wynndon's abduction. I would apprise you of it tonight. Dine with me at eight o'clock.*

He showed the message to his assistant. Spry cocked an eyebrow. "Supper started an hour ago, sir."

"I trust she didn't delay it for my company." Michael tossed the note, folded, back to a corner of his desk. "'Family business.' God's teeth, maybe this is about Jacobites after all."

Spry frowned in the direction of the perfumed message. "Then I'm confused, sir. Is Travis a Jacobite? Or is he hired by the King's men to kidnap the boy? Or is he a third party?"

"I don't know." Michael studied the ceiling a moment. "It baffles me, too. It's as if we're working multiple investigations at the same time, and the pieces of evidence appear interchangeable." He regarded Lydia's note. "But I shan't tarry with Lady Faisleigh. You and I have a long night ahead of us. If I'm not back in half an hour, go on to the barracks and make certain the next two surveillance teams are prepared." When Spry didn't respond, Michael rotated his head to look at him. "Spry?"

"Yes, sir." Spry met his gaze. "You realize that Mr. Neville is an Indian, don't you, sir?"

"Ah!" Michael's head drew back. Leave it to his assistant to spot what he should have recognized all along in the ranger. Gratitude surged though him for Spry's observational skills. Puzzle pieces that had lain disconnected too long fell into place, and his comprehension of Adam Neville's motivations expanded ten times. His blood warmed, revitalized. "Thank you, Spry."

"Don't mention it, sir. Mr. Neville doesn't look full Indian to me. Maybe his father was a white trader. Being Indian could be why he seems to fight for no clear cause. He certainly isn't fighting for any white man's cause."

"Exactly. His Indian background also explains the enmity between him and Fairfax. I've told you that Fairfax framed Creek Indians in Georgia for his murder of a Spaniard. Those Indians know." Michael steered his gaze to his closed bedroom door. He'd never confessed the rest to anyone, not even to Spry. The Creek knew because he, charged by the tribe's chief to solve the Spaniard's murder, had ridden, alone, to their village near Alton last summer and informed the tribe's Beloved Woman of the truth after he'd been forced to mouth his captain's erroneous statement that the Spaniard had been murdered by his cohort.

In Alton, Fairfax had missed having the Creek capture him by mere hours. Damn his fortune.

Spry shook his head. "Indians don't just walk away from that kind of slight, sir. Insulting their honor is suicide. Word of those who slight them spreads among tribes."

Michael cocked his eyebrow at Spry and lowered his voice. "Now we know why Neville has stuck with Lord Cornwallis's army all these months." He led the way to the door.

"Unfortunate, sir, that we couldn't have transported a war party of Creek to our situation near Hillsborough last month."

Michael grunted his agreement, opened the door, and extinguished the lamp. Unfortunate, also, that after all the horror Fairfax had generated, he could only be executed once. Maybe that was why Michael resisted the triumph Neville claimed from his one well-aimed rifle shot at the Guilford battleground. One execution seemed wholly inadequate to address the heinousness of murder, especially the Goliath force of evil embodied by Fairfax.

***

Downstairs, he informed Enid that he and Spry anticipated being out for much of the night, due to an investigation. As the housekeeper barred the doors by ten each night, he assured her that he and Spry would get what rest they could in the barracks. Enid let him out into the night, and he sought the house where Lydia and her party were lodged.

De Manning opened the door in stiff-shouldered, jaw-jutted silence. Michael followed the direction of the tutor's outstretched arm into the candlelit parlor. Dorinda rose from a chair near the couch, met Michael before he was two steps in, and gave him the barest of curtsies. "My lady, Mr. Stoddard has arrived."

Lydia didn't look up from where she sat on the couch facing the fireplace, back straight, embroidery occupying her hands. "Lieutenant, do join me. Dorinda, Mr. de Manning, leave us and close the doors. Dorinda, have Felicia prepare my room for the night."

"Yes, my lady." Her expression neutral, the maid swept her scrutiny over Michael. She curtsied once more to Lydia, although Lydia's back was to her, and continued past Michael. He swiveled to view the black scowl contorting de Manning's countenance and Dorinda's hand caressing the tutor's forearm. "Come," the young woman murmured near his ear. De Manning backed into the foyer. Dorinda closed Michael into the parlor with Lydia.

If de Manning had a bright spot in his life, it was Lydia's lady's maid. And Dorinda, lacking in dowry, could hardly go wrong with the tutor. Michael hoped de Manning realized their mutual benefit soon. He returned his attention to the unlit fireplace.

"Such a novel experience you've provided me, Lieutenant. You're the first man to ever decline a personal invitation from me without sending word." Lydia, who continued to apply her concentration to her embroidery, snapped a thread with a jerk and punctuated her next sentence with the force of it. "Do have a seat."

What a shrew. Michael allowed himself one deep, long breath to force down his ire before walking around the couch and assuming a rigid stance between Lydia and the fireplace. She declined to acknowledge him, so he fished the silver button from his pocket, bent over, and held it beneath her nose. "From your son's waistcoat, I believe."

She gasped and dropped the needlework to the cushion beside her. Then she picked the button from between his fingers and closed it into her hand. Her shoulders sagged. Her gaze searched his face.

He straightened. "Late this afternoon, he left the button for us to find in a barn to the northeast, within a few miles of where he'd been abducted. Spry and I missed rescuing him by less than five minutes."

"Five minutes?" Her voice squeaked. Her eyes filled with tears.

"Has Mr. de Manning produced any new evidence that Lord Wynndon was at the wharf last night?"

"No." Her jaw trembled. She blinked away the glisten.

"Surely you can see now that your son was never at the wharf. All evidence that Mr. de Manning produced from that area appears to have been planted to throw us off the search. As I found no evidence of physical violence done to the boy in the barn, I conclude that the blood on the cloak is not his."

She bowed her head. "Thank heaven."

"I haven't found substantive evidence to support my initial suspicion that Mr. de Manning has betrayed you and your son. Rather, I believe he's been duped. But there may still be a traitor in your household."

Her head perked. "Who?"

"I don't know. I now suspect the villain in this crime of abduction isn't the Reverend Greene, but someone jealous of his success with his congregation, someone eager to establish his own radical Protestant congregation. His name is Travis."

She squinted at him, rose, and slid the button into her pocket. "Travis?" She looked away. "I've heard that name before. Ah, if only I could remember where."

Michael pitched a calm he didn't feel into his voice. "He's supposedly from Yorkshire." He studied Lydia's reactions. "Perhaps he's a Jacobite."

"Jacobite?" She whirled back on him. "Oh, not that again! I've told you that I'm not conspiring with them. You've some gall, accusing me of colluding with Jacobites because of my forebears' alliance!" She stamped her foot. "Enough of this! You've made a fool of me!" Her teeth flashed in a snarl, and she squared off with him. "You. Lord Crump. And your family."

His stomach tensed. The wrong kind of warmth flowed through his face. After more than a decade, Lydia had, indeed, recognized him. He opened his mouth. No words emerged.

She flung up both hands. "What did all of you expect to gain by telling me you'd succumbed to a fever?"

He made himself stand his ground and steadied his breathing while he focused on pinning down a whirl of thoughts. His brows pinched together. *Fever,* she'd said. What was she talking about?

"I'd every intention of bringing you into my husband's household, ensuring that you received a gentleman's education, seeing you settled as a solicitor or an accountant. Instead, when I visited Lord Crump in the summer of 1771, I was told that you were dead. *Dead!*" She yanked a pillow off the couch and flung it across the room. It landed near the doors. "Ten years later in America, in a backcountry hamlet without a single paving stone on its streets, I find you alive, thriving, an *officer* in His Majesty's army."

She hurled another pillow. It whumped to the floor near the first pillow. Her snarl enlarged. "All of you perpetrated deception of the vilest kind. What have you to say for yourself?"

He blinked at her, his voice still refusing to cooperate. Lydia had recognized him. And she'd been told that he was dead?

Chapter Twenty-One

MICHAEL HAD BEEN certain that Lydia would not, could not recognize him. Where had his logic run afoul? Panic expanded in his throat. Instead of a two-day-old association of investigator and crime victim, he and Lydia had a murky relationship that meandered back more than a decade. He felt five inches shorter, pimply-faced, and narrow-chested. The Bard had said it about the tangled web.

No. This was insane. He'd lost his footing. Lord Wynndon's life depended upon him standing firm. His first step that moment was to make certain he'd understood what Lydia had said. He coughed to loosen his throat. "Lord Crump and my family told you that I had *died?*"

She glared down her nose at him. "Do you deny knowledge of this subterfuge?"

He straightened his shoulders. "Yes, I do." Why in hell had everyone told her that? His imagination conjured the image of a headstone with his name upon it and a too-brief span of years, 1754 to 1771. His bones quaked. "Have I a grave in a cemetery?" Surely the deception hadn't gone that far.

She scraped a frigid, blue-eyed stare over him. "They claimed you died in Scarborough after being sent there to recuperate. I didn't have time to travel there and look." Her lips pursed with three centuries of Blackhall disdain. "How did you come to be an officer in the Army?"

"Lord Crump summoned me to his study in the spring of 1771. He said I was too clever to spend my life sweeping the mews and caring for falcons. He and my uncle Solomon had purchased my ensign's commission. A few years later they purchased my lieutenant's commission. They wanted me to make something of myself."

As he heard his own words, his skin crawled. In one sharp motion, he turned away from Lydia, to the fireplace, guarding the expression that must be flooding his face. Had he at last uncovered why he'd been bundled off into the Army? Had his family and Lord Crump recognized what Lydia was and, in purchasing his commission, spared him the fate of Nigel de Manning? Damnation.

"Then you really didn't know of this deceit, did you?" The harshness fled her voice, replaced by summer-evening silk that made Michael's skin crawl more. She murmured, "Michael, Michael."

He corralled an urge that flared out of nowhere: a desire to sweep her up into his arms, to affix a set of marionette strings upon himself. That was what Lydia expected, what the sixteen-year-old youth who lay beneath the imaginary headstone would have done.

Unless the twenty-six-year-old man continued to assert himself, she'd manipulate him. And oh, how being manipulated roused his resentment. He gritted his teeth. Lydia would concoct lies, starting with the most obvious, an attempt to convince him that Lord Wynndon was *his* son, not de Manning's. She'd start there, because she'd already expressed her doubt that the search for the boy was receiving the highest priority she felt it was due from his attentions. Shifting Lord Wynndon from the status of "kidnap victim" to "son" would surely cause him to shuffle his priorities in her favor.

If he allowed her to meddle, it would hamper his ability to rescue the boy. Despite their history, despite her social standing, he must continue to stand his ground and assert authority. The bearing of Major Craig's criminal investigator reassembled, he faced her. "I had no knowledge of this deception. They never mentioned you to me in their letters."

"Then you are as much a victim as I am." She drifted closer, her lips parted, her voice husky.

Again, he squashed down an urge to embrace her and maintained a rigid posture. Whether either of them was a victim remained to be seen. "As a criminal investigator, I find it difficult to believe your claim that you would have provided a commoner access to a gentleman's education. You'd no motivation to extend such generosity to me.

"And in truth, all that is past. Discussion of these matters contributes nothing to the present dilemma of finding a way to wrest your son away from a madman." He clasped his hands behind him and strolled for the front window, increasing the distance between them.

"But why would I not have made so generous a provision for you?" Tenderness suffused her tone. "You gave me what I desired the most. You gave me Wynndon."

He laughed that she was so predictable and shook his head. "Frontier America isn't a peer's parlor in London. No one here has time for parlor games. Not your son, nor Travis, nor my assistant and I. You admitted to me today that Mr. de Manning is the boy's father. Now, do you want my help rescuing him or not?"

Still smiling, she pulled the portrait from her pocket and extended it in his direction by the ribbon. "Look at it, Michael. Is that Nigel de Manning's face? *Is it?*"

His gaze tracked the swaying portrait. Features of the boy's face leapt out at him. He'd been certain they were de Manning's features. But were they? He yanked his attention away, to the wall over her shoulder. Damn the woman, manipulating him.

Lydia whispered, "You *do* see. It's the face of your father. And you."

Resentment and fear knotted his stomach. He locked gazes with her. "You hold commoners in low regard. You wouldn't select a commoner to help you resolve your inheritance dilemma. Plenty of gentlemen wouldn't have hesitated to assist you. I saw who attended you in Lord Crump's parlor those summers. Noble *men*, not peasant *boys*."

She laughed and crammed the portrait back in her pocket. "Has the Army locked you in a monk's cell, that you don't know what a woman appreciates, why she'd select a boy and not a man?" She grinned. "You were so accommodating and such a quick learner. I cannot say the same for most men."

Flame rolled up his head and set his ears afire. "You've fabricated this twaddle about the boy's paternity to dodge my questions about the Jacobites."

"Jacobites, Jacobites." Hands on her hips, she swayed a few steps closer and jutted her chin at him. "What of Eòbhann MacCoinnich?"

He scowled. "Who is Eòbhann MacCoinnich?" His tongue stumbled over the Gaelic name. "MacCoinnich—that's a Highland Scots name, MacKenzie." He caught himself. *MacKenzie?* De Manning had flung the name at him earlier. What game were Lydia and the tutor playing with him?

Head tilted, she studied him. "You mean your family doesn't speak of your great-grandfather and the MacKenzies?"

"Oh, MacBalderdash! My family isn't Scottish. We've been in Yorkshire for two centuries." He spread his hands. "I suppose now you'll weave a tale that I'm secretly a Scottish prince." He waved toward the window. "I'm as common as the dirt out there on Second Street."

"Not nearly so, as my private investigator informed me—"

"Private investigator? More nonsense. Now, then. In the note you sent me earlier, you stated that you must apprise me of an issue of family business pertinent to your son's abduction. What is this issue?"

She closed the distance between them, her countenance sober. "I hired an investigator to research the lineage of Abraham Stoddard. For awhile, my man couldn't get past your grandfather, Andrew Stoddard. Then he found out that your surname comes from your great-grandmother's *second* husband. Her first husband, the father of your grandfather Andrew, was Ewan MacKenzie, a baron with a respectable estate in the Highlands."

Michael's scowl returned. MacKenzie? Baron? Highlands? Definitely not an angle from which he'd expected her attempt at manipulation. He growled. "The flaw in your story is that I've never heard so much as the hint of such a grand tale among all the tales told in my family. If it were true, someone would have mentioned it by now."

She smacked her lips as if she'd tasted ambrosia. "Not so, my dear Michael. There are some things that are best kept quiet for several generations. Ewan MacKenzie fought at the battle of Sheriffmuir in 1715 alongside the Earl of Mar for the Stuarts. Yes. He was a Jacobite—"

"Stop right there." He shook his head and held up his hands, palms out. "Next you'll be telling me that we're half-faery. Your story is hogwash. We've no bloody Catholics in my family."

She smirked. "No, not anymore. They wisely converted to the Protestant faith. Ewan's Jacobite kinsman, William MacKenzie, had the good fortune to escape to France after the battle. But your great-grandfather died at Sheriffmuir. Unlike William, he never had the opportunity to seek a pardon, never had descendants repurchase his lands and restore the family title."

Michael whipped out his watch and checked the time, then snapped the lid shut. "I've lost a quarter hour of investigative time listening to you spinning nonsense. Get to the point."

She took another step toward him and spoke quickly. "In 1715, just ahead of assassins, kinsmen smuggled Ewan's widow and six-year-old son, Andrew, out of Scotland into Yorkshire. While the lady was still mourning her dead lord, she was married in the Protestant faith to a Yorkshire widower named Henry Stoddard, who adopted her son, Andrew, and gave him the surname that protected his life."

Michael turned to the window and stared out at night while poking at his memories for Andrew Stoddard, who had died when he was seven. When memory summoned the old man's speech, Michael realized that the soft trill that came and went in his grandfather's voice might have been the remnant of a Highlands accent, much hammered down by decades of Yorkshire's own burr. Or maybe not.

Confusion shifted his thoughts around. Surely his family would have said *something* to him about such a heritage. Lydia was lying, probing for a way to control him.

Another memory squirmed into the foreground of his thoughts. Once, he'd chanced upon his grandfather while the old man was sorting through a wardrobe. Among items he'd placed upon the bed was a silver brooch bearing the design of a rose, similar to the one Lord Wynndon had dropped. When Michael had picked it up and examined it, his grandfather gently scooped the brooch from his palm and patted him on the head. "There's the good lad. Thank you for finding my trinket."

Come to think of it, Michael had never seen the "trinket" again.

Bewilderment clutched at his throat. What else would he remember if he had a moment to sit and think about his childhood and his grandfather? Did he *want* to remember, to validate Lydia's story? How much did his sister, older by two years, know? He had much to ask Miriam in his next letter home.

Aware of Lydia's presence near his left elbow, he swiveled a quarter turn. She smiled up at him. "All these years, you must have considered our time together those two summers as some sort of bizarre indulgence on my part. Perhaps you can now see that there was nothing arbitrary about my selection of you. I did have a motivation for wanting to give you a gentleman's education." She exhaled a long breath while her gaze strolled the length of him. "But the cream rises to the top. Here you are, an officer and a gentleman, so it was obviously meant to be."

He turned back to the window and scrubbed his face with one hand. Family business, bah. She'd lured him to her with that note. Regardless of whether what she'd told him was true, no other soul on the face of the earth need know a bit of it. And some elusive element of her story about wanting to bring him into her household nagged at him.

"You realize," she murmured, "that you're the direct, sole male descendent of Ewan MacKenzie. You could petition the Crown for a pardon, have your title restored."

Petition the Crown? Oh, hell. Michael's immediate plans with Lydia's information would be to verify her story about the MacKenzies with his family. A huge portion of him hoped Lydia was lying again. He'd no idea what he'd do with himself all day in a crumbling old Scottish castle. Count sheep on a foggy mountainside, perhaps?

Lydia's hand slid up his sleeve to his shoulder and fondled his epaulet. "Why haven't you advanced to the rank of captain by now?"

He stared stupidly at her fingers a few seconds, then guided her hand off his shoulder and shifted half a step away. "Like many junior officers, I find myself short of funds. Plus my uncle and Lord Crump are unable to finance the purchase of additional commissions."

"Surely you've ambition to advance within the Army?"

"Of course I've ambition." As always, he wondered how much of it could be furthered by progression up the officers' ranks. From what he'd seen, men who reached the ranks of senior officers often lost touch with the people who needed their help the most.

She drew back a bit and regarded him with the inner edges of her brows compressed downward. Then she tilted toward him and squeezed his upper arm once. "How competent you are, Michael. From what I've witnessed of your analytical abilities, I fully expect you to rescue our son—"

"No, no. He's *your* son." A white-hot needle of panic stabbed up his spine. He moved two steps away from her, severing the physical contact. "Even if you're telling the truth, I made no contribution, aside from a roll in the straw."

"I've a proposal for you."

His palms grew sweaty. "What sort of proposal?"

"A *business* proposal." Her smile vanished. "After you've rescued Wynndon, I shall fund your commission for the captaincy. Perhaps further, if you and I collaborate well as business partners."

Any officer would be daft to dismiss a potential benefactor with pockets as deep as Lydia's. "So you're offering the commission as a reward, a gift for the boy's safe return? See here, I'm grateful for your generosity, but rest assured that—"

"Yes, yes, a sense of honor and duty are what really motivate you, and they'd inspire you to try your hardest to rescue anyone thus imperiled, and it isn't at all about money." Her lip curled. "Gods. I've heard enough of that rubbish in Parliament. It's always about money."

Michael gaped. "This isn't Parliament. It's Frontier America. A lunatic has kidnapped your son."

"This is His Majesty's Army in Frontier America, where all men have a price, just as in Parliament. Men are men."

Indignation smoldered in his gut. Major Craig, like Lydia, was of a mind that most men who voluntarily engaged in heroic acts did so for monetary gain. The greater the heroics, the greater the gain.

"But to clarify, I'm not offering you a reward. I'm tendering a business proposition, with terms."

Michael's mouth went dry. He blotted his palms on his breeches. "What do you have in mind?"

Her expression grew pensive. "I assure you that my brother-in-law is quite greedy to possess the family title. Wynndon's current perilous situation resurrects the reality that my husband, my son, and I are vulnerable at holding the title and the estate. After my husband learns of this incident, I know exactly what action he'll insist upon from me." She advanced on him and fluttered fingertips over the front of his coat. "He'll resurrect our discreet agreement, insist that Wynndon have a brother or sister."

Michael's jaw dangled. He tried to retreat in the direction of the parlor doors but snagged the heel of his boot on a corner of upturned rug at the leg of a small table. After righting himself, he stepped around the table.

The Earl of Faisleigh wouldn't rest easily upon learning that his wife, separated from him by the Atlantic Ocean, had become reunited with her young buck from a decade earlier. Faisleigh might tolerate Lydia's vagaries with de Manning. He and the tutor were of a similar age. But he wasn't about to let his wife keep a mistress young enough to be his son.

And *mistress* was exactly what Michael would be, yanked about on Lydia's short leash. With shock, he comprehended that some form of the arrangement was what she'd intended years earlier, when she'd planned to recruit him into her household. Installed in Ridleygate Hall, he'd have been accessible to her day and night. Some gentleman's education that would have been. Yes indeed.

He set his jaw, grateful for the generosity of Lord Crump and Solomon Stoddard. "Surely you jest."

"Not at all. My husband will be thankful to discover that you're alive and fit. And he'll be well pleased to have another son as intelligent and healthy as Wynndon. Or even a daughter."

"Your *husband* will take his first opportunity to ruin my career, have me cashiered from the Army." Sarcasm scorched Michael's tone. "And if by some remote chance he doesn't sink me, what would you do if your sought-after outcome doesn't hasten along, despite my diligence? Do I still receive the captaincy? How long must I then uphold my end of our business proposal to ensure your patronage?"

"I see. You imagine I won't fulfill my end of the bargain." Lydia caught up with him. Her fingers closed about his facings. "I shall draw up a contract, then."

Contract, hell. Her proposal was beyond ludicrous. It was horrific and repulsive, and it deposited a taste in his mouth like rancid cheese. That she could even consider such an arrangement while her own flesh and blood was imperiled suggested that despite her professed loyalty to Lord Wynndon, the boy was expendable. Any children she had would be expendable. For that matter, her husband, her servants, and everyone in her life was expendable, including Michael. The world circled about Lydia.

He backed three large steps, placing him within reach of the doors, in the clear of furniture and pillows, and bored his stare into her. "I've a far better idea for the direction of your energy tonight. Ponder where you heard the name of Harley Travis from Yorkshire. I need information about this rogue."

Lydia sighed. "I shall think on it." From her pursed lips and folded arms, she'd just approved the week's menu at Ridleygate Hall.

"If matters go well, on the morrow in the afternoon, Travis will show me your son, unharmed."

She tossed her head. "Excellent. And of course, I shall be there to verify his identity."

No. Lydia's presence at the meeting would inject an additional layer of wild emotion and entail that Michael increase the size of his patrol to protect her. As much as he disliked the tutor, Nigel de Manning was a better choice for providing recognition. "You'll stay here where you're safe. Mr. de Manning will accompany me to identify the boy."

She jammed fists to her hips. "I'm Wynndon's mother! My presence will give him hope."

"Your presence will give his kidnapper another target. Don't underestimate Travis. He's irrational. Your son witnessed him murder a man this afternoon."

Lydia's eyes widened, and her hands drifted up to fold over her chest atop her heart. "Murder?"

He gave her a curt nod. "Trying to guarantee your safety at a meeting on the morrow introduces an unnecessary variable into the event. I'm not certain how long Lord Wynndon will be safe in Travis's custody. This step buys us an additional day to learn where he's hiding the boy. Now I must be off." He bowed his head and executed a quarter turn for the doors.

"Wait! Murder? How ghastly! I-I don't see how I shall be able to sleep at all tonight for the horror of it. Poor Wynndon." Eyes shimmery again, she extended a hand for him. "Where are you going?"

The devil—did she expect him to attend her? He set a quiet tone. "I've traps to set for a lunatic."

Her eyes shone like glacial ice. "Do you honestly believe Lord Crump would have purchased two officer's commissions for a *commoner*?"

Now that she mentioned it, he had wondered about Lord Crump's generosity. For several years.

"Someone told him of your family's barony, Michael. It wasn't I."

Was Lydia lying about that? But if not Lydia, who might have possessed enough sincerity to convince Lord Crump that his falcon boy was the descendant of a baron?

Michael didn't have time to dwell on the possibilities. He raised his chin. "And should you find yourself unable to sleep tonight, best you spend your wakeful hours thinking on where you've heard Travis's name. Good night." He pivoted for the parlor doors, yanked one open, and let himself out.

Chapter Twenty-Two

AT MRS. CHISWELL'S house just before Enid locked the doors for the night, Michael retrieved his fusil, cartridge box, and hanger. "Irrelevant to the investigation" was his response to Spry's query about what family information Lydia had imparted upon him at their meeting. Michael allowed his frustration over the encounter to color his response so Spry would infer the flavor of Lydia's irrelevance to be romantic.

The two soldiers wished Enid a good night and headed out. Michael sent Spry to White's Tavern to spy on Adam Neville for a few hours from the porch. Then he reported to the barracks, where he shut from his head Lydia's attempt at manipulating him over her son and composed a note for the abductor: the conditions, time, and place Sunday for their meeting. He made his order unambiguous and resolute. Terms wouldn't be met and negotiations wouldn't continue until he verified the identity and good health of the hostage.

However, he was ineffective at damming the trickle of reminiscences, scraps of moments spent with his grandfather. After he'd written and sealed the note, he permitted himself to indulge in memories for a few minutes.

A golden autumn morning, and fishing in a stone-spattered, chatty River Nidd. His first horse ride, encircled in Andrew Stoddard's sun-warmed arms, a meadowy sea of summer-yellow flowers below them. The crunch of frost beneath their shoes on a heathery knoll, hounds panting at their heels, the whistle of a hawk high above in a slate-gray sky.

No tartan. No haggis. No bagpipes. But weaving in and out of his memories was the faint, soft trill in his grandfather's voice.

MacKenzie. Baron. Highlands.

Would Lord Crump have purchased two officer commissions for a commoner? Even for a nobleman as kind and generous as Lord Crump, purchase of the commissions had constituted an exceptional deed. Suspicion had grown on Michael that there was more to the purchase of those commissions than his benefactor's gratitude for his sleuthing skills.

If Lydia's story about the MacKenzie barony was true, and she hadn't confided her findings to Lord Crump, Michael could imagine only one other source of the information. He pictured Abraham and Solomon Stoddard using the positive outcome of the embezzlement incident to plead the case to Lord Crump of resurrecting the impecunious branch of the MacKenzie family. That might have led to Michael's appointment in the old nobleman's study and the purchase of his commissions.

But if family members expected him to restore glory and eventually wealth and the barony, why had no one told him any of it until now?

Niggling inconsistencies in his background might be explained by the MacKenzie connection. Perhaps that connection was why his sister, in her most recent letters, pestered the blazes out of him to marry well and produce the next generation. MacKenzies, not Stoddards. Impoverished, perhaps, but capable and ready to assume a barony.

Alas, the joke was on Ewan MacKenzie. His supposed great-grandson was a mere junior officer and criminal investigator in frontier North Carolina, where glory, wealth, and titles were in short supply.

However, Henry Stoddard would have been proud of him.

Unfortunately, brooding over the entire black, bloody mess in no way helped him achieve his goal of rescuing Lord Wynndon. It also didn't change the facts that Major Craig was headed back to town and Lord Cornwallis's army would soon be visiting Wilmington.

He rose and sent out relief surveillance teams for the tannery and tavern. Around eleven, the men who'd observed the tannery during the first shift reported that all had been quiet there. Near midnight, the first shift from Rouse's Tavern returned with the report that jollification at the tavern was well underway, at least forty patrons inside the building. As of eleven o'clock, neither Jones nor Love had put in an appearance, and the soldiers had spotted no children. But the night was young for rebels in revelry.

White's closed at one, and Spry returned to the barracks about twenty minutes later to report that over the course of the night, Neville had consumed enough small beer to fill a pitcher, but interspersed his beer with what appeared to be four of Kate's refreshing summer drinks. The ranger had played multiple games of darts and checkers and stayed clear of brawls. At closing time, he'd ridden off on his horse like any law-abiding patron. Neville the double spy had taken Michael at his word, having no desire to wake up in the pen Sunday morning. Good for Neville. Maybe he'd do the Eighty-Second a favor and leave town.

Michael fidgeted with busy work at the barracks, trying to delay the march of time toward the encounter of the day that he'd wished the most to avoid. But all too soon, he and Spry headed out for their two o'clock rendezvous with Smedes the wainwright in front of his shop on Front Street—and what came after. The entire walk there, anxiety sealed Michael's lips.

He'd been a fool to allow his emotions to enfold any of White's family. But he didn't see how he could have avoided it. Even had he somehow been granted a physical transfer of duty to Charles Town or Savannah, he wouldn't have received a reprieve of emotion. Because he'd allowed himself to succumb to involvement with Kate and her family instead of holding back, he'd earned himself a new emotional experience. It felt as though a dozen needle-slender rapiers had bypassed the barrier of his ribs and impaled his heart, but had not withdrawn to grant him the grace of bleeding to death. Damned if it didn't resemble the state that maudlin poets and junior officers lamented. Fool, he told himself. Fool.

After he and Spry reclined in the bed of the wainwright's waiting wagon, Smedes pulled the tarp over them and set off on his minute-long drive to White's Tavern. Spry said softly, with conviction, "We've been here before, sir." Ostensibly, he was referring to a wagon ride during their perils near Hillsborough in February, and Michael grunted his agreement. But in the next instant, he wondered whether Spry had intended a secondary meaning, especially after his companionable silence during their walk to the wainwright's shop. He suspected that his assistant knew the impalement of the dozen needle-sharp rapiers. Knew it and had endured it. Perhaps it was one of those bits of life that both damned and exalted a man, left him fuller on the other side of the torment.

The wagon rolled to a stop. A slight vibration indicated that Smedes had lit down from the driver's seat. Michael heard one of the horses give a sleepy snort, and Smedes's soft knock upon a door, followed by hinge-squeak and Kate's murmur of greeting. Her voice drew nearer, the fragment of a sentence about hiring an additional barmaid, and Kevin spoke, his voice also low. "Yes, I've never seen business so hearty."

Michael mustered the detachment with which he'd engaged in battles. The tarp jiggled, then furled in two quick movements, exposing the soldiers to the starry sky. Michael sat up, followed by Spry.

His vision, well adjusted to night, discerned the initial blank expressions of both Kate and Kevin near the tail of the wagon bed as they comprehended that the delivery wasn't about whiskey. In the next instant, Kate gasped, and Kevin flung his arm out horizontally, a shield for his sister. Another rapier pierced Michael's heart.

The two soldiers scooted to the edge of the bed, climbed out, and donned their hats. Kate and Kevin retreated from them several steps. Michael regarded the wainwright. "Thank you for the ride, Mr. Smedes. Go home now. Sleep well."

Smedes exhaled in relief and tugged the brim of his hat. Then he hustled to the driver's seat and reins and clucked his tongue at the horse team. The wagon creaked off into the night.

Michael and Spry stared at Kate and Kevin. In a rustle of silk gown, Kate twisted to look up at her brother. Garnets in her earlobes glinted. "I'll handle this, Kevin."

"The devil you will. Go inside and—"

"I'm here to talk with both of you. None of us has time to waste." Michael extended his arm toward the tavern, where faint light glowed through one window. "Let's take this conversation off the street, shall we?"

They complied without speaking. Kevin opened the door and held it for the others to enter, then shut them into the eerie, yeasty night of a tavern af-

ter-hours. All four gathered around a small table bathed in the golden illumination of an oil lamp. Michael and Spry removed their hats.

Michael flicked his gaze over the chin-up solidarity of brother and sister
across the table from Spry and him, then pitched his tone quiet. "The scope of
my law enforcement concern is well represented by what occupies jail and the
pen. As I told Mr. Smedes this afternoon, I don't give a damn about arresting
whiskey smugglers who evade taxes in North Carolina. But when a whiskey
smuggling business suddenly includes highway robbery, abduction, and murder, it becomes my concern."

Kate and Kevin gawped at each other, then yanked their attention back to
Michael, both blurting a babble of, "Murder? Robbery? Abduction?"

He held up his hand to quiet them. "How long have you known that Harley
Travis is using profits from your whiskey business to fund the development of
an army of young boys for Governor Abner Nash?"

Their jaws dropped. Kate blinked rapidly. "Wh—army? Boys?"

So they didn't know. "Fair enough. Then you'll be just as pleased to learn
that Friday afternoon, Mr. Travis used that army of boys in an incident of
highway robbery, during which time a ten-year-old boy was abducted from his
family. Mr. Travis has demanded ransom in exchange for the boy. But because
of the existence of this 'army,' we believe that even if the ransom is paid, the
family will never see the boy again. We must rescue him."

"But you said 'murder,' Michael." Kate's voice quavered.

"I did. Yesterday afternoon, while the kidnapped boy was forced to watch,
Mr. Travis shot Ralph Gibson in the head."

"Oh, dear God." She folded into the embrace of her brother.

Kevin gripped her shoulder. His knuckles went pale for a second or two.

Michael's stomach knotted. He shut out the wide-eyed horror of the pair
and blunted his voice. "Where can I find Harley Travis?"

"We aren't certain," said Kevin. He licked his lips and released Kate.
"God's truth, sir."

"Where did he live in Wilmington?"

"He rented a room over the baker's shop. It's since been cleaned out and
re-rented."

Michael ejected a sigh of exasperation. "How do you pay him for your
sales, then?"

"Kate and I cut the tavern a percentage of sales, based on the contract
drawn up by the original principals of the venture. Wednesday nights, we leave
Mr. Travis his share in a sack on the rear step of the tavern. Once a quarter, we
include an accounting."

Michael and Spry eyed each other. There sure was a good deal of money
lying around in sacks on doorsteps in Wilmington each week. Alas, no one had
time to wait until the coming Wednesday night to bait a trap for Travis. In fact,
Michael's instincts warned him that Travis would have exhausted his patience
with Lydia's son long before Wednesday.

He withdrew the dead farrier's map from his haversack and spread it open
on the table. "Mr. Gibson's map. Spry and I suspect that each of these circles represents a hiding place where your uncle and Rephael Whistler once
concealed stills and whiskey from revenue collectors." He bent over the table

and stabbed several locations with his forefinger. "Some may be spots where a ten-year-old boy can be held and concealed without undue discomfort. What I need from you two is assistance in determining which of these are the most likely locations for Mr. Travis to use to that end." He straightened, arms at his sides, and waited.

Brother and sister sat at the table, pulled the lamp closer, and bent over the map. Kevin tapped a circle near the Widow Collier's tavern. "Storage shed."

"No." Kate nudged him with her elbow. "I spoke with Mrs. Collier's maidservant at market in early February. She mentioned that the shed had collapsed in a rainstorm mid-January."

Kevin looked up at Michael. "You'll want barns, then, won't you?"

"I want the very best leads, whatever they are. I don't have many men at my disposal for a search, and the boy has even less time."

Within ten minutes, Kate and Kevin had endorsed eight circles on the map. That they were unable to account for what structures were represented by eleven of the map's thirty-three circles made Michael a little uneasy. But he folded up the map with hope that Lord Wynndon was at one of the eight.

His watch informed him that the time closed on two thirty. He and Spry were due back to the barracks to accompany another team out to the Rouse house with the basket and note. Kate and Kevin were still seated. He looked them over. "Did Mr. Travis ever mention to you a young lady that he wooed when he lived in England?" They shook their heads in negation. Well, that had been worth a try. "You realize that you two know a good deal about Mr. Travis. More than he would care for you to know, I'm certain."

Kevin sat tall. "We'll guard our backs."

"Good. Guard your aunt's back, too, even if she knows nothing of this." He took a deep breath and sidled a half step closer to Spry to unify Kate and Kevin's view of the scarlet in the room. "After I've arrested and imprisoned this scoundrel, I must write a report. For the good of all parties involved, I insist that the report be accurate when I reference a certain *terminated* whiskey smuggling operation." He watched Kate's lips part and Kevin's jaw clench, and he plunged on before their resistance escalated. "You see, right now I'm looking the other way. But the King's men are moved about all the time. None of us knows who will be the lead investigator in Wilmington three months hence. An investigator other than myself may *not* look the other way."

Across the table from him, gazes lowered, and shoulders sagged. He'd made his point.

With Spry at his side, he walked to the door. "Ah. One more thing." He swiveled to them. "As long as Mr. Travis remains at large, he may commit additional crimes. Both of you must mention this conversation to no one while the investigation is ongoing. Otherwise, you may inadvertently assist Mr. Travis in eluding capture. Do you understand?"

They nodded.

"Good." Across the table, Kate's face emerged from shadow. Her gaze sought his, and her lips parted and softened. Perhaps she'd eventually forgive him for that deception with Smedes's wagon. He dropped his hat on his head and touched the brim of it. "Thank you for your cooperation. Good night."

They let themselves out, closed the door, and strode for Market Street.

Before they'd walked the distance of two shops away, Michael heard the groan of door hinges behind him and the patter of pursuit in the dirt street. The men halted and faced Kate's approach.

She bustled up to Michael, petticoat clutched in one hand to give her mobility. Despite the chill of the night, she wore neither a shawl nor a modesty scarf. She released her petticoat and wrung her hands once. "You've been transferred out of Wilmington, haven't you?" she said, her words breathless. The pale oval of her face tilted up to him.

"Not to my knowledge. I merely cited what is plausible." By starlight, he recognized the arch of desperation in her eyebrows. A wave of astonishment soared from the soles of his feet to the top of his skull. Kate didn't want him to leave.

"I—we didn't have the chance to discuss—you know, when you helped Friday night and moved that—that bag of rice." She shifted the silk of her lips and the creamy skin of her cleavage closer and whispered, "Might we discuss the matter you suggested? Tonight?" Her gaze slanted to where Spry stood a few feet away in discomfited stiffness.

She was inviting Michael to share her bed. That night. In Michael's peripheral vision, Spry radiated awkwardness, confirming it.

A primal paean pounded in Michael's pulse. Memory repeated every glorious second of that kiss in the grain shed Friday night. The pincushion that passed for his heart shivered in delight, enjoying each new rapier thrust, offering no resistance.

In the next moment, the buckshot of cynicism peppered him with the conclusion that Kate had resorted to seduction as a way of encouraging him to forget about that little business her family had on the side. Meanwhile, his groin argued that all men succumbed to a bit of bribery every now and then.

But after a forced swallow, the words of Major Craig's criminal investigator emerged from his mouth. "I'm not at liberty for discussion this moment. I'm occupied with the investigation through at least dawn today."

"Dawn?" Pain pinched her expression. "But—"

"Later, perhaps, I—" He worked his mouth to rescue faltered words, but his repertoire included no experience at extricating himself from trysting with a woman he desperately desired and probably shouldn't touch. "I—ah—good night." He spun about and stalked past Spry, who, from the surprise widening his eyes, might have managed the muddle with far more finesse. Michael didn't look back.

By the time he cut over onto Market Street, he'd corralled his seditious pulse, heart, and groin. He'd also been aware of Spry at his side for at least half a minute. They completed the walk to the barracks without conversation. Soldiers standing guard saluted Michael, and one opened the door for him. He and Spry entered.

Four men chosen for the next surveillance shifts rose from where they'd been sitting around a table with a lamp. They saluted Michael. One hefted a small covered basket. Where the circle of lamplight ended, the snoring of men of rank and file began. Even though the shutters were open to the night, the barracks stank of sour breath, and of feet that had worn the same sets of stockings for too many days in a row.

Michael motioned the men at the table out the door. In the starlight, he ordered two to fetch the horses and the other two to the tannery on Front Street. The quarter moon had set before he, Spry, and the two soldiers headed on horseback for the surveillance post near the Rouse house. Like a phosphorescent faery trail, the sandy road beckoned them northeast. They took the route slowly to avoid loose sand and arrived at the pine copse around three thirty.

Although the tavern was silent, shuttered, and dark, its hitching posts empty, the soldiers that Michael's party relieved told a tale in hushed voices of revelry lasting until almost three in the morning. Sounds of raucous merriment and music from inside, pistols fired into the air outside, and a partially clothed, drunken couple chasing each other around the tavern building and out into the barn.

Michael winced at the thought of what Eve Whistler's children and Lord Wynndon might have witnessed. However, the soldiers reported seeing no children and only the one plump, drunken woman.

They also reported that Devil Bill Jones and Captain James Love had spent about two hours inside, Love's hearty laughter distinguishable even above the din of others' high spirits. That news alone knocked back a good portion of Michael's anxiety. It appeared that Jones and Love frequented the tavern. A patrol of armed men from the Eighty-Second should be able to manage a tavern full of drunks while apprehending a couple of carbine-carrying blackguards.

Michael dismissed the earlier patrol and sent them back to Wilmington. Then he insisted that the three men remaining with him be still and listen a few minutes. Wind and infrequent, distant owl hoots were the only sounds breaking their lonely night vigil. He assigned Spry the task of delivering the basket beneath the mulberry tree. In case anyone in the tavern was watching, he and his assistant mapped out a way for Spry to backtrack and approach the area from the west.

Spry sneaked out for the delivery. Just prior to four o'clock, he sneaked back to rejoin them. From the four men's location of concealment, the pale, foot-high, round basket was visible beneath the tree. The soldiers of the Eighty-Second settled in for the task of waiting. Michael fidgeted to remain alert and stifled his yawns.

About four twenty, a rooster in the coop behind the tavern grated out his first greeting of the day—proximate enough to be excruciating for anyone inside the tavern building who'd imbibed too much and was trying to sleep it off. Minutes ticked past in Michael's waistcoat. A mile or so distant, another settler's cock crowed. Thus emboldened, Rouse's rooster sounded off again. A cow in the barn announced that she was ready to be milked.

The door on one of Rouse's outbuildings groaned open. Michael and his men came alert. Holding a lantern high, Eve Whistler exited and trudged for the barn. A mid-sized dog, its bushy tail wagging, appeared from the wiregrass wilderness to the east and followed the widow inside.

All three children emerged from the outbuilding and proceeded to the barn, stretching and yawning. In less than a minute, Mrs. Whistler's boy, who was the same age as Lord Wynndon, reappeared in the barn doorway. He turned around to receive an embrace from his mother—the kind of desperate, lengthy embrace that a mother gives a son who is headed off to battle. Then she released him and returned to the barn. The boy sprinted around the south side of the house.

The soldiers watched him trot out to the road and head south on it. "Where's he going?" muttered Spry.

Michael whispered, "Quiet." But like the men with him, his gaze tracked the lad until he disappeared in the road's bend. Surely Eve Whistler suspected by now that thirteen-year-old Zeke wouldn't be coming home again. Michael wondered about the mission on which she'd sent her only living son before dawn had hued the sky.

Ten or so minutes passed. The little girls emerged from the barn holding the ends of a pole that ran through the handle of a milk pail. Taking their time, they transported the pail around the south side of the house and up onto the front porch, where they rested it on the lowest step and climbed two more steps to sit on the top step. One of the privates said, low, "Bless 'em. I don't think they spilled a drop."

The widow reemerged from the barn soon and lugged another milk pail to where her daughters sat. Her bucket joined theirs. She trudged out to the road, stretched her back, and stood like a sentinel, gazing in the opposite direction of Wilmington.

About quarter to five, Michael heard the approach of hooves, tackle, and axle-creak from the northeast. A mule cart appeared on the road, a man guiding the beast afoot, two boys a bit older than Lydia's son walking to either side of the cart and carrying lit lanterns. The man braked the vehicle before the Rouse house, blocking the soldiers' view of the basket. He and Mrs. Whistler exchanged greetings.

By lantern light, they went about the business of inspecting the milk in her pails and exchanging milk for coins. The boys hauled pails out to the cart, poured milk into a canister in the cart, handed back pails, secured the canister, checked over the cart, and released the brake. With a wave for the Whistlers, the dairyman, his lads, and the mule cart continued south. Eve Whistler and her daughters walked around the south side of the house toward the barn.

The milk pickup had included the basket. Beside Michael, Spry muttered, "Shall we track them, sir?"

"No." The redcoats watched the dairyman and his party until they were lost to sight around the bend. Then Michael addressed his men in low tones. "We number only four. It's dark. We don't know what awaits them farther south, in the dark. The point of this venture has been to get the note into the hands of Travis. It's now on its way." He glanced at the eastern sky, which was beginning to pale. "And we shall soon be on our way, too."

Chapter Twenty-Three

IN THE BARRACKS at a quarter to ten on the morning of Sunday, April first, otherwise known as Fools' Holy Day, Michael took quill and ink to Lydia's perfumed request for his company at a nine o'clock breakfast and, at the bottom of her note, instructed her to notify de Manning that he must be ready to ride out with a group of armed infantrymen at one that afternoon for their meeting with Travis and Lord Wynndon. Furthermore, Lydia was to order de Manning to acknowledge Michael's authority as leader of the expedition and during negotiation. Michael sent the note off with a runner boy. Then he assigned Spry to maintain extra vigilance on de Manning later, including restraint, if necessary.

At ten o'clock, he met with two teams of ten soldiers, assigned each team two of the eight circles on Gibson's map, and detailed his plan for their systematic and stealthy search operations, to commence upon conclusion of the meeting. The Eighty-Second had never possessed a surfeit of mounts, and as Major Craig and his dragoons had commandeered most of what the regiment did have, Michael's expedition to meet with Lord Wynndon and Travis would use every remaining mount. Therefore the two teams of men must march out to search the areas closest to Wilmington. On the morrow, horses would be available for them to search the more remote areas.

At eleven, while many civilians were standing rather than sitting during the service in the Anglican church due to lack of pews, Michael was in Major Craig's office rubbing eyes grainy from three hours' sleep and poring over the register of miscreants with the growing sensation that he was the one on a fool's errand that holy day for fools. Ralph Gibson wasn't listed, and neither were the business partners who owned the tannery shop on Front Street. The entry for Harley Travis read, "Fled prior to occupation. Rebel group affiliation unknown." Alexander Rouse's entry stated, "Rebel sympathizer, owns tavern 8 mi NE." Useless, those particular register entries. Tempted as Michael was to append them with what he'd learned thus far about the men, he resisted. The investigation was far from complete.

The holes in the investigation explained why his luck felt spotty. He'd yet to interview Dorinda and Felicia about what they'd witnessed in the carriage during the abduction. He'd also yet to interview the groom, the second coachman, and the remaining outriders. Somewhere in the testimony of those people, perhaps a clue lurked to advance the investigation and improve his fortune. However, those interviews must wait until after the meeting with Travis and Lord Wynndon.

His providence was definitely better at Mrs. Chiswell's house, where Enid propped him vertical with three cups of coffee and a plate of biscuits smothered in sausage gravy. Amazing how clean teeth, a clean shirt, and a clean shave improved his mood beyond that. It reminded Michael that within a few days, the pampering he and his assistant had enjoyed in the house on Second Street since late January would be a memory: Mrs. Chiswell and Enid gone to Boston, the house locked and for sale. He must remember to thank them both.

When he, Spry, and nine men of the Eighty-Second rode up to Lydia's residence at one, de Manning was waiting beside a saddled horse: rifle in hand, a scabbarded infantry hanger at his waist, and pistols in saddle holsters. Also waiting with horses and firearms were Ames, the second coachman, and all six outriders.

And there was Lydia, posed in the doorway in pink satin and pearls, her lips pursed.

Astride the mare Cleopatra, Michael looked over the household. His rationale for excluding all the men except the tutor was simple. He didn't want to worry about reining in a group of civilians. "Mr. de Manning, mount your horse and fall in beside me. The rest of you, I'm heartened by your enthusiasm, but your participation is neither required nor permitted on this venture."

"Take them anyway." Lydia sashayed down the steps. "They wish to be of service."

"Thank you, Lady Faisleigh, but no." Michael watched the head coachman fidget from one foot to the other, his fingers tightening around his firearm, and he caught the man's gaze. "Ames, understand me. This is not your time to be of service. When I need you fellows again, you've my word that I shall call."

Ames's frown faded. He nodded.

Lydia completed her parade to the end of the front walkway. Before she could challenge him again, Michael clicked his tongue and sent Cleopatra out into the street.

In a few seconds, de Manning rode up beside him, his posture and equestrian skills flawless. Michael led the party onto Market Street, where he and the tutor regarded each other without words, a brief concurrence of mutual dislike.

De Manning couldn't set his dislike aside, even though he was certain that Michael was a fellow MacKenzie. That was when Michael realized why subjugation to the English throne had been inevitable for the Scots, despite their centuries of struggle and protest. It was bad enough that the clans fought each other. But they also fought themselves.

***

About one twenty, the party rode into a small clearing of wiregrass, rocks, and infrequent prickly pear cacti. An abandoned hovel squatted about twenty-five feet to the east of the New Berne Road. It was the site Michael had selected for the meeting. After securing the immediate area, all twelve men searched out to and beyond the nearest trees, thirty or more feet away, to make sure that Travis hadn't preceded them and sneaked in guards or traps.

Five soldiers in the patrol were proficient marksmen. Michael repeated earlier instructions he'd given them about not firing unless they had a clear shot of the outlaw leader, or unless their own party came under attack. He sent the marksmen, with their horses, into cover of the surrounding trees to assume posts with their rifles. He, Spry, and de Manning stood just outside the hovel. Two remaining privates waited with them while the other two acted as sentinels at the road, muskets ready. Their horses were picketed behind the hovel.

Just after two, the sentry to the south sprinted back with news of an approaching party. Michael drew him and the other sentry in and, hearing sounds of hooves and the creak-jingle of tackle, ordered Spry and de Manning into the hovel and the four redcoats to wait just outside, able to take cover, if necessary. He ducked inside with his assistant and the tutor and peeked around the edge of the open doorway, its closure long gone.

A pair of young men Spry's age wearing the hunting shirts of backwoodsmen rode into the clearing on horseback, rifles ready in their laps, their gazes scouring the clearing, the hovel, and the visible soldiers. They halted their horses about twenty feet past the building. One of the horses looked like Alexander Rouse's gelding, tended by Gibson the morning Michael and Spry had first visited the farriers' shop.

A fine coach-and-two, followed by another pair of armed young men on horseback, rode in. The driver, also armed, brought the coach to a squeaky stop in front of the hovel. The rear guard halted about twenty feet behind the coach. A lad about twelve years old, his clothing just as ragged as Zeke Whistler's, and a pistol jammed in his belt, hopped off the rear of the coach. He marched through sandy dust to the coach door, faced the hovel, and held the posture of attention, his stare penetrating the walls.

Michael allowed dust to settle. To his right, de Manning peered out through a split in the siding, while to Michael's left on the other side of the doorway, Spry was observing through a rotted knothole. The window shades of the coach had been drawn to conceal the interior. As many as four people might be seated inside.

One shade twitched an inch—someone looking out. That was Michael's signal to step into the doorway and play out more of the game that he believed Travis wanted to hear. "Good afternoon, Mr. Greene, or perhaps you're Mr. Greene's representative. I'm Lieutenant Stoddard. Thank you for agreeing to this meeting. I trust you're prepared to show us the hostage? Do produce him at this time."

The footman opened the door and positioned the step. The shadowy interior of the coach writhed, resolved into a dark-haired boy—hatless, coatless, and gagged—his arms restrained behind him. A man with the top half of his head covered by an executioner's hood descended the step to the ground with the boy held close before him, the point of a knife caressing his carotid artery. A leather harness crisscrossed the lad's dark blue velvet waistcoat, a waistcoat with silver buttons that matched the one Michael had found in the barn the previous day. The harness allowed the man to control him.

Blinking in the sunlight, as if he'd had his head covered by a sack during the coach ride, the boy shook hair from his eyes. A bruise snaked up from beneath the gag and across his left cheekbone. His attention skimmed over the four redcoats outside the hovel then riveted to Michael, the only man wearing an epaulet. Pain filled his eyes. He lifted his chin anyway.

A current of electricity energized every blood vessel in Michael's body, flattened the breath from his lungs, stripped speech from his throat. He moved out of the doorway, drawn forward one pace. Twenty-five feet away, the eyes of Abraham Stoddard pleaded with him to end the two-day nightmare.

Until that moment, Michael had been certain that Lydia was attempting to manipulate him with a lie.

Behind him, de Manning's breath went raspy. "Dear God, he's bound like an animal—Why? *Why*?" The tutor slammed into Michael in attempt to barrel past.

"Spry!" Michael snagged de Manning's upper arm.

De Manning extended his other arm, shredding rotten wood on the threshold in passage. "Wynndon!" Spry hauled de Manning back inside. "Let go of me, you lout! Wynndon!"

Michael glimpsed the hostage's wide-eyed acknowledgement of de Manning before he had to return inside and ensure that Spry had the tutor under control. "Mr. de Manning, as you were!" Alerted by a muffled cry outside, Michael pivoted and sprang from the hovel. The executioner was hauling the wriggling boy back into the coach. Michael said, "Lord Wynndon! Remain strong!"

Lydia's son landed with a whump and a groan on the floor of the coach. At least one person on the inside dragged the boy in, assisting the executioner's efforts. The hooded man leapt up into the coach. Someone inside handed him a hunting sword shorter and narrower than de Manning's hanger, its tip pointed like a rapier. In partial cover of the doorway, he twisted toward Michael, grinned, and brandished the sword in swishing arcs. "So, Stoddard, are you satisfied as to the identity and soundness of the hostage?"

The accent from southern Yorkshire suggested that the executioner was Harley Travis. Michael made himself breathe slowly, despite his hammering heart, and relaxed his fists while his gaze memorized Travis's height and build.

And his clothing. From his ruffled shirt to calf-hugging soft boots, it had been tailored to emphasize his athletic physique. How he loved to play with that sword, too. In fact, all Travis lacked was a goddamned bow and quiver of arrows to look just like an eighteenth-century Robin Hood. "Yes." Michael rolled back his shoulders and, in a new light, took in Travis's retinue. His Merry Men. "I am satisfied."

Braced by one hand on the side of the coach, Travis swept the sword blade outward, a gesture as noble and high-minded as any blackguard could make.

"Excellent. Then on the morrow, you will deliver the ransom beneath the mulberry tree two hours before dawn, in a basket. Well before then, though, you will receive instructions about the exchange of the boy."

On the morrow? No. Michael must stall for longer, give his soldiers time to find the great hollow oak where Robin Hood stored his stolen goods. "It's Sunday. No financier is available on Sunday. Access to the ransom amount is out of Lady Faisleigh's hands until at least the morrow. More likely Tuesday."

"Lady Faisleigh is carrying the full amount with her. I know it. The boy has confessed."

Michael refused to believe that Lydia had confided in her son the amount of money she was carrying. "Of course he confessed. I saw the bruise on his face. He'd have made up any story that stopped you from beating him. Now I'm telling you she has a fraction of that amount with her. We must have patience with this process."

Travis laughed. "Shame on you, Stoddard. Didn't your mother teach you not to lie?" He bowed inside.

"Wait!" Panicked that he'd fouled the negotiation, frustrated with Travis's arrogance, Michael spread his hands and took several quick steps forward. "Do you really think any lady would travel with so much money except in the protection of an army? Lady Faisleigh must have the time to speak with financiers on Monday and Tuesday, so she may comply with your demands. And you must give me a better way to contact you than a basket beneath a mulberry tree—a more secure way to ensure that you receive the funds. Consider all the traffic on this road!"

Travis cocked his head and said nothing for several seconds. Then his eyes narrowed, and he straightened his neck. "You want more time?" He frowned. "Very well. I shall give you until Tuesday morning, two hours before dawn beneath the mulberry tree. And you also want more security in the delivery? Hmm." Travis's eyes glittered in the holes of the mask. A gravelly smirk penetrated his voice, and his words came more quickly. "Very well. Lady Faisleigh's maid will courier the basket with the money. We're done talking, Stoddard." Travis vanished inside the dark interior of the coach. "Home, lads!"

The footman placed the step inside, slammed the door shut, and hopped on the back of the coach. The driver snapped the reins. With a jolt, the coach rolled off northeast, the pairs of guards riding before and after.

Lady Faisleigh's maid will courier the basket with the money. Why had Travis altered the delivery terms in such a way? Michael had expected him to change the delivery location to a building to comply with his request for greater security. It seemed rather obvious to Michael that if he permitted Dorinda to courier the money, both she and Lord Wynndon would be murdered.

Behind Michael, de Manning growled. "Mr. Stoddard, I insist we give chase."

Michael kept his back to the tutor, watching trees on the northeast edge of the clearing engulf Travis's rear guard. "I shall do nothing of the sort. If we chase after that rogue, he'll kill the boy."

"He's torturing him!"

Michael turned on his heel to stare down de Manning who, with Spry, stood just outside the hovel. "Mr. de Manning, was that masked man one of the two men who entered your carriage Friday and knocked the wind from you?"

The tutor squinted at him, then blinked in the afternoon sunlight. "No, he was not. One of those was tall and spindly. The other was fat."

Ah ha. It had been as Michael suspected. Travis hadn't participated in the abduction. He'd schemed it, then sent men and boys from his army to carry it out.

Anger and grief had drained from the tutor's posture. "Was that rogue the Reverend Greene?"

Michael shook his head. "I've learned that Greene isn't the architect of this outrage." He pointed over his shoulder in the direction the coach had driven. "That man's name is Harley Travis. Did you recognize his accent?"

De Manning's eyes lit with curiosity. "He's a commoner from Yorkshire."

"But do you know him?" The tutor shook his head. "Recognize his name?" Again, de Manning's denial. "Any idea why he'd ask for Dorinda to courier the money?"

"None. But you mustn't allow her to act as courier. He'll kill her. Or worse." De Manning lowered his gaze. "She's a good woman."

The tutor was overdue at taking that realization to heart. Michael softened his voice. "Don't worry. I shan't let them have her. And I shall get Lord Wynndon back."

"How?" The sneer in de Manning's voice snapped at him. "You've just let all of them escape."

Michael scanned the angle of the sun. Time to head back. And it was long past time for him to interview Dorinda. "I've bought us one more day, Captain. Furthermore, although Mr. Travis doesn't realize it, in this brief meeting, he gave me a new angle from which to view this puzzle."

"Bloody hell, you're confusing me. The only 'angle' I saw was Wynndon, in pain."

Michael thought of the contortion of the boy's arms and repressed a shudder. "Yes. It was difficult for you to witness that. Thus I insist that you censor your description of him for Lady Faisleigh."

The tutor studied him, and some of the virulence faded from his eyes, although he kept his jaw firm. "I shan't tell her about that abominable harness, if that's what you mean. Or the bruise on his face."

"Good. Then you and I shall have the same story." Michael smiled without humor. Amazing. He and Nigel de Manning had finally agreed upon something.

***

During the return trip, Michael attempted to ponder what he remembered of Robin Hood stories. If Travis styled himself as the legendary outlaw, whether he were aware of it or not, it stood to reason that he'd have weaknesses parallel with those of Robin Hood. Michael should be able to exploit those weaknesses.

However, his brain, short on sleep, couldn't pin down those weaknesses and, instead, kept dragging him back to the image of the boy, bound and gagged. How surprising that neither de Manning nor Spry had remarked upon the resemblance. Lord Wynndon, so clearly a chip off the Michael

Stoddard block.

Michael's stomach flip-flopped. He'd contributed only to the boy's bloodline. De Manning was, for all practical purposes, Lord Wynndon's father. And Michael was glad to leave it that way.

Yet he felt haunted over the way blood had called to blood in that clearing: all-too-capable of placing himself in the boy's shoes emotionally. In his quiet moments, he hadn't allowed himself to dwell much on the bruise left upon his soul by the loss of his own father. Yet it was there, throbbing with the same wail of abandonment and terror that he'd seen in Lord Wynndon's eyes. What eerie truth there was to the old proverb that blood was thicker than water.

Close to three o'clock, the party of twelve riders reached Lydia's house. Soldiers relieved Michael and Spry of their mounts and gear and headed back to the regiment's stables. The groom in Lydia's retinue, who'd been waiting on the front porch, took de Manning's horse around back. Then Michael, Spry, and de Manning entered the house. The tutor gestured them into the parlor minus his usual hostility and climbed the stairs to notify Lydia of their return.

In the parlor, the soldiers startled the housemaid, Felicia, occupied at plumping pillows. The girl dropped a pillow on the couch and stiffened near the fireplace, gaze darting between Michael and Spry.

Travis's selection of Dorinda as courier had been prodding Michael's thoughts during the return trip. Felicia was possibly the only person beside de Manning who had Dorinda's confidence. Maybe the girl could shed some light on Travis's peculiar request. He gave her a quick smile. "Felicia."

Petticoat clenched in one fist, she bobbed a curtsy. Then she scurried for the door.

He moved to block her exit. "One moment."

She halted facing him, back stiff and eyes downcast. Her hands clenched her apron.

Michael pitched a soothing tone. "We saw Lord Wynndon. He's in good health." Lit with hope, Felicia's gaze made a foray for his before she bowed her head again. "We also saw the scoundrel who holds Lord Wynndon hostage. He made a peculiar demand of us. Might you help us in understanding his demand?"

"Sir," she whispered.

"Why should this blackguard insist that Dorinda be the one to deliver the ransom money for Lord Wynndon?"

Her head shot up, and she blurted, "Perhaps Dorinda's a damsel to be rescued, like Queen Guinevere or Maid Marian."

Michael yanked his stare to Spry, who was squinting at the girl. His scrutiny snapped back to her. Eyes wide, she clapped her hand to her mouth. "A damsel to be rescued, Felicia? Is Dorinda in league with this rogue?"

Hands crossed over her heart, Felicia shook her head. "N-no, sir."

"Then explain yourself."

"P-please, sir, I misspoke."

Michael stepped toward her, followed by Spry, and ceased making his tone soothing. "We don't think you misspoke at all, Felicia. Look at me. Tell us exactly what you meant."

Her jaw hinged open. She backed a step from him. Her body trembled.

From upstairs, de Manning's voice carried. "Felicia! The lady requires your help this instant. Where are you? Come, girl!"

His voice interrupted Michael's hold on Felicia. She used that second to dash past the soldiers and out the door. Her footsteps tapped an ascent of the stairs.

Michael expelled a breath of frustration. What had that been about? Was Felicia concealing something, or was she held mute by fear? He must speak further with her that afternoon.

"Hsst, Spry, before they come downstairs." With a jerk of his head, Michael motioned his assistant, who'd been taciturn during the return trip, over beside him. "Your observations of this afternoon. What was your impression of Travis and his soldiers?"

The private's head perked. He snorted. "You shall think me daft."

"No, I shall think you perceptive, as usual. What did you see?"

A smile kinked one corner of Spry's mouth. "Robin Hood and his Merry Men."

Michael snapped his fingers. "I knew it! And as I recall, you mentioned Robin Hood two days ago, when we were in the infirmary looking over those bodies."

"Sir, I meant that comment on Friday in jest. Not so about what I saw this afternoon."

"Well, then, what do you remember those old stories saying of how one goes about imprisoning Robin Hood?"

"You don't imprison him, sir. At every opportunity, his enemies such as the Sheriff of Nottingham either fail to capture him or fail to retain him."

"Nottingham? Bah." Michael scowled and crossed his arms. "Robin Hood was from *Yorkshire.*"

Spry raised his eyebrows. "Yorkshire, sir? But I thought Robin of Locksley was—"

"Loxley, spelled l-o-x-l-e-y, is a village in southern Yorkshire, near Nottinghamshire. Certain envious people in Nottinghamshire have naught better to do with their time than thieve a robust legend from a neighboring county. And you do realize that we shall only have one opportunity to apprehend Travis before he kills the boy." The private let out a long, sad sigh of agreement. "Robin Hood can be captured and imprisoned. He has a weakness. We find it, and we make the most of it. Think on it. I want your suggestions at the end of this meeting."

"Yes, sir."

"Any other observations?"

Spry flicked his gaze the length of Michael and opened his mouth to speak. The sound of multiple pairs of footsteps descending on the stairs dragged his glance to the parlor doorway.

"Save it for later." Michael held up a hand, palm outward. "Here they come." He took up position before the fireplace, arms at his sides, while Spry returned to the window.

In glided Lydia in her cloud of pink and perfume. Felicia, Dorinda, and de Manning followed her in and, when she took a seat on the edge of the couch, arrayed themselves around her. She tilted her chin up to Michael. Her eyelashes were damp. "Mr. de Manning told me that you saw Wynndon this afternoon and that he was sound of body."

"Mr. de Manning is correct. Your son was restrained and frightened, and his abductors had taken away his hat and coat, but all that is to be expected under the circumstances."

A sigh escaped Lydia. In her lap, she massaged her palm with her thumb. "What do we do next?"

He pinned his gaze to hers. "I've bought us one extra day. This morning, before we set out for the meeting, I sent men of the Eighty-Second out to follow solid leads for where your son might be held. If those leads don't bear fruit, we've more to pursue on the morrow. In addition, at this afternoon's meeting, the villain inadvertently allowed my man and me to comprehend something of his personality and the way he thinks, thus giving us a new and possibly more effective way to combat him and approach a rescue."

"Mr. Stoddard," said de Manning, "what you speak of, I recognized none of it at the meeting." The tutor's frown reflected curiosity, not antagonism. "Do enlighten us."

Michael glanced from de Manning to Spry, in passing noting the bland expression of Dorinda. He returned his focus to Lydia. "Very well. The man who abducted your son fancies himself some sort of Robin Hood."

De Manning roared, "Robin Hood?" Lydia laughed with scorn. But Dorinda's eyes bulged, and she yanked her head to one side, her jaw hanging.

Michael dragged his scrutiny off her and back onto Lydia. "Lady Faisleigh, on the morrow you've an appearance to maintain in the event that spies for your son's abductor are watching your movements." Lydia sobered and cocked an eyebrow at him. "There are several financiers in Wilmington. You will seek them out. I care not what you discuss during your visits with them so long as you spend at least half an hour inside each office."

She nodded. "So I'm to use this extra day that you bought to appear as though I'm obtaining the demanded ransom amount, as the financiers haven't been open for business on Sunday."

"Precisely. Did you tell your son the amount of money you're carrying with you?"

Lydia turned her head slightly and frowned, regarding him from the side of her eye. "No. Why should I do that?"

Michael nodded, then shifted his attention to Dorinda, who refused to meet his gaze and fidgeted clasped hands before her. "And as I've been remiss at completing my interviews of other members of your household regarding the abduction Friday, I shall resume the process, starting with Dorinda." The maid darted a look at him before contemplating the floor as though it had begun to undulate beneath her feet. "I ask that you, Mr. de Manning, and Felicia allow Spry and me a private audience now with your maid. I shall interview Felicia directly afterward."

"Of course." Lydia rose with a sour smile, leaned toward Michael, and murmured, "I suppose it's someone else's turn for a private audience with you." She strolled around the couch and hovered close to Dorinda. "Cooperate. He doesn't bite." With a wave of her index and middle fingers, she gathered de Manning and Felicia to her and bustled them out.

Chapter Twenty-Four

THE DOORS CLICKED shut on their departure. Michael pitched an easy tone. "Dorinda, do have a seat on the couch. This shouldn't take us long."

She drifted over and perched upon the edge of a cushion without making eye contact with him or Spry, who was still at the window. Hands folded in her lap, she fixed her gaze on bricks at the base of the fireplace. Color had abandoned her face, and she gnawed her lower lip. Guilt or fear?

With his head, Michael gestured Spry closer. Then he assessed the young woman before him. "Spry and I no longer consider Mr. de Manning complicit in Lord Wynndon's abduction."

Her head tilted up, and gratitude lit her face. "You don't?"

"He's a good man, very devoted to the boy. It must tear at him horribly that he was unable to prevent Lord Wynndon from being wrenched from the carriage."

"Oh, yes, it does, I assure you." Dorinda scooted back on the cushion and sat tall.

"We've heard the testimony of Lady Faisleigh and Mr. de Manning about those terrifying moments when your carriage was forced open and bandits took the boy away. Tell us what you saw."

"Why does it matter? They've already told you everything."

"Dorinda, everyone who experiences a criminal act as a victim perceives that act differently, participates differently. You're the only one in that carriage who stabbed a bandit in the hand with embroidery scissors. Based on your action, we've been able to identify the man whom you stabbed." Her eyes widened. "So you see, what you did in the carriage during those seconds matters very much. And it's important in helping us understand the full scope of the abduction."

"Very well." She cleared her throat. "Where would you like me to start my testimony?"

"After you stabbed the bandit in the hand, what did you do with the scissors?"

She stared through him a moment, then blinked a few times and refocused on him. "Why, I-I must have kept them in my hand because—" She gulped and looked away. "Oh. God help me."

"You used the scissors again, didn't you?" Michael glanced at Spry and the dawn of wonder on his assistant's face. "You used the scissors on two masked men who entered the carriage after Mr. de Manning shot the first bandit who tried to enter. Yes?"

"Yes." Dorinda's breathing became labored. "The men shoved Felicia aside, poor mouse. Then they hurt Nigel. He couldn't breathe, Mr. Stoddard!"

Michael frowned, trying to envision a woman as mild-mannered as Dorinda leaping to defend a downed de Manning like an extreme incarnation of Queen Boadicea, whose battle rage had shocked Romans in eastern England more than seventeen centuries earlier. "Are you saying that you attacked them with the scissors because they knocked the wind out of Mr. de Manning?"

"No!" Still breathing hard, she sought Michael's gaze again. "Only after they came for me. It was self-defense, I swear it!"

"So you interposed yourself between them and the boy, as a shield?"

"No, they came for *me*! They tried to drag *me* from the carriage!" Her eyes filled with tears. "I stabbed them over and over with the scissors until they left me and—and—they took the young master. I should have sacrificed myself. I have failed my lady!" She dropped her face in her hands and sobbed.

Hair stood up all over Michael's neck. The truth of events in the carriage slammed through him and righted pieces of the puzzle in his head. While Dorinda gave vent to her misery, he sidled to Spry, by then standing a few feet away at the end of the couch. He muttered, "Ye gods, Spry."

"Ye gods have naught to do with this, sir," Spry whispered. "'Twas all ye Merry Men muddling their mission."

"A mission befouled by embroidery scissors in the hand of a maid. Those Merry Men are damned fine recruitment material for the Continental Army and Governor Nash."

Spry grunted. "Cream of the crop. Robin Hood must still be incensed over their error, sir."

Michael rubbed his hands, his gaze on Dorinda, who'd raised her head and was sniffling. "I think you and I can connect the pieces from this point onward, but I still want to hear it from her."

Dorinda eyed Michael, scuttled away a few inches when he approached, and sniffled some more. "Are you going to arrest me for assault?"

Michael laughed. "Oh, goodness, no Dorinda. I wish you might have had at those rascals with a fixed bayonet, poked a few more holes in them." She drew back further, her expression a wobble of mistrust and hope. He pulled a chair over and sat facing her, almost in the fireplace because he didn't want to crowd her. "What Spry and I need from you now is your history with Harley Travis."

She groaned. "Oh, so it *is* him." Her expression screwed up as if she'd swallowed sour milk.

"Yes. And seven or eight years ago, I believe he sought your hand in marriage? Tell us."

She dragged the side of her forefinger beneath her reddened nose and sniffed one more time. "Mr. Travis apprenticed to my father, a maker of fine carriages and coaches in Yorkshire. He came to my father's employ from a wainwright in southern Yorkshire, in a little village called Loxley."

Loxley. Michael wiggled his eyebrows at his assistant and stifled a gloat when Spry conceded the point with sagged shoulders and a shaken head. His attention back on Dorinda, Michael said, "I'm familiar with Loxley. Continue."

"He first took note of me when I was in my fifteenth year. All was quite proper at that point. He sent me a poem he'd written. It was excellent poetry about sparrows in the springtime. I showed it to my father and mother and sisters. They were well pleased. You see, I've three elder sisters, and I've no dowry. Mr. Travis assured my father that he was unconcerned with a dowry. So my father approved the courtship, but he insisted that the marriage wait until I was eighteen."

Michael sat back. Three years was a long bit of waiting for a lunatic who fancied himself a legend. "How did this courtship degenerate?"

"Mr. Travis continued to send me poetry, but he gradually altered the topic. Instead of writing about the beauty in nature, he wrote about the cruelty in man, and the wrath of God, and man's need to be controlled, to have choice stripped away, to be ruled. Mr. Travis became God's anointed lord of all earth, and I became his lady, and together we would build an empire."

Spry coughed in a polite way, but even without looking at him, Michael knew that his assistant's opinion of Harley Travis had plummeted about three hundred feet. "Let me guess, Dorinda. Mr. Travis wanted you to run away with him to the greenwood."

She blinked at him, lips parted. "How did you know? Oh, yes, I see. Loxley and Robin Hood. He wrote me poems about that, too."

"Of course he did. And when did your father brake this runaway wain of delusion and superciliousness?"

"Early in my sixteenth year. Mr. Travis had begun following me everywhere, sneaking me more poetry." She shivered. "Father arranged to have me placed in Ridleygate Hall as Lady Faisleigh's maid. Then he terminated both the betrothal and Mr. Travis's employment."

"Ooh." Spry spoke the word soft and clipped, as if he'd tightened stomach muscles to withstand a blow.

"But he also arranged for Mr. Travis's employment in America and purchased his passage here."

That was convenient. Michael wondered what legacy Britain was bequeathing upon America, foisting off all her religious fanatics, lunatics, and a goodly number of thieves, rapists, and murderers upon the land for so many decades. Naturally, the Crown had little way of tracking those miscreants after they landed upon American soil or learning how many ended up serving beneath General Washington. Or pretending to serve beneath him.

Michael studied her, frowning. "Before this incident, did you know where Mr. Travis went in America?"

"No."

"How much money is Lady Faisleigh carrying with her right now?"

Dorinda held his gaze, her eyebrows drifting downward. "Money? Why, I don't know, sir."

"She confides in you."

Dorinda blinked. "Yes, about some things." She shook her head. "Never about her finances."

It looked as though Travis had indeed, by sheer accident, hit upon the exact amount of money that Lydia had brought, assisted by desperate guesswork from her son. "Mr. Travis's former business partner here in Wilmington informed me that even after he moved here, he bragged of enlisting the aid of friends and family members to keep him abreast of your activities."

Dorinda sighed and hung her head. "They seemed to be everywhere I went, always smiling at me."

Unpleasant, at best. Travis, his friends, and his family clearly had too much time on their hands. "Spry and I believe that Mr. Travis sent his men to abduct *you* on Friday. They grabbed Lord Wynndon because you fought them off with such ferocity. Do you agree?" Her head bobbed in affirmation. "Then how did Mr. Travis know to expect you on the road?"

"I don't know."

"You told someone your itinerary."

"Back home, I-I was so tired of seeing them everywhere. Two weeks before Lady Faisleigh left Yorkshire, I told them I was sailing across the Atlantic and would never be back."

Michael squinted at her. "You told them you were coming to Wilmington, North Carolina?"

She lifted her head and studied him, exhaustion hollowing her eyes. "I said East Florida. Such is hardly an itinerary."

Spry cleared his throat. "Sir, there are but a finite number of ports in the colonies where passengers of nobility might care to disembark. There's only the one main highway down the coast. And it isn't difficult to learn where Lord Faisleigh has estates in America."

"Your man is correct." Dorinda gestured to Spry. "Lord Faisleigh's estates are in Charles Town, South Carolina and St. Augustine, East Florida."

Spry said, "Sir, you mentioned that Lady Faisleigh disembarked in Boston and attempted to book passage to a port farther south before she was forced to rent her conveyance and travel on the King's Highway. A blackguard who wished to intercept her on the New Berne Road could, in theory, estimate the time period when she might be due in the area—"

"And lie in wait to ambush her?" Michael pushed to his feet and faced his assistant. "You're suggesting a great deal of coincidence operating in Mr. Travis's favor."

"Yes, sir, but we don't know the range of Mr. Travis's contacts within the colonies, with whom he might have communicated to bolster his information and help coordinate and fund his efforts."

John Wynndon, perhaps? That would put another piece of the puzzle in place. If John had instigated the plot, it must have been because he'd intended Lord Wynndon's abduction, giving the Merry Men *two* targets in the carriage Friday afternoon.

"But it looks to me as though his patience and contacts paid off." Spry glanced to Dorinda, then back to his commander. "Or almost did. Bad luck, alas, for Lord Wynndon."

Michael grabbed the chair and returned it to the side of the fireplace nearest Spry. Then he spent half a minute digesting and melding Dorinda's story and Spry's theory, his gaze flying back and forth between them. *Perhaps Dorinda's a damsel to be rescued,* Felicia had said. That was when Michael realized that Travis's string of luck and almost-luck in the past few days no longer mattered. The Fates had handed him what he'd asked for minutes earlier.

"Spry!" Michael swung his grin between Dorinda and the private. "I insisted earlier that Robin Hood has weaknesses. Well, we have one of his weaknesses right here in the room with us." He extended an arm for Dorinda. "We have Maid Marian."

Dorinda's nose crinkled, and she shook her head. Spry took a step forward, his expression tight. "Sir, you mustn't bait a trap for him with her. It's a move that only the dastardly Sheriff of Nott—er, the most wicked and depraved of blackguards would scheme."

"Like our friend Mr. Fairfax," Michael said, low, remembering Helen Chiswell's testimony.

Spry nodded once and held his gaze, unflinching. "Sir, you cannot allow her to fall into Mr. Travis's hands."

Michael held up his forefinger. "You and I are in complete agreement. Dorinda must be kept away from Mr. Travis at all costs." He closed a balled fist into the palm of his other hand. "In fact, we've been amazingly fortunate thus far in that he hasn't attempted to storm Castle Wilmington with his army in search of the damsel." He rubbed his chin a moment and swaggered out another grin. "We must prevent him from rescuing her. What do you think—an armed guard of a half-dozen men of the Eighty-Second on the premises at all times?"

An easy smile spread over Spry's face, and the clench of his shoulders softened. "Sir. Yes, sir. Shall I select the men for the shifts?"

"Immediately." Michael snorted. "Bait a trap—bah. I'm juggling far too many balls to add one more. I wager that one of those other leads will bear fruit." He faced the maid and smiled. "And I wager that if we gave Dorinda a moment to think about it, she could remember something about Mr. Travis that would aid us in apprehending him."

She stood. "Of course, Mr. Stoddard. But I don't understand what you have planned for me."

"My dear, you're under house arrest. I must insist that you remain inside and cooperate with the soldiers who will arrive in a little while and act as your guards."

Her mouth made a little "o." "Er, perhaps this is a jest for Fools' Holy Day?"

"It's Fools' Holy Day, yes, but you're still under house arrest. It's only until we apprehend Mr. Travis and secure him in the pen or jail."

"Oh. I see." She lifted her chin. "Thank you." She rolled her gaze away for a second or two. "At least it seems I should be thanking you. But all the same, I believe I shall keep my embroidery scissors close at hand for the next day or so."

***

In Michael's brief interview of Felicia immediately afterward, the house-maid corroborated enough of Dorinda's story to clear both maids of disreputable dealings with Travis. Michael had no desire to reveal Dorinda's role in the affair to Lydia. Doing so would almost certainly bring wrath, unwarranted, upon the lady's maid, and Lydia would insist that they trade Dorinda for her son. So he spun twaddle for Lydia and de Manning about the potential for Travis to attempt Lydia's abduction next. De Manning, who hadn't removed his hanger from their meeting at the clearing, swallowed the story like a large-mouthed bass gulping a worm, eager to contribute his martial prowess to Lydia's defense.

Michael made Lydia promise to remain inside the house with Dorinda and Felicia and cooperate with the men who'd soon arrive from the Eighty-Second to guard them. Lydia appeared delighted at the prospect of being guarded, escorted around Wilmington the next day by soldiers for her meetings with financiers.

At the barracks, he circulated a description of Travis's carriage among the men and produced bulletins with the description, which he ordered posted about town. Travis must find it difficult to conceal a coach of that size in the countryside.

Spry selected three shifts of men for guard detail, most from among those who had participated in surveillance the previous day. As he was completing the assignments, the two teams of scouts that Michael had sent out returned footsore and thirsty, but successful at having located all four of the structures on the map. The soldiers had spotted no one around any of the structures, but in the one farthest out from Wilmington, a storage shed, they discovered Lord Wynndon's hat and dark blue velvet coat, a blanket, and a small cask of water.

They had followed Michael's instructions. Left all of it behind. The men and boys who imprisoned Lord Wynndon would be none the wiser.

Bless Kate Duncan and her brother for identifying viable leads on Gibson's map.

Kate.

Michael's concentration rifted. He dragged it back from Front Street at two thirty in the morning, Kate embraceable and yielding and so close that he fancied he'd felt the warmth of her breath on his skin. Then he squared his shoulders and reassigned a smaller group of men from within the two patrols to a search of the remaining four circles on Gibson's map, riding out Monday morning at nine.

Before he and Spry left the barracks for Mrs. Chiswell's house, Michael ran into Major Craig's adjutant. In late January, when Craig had assigned Michael as his lead investigator, the major had specified that he wanted Michael more accessible to the civilians of Wilmington than quarters in the barracks would allow. Hence the housing arrangement on Second Street. But that was about to expire, so Michael requested a new billeting arrangement for himself and Spry.

After he and his assistant left the barracks, Spry settled into another un-characteristic silence. The two men walked through half a block of late-afternoon shadows on streets that were mostly empty of pedestrians and vehicles before Michael said to him, "A penny for your thoughts."

Again the private flicked his gaze the length of him. "You may not consider my thoughts worth a penny, sir."

"To the contrary, you've been mulling over something since our encounter with Robin Hood and his Merry Men this afternoon. Your thoughts are probably worth at least a guinea by now. Out with it."

"Permission to speak frankly, sir." Spry stared straight ahead.

That sounded grim. Michael twisted his torso to regard his assistant. "Permission granted. God's teeth, Spry, what in the world—"

"My observation, sir." Spry kept his voice low. "Lord Wynndon doesn't look much like Mr. de Manning. He looks like *you*. Sir."

Michael unwound his torso and also stared straight ahead. Beneath the soles of their boots, crushed shells in the dirt street popped and cracked like musket fire on a battlefield. Silence as stiff as a wall of hardened clay assembled between the two men. Several slow breaths filled Michael's lungs. "You will not repeat that observation to anyone."

"Sir."

In his peripheral vision, Spry's rigid posture told him that the private would carry the secret to his grave. Tension loosened in Michael's chest. "Despite daily enthusiasm for the game of begetting offspring, Lord Faisleigh apparently lacks one critical element for success. Thus he and Lady Faisleigh crafted a sort of compromise common among the nobility."

Receptive silence from Spry unraveled more tension in Michael's chest. He'd never told the story to anyone before and was surprised at what a weight he'd carried in his years of silence. "Late one afternoon, I looked up in the doorway of the mews. There she was, wearing only her shift. Half out of her shift, to be more accurate. And I'd just spread fresh straw."

That time, Spry's cough didn't sound much like a cough. And his expression looked the way it had the previous day, when he'd found the straw dummies in the abandoned tannery.

Michael pursed his lips. "It appears that you find the story amusing."

"No, sir. I find it amazing. You at sixteen years of age, a commoner, and she a baroness. Whew." Spry sobered, released a sigh. "How that must have cut you to see the boy tortured, in the hands of Travis this afternoon."

"I didn't know that my contribution in the straw had mattered until that moment I saw him." Michael heard his own voice go hollow. "He has my father's eyes."

They turned onto Second Street. Spry said, "After we rescue him, sir, you must go your separate ways."

"It matters not. I wouldn't know what to do with a sudden son. Nigel de Manning is his father. Lord Wynndon mustn't lose his father. It's too much like being orphaned." Michael swallowed at a hitch that had torqued his throat on his last two remarks, aware of Spry's scrutiny.

Their conversation at a lull, they continued to Mrs. Chiswell's house, where they washed away some of the travel grime around back. In the gathering dusk, on their way between the kitchen and the house, Spry said softly, "When did you lose your father, sir?"

Even more tension drained from Michael. He paused to scrape his boots on the back step, and his stance brought his eyes level with those of his assistant. "December. I received word a few days ago."

"Bloody slow, the post. My condolences, sir."

Michael nodded, continued to hold Spry's gaze, and waited, his own silent query hanging in the air. His assistant had told him precious little about his life in Nova Scotia, before he'd joined the Army.

"I lost mine when I was seventeen," Spry whispered. "Fishing accident. Like being orphaned, yes, sir."

There was far more to it than a fishing accident, Michael could be certain. His assistant didn't lie very well. And had Spry been orphaned? "So what did you say were your options? Soldiering or juggling, I believe?"

Spry grinned. "Sir. You remembered. Join the Army, or take up juggling and become a Fool."

"You haven't told me your third option, the course you abandoned to join the Army."

Humor drained from Spry's face. He steeled his face muscles, tried to make his expression blank. But the eye twitch betrayed him.

Fishing accident. Michael rocked back on one heel and cocked a fist on his hip. "You aren't the only fellow who's taken the King's shilling at a run, Spry. Before your beasts catch up with you, wouldn't you rather that I hear about them from you?" Spry lowered his gaze, rolled his lips inward, and gnawed his lower lip. "Your choice, lad. Remember. I've looked the other way for a woman who tried to kill a fellow officer and a brother and sister who smuggled whiskey."

The back door groaned open, and Michael hopped off the step to clear the exit. "Whiskey?" Enid poked her head out. "Thought I heard you out here. Been helping Mrs. Chiswell pack books this afternoon, so I'm afraid it'll be cold leftover beef for supper tonight."

Spry perked up. "Enid, a supper of cold leftover beef from your kitchen is better than ambrosia from the gods."

Enid's jaw dropped. Then her cheeks rosied, and she tidied her mobcap. "Well."

"What Spry means, Enid, is that he and I are grateful for all the meals you've prepared for us."

The Welshwoman cleared her throat. "Well. Well. Er, that's—that's kind of you to say, Mr. Stoddard. Sweet, even." Enid blinked away a glimmer in her eyes. "Now, before I embarrass myself, step inside, won't you? I shall give you the note you received while you were out this afternoon and fetch your supper."

A note to Michael received that afternoon was probably something Spry should read, too. Michael signaled his assistant with a nod of his head. "Come along."

Chapter Twenty-Five

ENID POURED MICHAEL a glass of wine in the dining room, then fetched a sealed note from Mrs. Chiswell's study. After a sip of his wine, Michael popped the seal open on the note, and his eyes bugged at the correspondent: Mrs. William Hooper. He waited until the housekeeper left for the kitchen to smooth the note open on the surface of the table for the two men to read:

> At my Home early this morning, the Child of a certain Widow arrived and asked me to convey to you Confirmation that the Person whom you seek was indeed present for six Hours Saturday Night inside the building eight Miles distant from Wilmington. In exchange for this Information, the Widow humbly petitions you for return of the Property of her eldest Child.

Neither soldier spoke for a few seconds. Michael expelled a breath. "Bless Eve Whistler."

"Indeed, sir. So that's where her younger son was headed before dawn this morning." Spry frowned. "But our men performing surveillance didn't see Lord Wynndon arrive or leave."

"Our men cannot see what transpires on the north side of the house, or traffic approaching from the north." Spry nodded. "The widow must know her older boy is dead. Not that I believe the Psalter will be of much comfort to her now, but I shall honor our pact and make certain that she receives it."

"Brave woman. She's taken quite a chance, contacting you."

"And now we know where to locate Lord Wynndon during tavern business hours. If our men don't find the boy on the morrow at one of those remaining sites marked on Gibson's map, a raid on the Rouse house is in order for Monday night.

"And during such a raid, the odds have increased that we shall also encounter William Jones or James Love. I've no longer the leisure to wait for both to be present. Whoever is there will be arrested. After we've rescued the boy and imprisoned Travis, we shall redouble our efforts on Jones and Love."

"Yes, sir. Monday night. But not tonight?"

"Tavern's closed tonight. Travis is cocksure, believes the Fates have graced him in his kingdom to the northeast, so much so that he let his guard down Friday and Saturday night—possibly entrusting others to keep an eye on Lord Wynndon while he snatched a few hours of badly needed rest. He wants to be present for Dorinda's delivery of the ransom early Tuesday morning, as his Merry Men have already bungled the operation of abducting her once. Monday night, he may again rely upon others at Rouse's Tavern to guard his hostage while he grabs a few hours' sleep."

Spry frowned. "How do you know for certain that Travis will do all that?"

"I don't. It's an instinct."

"Suppose we do find the boy at Rouse's. Where will we find Travis?"

Michael's gaze slid from his assistant to Anne Hooper's note. "Somewhere nearby."

"His repose guarded by Merry Men?" Spry sniggered. "The loft in the barn behind the tavern."

"That's a good guess, Spry. I doubt Mrs. Whistler will allow him to share her bed."

Both men laughed at the thought. Enid returned with a plate bearing a two-inch-thick pile of sliced, cooked beef wedged between hefty slabs of bread, accompanied by pickled cucumbers and pears. Michael pocketed Anne Hooper's note.

Enid thumped his plate to the table with a grin for Spry. "And yours is waiting in the kitchen."

Michael dismissed his assistant and reached for his chair. Spry bounded from the dining room with a chuckling Enid following. Michael set to his meal.

It wasn't enough. He was famished, and Enid had outdone herself, slathered the beef with a divine mustard sauce. The rate at which he gobbled the meal far outpaced his stomach's ability to register satisfaction. When Enid hadn't returned with a second helping, he pushed up from the table and went in search of more.

At the entrance of the dining room, he almost collided with Helen Chiswell, *en route* for the back door. They fumbled their pardons. His gaze dropped to a wrapped package about a foot square and three inches deep, tucked beneath her left arm. She turned toward the door and resumed walking. Odd. Had that been a flash of panic in her eyes?

Before he'd taken a third step in pursuit, the back door opened to admit Enid, another full plate on her tray. Mrs. Chiswell slipped out the opened door into the dusk, and Enid bore down on Michael, beaming. "Sorry to keep you waiting, sir. Had to get that man of yours settled with a third portion. Otherwise I'd have brought you this earlier. Where'd you two run off to today, that you made Spry so ravenous?"

The aromas of beef, fresh bread, and mustard sauce wafted past Michael. He regarded the back door, drawn closed behind Mrs. Chiswell's exit. He considered the full plate Enid placed on the table.

"And you're hungry, too, sir. The King's men oughtn't to be traipsing around with empty bellies. Have a seat."

Michael's stomach growled. He returned to the table.

The housekeeper scooped up his empty plate. "Got pieces of leftover tart for you and Spry each. You sit there and enjoy your meal. I shall bring dessert in, straight away."

Michael made a good show of wolfing his second portion: not a difficult act because he was still hungry. Enid left after his second bite. He listened for the back door, took one more bite when he heard the door close, then pushed away.

The hinges on the front door had been greased the previous week, contributing stealth to his exit. After swallowing the mouthful, he circled back through the side yard. Instinct pestered him. What was Helen Chiswell about?

He peered around the rear corner of the house. Framed in the kitchen window, Enid laughed and conversed with Spry, who sat at the small table in the kitchen. Alongside a little stone path in the garden area of the back yard, shielded by the trunk and spring-bare branches of a fruit tree, Helen Chiswell sat on a wooden bench with a man. In the gathering dusk, Michael couldn't distinguish his features, but he watched her pass him the package. The man opened one end to inspect the contents. He withdrew a piece of paper partway and bent his head closer.

Michael brushed breadcrumbs off his mouth and strode for the couple. Within a few feet of leaving cover of the house, his view cleared. He saw the man's dark hair, his lanky frame angled toward Mrs. Chiswell bespeaking a long acquaintance between them. And that disarming, easy smile—all for the lady that moment, but deployed with winning results at card tables from Philadelphia to St. Augustine.

So immersed was David St. James in his companion that he didn't spot Michael until Michael scuffed dirt ten feet from them. They both started. Mrs. Chiswell gasped. St. James bolted to his feet, his right arm pinning the package to his torso.

Was something amiss here? Michael smiled. "How nice to see you again, Mr. St. James."

"Likewise, Mr. Stoddard." St. James, still clutching the package, bowed.

Michael's gaze swept over the other man, took in the well-tailored wool suit, linen shirt, and silver buckles on the shoes. All expected for David St. James's appearance. What was new was the way those fine clothes hung on his frame, and the bags under his eyes. Not all was well in his world. Such was the lot of neutrals. Especially a neutral whose father had printed seditious material on his press and was thus wanted almost as badly as the signers of the Declaration of Independence. Michael extended his right hand. "How have you been?"

He noted the way St. James stopped himself from shuffling the package, twisting instead to hand it to Mrs. Chiswell, her posture and expression as wooden as the bench. Then he unwound to face Michael again, grace him with a grin that said he'd just won at piquet. He shook his hand briefly. "As well as can be expected. And yourself?"

"Enid's been feeding me."

"Why, you lucky fellow! Yes, I can see that. You look the very picture of health."

"She's been feeding my assistant, too. And that reminds me. Wait right there. I want to introduce you two."

As Michael pivoted, he heard a small cough of exasperation from St. James, but he didn't wait for a protest. Within seconds, he crossed the yard to yank open the kitchen door, all the while keeping St. James and Mrs. Chiswell in his peripheral vision. "Spry!" His assistant jerked his head up from savoring a mouthful of fruit pie, and he set down his fork to regard Michael. "Step out here. I've someone for you to meet."

Enid, over by the fireplace, kept her expression dispassionate. Spry wiped his mouth on a napkin, scooted back his chair, and scuffed from the kitchen after Michael.

Hands at his sides, St. James awaited them at the bench. Mrs. Chiswell sat in position much as Michael had left her, except that she'd placed the package on the bench beside her. When Spry had assumed a stance beside his commander, Michael said, "Mr. St. James, this is my assistant, Spry. Spry, Mr. David St. James." The two nodded to each other, sizing each other up. "So, sir, what brings you to Wilmington?"

St. James glanced to Mrs. Chiswell, then studied the ground. "I came to say farewell to Helen. You know she's leaving Wilmington."

David St. James was an accomplished actor, even though that wasn't his profession. From his slumped shoulders and what Michael knew of his history with Mrs. Chiswell, he realized that St. James had spoken at least the partial truth. But instinct still nagged him. His gaze homed on the package. "What's in that package?"

The other man swallowed. "Mementoes." His voice tightened. "Please don't question me further about it."

"Very well. Hand me the package, madam."

She jutted her chin. "It contains letters, Mr. Stoddard. David's *personal* letters to me."

Michael gauged the thickness of the package. "That's certainly a good number of personal letters."

She sat forward on the bench, her gaze pinned to Michael. "More than a decade of letters."

He extended his hand. Rather than giving him the entire package, she sighed, plucked several sheets of paper from it, seemingly at random, and presented them to him. Then she rose and faced the house, her back to the three men, the package left behind on the bench.

Enough daylight remained for Michael to read the masculine script on the top page: *In the shelter of your arms, I am restored, refreshed...* Michael slid that paper beneath the others and found more of the same script on a different letter: *Shall we make an entire morning of it, then? I shall tease your breasts with my tongue and...* Heat rushed up Michael's neck, and he shuffled paper again to spot phrases promising far more of Eros. With a quick step forward, he dropped the papers atop the package.

St. James was staring through the kitchen building, past the Morris's yard, past Brunswick, out to sea. "I was a fool, Mr. Stoddard. I waited too long. Take my advice. If you love a lady, don't wait to ask for her hand in marriage."

Mrs. Chiswell's back was still turned to the men. His insides squirming, Michael backed off to stand next to Spry, who looked at least as uncomfortable as he felt.

St. James bent over and shoved the love letters back in the package. With it tucked beneath his arm, he straightened, then rotated his head to Mrs. Chiswell. His voice grew harsh edges. "Did you tell Mr. Stoddard everything?"

"Yes. In my study. Yesterday morning."

St. James faced Michael full on. Tension cut lines into his handsome face, deepened the haggardness of it. "Then *you* know what happened to Helen in January, near the Battle of the Cowpens. You must make certain she gets out of Wilmington safely."

"I will do so, sir, to the best of my ability."

"Good. Thank you." The gray-eyed stare of David St. James flicked to Spry, then returned to imprison Michael.

St. James had more to say to him. Alone. "Spry, escort the lady back inside the house."

"Sir." His assistant moved to Mrs. Chiswell's side, the whisper of dried grass beneath his shoes. "Madam?"

From the corner of Michael's eye, he saw them walk away. The back door squeaked open. Spry and Mrs. Chiswell disappeared inside. The door closed.

St. James spoke in just above a whisper. "Word is that Lord Cornwallis's army is headed this way. Lieutenant Fairfax rides in that army." He exhaled a deep breath. "Kill him."

So St. James was singing the same song as his former mistress. Michael crossed his arms over his chest, the action sending his torso back a few inches from the other man. "Word is that Fairfax was either killed or seriously wounded in the battle two weeks ago. And Mr. St. James, your request is out of line."

"You're absolutely correct on that. He's your fellow officer. Of course you won't consent to overt involvement in such a scheme. But Mr. Stoddard, you and I both know that unless he occupies a patch of ground six feet underfoot, he'll continue his machinations and barbarity.

"You've known what he is since Captain Sheffield forced you to cover up his murder of the Spaniard in Alton last summer. Helen told me what you tried to accomplish last December in the backcountry of South Carolina. You want him dead, too. You need a team to help you with the dirty end of the job. So seek out my brother-in-law, Mathias Hale."

Mathias Hale? Michael's memory sputtered details. Blacksmith from Alton, Georgia. Half-Creek Indian. He was St. James's brother in law? More memory plus deduction filled in the gaps. Hale must have married St. James's widowed sister, Sophie Barton, after that escapade in Havana last summer. Both of them were still on the run from redcoats somewhere in the western Carolinas. Under such circumstances, how did St. James expect him to contact Hale? This was ludicrous.

Fortunately protocol again provided Michael with an avenue clear of implicating himself in the morass of plots to murder a fellow officer. "As you've retrieved your old love letters, I think it's time for you to leave, sir."

Tension on St. James's face dissolved, left him with lips upturned in a happy-go-lucky countenance. He roved his gaze over Michael. "I admire you, Mr. Stoddard. You've discretion, perseverance, scruples, and valor. With those qualities in your favor, you'll accomplish whatever you set out to do." He bowed. "Good chatting with you again, sir. And good fortune to you." The package beneath his arm, he sallied for the front yard.

Michael watched him until the gloom of oncoming night embraced him. At a brief, plaintive sound behind him, he lowered his arms to his sides and faced the kitchen. In the doorway, Enid dabbed her handkerchief beneath one eye and sniffed. "He's a good man, Mr. David is. Always treated my mistress well." She bowed her head and vanished into the kitchen.

Michael had no cause to question St. James's character. Yet despite his "goodness," he'd handed the prize of winning Mrs. Chiswell's heart to Jonathan Quill. Michael pondered what he'd said, part-testimonial, part-counsel: *Take my advice. If you love a lady, don't wait to ask for her hand in marriage.*

He'd pronounced himself immune to love. But did he love Kate Duncan? The hunger grinding away behind his ribs, the desperate catch to his breath, the sadness beneath his eyelids—was that love? Heaven help him if it was.

***

He closed Spry and himself into the dusk of the parlor—Enid had not yet lit candles or drawn the curtains for the night—and glanced out at the darkening street. "Your impressions of David St. James." He leaned against the sill to study his assistant's face.

"Heartsick, sir. And nervous. Why he didn't bolt like a rabbit when you fetched me I'll never know. Surely he knew that we could have imprisoned him, tried to torture the location of his father from him."

"Perhaps."

Spry shook his head. "I hope I never ruin a relationship with a woman as Mr. St. James has done. But how's a man to know, eh? It's a mystery what women think. Seldom do they tell us until it's too late."

Michael snorted at the sense of Spry's words. "Well, we can add Mr. St. James to the list of people who want Fairfax dead. He offered assistance to me of one Mathias Hale, his brother-in-law, a half-breed Creek Indian from Georgia. The catch is that Mr. Hale is now hiding from every redcoat in North America in the backcountry of the Carolinas."

Spry laughed, short. "Those Indians do have a score to settle with Mr. Fairfax. But this begins to resemble one of those myths, sir, wherein the gods give the hero the impossible task, like separating out several kinds of grains from a large pile in the dark."

Motion outside caught Michael's eye: one of the camp boys about ten years old trotting up the walkway to the front door. "Hah. Here comes a messenger." He detached himself from the windowsill, his walk for the parlor doors brisk.

He opened the front door as the lad was preparing to knock with a raised fist. "Oh, Mr. Stoddard, sir. Someone directed me to bring you this message." He pulled a sealed note from his haversack and handed it to Michael.

Michael's gaze bounded above the boy's head to Ames, Lydia's head coachman, that very moment exiting the street and striding up the walkway. "Thank you, lad." Michael shoved the note into his waistcoat. The boy turned about and jogged past Ames for the street.

"Evening, Mr. Stoddard." The coachman hopped onto the step and touched the brim of his hat.

"Evening, Ames. Is all well at the house? Lady Faisleigh comfortable, soldiers at their posts, and so forth?"

"Yes, sir." Ames extracted what looked like a multi-page, sealed letter from his waistcoat. "My lady bade me deliver this to you."

Annoyance pricked Michael at the letter's thickness: at least three pages, from the feel of it. And from the smell of it. She must have drenched every page in perfume. The bad thing about cooping Lydia up in that house was that it gave her imagination too much free time. He looked from the letter to Ames. "Did she direct you to wait on a response?"

"Oh, no, sir. In fact, she said specifically that she knew you wouldn't want to respond immediately, that you'd want to read it several times."

Michael recalled the eroticism in David St. James's letters. Heat encased his ears, and he found himself thankful for the descent of night. "Well, then, thank you, Ames. Good night."

The coachman bowed. "Good night, Mr. Stoddard. Rest well."

Michael shut the door and, with a sigh, held Lydia's perfumed missive out from him. Spry, who'd stood beyond Ames's sight to the left of the door, said, "If you'll wait in the parlor, sir, I won't be but a moment fetching us a light from the kitchen."

He strode for the back door. Michael, remembering his unfinished supper, slipped into the dining room, gobbled the rest of the beef, and belted down the half glass of wine remaining. Enid's promise of pie hadn't yet materialized. He hoped she'd reserved some for him in the kitchen.

Spry met him in the parlor with a lit taper, touched it to the wicks of three candles on the mantle, and placed the taper there also, in a holder. Standing before the unlit fireplace, Michael broke the seal on Lydia's letter, opened it, and recognized from the outset that it wasn't a letter. It was a contract.

A contract to provide one rank advancement in exchange for one impregnation.

"God's teeth," he muttered.

"Bad news, sir?"

Michael's gaze skimmed over explicit detail for duration and frequency of coupling, and positions and devices to employ in assisting the process. Her intent was transparent: the sanctioning of a feral affair. The Huntress and the Falcon Boy, Part Two. He visualized the painting it would inspire and grimaced. "God's foot."

"Better let me have a look, sir."

From the flush tingling his scalp, Michael knew his face must be redder than berries on a holly bush. He clutched the contract to him with what he was sure was the wild-eyed ferocity of a street-hardened mongrel. To be sure, he'd have to hide the thing upstairs until he could read it thoroughly. Then he just might burn it. "You don't need to read this. You can smell it at ten paces."

"Yes, sir." Spry's mouth reprised the compressed, squirmy look of stifled humor.

Michael folded the contract and, not wishing to infuse his clothing with Lydia's scent, dropped it on the couch with a glare that told Spry he'd bite his hand off if he dared touch it. Then he withdrew the other note from his waist-coat, loosened the seal, and opened the single paper, scrawled with a brazen, masculine hand that registered as familiar with a shock:

> *Stoddard, such insult you deliver me. Abduction, highway Robbery, unlawful Imprisonment, and Extortion? Being a Man of God, I've never sullied my Hand with such Practices. However, I've an excellent Idea who's at fault here. Shall we race to find him and dispense Justice, then? And the Victor is awarded Possession of that fascinating Prize he's been keeping from you!*

The signature froze the fire in Michael's scalp. "God's arse." Ice sluiced his neck and shoulders. He passed the note to Spry.

His assistant's gaze darted over the message. He let out a deep breath. "God's arse, indeed, sir. Leave it to the Reverend Paul Greene to make his appearance now and upend the stage."

Chapter Twenty-Six

SPRY STRAIGHTENED HIS shoulders and braced his feet apart. "Orders, sir."

Michael retrieved Greene's letter and reread it. Then he folded it and pounded back the doubts that turned his gut queasy. "We shall trust in the groundwork we've laid thus far. Tonight we sleep."

Spry frowned. "Sir?"

The only way Michael would have unwavering support from Spry was to show him why he believed they stood on firm ground. "Greene may entertain good guesses of where to find Travis, but he doesn't know for sure. He also believes he's surprised me with his peek-a-boo announcement that he isn't the culprit, that the surprise generated by the announcement has given him an advantage."

"Sir, surely this very moment he has assembled his rogues, and they're planning their attack."

"Planning where they'll *begin* their search, yes." Michael tapped a corner of Greene's note on his cheek a few times. "But unlike Travis, Greene's no fool. He won't start searching until he has daylight. We've already been searching. It's borne fruit. We know where else to search. And we've a very good idea where to find both Lord Wynndon and Travis Monday night."

He collected Lydia's contract, slid it beneath Greene's letter in his left hand, and again faced Spry's dubiousness. "In February, near Hillsborough, we fought together in a savage skirmish. We could easily have been among the men who died. Afterward, we limped ten miles back to town, where we learned that a villain was within our grasp. What were my orders?"

The hitch in Spry's shoulders dissolved. "Sleep that night. Capture him early on the morrow." Spry smiled. "Sir."

"Last night, you and I had perhaps three hours' sleep. I've driven men of the Eighty-Second hard these past few days. Do you feel up to a night march, and thrashing the brush in the dark?"

"No, sir."

"Good. I assure you that Greene and I share the sentiment. As I said, he's no fool." At least, Michael hoped he knew Greene well enough to predict how he'd proceed. Michael clapped his assistant's shoulder, then released it. "Get your rest. The morrow will come soon enough."

***

He slept like the shale and grit stone that slumbered deep beneath peat-brown soil in Pateley Bridge, awakening clear-headed just after five Monday morning the second of April, in good time to write his mother, sister, and uncle, question them about Ewan MacKenzie. With luck, he'd hear from at least one of them by late June or early July.

Before breakfast, he and Spry walked to the barracks, where he advised his teams of mounted infantrymen that Paul Greene had stepped onto the stage. Then he watched them ride away, their mission to investigate the four remaining sites to the northeast. His orders, should they encounter any from Travis's or Greene's band: engage, apprehend, transport to Wilmington. And bring all evidence back with them. Meanwhile, Spry managed the changing shifts of guards for Dorinda and found two more soldiers to stay with Lydia when she ventured forth to visit financiers later that morning, thus allowing four men to remain at the house guarding the maid.

Sunday's surveillance shifts at the abandoned tannery on Front Street and the Rouse house had yielded no visitor activity. At the tavern, the soldiers had seen only Mrs. Whistler and her children. Michael renewed surveillance at the tavern and pulled in his men watching the tannery—but not before he'd summoned a locksmith to change the padlock there.

Major Craig's dragoon messenger rode up to the barracks and dismounted. With a salute for Michael, Rowe related news that Craig was still several days out from Wilmington, although dragoons were moving closer to town. The news relieved Michael. Maybe he stood a chance of producing that halcyon town image that Craig desired upon his return. At least as halcyon an image as could be fabricated with Cornwallis's hundreds of injured and dying soldiers lying around.

Rowe produced the major's latest message for Michael: *What news of the vermin?* Michael located quill and ink in the barracks and scribbled his response: *Vermin sighted Sat night, same location. Eradicative measures in process.*

After Rowe had been dismissed by Michael, he sniffed at lumpy, beige corn mush over the regiment's kitchen fire outside, turned down the corners of his mouth, and mounted his horse. He rode away gnawing dried meat from his saddlebag. Michael couldn't blame him and reflected that Enid had spoiled Spry and him rotten. Both men headed to Mrs. Chiswell's house.

After partaking of the Welshwoman's breakfast, they walked to the farrier shop on Front Street. The apprentice whom Gibson had sent on the wild goose chase for nails greeted them, then brought them back into the stable area, where his master and the other apprentice had just finished shoeing a mare. Hiram Duke spotted them, flinched out a smile, and rubbed the back of his head.

Michael nodded to him. "I'm glad to see you up and about, Mr. Duke."

"Thank you." After handing over the mare to an apprentice, he motioned the soldiers to follow him into the front of the shop, just as cluttered as Smedes's wainwright shop on the other end of Front Street. The farrier leaned on the counter. "Wish I could take the day off and rest, but there's too much work to be done. The wife says she's never before been grateful for my hard skull as she is now."

"You should feel less pain in a few days." Michael studied him. "Our condolences on the loss of your business partner. We hope you can find someone to replace him soon."

Duke nodded. "Ralph was efficient and thorough, and he knew how to handle horses. Difficult to find that combination in a partner. My shop prospered because of it. Plenty of business coming in. I should have paid more attention."

"Paid more attention to what?"

"His frame of mind. His deeds, especially those of recent weeks." Duke blinked at a beam of sunlight trying to pierce the dingy front window. "I may as well admit it. I'm neutral in this war. I don't take up arms against anyone. I don't spy for anyone. And I don't much care who's in charge as long as I can operate my business." He rotated his gaze to Michael. "I thought Ralph was neutral, too. That's why I went into partnership with him."

"People change. When did Mr. Gibson's political persuasion appear to vary from neutrality, sir?"

"Shortly after you fellows occupied Wilmington. But it wasn't blatant, like the stance of those fellows on the Committee of Safety."

Gibson hadn't fled with the rest of the rebels. Michael braced an arm on the counter near Duke. For a second, his gaze met that of his assistant, who stood near the door. Travis had probably insisted that Gibson remain in Wilmington as his spy. "When was the last time you saw Harley Travis?"

Duke's eyebrow cocked. "Ah. So you know about Ralph's acquaintance with him. Probably the last time I saw Mr. Travis was the third week of January. Frankly, I never liked him. A braggart. Those two started associating a couple years ago. The more Ralph kept his company, the more pessimistic he became. He took to spending Saturday nights at Rouse's Tavern northeast of town with Mr. Travis and his acquaintances. Sandy Rouse lets regular patrons sleep off their drunkenness in the tavern, sometimes out in the barn. Monday mornings, Ralph was usually in a foul humor from all that drinking." Duke rubbed his jaw. "In retrospect, I don't suppose it was a good idea to make a bet with my partner in the cockfights."

"Who do you think would have murdered Mr. Gibson?"

"I don't know."

Although it had probably been Travis, Michael wondered whether he'd ever know for certain. He hoped Travis hadn't forced one of his boy initiates to squeeze the trigger. "Who else from town belonged to Mr. Travis's circle?"

The farrier shook his head. "They're all gone. They left ahead of your arrival."

"Where does Mr. Travis live now?" Duke shrugged. "Is he, perhaps, a tenant of Mr. Rouse's?"

"To my knowledge, sir, Mr. Rouse's only tenants are the Widow Whistler and her children."

Frustrating. Travis had to hang his hat somewhere. Michael described Travis's coach to Duke, hoping that the farrier would have seen it, but he had not. "Also Mr. Duke, the Eighty-Second has been unable to locate any next of kin for Mr. Gibson in the area. What light can you shed on that?"

"I don't think Ralph had kin in the area. There's a brother who lives west of the Haw River. Ralph was betrothed, but two years ago, his dear lady succumbed to malaria. Then her family moved west. Elizabeth invited Ralph to supper with us a few times, but after the first time, he declined. I think it bothered him to see my growing family."

Gibson, alone and bereaved. Ripe for Travis's poisonous camaraderie. Michael raised eyebrows at Spry. His assistant shook his head, confirming his conclusion that the farrier had told them everything that might possibly be of value in the investigation. After conveying their wishes for Duke's continued recovery, Michael and Spry left.

Just after noon, one of the patrols Michael had sent out rode back into town with a bedraggled, filthy boy. They'd encountered him near the site where Lord Wynndon's coat and hat had been found the previous day. In fact, he'd had the coat and hat in his possession when the soldiers intercepted him. They disarmed him of pistol and knife, then hoisted him on horseback before one of the soldiers. The soldiers brought Lord Wynndon's coat and hat with them.

Michael recognized the boy as Travis's footman at their meeting the previous afternoon. To Michael, it seemed obvious that Travis had sent him to recover the articles of clothing for the hostage. Michael considered the odds of successfully tracking the boy's return to Travis. Travis's band knew the land too well, and the general sparseness of foliage would have offered his men too little cover for stealth. Unless Travis's spies spotted the apprehension of the boy, Travis would have to guess at what had happened to his young soldier and the hostage's clothing.

Michael didn't expect his prisoner to talk at first. The boy didn't disappoint him. Michael sent him to the barracks with two soldiers as guards, instructing the men to spend time describing conditions in the pen to their charge.

Mid-afternoon, the final of Michael's patrols returned escorting an unexpected prize: Travis's coach, found in a barn near Collier's Tavern several miles north of the Rouse house, as well as several horses secured in the barn with the coach. On horseback with the patrol, bound in their saddles, were three men of the Reverend Greene's patrol who hadn't escaped a skirmish with the soldiers on the road back to Wilmington. Greene's men weren't talking, either. In the pen they went.

A messenger brought a note from Travis to Michael. It bore instructions for their retrieval of Lord Wynndon Tuesday morning at nine o'clock, dependent upon Dorinda's pre-dawn appearance beneath the mulberry tree with five hundred pounds. By then, Travis would have been certain to hear of the loss of his coach and horses. He'd realize that the boy he'd sent for the clothing had been captured, that his hiding places were compromised.

Would Travis kill Lord Wynndon that afternoon? Michael pondered the effort the would-be Robin Hood had gone through to place himself in the position of demanding money and Dorinda. Michael decided no. Travis's arrogance and greed inflated his expectations, led him to believe he could achieve both goals.

But the tension and uncertainty of Michael's numerous, savage gambles scraped his gut raw all afternoon.

Only one thing he knew for certain as the sun sank in the west. The investigative field that he'd tilled and planted must yield Lord Wynndon within twelve hours, or he'd lose him.

***

The collar of the boy's shirt was torn, gray with grit. Pale specks in his greasy brown hair suggested the activity of lice. From where Michael stood, he studied the way the young prisoner fidgeted, sitting in a chair on the opposite side of the table in the barracks. "What's your name, boy?"

"Sam." Although he didn't look up, the boy yanked his gaze to the right.

The name was false. Michael resolved that it was the last lie the boy would tell him. He shook out Gibson's map and placed it, unfolded, on the table before the boy. In one smooth motion, he slid a lit candle closer. The prisoner eyed the soldiers standing to either side of him, then ricocheted his gaze over all the black circles on the map.

"Travis is holding the prisoner at a location marked by one of those circles. I give you my word that you won't go to the pen tonight if you identify where I'll find the prisoner on that map."

"Might you give me some of that mush, sir? I'm powerfully hungry."

His hands were thin, and his fingers shook, probably a blend of fear and fatigue. Michael braced one hand on the table and leaned toward the boy. "No." When the boy gawped up at him, Michael scowled. "I see there's been a misunderstanding. Private Jenkins claims you offered to help. I don't consider begging for food helping. And I don't have time for your tricks." He straightened.

"Wait! I-I don't think the shed that General Lord Travis uses is marked on this map."

General Lord Travis. God almighty. Michael pounded both fists to the table and loomed over him again. "I've changed my mind about putting you in the pen."

The boy shrieked. "Here!" He pointed to an area that appeared to be about a quarter mile northeast of Rouse's Tavern. "Here! It's a r-rotted shed, and—and sometimes that old woman's d-dog sleeps in it so p-please d-don't p-put me in the p-pen with those m-men please!" Tears streamed tracks through the grime on his face and uncovered a mole on his left cheek.

Michael regarded the soldiers, who smirked at the boy. Yes, indeed, his men had done their duty, communicated well the slow and horrific fate of a twelve-year-old boy thrown in the pen. "Where else will I find Travis and the prisoner, boy?"

"That's a-a-all I know about."

Wretch. Michael again straightened and did his best to look down his nose at the sniveling boy like every haughty, aristocratic British officer who'd crossed his path, including Nigel de Manning. Behind him, the door whistled open, but he didn't turn to see who'd entered the barracks and progressed to a stance a few feet behind him. He'd come to recognize Spry's tread. "We know Travis has been bringing the prisoner to Rouse's Tavern. What time will he bring him there tonight?"

"Before ten o'clock. Sir." The boy hung his head and knuckled his eyes.

"Boy! Look at me!" The boy's head snapped up. He shrank into his shoulders. "You know what I shall do if you're lying."

"But I've told the truth, sir. G-God's truth!" His face and lips lost color, and he trembled.

Michael had a feeling that the boy had spoken truthfully about the rotting shed. And if Travis possessed half a brain, he knew his soldier hadn't withstood interrogation. At the shed that night, Travis might see fit to set a trap for men of the Eighty-Second.

He executed a partial turn to Spry, his eyebrow cocked. In response to the unspoken query, the private handed him one of the area newspapers archived by Major Craig's adjutant and dated from February. He pointed out the fugitive servant and slave section of the advertisements. Michael read about a miller in Brunswick County whose servant boy had run off for the third time. Ted Newcastle was twelve years old and skinny, and he had brown hair and a mole on his left cheek. The miller was willing to pay four pounds for his return plus reasonable charges.

Michael returned the paper to Spry and studied Ted Newcastle, who was picking at the scab of an insect bite on his wrist, his face still downcast. He made his voice crack the air like a cat o' nine tails in a flogging. "Ted!"

The boy's head yanked up in acknowledgement of his true name. Then his gaze unfocused and slithered around, and he slumped his shoulders as he realized he'd revealed himself.

"A miller in the next county will pay us four pounds plus expenses to have you returned."

"Oh, please don't send me back, sir. He makes me work much too hard!"

"Excellent!" Michael whipped the map from beneath Ted Newcastle's gaze and folded it. "Jenkins, find this lad some mush and pork. He mustn't faint from hunger before we can return him to his master. And both of you men make certain you keep an eye on him. He's proficient at running away." He pivoted and, on his way out, muttered to Spry, "Good work, lad."

In the dusk outside the barracks, he recognized Kate Duncan standing away from the in-and-out traffic, her arms crossed, her foot tapping. Any enjoyment he derived from the sight of her was dashed away as soon as she spotted him and rushed forward, her countenance taut, her gaze darting to Spry, who'd followed him out. Her voice was low. "Did you tell him, Spry?"

"No time, Mrs. Duncan. You can tell him."

Michael guided her by the elbow out of the path of soldiers headed for the barracks. "What can I do for you?"

She grabbed fistfuls of her apron. "In early February, you asked me to watch for a specific man who'd been through town before. Well, he's drinking rum at White's this very moment."

Michael studied her face. Immediate memory offered him no record of such a request of her.

Kate raised her hands in exasperation. "You said he was dangerous, an assassin for the rebels." She sucked in a breath. "A big Frenchman with black hair, like a pirate."

Damnation! His eyes bulged with recollection, Michael swung back on Spry. "Claude Devereaux!"

"Yes, that's the name you mentioned!"

Spry's jaw dropped. Michael gripped his shoulder. "Party of six accompanies us, mustered on the double!"

"Sir!"

They ran for the barracks. Inside, Michael signaled the first six men he spotted who were fully dressed, wearing shoes, and not guarding the boy. Muskets and cartridge boxes were snatched up. Spry grabbed a coil of rope. All eight hustled from the barracks. In the lead, Michael clanked past Kate, who had set off back to the tavern. "Thank you, madam!"

On the night of February first, Claude Devereaux had picked up Michael bodily from where he'd been crouched in foliage performing surveillance and heaved him into a clearing so Paul Greene and his men could open fire on him. For years, well before that incident, the French assassin had been accruing reasons to be captured and executed. Surely his appearance that night, as Michael was prepared to venture north and rescue Lord Wynndon, was a harbinger of disaster. No way in hell was Michael letting him roam free.

The eight jogged for Front Street. Everyone they met cleared out of the way, as did three fellows chatting at the post before White's when they realized the destination of the armed party. Spry bounded ahead and pulled the door open. Michael and the men spilled into the tavern and spread out across the entrance. Fiddle music and conversation dwindled off in a collective gasp. Civilians gaped. Several dove beneath tables.

Michael motioned two off-duty soldiers who'd risen back to their benches. "Everyone stay where you are." He swept his gaze over the assembly of people twice. The Frenchman wasn't present in the room. He ordered three men from his patrol to check upstairs and two to look in the downstairs rooms. They rattle-stomped across the common room. Michael and the other two soldiers progressed through more slowly, their gazes combing the crowd.

When they reached the opposite side of the room, they converged with the other five soldiers. No Devereaux.

Aunt Rachel strutted through the back door, leaving it open to the approach of night. She sized up the patrol and lifted her chin to Michael. "What is this about?"

"Madam, have you seen a large, muscular fellow with black hair—"

"Indeed I have. He went that way, past the kitchen at a run." She pointed out the back door. "Not five minutes ago."

"Thank you. Men, let's go!"

They searched buildings on the tavern grounds, neighboring businesses and houses, and the other taverns in Wilmington without finding the Frenchman. Night had fallen by the time Michael called off the search.

He'd no more time to chase Devereaux around Wilmington. He, Spry, and a party of eleven soldiers plus de Manning and Lydia's coachmen, groom, and outriders were due to ride from town at eight, their destination the Rouse house. What had been Devereaux's purpose for slaking his thirst for rum in a tavern where he must surely suspect that someone would report him?

The soldiers circled past White's. Michael ordered all the men except Spry to the barracks and sent weapons and ammunition back with them. Then he and Spry slipped into the hubbub of the tavern, this time attempting to make their presence inconspicuous.

He passed another gaze over the crowd. After ascertaining that the Frenchman wasn't present, he checked the time: seven thirty. Kevin Marsh wove his way to them. "Mr. Stoddard, what happened? I was reprimanding an employee and saw your patrol go—"

"Excuse me, Mr. Marsh, I—"

"It's Kevin. Call me Kevin."

Michael repressed a sigh. "I must speak with your sister immediately. Kevin."

"I shall fetch her." Kevin bustled across the room for the rear door of the tavern.

Not a single serving wench so much as looked at Michael while he and Spry waited near the door. Within half a minute, Kate was navigating the common room to Michael. When she reached him, she pointed out one of the tables along the right side of the room, opposite the fireplace. "He was sitting at that third table, the left edge of the bench, his back to the wall. He ordered two shots of rum."

"How long was he here before you left to find me?"

"No more than twenty minutes."

Michael scrutinized the defensibleness of the seat. Devereaux, his back to the wall, a window within easy reach, had drunk two shots of rum in a predominantly loyalist tavern beneath the watch of the Eighty-Second. Why? So he could thumb his nose at them, dare them to catch him, knowing he could elude them?

No. The assassin had intended a message in it. How he'd evaded the sentinels on the roads, Michael could only guess, but security must be tightened after this incident. He became aware of Kate's proximity and shifted his attention to discover her standing but a foot away from him.

"Did you catch him, Michael?" Her voice was soft.

"No." His body angled to hers before he could remind himself to remain remote.

Her face tilted to his again, as it had in the middle of Front Street at two thirty Sunday morning. "I shall keep a close watch for him."

"I doubt he'll return. But thank you again for your vigilance."

Her hand brushed his lower arm. "Won't you and Spry stay for a drink? You and I can talk later."

Damn the timing. Again, he felt Spry's discomfiture as an observer. "We're headed out. Now."

"Dear heaven." A shimmer appeared in her eyes. She blinked several times at it. "You must've located Travis."

His lips pressed together, and his heart shivered in response to her tears, to the new thrusts of rapiers and their gift of agony and delight. For the second time, he turned his back on invitation, desperate to skitter from beneath the great, inevitable wave that bore down upon him. "Good evening." He tugged on the door handle, Spry following, and gave himself to a night that promised only terror and trickery.

Chapter Twenty-Seven

"THERE ARE ABOUT ten patrons in the tavern right now, Mr. Stoddard."
The soldier reporting surveillance was Wigglesworth, who, with Spry, had
discovered Ralph Gibson's body late Saturday afternoon. The private waved
in the direction of Rouse's from the copse of pines, his voice low. "Captain
Love is among them, but not Mr. Jones."

Light glowed in both windows on the south side of the tavern and framed
shadows of people on the interior. Michael listened. Men inside whooped
at some jest. James Love's hearty laughter rose above the merriment. Love
sounded well into his cups.

Where was Bill Jones? Inconvenient, that the scoundrels weren't together
in the tavern, as they'd been Saturday night. But Michael would take what he
could get. "Have they weapons?"

"Yes, sir. Most carried in firearms."

"How long has that group of men been in there?"

"At least two hours, most of them. There's been some coming and going
of patrons. Seems to be a core group remaining, though. I heard one say that
Rouse received a shipment of brandy earlier today."

"From the sound of them, they're already good and drunk on it." Spry's
grin was audible. "We could take them now, sir. I doubt they'd offer serious
resistance."

Michael shifted his scrutiny northeast. Ted Newcastle had claimed a shed
was located out there that housed Lord Wynndon, Travis, or both. Michael
also scanned the barn and outbuildings. The only source of movement, light,
and sound in the area came from the tavern.

Robin Hood, he wagered, was resting, guarded by Merry Men. Or he and
the gang might be waiting after setting up a trap. Overhead, just west of its
transit, a moon one day past the first quarter contributed some illumination,

and the sky was clear, availing them of starlight's radiance. But regardless, it was night. Finding Travis without having men trip over each other might present a challenge.

De Manning said, low, "What about children, soldier? Have you seen any this evening?"

"Yes, sir," said Wigglesworth. "About half an hour ago, we watched a party of approximately a dozen men or older youths, plus a small boy, march in from the wilderness up there to the northeast. Behind the tavern, they met with the old woman and her three children and handed off the boy to her."

Michael sucked in a breath. "Where are the woman and children now?"

"Inside Rouse's Tavern, sir."

From Wigglesworth's report, it appeared that Travis had delivered Lord Wynndon to the tavern a bit earlier than usual, either to gain more sleep in anticipation of a busy pre-dawn, or to lay his trap for the Eighty-Second. Lydia's son was now separated from Travis: a double-edged sword. For while the separation meant that the boy wouldn't be present during any aggressive action at the shed to the northeast, it also meant that for Michael to apprehend Travis, he'd have to leave Lord Wynndon behind in the tavern.

"What are you waiting for, Mr. Stoddard?" The soft click of de Manning's loosened hanger reached Michael's ears. "Let's rescue Wynndon from the tavern right now. We're more than a match for ten drunks."

Michael rotated his head sideways toward the tutor. "I doubt such an operation would be quiet. Mr. Travis, whom we believe to be close by to the northeast, may hear us fighting with Captain Love's party and either flee or rush in to engage us with his party. The boy will become imperiled. He is not so this moment." Indeed, he was entrusted to Eve Whistler for a third night.

De Manning grunted in protest. "Do you intend to apprehend Mr. Travis in his lair, then?"

"I do."

"Then split your party. I shall command the group that rescues Wynndon. You shall command the group that captures the criminal."

Michael heard the combative edge to de Manning's voice and pivoted to face the tutor full-on in the darkness. In the copse around him, men gave them room, even Lydia's men. Michael kept his voice low. "Historically, splitting a military force has almost always led to disaster. As I'm in command of this military force, we shall not split our party."

"You mean to engage Mr. Travis first?" De Manning swung his arm toward the tavern. "Then those rogues will hear you and spirit Wynndon away."

They were so close to rescuing the boy. So close. That knowledge tainted de Manning's reasoning with frustration and pain. Even Michael felt it hammer at his logic.

In the next instant, Love and his companions let loose a huge explosion of hilarity. The night air vibrated with it, and even after the mirth had subsided, rebel voices rang out. "Look at Ed, sleeping peaceful as a baby!" "Ah, I've had enough that I'll be joining him, soon." "I want to sleep like that." "Then drink up, lads. We may have lost our all to that scoundrel, Craig, but at least Sandy Rouse will let us rest here a few hours." A boisterous series of toasts for Rouse's good health circulated the tavern.

"Listen to them, Mr. de Manning." In the dark, Michael glared at the tutor. "Do you think they'll hear much of anything that transpires to the northeast, much less be able to offer Mr. Travis assistance? By the time we return here, they'll all be snoring. Makes our job so much easier. And I'm ever hopeful that William Jones will have joined them in the interim and downed a few whiskeys."

He heard capitulation in de Manning's sigh. He squared his shoulders. "Lindsay and Wigglesworth will remain here for surveillance. Dylan, you'll join Lady Faisleigh's groom back around the bend and help secure the horses."

"Sir," murmured the three privates from the shadowy ensemble.

"That leaves twenty of us to successfully execute an operation with multiple goals. Most importantly, the safe rescue and return of Lord Wynndon. But also the subduing and apprehension of Mr. Travis and his band, who abducted the boy and have engaged in highway robbery and extortion. Likewise, the subduing and apprehension of Captain James Love, who has repeatedly galloped the streets of Wilmington while firing upon soldier and civilian alike. And, should he make an appearance, Love's accomplice in devilry, William Jones."

Michael craned his neck for a glance at the tavern area. "Our first step will be to ensure that Mr. Travis and his henchmen aren't in that barn and those outbuildings. Men, for King and country, now. I need six volunteers."

***

From concealment in the trees, Michael and his party watched while six redcoats crept around the outbuildings, eased open doors, and snooped inside. Mrs. Whistler's dog bounded over and woofed a couple times. To shut him up, one soldier enticed the dog to him on the south side of the barn using food from his haversack, got the beast to roll over, and scratched his belly. Spry muttered, "Henshaw, what are you doing? The dog will want to come back to Wilmington with us."

Wigglesworth snorted. "Eh, what's another camp dog, Spry?"

"Quiet, both of you," said Michael.

The back door to the tavern crashed open. A man staggered out to the step and called over his shoulder, "Save one more for me, lads. My back teeth are drowning!" Then he tottered for the jakes.

Henshaw, closest to the jakes, hung onto the dog and hunkered down. Three other visible soldiers dropped to a crouch and stayed still on the east side of other outbuildings. The drunk pawed open the door to the jakes and relieved himself inside while crooning a ditty about a Catholic priest and three bosomy, young nuns.

Men around Michael snickered. Considering the inebriation of the fellow, Michael reevaluated whether he should engage Captain Love first. But if anyone in Love's party fired a shot, Travis might take it as a warning. No, they had to apprehend Travis first, firing as few shots as possible.

The drunk tumbled from the jakes, picked himself up, and stretched his arms to the heavens. "Kiss my arse, King George!" Then he blundered into the tavern.

Michael's six volunteers sneaked back to the copse of pines. The dog followed them halfway, then turned about and scampered back to his domain. The soldiers reported the barn and outbuildings empty of people. The outbuildings were secured.

In Rouse's Tavern, most of the patrons had settled down. Only the voices of Captain Love and one or two companions could be distinguished. Even their laughter sounded mellow, sleepy.

In the pine copse, soldiers and Lydia's men waited, silent, their regard on Michael. He said, "For the next step, we shall fetch Mr. Travis and as many of his band of boys and men as we can round up. He's likely expecting us in a shed just to the northeast. So I need a scout first."

***

The scout reported no sentries posted around the shed. Situated well off the road, the structure was located much closer to the tavern's outbuildings than Michael had expected, perhaps only an eighth mile away. The proximity confirmed for him that he'd been wise to not move against the men in the tavern first. It would have created a ruckus that alerted Travis's band.

More significantly, as the scout had also reported, the shed backed against a group of pines and live oaks. Michael gambled that the shadow conveyed by those trees concealed at least some of Travis's band, that this was the trap Travis had laid for the Eighty-Second.

Dorinda had told him that Travis was fond of stories in which Robin Hood and his Merry Men surrounded and disarmed their enemies. Crouched in sand behind a spindly bush, hoping to avoid more encounters with prickly pear cacti like the one that had rendered the back of his left hand scratched and stinging, Michael watched the progress of Robin Hood's enemies. Spry and five seasoned soldiers advanced in a line for the shed, muskets readied with fixed bayonets, wiregrass rustling beneath their shoes.

When the six were about thirty feet from the shed, a lone figure clambered to the creaky roof of the shed from the tree shadows. "Welcome, boys!" Again wearing the executioner's mask, Travis straightened, wobbling a bit as if unsure of his footing on the sloping roof. Light from the moon and stars imparted a dull gleam upon the blade in his right hand. "Looking for General Lord Travis? Here I am!"

Travis, Michael decided, was even more enthralled with himself than was Narcissus of the Greek myth. As planned, Spry loaded theatrical flourish into his voice. "King's men, apprehend that rogue!" He pressed his team forward.

Travis raised his sword and snarled. "Brotherhood of the Greenwood, kill these fools!"

The woodsy darkness behind the shed convulsed, divulged more than two-dozen shadows. Fewer than a third possessed the stature of grown men. But boys or no, Michael hadn't expected quite so many, and panic bolted from his head to the soles of his feet. He squashed it down and stretched his neck to get a better strategic view.

Travis's gang encircled Spry and his men. The soldiers assumed a defensive circle, bayonets outward. The outlaws hesitated, kept at least twenty-five feet away. Four small boys retreated without realizing that it brought them closer to Michael's hidden party.

"What are you waiting for?" Travis attempted to swish his sword but stiffened and curtailed the motion when it almost pitched him off the shed. "I taught you how to foil the bayonet. See there, your enemy numbers only six. Kill them!"

The gang closed. Most lifted clubs. A few had brought short swords. Michael cupped hands around his mouth. "Present!"

In seconds, he and the additional men, including de Manning and Lydia's men, had risen from their concealment. They scuttled forward, bayonets leveled, firearms ready, formed a semicircle, and closed upon Travis's band. Hemmed in, the outlaws ceased approaching Spry and his men and cast about, their formation wavering. The four small boys dropped their clubs and bolted.

Michael's men allowed their departure, then sealed the envelopment. He elevated his voice. "Mr. Travis, you and your party are under arrest! In the name of King George, I order all of you to drop your weapons immediately and—"

"Kill Stoddard!" Travis stabbed his sword in Michael's direction. Travis's gang huzzahed and charged redcoats and Lydia's men.

Michael caught a glimpse of de Manning swinging his officer's hanger and hacking into an outlaw's arm. Then his attention was all for three boys who ran at him with clubs. At too-close quarters to aim his fusil, he swung it by the barrel, slamming one of the boys in the head with the butt. He caught a bruising blow from a club on his left shoulder, then tripped the second boy, who landed in a cluster of cacti with a screech. The third boy, probably about seventeen years old, held back, a large knife in one hand, a club in the other, eyes blank in a deadened face.

Michael had seen that look far too often on battlefields. Around them, the fist fighting, weapons clash, and cries of the wounded rose, and smells of blood and piss dampened the night air. He transferred his fusil to his left hand and drew his hanger with a metallic whoosh. The boy held his ground. Michael lunged. The boy attempted to parry with his knife, then released it with a howl of agony when the hanger's point gouged a gory trail up his forearm. He stumbled backward, dropped his club, clutched his arm, and staggered off sobbing.

The boy who'd landed atop the cacti was limping away, club discarded. The third boy was shaking his head, trying without success to raise himself to his hands and knees. His hanger ready, Michael raked his gaze across all the pockets of fighting between men and boys.

Ames and an outrider were huddled over a supine Nigel de Manning. Four of Travis's men, armed with swords, were trying to get to them. Spry, swords in both hands, was holding all four outlaws at bay.

Michael gaped.

In a singing clash of metal, Spry parried jabs and thrusts from all of Travis's men simultaneously. He executed a dazzling feint. The sword in his right hand spiraled the blade out of one opponent's hand while steel wielded in Spry's left hand plunged into another man's shoulder.

Michael's gape enlarged.

God in heaven. Where had Spry learned swordplay like that?

Motion on the shed dragged his attention away. Like a chameleon, Travis was easing himself over the edge of the roof. No one else had spotted him. Within half a minute, he'd have slithered to the ground and run away. Michael jammed his hanger into its scabbard, drew up his fusil, aimed, and squeezed the trigger.

Click. Flash in the pan. Michael swore, then sprinted for Travis.

At a run, he reached the outlaw just as a plank on the roof popped and splintered, dumping Travis onto him. They thumped, tangled, into the wiregrass, the impact rattling every bone in Michael's body. Momentum tore the fusil from his hand. Travis's sword clanged to the ground near the shed.

Travis flailed at him. Michael punched his face and connected with his jaw. Even though the eyeholes of Travis's mask had shifted sideways, he punched back, and Michael's ears rang with the blow. In and out of the trees' shadow, the two men thrashed around in the wiregrass slugging torsos, arms, faces, sand, and cacti, blocking each other from grabbing daggers, the fighting too tight for Michael to draw his hanger. He felt his lip, one eyebrow, and the knuckles of his right hand swell. He kept pounding away at Travis.

After what seemed like hours, he pinned the other man on his back long enough to punch the pit of his stomach. Resistance emptied from Travis in a whined reverse-gasp. Michael rolled away and up to a crouch quickly, spat blood, and raked hair from his eyes. "Again, Robin Hood!" A swollen lip and chewed tongue slurred his words. "Come! Have at me, you shit!"

Travis managed the feeble limb movements of semi-consciousness. Michael found his fusil and scooped it up, out of range. He also confiscated Travis's sword. The outlaw flipped to his side with a groan and foundered about in attempt to rise. Michael booted him in the kidney. Travis collapsed and lay still.

For a half minute, he watched Travis from a crouch, catching his breath, ready to club him with the fusil should he offer more of a fight. Then Michael straightened partway, joints creaking, and grunted at every cactus spine and sandbur that had wedged beneath his uniform coat. He swore and spat blood again, ran his bitten tongue over his teeth. At least he hadn't chipped any.

He squinted outward. The skirmish had subsided. Twelve to fifteen of Travis's gang were in custody, forced to sit or lie in the grass while their wrists were bound behind them, some of them moaning from injuries. Spry appeared to be overseeing the process. Between Michael and the prisoners were two outlaws sprawled motionless in the grass. Farther distant, men were hunched over a figure on the ground.

Michael straightened to his full height. A chill scraped his spine. De Manning was still down.

"Henshaw! Rollins!" he hollered at the nearest of his men, who were prodding one outlaw's motionless body with their muskets. He waved his arm not holding the fusil and winced at bruises and stiff muscles. The soldiers trotted over. He pointed to the outlaw leader and handed Henshaw Travis's sword. "Drag Travis over to the rest of the prisoners. Tie him. Make sure he doesn't wander off after he wakes up."

"Yes, sir!"

"What's wrong with Mr. de Manning?"

"Knife to the leg, sir." Rollins shook his head. "Lost a good deal of blood."

The chill in Michael's spine dug deeper. He bolted for the downed tutor, the fusil in his hand clanking in rhythm to each harsh breath he exhaled. Not de Manning. No.

Sand beneath the tutor's right leg had darkened with blood. The shirt that bandaged his right thigh was soaked with it. The air stank of metal, sticky and dribbling despite Ames applying full pressure to the wound. The blade had nicked de Manning's artery. Horror and anger twined in Michael's gut.

He heard the slap-pound of someone's footsteps approaching at a run from the direction of the tavern, glanced up to see what looked like Wigglesworth, who, since he'd quit his surveillance post, couldn't possibly be bringing good news. Regardless, Michael sank to his knees beside the tutor, slid fingers to his wrist, and found his pulse hammering away. He placed a hand on his shoulder. "Captain de Manning." He shook his shoulder gently.

De Manning's eyelids flickered open. His voice rasped. "I see you've fought the devil, Stoddard. Hell is a cold, c-cold p-place."

Damn. Shock. Michael turned to one of the outriders. "Find something to cover him." The outrider stripped off his own coat and placed it over de Manning's torso.

"Stoddard." De Manning's lips stretched, bared his teeth. The pallor of his face was almost luminescent. "*Luceo non uro.*"

"Er, that's Latin. *Luceo,* to shine. No, I shine."

"'I shine, not burn.' M-Motto of MacKenzies. Remember. C-Cousin. C-Cannot catch my breath."

Wigglesworth puffed to a stop before their group. "Mr. Stoddard, up at the tavern, sir, come immediately!"

Michael held up his hand to silence the private, then replaced his palm on de Manning's shoulder. "Mr. de Manning, you must stay with us."

The tutor gusted out a laugh. "I f-finally remembered. L-Lord Crump's falcon boy." He held up his hand to Michael.

Michael grasped it, appalled at its iciness. His throat clenched. He forced himself to swallow. "Lord Wynndon needs you, sir."

De Manning pulled him closer, his words whispered, only for Michael. "Tell her. I love her."

"Oh, thank God," said Ames. "The bleeding has stopped. Don't move, Mr. de Manning."

Michael pushed back from the tutor but held the embittered savagery of his dark-eyed glare one long moment. De Manning must fancy he was still dealing with the servant boy in the mews. Well, he could deliver his own message. Michael placed the tutor's hand at his side, grasped his fusil, and stood. After stepping away so the injured man wouldn't hear, he lowered his voice and addressed the private who was still catching his breath. "Report, Wigglesworth."

"Sir. Just a few minutes ago, Major Craig's dragoons and twenty-five infantrymen arrived at Rouse's. They've lit torches and surrounded the house."

Michael stared at him. "Our men? You're certain?"

"Yes, sir."

Michael recalled the two notes he'd sent Craig apprising his commander of the location of the "vermin." His body went as cold as de Manning's hand had been. No. This couldn't be happening, dragoons unleashing a raid upon Captain Love and the rebels in the tavern while Lord Wynndon and the Whistlers were inside. He pivoted toward the soldiers closer to the shed. "Spry!"

"Sir!"

"To me, now!" Without waiting for Spry, because he knew his assistant would catch up with him, he motioned for Wigglesworth to follow and ran for the tavern.

Chapter Twenty-Eight

ABOVE THE THUMP of his own footfalls, Michael heard a bawl of pain from the vicinity of the road. Five dragoons scrambled out to intercept him from behind the tavern, hands ready on the hilts of their sabers. In the dark, they'd assumed his party was rebel reinforcements.

Having no desire to engage in combat with dragoons of the Eighty-Second, Michael braked his run, followed by Wigglesworth and Spry, both breathing hard. He flung up his hands. "Stop where you are! Lieutenant Stoddard here, with my men!"

The dragoon in the lead skidded to a stop and signaled the rest of his party to halt. "Yes, sir!"

The parties closed, and Rowe, who'd acted as Craig's messenger, came forward. "Mr. Stoddard, sir, Major Craig sends his thanks and congratulations. Your information allowed us to find Captain Love here. We're ordered to engage in action against him and the rebels in his company."

"Where is Major Craig this moment?"

"This moment, sir? Uh, twenty-five or thirty miles to the north, I believe."

"Then you will stand down, all of you." Michael stabbed his forefinger toward the building's back door. "There's a woman and four children in that tavern!"

Rowe shook his head. "That's unfortunate, sir. We've already initiated the—"

"On my authority, you will stand down immediately!"

The dragoons stared at each other in confusion. A clash of metal and wail of agony sounded from the road. From inside the tavern, Eve Whistler's voice rose: "Go away! N-no! G-go away!"

Horror fueled the slam of Michael's heart against his ribcage. He shouldered past the dragoons and sprinted ahead. "Spry! Wigglesworth!" He flung down his fusil in the grass so he could pump his arms and gain speed toward the back door.

Two infantrymen with torches blocked the door. "Open, in the name of the King!" Michael hollered. "Out of my way!" One of them shouted. Michael didn't comprehend. But at the last second, they tugged the door open and moved off the step.

Inside, past the threshold, Michael had to vault over a civilian man who lay facedown on the wood floor writhing and bleating, a pool of blood spreading from beneath him. A crimson blur of infantrymen with muskets and fixed bayonets filled the common room. A man shrieked from behind an overturned table to one side. Another, on his knees near the stone fireplace, mouth gaped and eyes bulging, flung up an arm before his face, a futile defense against an incoming bayonet.

Michael dove behind the doomed man, his destination the unlit fireplace, where Eve Whistler cowered in the cold ash with her three children and Lord Wynndon. Facing them, he spread his arms above them and braced his feet, making his body as large a shield as possible. The woman and children huddled tighter together beneath him. Spry bumped to his side and spread his arms, too, joined by Wigglesworth.

A fist or elbow smacked into Michael's shoulder from behind. He tensed, held his ground. Blood sprayed the back of his coat, neck, hair, and right cheek, and it sprinkled the mantle. He gritted his teeth and shut his eyes, expecting a wayward bayonet thrust through his back. Below him, the woman babbled, "G-go away. G-go away. G-go away."

Men screamed to heaven, begged for mercy. They received curses, and metal that ripped their flesh wetly. Life fled them in bubbly coughs and sobs, drowned screams. The world stank of blood and scorched wood, vomit, sweat, and insanity.

A child crawled up against Michael, clung to him with fingers the strength of ancient oak roots. Through his eyelashes, Michael recognized the only dark-haired child in the group. He scooped his left arm downward and clutched Lydia's son to him.

The building vibrated with the stomp of infantrymen and the final jabs of their bayonets into the bodies of rebels who were no longer resisting. Michael thrust Lord Wynndon at Spry. "Out!" Spry pivoted for the back door with the boy, Wigglesworth at his side as added protection. Lord Wynndon moaned.

Michael bent over Mrs. Whistler, his peripheral vision granting him the image of Lord Wynndon reaching for him over Spry's broad shoulders, his mouth a soundless scream. "Out, Mrs. Whistler!" He grabbed her bony shoulder.

She flinched from his touch and batted his hand away. "G-go away. G-go away. G-go away." Her three children burrowed against her, eyes vacant and glazed, like their mother's eyes.

Michael couldn't compel the Whistlers to come with him. From the outside, Lord Wynndon's wail reached him. Michael's heart, blood, and bones comprehended the message, the boy's need for anchorage. He fumbled in his waistcoat pocket, withdrew Zeke Whistler's Psalter, and pressed it into the palm of the dead boy's mother. Then, dodging bloody metal in the landscape of hell painted by the Eighty-Second Regiment, he ran for the back door.

***

With his saddle as a shield, Captain James Love had used his sword to hack his way past soldiers on the front porch. He progressed as far as the road. Near the mulberry tree, he collapsed and died, full of bayonet and saber wounds. Two of his rebel cohorts were cut down on the front porch. Five more were dispensed inside the house.

Dragoons interrogated two civilian men they'd spared. Michael stayed out of it, focusing on supervising his own party's appropriation of Alexander Rouse's wagon and horse from the outbuildings so they could transport back to Wilmington an unconscious Nigel de Manning and two of Travis's outlaws who were in no condition to stand. The activity helped settle the tremble that always possessed his body after battle. It also held at bay the suspicion that if he hadn't stopped to speak with de Manning, he might have snatched Mrs. Whistler and the children from the tavern before the carnage began.

As his party prepared to depart, dragoons presented Michael with nine of the Reverend Greene's men whom they'd caught in the brush spying on the raid at the tavern. The men were roped in with Travis and his gang to hike the eight miles to Wilmington, escorted by Michael and his men. A detachment of six dragoons, headed by Rowe, accompanied them. Michael was grateful for the extra security. No telling how many more of Greene's men lurked in the midnight wilderness, ready to pounce on the party, liberate their own men, and grab Travis.

Thus he insisted that Lord Wynndon ride to Wilmington astride Cleopatra, in the saddle before him, and Michael kept his arms around him. The boy sensed his resolve to deliver him safely to his mother. Five minutes into the return trip, he fell asleep against Michael's chest.

Michael's thoughts circled from all the children he'd witnessed fighting for the Continentals on battlefields since 1777 to Travis's gang of mostly boys to the increasing number of children he'd noticed caught up in service to the King. So many years he'd been fighting the insurrection. He could see no end to the ferocity. By casting their children into the fray, surely both sides were seeking extinction.

Lydia's offer to fund his advancement to the captaincy stirred only ambiguity through his soul. Sometime in the past year, he'd lost his taste for soldiering. What he wanted from life was to help people by pitting his wits against criminals. Not as an afterthought, in the role of Major Craig's criminal investigator, where at any moment he could be summoned to slip back into the skin of a soldier. Nor in the limited capacity of those men who worked for Bow Street, chasing down London's thieves. Something that offered him focus and variety.

He wasn't sure whether such a profession existed yet in the world, or how to access it, if it did. Perhaps it awaited his definition and shaping. But he did know that he must guard his position as lead investigator with as much dedication as he guarded Lord Wynndon. The role that Major Craig had assigned him might be mere afterthought, but it was a step on his path to the profession he wanted. He couldn't possibly be the only man who sought it.

***

About one o'clock in the morning, the soldiers arrived at Lydia's house. Michael had trouble prying her son's clutch from his uniform coat facings, so he carried the boy up the front walk. As soon as Lydia appeared in the doorway and burst into tears, the boy traded him for his mother. Michael noted that although Dorinda shed no tears for the unconscious de Manning, her expression was somber, and she stayed right on the heels of the men who lifted him from the wagon and carried him inside.

For his final acts of the night, Michael transported Travis to jail and the rest of his prisoners to the pen. He was eager to clean death and cacti off himself, change into fresh clothing.

Movement awakened him about eight o'clock Tuesday morning, April the third, in a cot in the corner of the barracks. Spry, his own eyes bloodshot from lack of sleep, was pulling closed the canvas partition that gave his commander an officer's privacy. Michael, in his shirt only, pushed up to a sitting position and winced at his bruises and pulled muscles.

From the feel of it, a knot the size of an unshelled almond adorned his left eyebrow. His tongue, lip, and right hand were swollen. His arms and left hand itched with scratches from cactus spines. He hoped that Travis, after spending the night in the pen, felt at least five times worse than he did.

His assistant held out a cup of coffee. Not Enid's coffee, but any coffee would do that moment. Michael motioned Spry to sit on a stool beside his cot.

He sipped most of the coffee while studying the new Nick Spry: shoulders hunched, laconic, avoiding his gaze. "So did we rid ourselves of that little urchin, Ted Newcastle?"

"Sir. At dawn, a couple men headed to Brunswick County with him."

"Good. Worth the reward of four pounds. And he's far luckier than those lads we threw in the pen. How's Mr. de Manning?"

"From what I hear, he's still unconscious." Spry darted a look at him. "He might die, sir."

Michael waved away the suggestion and fought back a nudge of panic. He disliked de Manning, but he didn't want him dead. "I've seen plenty of men lose blood that way and recover. Much depends on a man's will to live. De Manning's tough."

He gulped the rest of the coffee, set the empty cup on the floor, and leaned toward his assistant, palms on knees. "Spry," he said, his voice low, "Teach me swordplay."

Spry jerked as if he'd been struck, then scooted the stool an inch away from Michael. "Me, sir?"

"Don't tell me your training in the Army included drilling with two swords to fight off four opponents simultaneously. That would be a lie." Spry worked his mouth but said nothing. "And you've already lied to me at least once. Your father didn't die in a fishing accident when you were seventeen. He's still alive, isn't he? Out with it. What's his given name?"

Spry stared at the rough, wood wall behind Michael. "John Philip, sir."

Michael considered all the liberties the English language took with the name John. Chill coiled up his spine when he hit upon the nickname "Jack." Because Wilmington was on the coast, he'd kept himself apprised of warrants for the arrest of criminals who claimed the coastal waters of the thirteen colonies as their territory. He poked Spry's knee but kept his voice just above a whisper. "Look at me when I'm talking to you. Your father is Black Jack Spry, isn't he?"

His assistant gulped. "Sir. Yes, sir."

"Brilliant. My assistant's the son of a bloody pirate and smuggler who has bounties on his head from five countries." Michael sat back and felt himself smile without humor. "Looks like you picked up at least one handy skill from the family business. And why are you here, Nick Spry? Are you spying?"

"No, sir. I'm here because I get seasick."

"Seasick?" Of all the responses Michael expected, that wasn't one.

Spry sighed. "From when I was a small lad, sir. Terrible sick. A ship doesn't even have to set sail. I but step aboard her and sicken immediately. I was trained in swordplay, true, but never before last night had I used it in fighting. After I'm ill, I stay ill until my feet again find land. The truth is that I cannot be depended upon in combat at sea."

Michael drummed fingers on his thighs briefly. "Nick Spry the seasick pirate." There was a sort of dark humor in it. But he wondered how much piracy and smuggling Spry had actually done before he'd joined the Army.

"No, sir. Not a pirate. The amount of rum I must consume to counter the sickness leaves me useless for a pirate's work. Or any work, for that matter."

Perhaps rum consumption was how Spry had managed the voyage from Charles Town to Wilmington in January. "So what happened to bring you to take the King's shilling? Were you drummed from the family camp?"

"Oh, no, sir. My father wanted me with him regardless. But it was torture for me, knowing that I'd be sick every mission. Comes a time when a fellow has to leave the nest anyway and make a name for himself. So I ran away last year and joined the Army."

Michael scowled. "When was the last time you communicated with your family?"

"March the twenty-third, last year. The day I ran away. I left them a note. Told them I was trapping fur in Quebec. I even left a two-day trail for them to follow, then lose, in the wilderness up there."

"Oh, come now. Black Jack Spry isn't known for giving up." Michael lowered his arms. "What are you going to do if they somehow track you here?"

Spry's blue-eyed gaze bored into him. "Then I'll tell them to kiss my arse. You're my commander now, sir."

"Well, that's quite heartening, but what if I'm killed in battle or transferred to another regiment? I won't be your commander, then."

"Sir. I've taken an oath. I'm a soldier of the King. I'm not a pirate. If you put me aboard ship, I won't even be human. The land suits me just fine."

"What did you tell your recruiter about your background?"

"That I was the son of a fisherman and didn't care for the life." Spry's gaze slid back to the wall over Michael's shoulder.

As Michael was learning, blood was thicker than water. Would Spry still cleave to piracy had he not been disposed to seasickness? Should pirate family members somehow be caught by the Eighty-Second, would Spry injure or kill a fellow soldier to help them evade the King's justice? Michael doubted that his assistant could answer such questions. Were he in Spry's shoes, he wasn't sure he could answer them.

And if he were the sort of officer who followed regulations to the letter, Michael's next move would be to summon the provost marshal's guards and have Spry arrested. They'd interrogate him for information to assist the military in the capture of his family. Then they'd hang Spry. Likewise, because Spry knew enough to compromise the security of his family's illegal business, his own family might hunt him down and kill him—before he could tell them to kiss his arse.

However in Hillsborough as well as near Rouse's Tavern, Spry had risked his own life and performed with valor in service to the King. He'd also saved Michael's life. Tuesday morning the third of April, Spry's intentions seemed clear. If Michael cared to retain his intelligent, capable, and humorous assistant, he'd have to write his own regulations.

But he'd already been doing that. He'd looked the other way for a woman who tried to kill an officer of the Crown and a brother and sister who smuggled whiskey. He was hard at work warping the fabric of military orthodoxy.

Sooner or later, the Army might notice. The realization shimmied a little chill through him. He'd give some thought to how to cover himself.

Spry spoke softly, the color in his face leached out. "What would you have me do now, sir?"

Yes, sooner or later, the Army might notice. But not that moment. Michael considered Spry's quirky statement about joining the Army or taking up juggling and becoming a Fool. "Do you juggle?"

"Not well, sir."

Michael scooped the coffee cup off the floor and thrust it at him. "Then it's a good thing you joined the Army. Bring me more coffee." Spry's gaze sought his. "And in our spare moments, you will teach me swordplay."

Color sifted back into Spry's cheeks. His lips quivered into a smile. "Sir. Yes, sir."

"Don't let me down, Spry."

His assistant lifted his chin. His eyes twinkled. "No, sir."

Chapter Twenty-Nine

THE FATHERS OF four boys from Travis's gang who'd been apprehended were waiting to petition Michael outside the pen when he arrived there mid-morning to question the more than two-dozen prisoners he'd taken the previous night. The fathers were small-plot farmers with calluses on their hands and the odors of the barnyard permeating their clothing, men whose names didn't appear on Major Craig's list of rebel sympathizers. Their sons, ages ten and eleven, were in tears from having spent seven hours in the pen. Michael made fathers and sons swear allegiance to the King, vow to never take up arms against His Majesty. Then he released the boys into their fathers' custody.

The older boys and men from Travis's gang weren't ready to talk yet. Neither were Greene's men. Michael moseyed on to the jail and found Travis just as uncooperative. Unperturbed, Michael left them all to the meager rations, thirst, filth, violence, and contagion of incarceration and returned to Mrs. Chiswell's house, where he savored another of Enid's divine creations with bread, beef, and mustard sauce.

Afterward, while Enid and Mrs. Chiswell continued packing books in her study, he returned to his room to discover his bed rumpled, as if he'd slept in it, except that he hadn't. Puzzled, he checked all his belongings to make certain nothing had been stolen. All appeared untouched.

Even Lydia's contract, which he at last took the time to read, sitting at his desk. Afterward, he folded the thing and stared at it. A commission in exchange for a child. The language might be different this time, but Lydia was looking for an excuse to sport with her falcon boy again.

For his diet, red meat as often as possible plus a daily combination of herbs and spices recommended to Lord Faisleigh by Mediterranean physicians. Assignations with Lydia were to last at least half an hour. Should either of them be less than forthcoming, enthusiasm could be sought from silk, leather, and wood devices, some of which possessed names that sounded Arabic or Indian. The Mediterranean physicians also recommended nine coupling positions to deliver the quickest results. However, Lydia must not be permitted to mount him unless she had failed to conceive after a month. What a sacrifice for Lydia. She'd enjoyed that position the most in Lord Crump's mews.

Michael's groin tightened. With a muttered oath, he stood and shoved the chair beneath the desk. His gaze passed between the contract, his tinderbox, and an unlit candle several times. In the end, he didn't burn the contract but buried it again in his belongings. Why he didn't burn it, he wasn't certain.

But he thanked heaven Lydia hadn't contacted him that day. He presumed she'd stepped back into her role of running her household and tending her son. And well she should.

He sent for the remainder of Lydia's men, one by one, and conducted brief interviews with each to round out his documentation of the abduction. Late afternoon, he returned to the pen to find that the owners of two young slaves who'd escaped to join Travis's band had appeared to claim their boys. Also, the father and uncle of two of Travis's older boys showed up to petition Michael for their liberation. The boys were Ted Newcastle's age. Although the day wasn't unduly warm, oppressive heat in the pen had convinced both boys that honest manual labor on the family farm was preferable to following Robin Hood.

Releasing them with vows of allegiance gained Michael two pieces of information.

One of the boys stated that he'd been present with Lord Wynndon, Travis, and two of Travis's men in the barn the previous Saturday afternoon. Travis himself had placed the pistol to Ralph Gibson's head and squeezed the trigger.

The other boy confessed that a few weeks earlier, he'd overheard his erstwhile leader discussing with Gibson his abduction of Lord Wynndon, his receipt of monetary support from someone named John Wynndon in England, and intelligencer reports from John Wynndon's agents in America. Alas, the boy hadn't heard more, and as far as he knew, he'd been the only witness to the conversation.

His testimony confirmed that Lydia's wastrel brother-in-law possessed more cunning than most people had credited him. Both Lord Wynndon and Dorinda had been targeted for abduction. Had Michael not seen evidence of the maid's clear preference for de Manning over Travis, he'd have suspected her of feigning her devotion to the Faisleigh household and leaking details of Lydia's itinerary to Travis and John Wynndon.

If John had truly set his mind to removing Lord Wynndon from the inheritance picture, the loss of Travis as a henchman might not stop him. Michael had no way of knowing whether anyone else he'd captured from Travis's band knew of John Wynndon's involvement, but he needed to apprise Lydia of the development soon so she could protect herself and her son.

That afternoon, a messenger arrived in Wilmington from Lord Cornwallis. The general anticipated reaching Cross Creek within a day or two. He expected Major Craig to send vessels with flour and rum to the town ahead of his arrival.

Craig had still not returned from his Harnett-hunting, cow-herding expedition to the northeast. Lord Cornwallis had received none of the major's letters warning that he'd been unable to safely transport supplies up the Cape Fear

River to Cross Creek. His lordship was headed for a foul surprise when he reached his destination.

The pace of provisioning and fence building accelerated in the area south and east of town, where Major Craig had ordered the construction of earthworks in early February.

***

Around noon on Wednesday April fifth, Mrs. Chiswell found Michael and Spry in transit between the jail and the pen and informed them that Jonathan Quill had arrived. That meant she'd be leaving Wilmington Friday morning by boat, closing up the house, and placing a padlock key in the hands of her land agent's representative.

The two soldiers hadn't yet been reassigned to a residence. With the impending arrival of Cornwallis, they weren't likely to receive a new billeting arrangement for awhile. So it would be back to the barracks for them. Ah, well. At least the barracks kept the rain off.

Michael had reached an impasse questioning Greene's men, Travis, and the remainder of Travis's band. To hell with them. Let them stew in their incarceration. He and Spry returned to Mrs. Chiswell's house, and chaos. Quill had brought servants, a coach-and-four, and a wagon and horse team. Michael had Spry assist Enid in packing essentials from the kitchen while he completed his report for Major Craig on Travis and wrote letters in his room upstairs. The soldiers' presence in the house enabled both to study Quill again, a man whom Fairfax had labeled a spy. As Michael suspected, nothing about the older man hinted that he was anything other than a civilian loyal to His Majesty.

Late afternoon, Michael had just trotted downstairs when he heard a timid knock upon the front door. Everyone else was in the back yard. He opened the door to find a pallid-faced, puffy-eyed Eve Whistler on the front step. In astonishment, he guided her by the elbow into the parlor, seated her in one of the chairs, then sat on the nearest end of the couch.

She didn't meet his gaze and spoke just above a whisper. "I cannot stay long. Mr. Rouse decided to accept the protection of the Eighty-Second. He abandoned his tavern and has moved here, to Wilmington. He was good enough to bring my children and me with him."

Rouse was in Wilmington? Michael must keep an eye on him. Right before the bloodshed started at Rouse's Tavern, the dragoon, Rowe, had relayed Major Craig's thanks for informing him of where to find Captain Love. But Craig had assigned Michael to hunt down both Love and his cohort. Jones was still running loose. Alexander Rouse might know where to find Devil Bill.

"I-I remember. You and your men protected us that night. It was very brave of you. Thank you."

"You're welcome, madam. And I'm grateful to you for protecting the kidnapped boy."

Her gaze, full of tears, swung up to his face. "Where did my boy Zeke die?"

"On the road, during the abduction. The Eighty-Second has already buried him. Do you wish me to show you his grave?"

A tear slid down her cheek. She dabbed it away with the back of her hand. "No."

"Are you and your children staying here in Wilmington?"

"Yes. We have no family to take us in elsewhere. Mr. Rouse was also good enough to find me scullery work at a tavern. Not at White's Tavern, of course. Mrs. Duncan there believes I had an affair with her husband after they were married. She hates me."

"Well, I'm glad you found some work and—"

"But I *didn't* have an affair with him." Her fists pounded her lap once. "He told people that to hurt her. He also told people that Zeke was his son, to hurt her." Her nose crinkled in a snarl. "Zeke was my husband Jed's child. All my children were Jed's children. I loved Jed with all my heart, Mr. Stoddard." Her eyes brimmed with tears. "When I lost him in that fire, I lost my heart as well as my life."

Michael squirmed and patted the back of her hand. "See here, you don't need to explain anything to me."

"Oh, but I do. You're the only one who will believe me. You've never been anything but respectful to me, and you haven't lived here long enough to hear the rubbish. I've had to keep silent all these years because I've been buried in that rubbish, and no one would believe me. They think Daniel Duncan died so heroically at Moore's Creek Bridge. But he was no hero."

Michael squinted at her. "How do you mean?"

Tears wet her cheeks. "Daniel betrayed his commander to the patriots. MacDonald found out and shot him like the dog he was. MacDonald knew that Daniel and I had once been romantically involved, so he sent me a messenger to tell me the truth."

Michael sat back and studied her. "Who else knows of this?"

"Besides MacDonald and his messenger, who both returned to Scotland years ago? Why, Mrs. Duncan, of course."

That certainly explained why Kate, Kevin, and Aunt Rachel had nothing positive to say about Daniel Duncan. And why they'd never tried to correct the townsfolk's impression of him as a valiant soldier. "Alas that sort of misconception is all too common in war."

She wiped her cheeks with the back of her hand and studied his expression. "You believe me."

"Your story makes more sense than the legend about him."

She sat forward. "Then I'll tell you also that Daniel Duncan was a cruel man all the way down to his blood. Fortunately, that cruel blood of his made certain that no piece of him carried on."

Again Michael squinted at her, uncertain whether he was hearing a lunatic's ravings. "I'm afraid I don't understand, madam."

"Before I married Jed, I lost one of Daniel's babies the same way his wife lost all four of hers. Before Daniel marched off with MacDonald, he told everyone that Zeke was his so he could torture her, make her think there was something wrong with her. Then some fool surgeon told her she'd be better off never lying with another man because if she managed to get with child again, she'd probably die." Mrs. Whistler flung up her hands. "Mrs. Duncan has nothing wrong with her. The wrong was all in Daniel. But she hates me because of his lies."

And now Michael knew what Kate had wanted to talk with him about after she'd kissed him last Friday. Christ Jesus. He heard the back door to the house squeak open, and an approaching conversation between Mrs. Chiswell and Enid.

Eyes wide like those of a rabbit's in torchlight, Mrs. Whistler stood. "I must go!"

Michael signed for her to remain where she was. Then he strode to the doors and closed them. He heard the two women walk past into Mrs. Chiswell's study. Enid said, "Mr. Stoddard must have gone in the parlor with a witness."

He waited a few more seconds, then cracked open the door. They'd closed themselves into the study. He signaled Mrs. Whistler, preceded her to the front door, and let her out. Then he leaned against the front door and shut his eyes.

He'd turned his back on Kate twice since her kiss Friday evening. She'd probably concluded that he didn't have time for her, but the truth was that he didn't understand himself. One part of his heart kept insisting that he make time for her, while another part coached him that it was for the best if he let her believe in a Michael Stoddard whose life was all work.

But could any man undo the devilry of Daniel Duncan?

***

About five that evening, Enid mentioned that she'd seen a carriage-and-six rumble down Market Street, drive past Mrs. Chiswell's house, and halt before the house occupied by "that noblewoman." Michael and Spry stepped out on the front porch for a look. Grooms and coachmen waited near the vehicle in the street, but there was no activity associated with the coach. The occupant had vacated it.

Spry frowned. "You think that's her husband's coach, sir?"

"She said the two parties would convene in Charles Town, in June." Michael met his assistant's gaze. "Plans change."

Spry cocked an eyebrow. "Yes, sir. Especially when your brother decides he's going to abduct and kill your heir so he can have your money." He snorted. "Lord Faisleigh can keep his mountain of money. It's a commoner's life for me." They chuckled and returned inside the house.

A couple hours later, Enid tapped on Michael's bedroom door and handed him a note. The Faisleigh seal imprinted the wax. The note was unscented. And the message, a request for an audience with Lieutenant Michael Stoddard at eight that night, was rendered in masculine scrawl and signed with Faisleigh's name.

Michael sighed, tossed the note to his desk, tidied his uniform, and cleaned dust off his shoes.

On the nose at eight, he presented himself at the front door five houses down. A young man in well-tailored livery conducted him to the parlor, then closed him in, such that he was alone with Lydia and her husband.

Lydia remained seated on the couch. Faisleigh stood. Michael bowed from the waist, and Faisleigh inclined his head. "Do join us, Mr. Stoddard." He gestured to a chair beside the couch.

In the time it took Michael to walk to the indicated chair, he inspected the other man. He saw a fellow of fifty years, average height and build, dark hair graying at the temples. A man with an insistent chin, cunning, black eyes, and a mouth quick to tighten. A perfect complement to Lydia.

Hair at the back of Michael's neck pricked. The Earl and de Manning resembled each other. He wondered whether he'd look similar to both men in another quarter century.

After they sat, Faisleigh's gaze meandered over him. "You have my profound gratitude for the rescue of my son."

Michael held his gaze. "How is he?"

Faisleigh glanced at his wife. Her frown looked sincere. She fidgeted her fingers in her lap. "He has nightmares."

Even had the boy not witnessed slaughter in the tavern, the hardship he'd endured would have granted him nightmares. "His captors weren't kind."

Lydia drew a shaky breath. "His face is bruised."

"The bruise will heal. As will the nightmares." At least Michael hoped Lord Wynndon would be free of nightmares someday. He focused on Lydia's husband. "Lord Faisleigh, based upon the testimony of one of the bandits, I must warn you that your brother, John Wynndon, appears to be complicit in the boy's abduction. Assume he's also plotting against you and your lady."

"Thank you for the confirmation, Mr. Stoddard." Faisleigh's lips peeled back to reveal his teeth. "John showed me his hand mid-January. That's why I'm here two months early. Fortunately I was able to set up a counter-plot before I left. On the morrow, in my correspondence, I shall light the fuse." He chuckled. "Alas, I didn't have time to arrange an explosion the magnitude of the Gunpowder Plot. But my brother will never deal injury to my family again."

The man's eyes were black ice. Michael shoved down a shudder and flicked his gaze back and forth between the couple. "How is Mr. de Manning?"

Faisleigh's smile vanished. He drew a deep breath. "Not well."

"I'm told that he lost a good deal of blood."

"Yes." Lydia voice trembled. "He hasn't regained consciousness."

Michael felt his jaw dangle. De Manning had been unconscious for almost two days? He tried to recall whether he'd heard of a man doing that and recovering completely. Perhaps one man. If de Manning didn't get water soon, his kidneys would fail.

Lydia dabbed a handkerchief to one eye. Michael felt a dull anger. Only now did she display concern, when de Manning was insensible to perceiving it. Michael bowed his head, squeezed his eyes closed, and dispelled the anger.

"Why, Mr. Stoddard, I didn't think you and Mr. de Manning cared for each other," said Lydia.

He blinked and stared at the unlit fireplace. "He's a fellow soldier. On that level, we've understood each other. And he fought like a tiger Monday night." On that final point, Michael wasn't sure. He'd only seen the tutor swing his sword once. But this was not the time to downplay de Manning's valor.

Lydia sighed. The direction of her voice changed. "Wynndon needs to return to his studies, my dearest. I feel it will help him recover." Her voice softened. "Perhaps for the interim, we might employ Mr. Stoddard—"

"No." The word was spoken by Michael and the Earl at the same time. They eyed each other and nodded once.

Faisleigh leaned to his wife and stroked the length of her lower arm with his forefinger. His smile, seen by Michael in profile, curved his nose like a hawk's beak. "You may leave us, my sweet. We have something to discuss."

Lydia's voice grew husky. "Of course you do." She rolled to her feet. Both Michael and Faisleigh stood. The Earl kissed her temple. Michael nodded when she swayed past him with a smile.

After she closed them into the parlor, Faisleigh motioned Michael back into his chair and resumed his seat. "Now, Mr. Stoddard, my dear lady sent you a contract a few days ago." He pinned Michael with his stare. "Did you read it?"

Oh, damn. How was he to play this? Michael waited a few heartbeats. "Yes, my lord."

"Good. I read a copy of it tonight over supper." The other man waved a hand in dismissal. "And you may call me Faisleigh." Again, his smile didn't involve his eyes. "Are we not almost like family?"

Michael said nothing. He tried to swallow. It got stuck halfway.

"Apparently, you have some doubts as to her good intentions."

Michael coughed. "Uh, Faisleigh, I believe it possible that you and I didn't read the same contract."

"Oh, yes we did. Her attention to detail is one of the many things I adore about her. And in this contract, she detailed the diet for you to pursue, the positions and devices you will employ, and so forth. I paid a great deal of money to consult physicians in several countries about their latest research." He sighed. "A pity it's wasted on me. But at least my sweeting and I can put all that scientific knowledge to good use with you."

Michael stared at him and felt the tips of his ears glow.

"So as for her intentions, I shall have you know that she spent numerous hours yesterday and today writing letters on your behalf. Letters to her contacts that will secure your advancement to the captaincy. I shall add my voice to them on the morrow.

"She and I are in complete agreement. You've saved the life of our son and returned him to us in good health. You need do nothing more to secure our funding for the captaincy. At the rate at which I shall push this through, you may expect the advancement this summer or early fall. Congratulations, Mr. Stoddard. And thank you again."

"Y-You're welcome. Are you saying you aren't holding me to the terms of the contract for this rank advancement?"

"That's correct." Faisleigh stretched an arm closer to Michael across the back of the couch and crossed his legs. "The contract applies should you wish to advance to the rank of major. And Mr. Stoddard, my guess is that you'll need to advance to the rank of major, at least. In addition, you'll need to petition the Crown to reinstate your barony. With your service record, I don't imagine it would be difficult at all." His teeth flashed once in the candlelight. "We can help you with that, too. You're a special project for us."

Michael said nothing, but the dull anger he'd felt earlier returned. Faisleigh was a pompous ass, presuming to know what he wanted of life when he himself wasn't sure. But he kept the anger from bleeding into his expression. He was grateful for the captaincy, especially since it didn't require his coupling with Lydia.

The Earl chuckled. "I know exactly what you're thinking. How can I possibly know what you'll need? Well, Mr. Stoddard, in my fifty-one years, I've dealt with a good number of military men. You, sir, aren't a military man. You're a thinker and an idealist. Oh, you're doing a splendid job fitting in with the Eighty-Second, but I wager that you give yourself away every time you're successful at a criminal investigation."

Michael's inner agitation increased. How would Faisleigh know? The two of them had only just met five minutes earlier.

"And why is that so? Because you cannot solve crimes by following a standard procedure." Faisleigh leaned forward. "Well, can you?"

"No, not really." Michael resisted the urge to glance down and make sure he was still wearing his clothing. How did this man know him so well?

Faisleigh sank back against the couch. "There you have it, then. I've an idea where you're going. As I mentioned, you'll definitely need a senior officer rank and a title to get there. Oh, yes, and you'd better start thinking about a wife. I presume you know the sort of woman whose background the nobility will find acceptable? Essentially, Mr. Stoddard, it comes down to this. I have something you need, and you have something I need."

The Earl shifted his gaze to the fireplace. "I'm not at all enamored of this town and am eager to seek the civilities of Charles Town. I hear that Lord Cornwallis may be arriving in a few days. It behooves me to linger a week and greet his lordship. Should you wish to pursue this arrangement, bring the signed contract to the back door at nine o'clock any night through next Tuesday." He returned his pitch-black stare to Michael. "You will, of course, employ the utmost discretion. With a signed contract, I shall then remain in Wilmington however long it takes." His teeth showed again. "Any questions?"

"No."

"Splendid. I believe we're finished for tonight. Let me show you out."

Chapter Thirty

MICHAEL SLEPT LITTLE Wednesday night for pondering the utter ruth-lessness of his new benefactors. Lydia, no pawn, was an equal and willing partner in the scheme with her husband.

At dawn the next morning, April sixth, Michael received word that Nigel de Manning had died. The news shocked him. He'd expected the tutor to rally.

A stream of business traffic from the Anglican priest and cabinetmaker be-gan at the house five doors down. Michael's shock converted to anger.

He toyed with the idea of inviting Ames and Lydia's other men to accom-pany him to jail and letting them have at Travis for about fifteen minutes, perhaps giving Dorinda and her embroidery scissors the first minute of that quarter hour. But after stewing briefly over how Lydia had ruined the tutor's life, he realized that he was angry with de Manning. No de Manning meant no buffer against Lydia and her husband, against Lord Wynndon, against the de-mands of the world that he make something of himself for which he'd neither planned nor desired.

But railing against a corpse was futile, absurd, so he queried among the men of the Eighty-Second, found a piper to play at the churchyard Friday morn-ing, when de Manning would venture into eternity with full military honors. It seemed fitting that the piper was a MacNeill: like the MacKenzies, a clan that had found itself on the wrong end of the King's bayonets at Culloden Moor.

In the street before Mrs. Chiswell's house, crates and trunks of the lady's belongings were added to a wagon already holding Quill's property. Echoes resounded through the house, despite the fact that Mrs. Chiswell was leaving all her large furniture pieces behind, to be sold with the dwelling.

Mid-morning, Spry escaped the dismal atmosphere by joining the camara-derie of his mates like Wigglesworth in the barracks. At three o'clock, Michael visited White's, which was busier than he'd ever seen it, and ordered a glass of claret and a bowl of soup. The wench who served him was far too rushed to flirt. When he queried her about Mrs. Duncan, she said something about the kitchen and Cook. Neither Kate nor Aunt Rachel made an appearance, although Kevin waved at him once from across the common room.

At eight thirty, he trudged upstairs in Mrs. Chiswell's house for his final night in a bed for awhile. The candle he'd carried sputtered out at the top of the stairs. No matter. He knew where to find the tinderbox in his bedroom.

But as soon as he shut himself into the room, the stink of garlic and brandy told him he wasn't alone. He tensed, his back to the door, and slid the candle to the desk. His hand went for his dagger.

The bed creaked. From it, a man's voice said, low, "Ah, Michel, at last. *S'il vous plaît*, do not draw your dagger. I would rather not have to kill you."

Michael stared across the room at his bed, pulse hammering, and let out a slow breath. In the darkness, a huge, body-sized mass of deep shadow was sprawled there. The curtains of his window billowed. Damnation. He must have forgotten to lock his window before leaving for White's. "You jackal. What is it you want?" Obviously the French assassin didn't want to kill him that moment, or he'd have done so, without inviting conversation.

"Such a soft bed you have." Claude Devereaux chuckled. "I, by contrast, have recently come from the battlefield at Guilford Courthouse and have been sleeping on the ground. But I have information that you will find of interest."

Michael slid his hand off his dagger. The hammer of his pulse eased. "Go ahead."

"We have a mutual enemy. Last summer, he killed *mon ami* Jacques le Couevre in Havana."

"Lieutenant Fairfax."

"*Oui*. I fell in with one of Greene's militia units for the sole purpose of finding a moment in battle to kill that English pig. The moment arrived. But my rifle shot found his horse instead."

Breath hissed from Michael. "Rot Fairfax's luck!"

"Luck indeed, Michel. The pig was knocked unconscious and his leg was broken when the horse rolled upon him."

Michael swore. His instincts and those of Helen Chiswell had been correct. Fairfax was still alive. The lady was leaving town just in time.

"Much later, I returned to his dead horse on the battlefield. My rifle shot had not been the only one to find the horse."

And Adam Neville thought he'd killed Fairfax. Bah. "Does that surprise you, Claude?"

"*Non*. This pig has enough enemies to fill a battlefield." The bed creaked again. The assassin's body coiled into a sitting position. "I have tracked Lord Cornwallis, as have many men who fought beneath Greene. We have been shooting English pigs in the rear guard of the army. His lordship is coming to you, here."

"I know it."

"He will arrive no later than Monday. The abomination is coming to you, too, in the wagons of the wounded. You will have an opportunity to assassinate that animal at last, while he is weakened."

Michael finally comprehended the sense of statements from Helen Chiswell and David St. James that it would require a team to kill Fairfax. He snorted. "As he'll be under guard, it's highly unlikely that any one person will be able to assassinate him. I certainly don't intend to invite the hangman's company by slipping a dagger between Fairfax's ribs while I pay him a friendly visit."

It was the Frenchman's turn to swear. He did so in his native tongue.

"Nor will assassination be easily accomplished by one person should Fairfax recover. Fairfax is too cunning to let his guard down that way, Claude."

"You wish to create a team. Is that so?"

"Oh, I understand that most assassins don't work in teams, but perhaps you might transcend your solitary nature for awhile to achieve a goal that men acting alone cannot achieve. A broken leg may keep Fairfax here in Wilmington for awhile." Not a thought that Michael enjoyed, but a distinct possibility. "Thus a team wouldn't need to hunt him down."

After several seconds of silence, Claude expelled a slow breath. "You have this team created, *Monsieur*?"

Michael smiled in the darkness at the pique of interest in the assassin's voice and the realization that if he played the game of piquet well, his hands would never get dirty. "I have prospects. But of course, my ability to travel is limited. I'm unable to personally recruit everyone and pull the team together."

"Where do I find these prospects?"

Michael rubbed his jaw. "Well, let's see. There's your dear, dead friend Jacques le Couevre's half-breed Creek nephew, Mathias Hale. He resents Fairfax for killing his uncle as well as torturing a Spaniard to death last summer in Georgia and blaming the Creek. The trick will be to find Mr. Hale. He's hiding with the Cherokee in western South Carolina and doesn't want to be found."

"I will find *Monsieur* Hale. And perhaps some of the Creek. Who else?"

"At Guilford, another of those rifle shots in Fairfax's horse came from a double spy, a ranger named Adam Neville."

"I know of Lieutenant Neville. He is a Catawba scout. I will find him, too." Claude stood, a hulk of blackness in the bedroom. "Then you and I will talk again."

Michael's heart gave a little kick. His back grazed the door. "Jolly good of you."

"You interest me, Michel. You improvise your lines in the play and do not read straight from the script. Perhaps I will kiss both your cheeks someday."

His nose twitching with revulsion, Michael plastered his back to the door. The last thing he wanted was a Frenchman's gratitude in such a form.

In a whisper of sound, Claude transported himself to the window. "But tonight, do not try to follow me." He pawed aside a curtain, swung a leg over the sill, and vanished from the bedroom.

Michael rushed forward and peered out. In his peripheral vision, he saw the dark shape of the assassin on the ground. In the next second, like a cat, Claude was gone.

★★★

Michael secured his window closed, then bustled straight to the barracks, pulled Spry aside, and informed him of Claude's visit. When they returned to the house, he also updated Mrs. Chiswell that Fairfax had only been wounded at Guilford Courthouse and was likely less than two days from Wilmington.

At dawn Friday morning, on the front step of her locked house, Mrs. Chiswell pressed the key to the padlock into Michael's hand, trusting him to deliver it to the representative of her land agent as soon as the fellow's office opened for business that day. Her northbound ship weighed anchor in two hours. Servants would need time to transfer her belongings and those of Quill to the ship from the shallow-draft vessel that awaited them at the wharf. Quill assisted her into the carriage with Enid, accepted the step from Michael, signaled his driver, and shut the door. The carriage rolled toward Market Street, followed by the loaded wagon.

Spry watched the vehicles turn the corner toward the wharf, then shouldered his pack and Michael's. Their trunks had been transferred to the barracks the previous day. "Luck to her and Mr. Quill, sir. They need a dose of happiness in their lives."

Mr. Quill and Mrs. Chiswell weren't the only ones who could use a dose of happiness. The highlight of Michael and Spry's day would be de Manning's funeral amidst the wail of bagpipes. Huzzah.

Early afternoon on the next day, Saturday the eighth, the train of Cornwallis's many wagons of wounded and dying soldiers trickled into Wilmington from the northwest road. Men of the Eighty-Second blockaded civilian traffic from Market Street so they could better direct the wagons southeast of town, into the area defined and protected by the earthworks Major Craig had ordered constructed. There, Cornwallis's army and civilian followers would establish their camp and set up an infirmary for wounded men of rank and file as well as a number of wounded officers.

The wagons came attended by dragoons and mounted infantrymen from different units. The Eighty-Second cheered them, bringing smiles to the grimy, gaunt faces of men who'd been in the saddle too long, soldiers who stank almost as bad as the sick and gangrenous men they guarded. What shocked Michael was the ragged, bleached-out appearance of Cornwallis's soldiers. Every coat he saw had been patched at least once. Some men wore tatters of uniform coats, their shirts and waistcoats visible through rotted seams. Especially in contrast to uniforms of the Eighty-Second, the proud scarlet of Cornwallis's army had faded to a ubiquitous orange.

The Eighty-Second's stores contained medicine and food to shore up, even rejuvenate, the Earl's army, and red wool aplenty to re-clothe them. But all the orange pallor that day in the streets of Wilmington resounded as a metaphor in Michael's soul. Premonition ghosted through him.

The remainder of the army arrived the next day, including many of the British Legion, provincial cavalry. The right hand of their commander, Lieutenant Colonel Tarleton, was bandaged. Nevertheless, Tarleton rode in his saddle in such a way as to make the black swan feathers of his headgear dance in the sunlight.

Lord Cornwallis sat straight-backed in his saddle and wore a smile of victory as well as a spotless uniform. Every inch of him radiated confidence. Residents of Wilmington and soldiers of the Eighty-Second welcomed him with huzzahs and waved hands.

But even on Lord Cornwallis, the King's scarlet looked exhausted.

***

By late morning on Monday, supplies once destined for the depot in Cross Creek had been wrangled over and portioned out, and company quartermasters were circling the Eighty-Second's own stores. Cornwallis billeted himself in a large house off Market Street owned by a prosperous merchant named Burgwin. Those injured officers with the most seniority or money were shuffled around civilians' homes. Local business owners, aware that they had a captive audience, descended on the officers and pitched products and services under the guise of a hearty welcome.

Alice Farrell and the Wilmington ladies postponed the guest of honor social they'd planned, waiting on Major Craig's return. Michael hoped they'd never reschedule the event. He discovered he was sharing his corner of the barracks with a rosy-cheeked ensign named Chirpwell from Dover who had a heavily bandaged left arm. "Grapeshot, sir. They wanted to take my arm, but I held still with no laudanum while they dug out all the pieces and stitched me up. Fifty-eight stitches the surgeon put in me, yet the infection is clearing. My mother will faint when she sees the scars. How did you injure your left hand?"

"I beat up a cactus," said Michael. Unable to bear another minute of Ensign Chirpy, he left the barracks.

At White's, every seat in the tavern was taken. Men from Cornwallis's army clustered between tables, in the paths of serving wenches. He could barely hear two fiddlers over the conversation and laughter. There was no sign of Kate. Her brother and aunt were also absent from the common room. He left the tavern.

Around three that afternoon, he learned that Lieutenant Fairfax was lodged in Helen Chiswell's house, along with several other officers. Time for a visit. He rescued Spry from an assignment to deliver shovels to Cornwallis's camp, knowing full well that they'd put his assistant to work digging latrines as soon as he presented the shovels. The two men headed for Second Street.

On their approach to Mrs. Chiswell's house, Michael could see two soldiers of the Thirty-Third Regiment of Foot standing guard outside the front of the house, and he spotted several more throughout the back yard. The infantrymen on the porch saluted during his approach. Michael returned the salute and walked up the steps. He addressed one of the privates, again keeping his voice low. "I understand that Lieutenant Fairfax of the Seventeenth Light is lodged here with a broken leg. I'm here for a visit."

"Yes, sir. Your name?"

"Stoddard. He and I served together on a past campaign. No doubt he will appreciate the call from a familiar face."

"No doubt, sir. Incidentally, his rank is now captain."

Michael's heart stammered a few beats. His glance at Spry showed him the momentary bulge of his assistant's eyes. Fairfax had been promoted to captain. His nemesis now outranked him. Damnation.

"And they've put him in the parlor so he didn't have to be carried upstairs. Surgeon left an hour ago." The private leaned toward Michael and muttered, "The break was a bad one. Been some talk of taking his leg."

Michael couldn't help but gape. Behind him, he heard Spry's exhalation.

"Yes. Sorry for that bit of news, sir. He's been refusing laudanum, too. He could use some cheering from an old friend." The private opened the door, gestured for Michael and Spry to enter, and said inside, "Stewart. Mr. Stoddard of the Eighty-Second is here to see his friend, Mr. Fairfax."

Stewart, another private, poked his head from the parlor through a half-opened door and saluted. "Mr. Stoddard, you say? Let me make sure he's up for a visit." He disappeared into the parlor.

Michael slid his gaze to Spry. His assistant had smashed his lips together to discipline a grin from popping through. Michael did the same. Until that moment, he hadn't considered the possibility of Fairfax having his leg amputated. *That* would stop him from ever mounting a horse again. If he survived.

Stewart reappeared in the doorway, his cheeks dimpled. "First time I've seen him smile in days, when I mentioned your name just now. Come in, come in."

Of course Fairfax would find humor in such a meeting. The arrogant cur thought himself at a complete advantage because of his promotion to the captaincy. Well, he wasn't the only officer receiving such a promotion, and Wilmington was Michael Stoddard's territory. He followed Stewart into the parlor, Spry a few steps behind.

The couch had been shoved close to the fireplace to grant a straw tick possession of the room's midsection. With his upper body propped by pillows, Fairfax sprawled upon the tick in his shirt like an indolent feudal lord, a blanket covering his muscular body from the chest down, his russet-colored hair freed of its military queue, his complexion almost cadaverous. Another set of pillows supported his left leg, splinted and bandaged.

The pale, green hoarfrost of his eyes leapt out and buffeted Michael like a blast from the arctic. His teeth flashed, followed by a chuckle like the shriek of fingernails across slate. "Stoddard! And Spry, too—what a pleasure to have your company." At attention, Spry saluted and received a flick of the dragoon's hand as acknowledgement. Michael gave his nemesis a quick bow of the head and had it returned with just as little flourish. "Sit if you like." Fairfax gestured to chairs wedged against the wall near the door, then jerked his head aside. "Stewart, leave us and shut the door."

"Yes, sir." The infantryman's response vibrated with relief that someone had made Mr. Fairfax cheerful.

Michael remained standing and heard the click of the closed door behind him. Misgiving twinged his soul, although he wasn't sure why. Except for the issue of rank, he possessed almost every advantage in the meeting. Didn't he?

Best he jumped on those advantages. "In February, I relayed a message to you from Major Craig, to be delivered to Lord Cornwallis."

"So you did. And I relayed your message to an infantry officer who was headed directly back to his lordship. Then I continued my reconnaissance. Unknown to me, the infantry officer was killed before he arrived in camp. The first time I realized that the message hadn't been delivered was when I awakened, jolted around in the wagons of the wounded, in a haze of laudanum, and was informed that the army was headed to Cross Creek."

Michael released a sigh of exasperation. Alas, that sort of thing happened far too often.

"However, I cannot complain of my accommodations in *this* house." Fairfax crossed his arms over his abdomen, braced an elbow on a wrist, and tapped fingers on his cheek. "In November, I had supper in the dining room. I searched for evidence in the study and upstairs. And I disassembled the entire Committee of Safety in this parlor."

He bored his stare into Michael. "Despite the encumbrance of a broken leg, I've managed to search the parlor for evidence of espionage today. Soon enough, I shall have the remainder of the house searched. Where is she, Stoddard?"

Too late to wonder whether Mrs. Chiswell had left anything behind that Fairfax might consider incriminatory. "Some place where you'll never find her."

"Boston." Michael said nothing. "And you abetted her escape. Sounds as though you fancy her."

"Sounds as though *you* fancy her—even while trying to kill her."

"She told you I tried to kill her?"

"You made her witness your sport at the Cowpens, and then she escaped what you'd planned for her." Michael clenched his fists briefly. "Everything that comes out of your mouth is dung, Fairfax. Like that story that she was a spy. I examined her correspondences several times. I saw no sign of espionage. Dung."

"I wonder what happened to that book of hers. She wrote a journal while she followed the Legion. She expected to have it published. You don't think any loyalist would publish a story about the Battle of the Cowpens, do you?" Fairfax cocked an eyebrow at him. "If I'd been Helen Chiswell, I'd have found a way to get that journal to Will St. James."

So that's what had been in the package Mrs. Chiswell had transferred to David St. James. Not a decade of letters to Eros. Michael sighed again and spread his hands. "Even if such a thing happens, don't imagine it'll be the only account published of the battle. You're a fool to chase phantasms like that."

Fairfax lounged back on his pillows and swept his scrutiny between Michael and Spry, his upper lip curling. Color dusted his cheeks: not the flame of fever, but a faint pink. The fingers of one hand trailed over a short stack of papers at his side. "You're fond of the rustics in this little town, aren't you, Stoddard? I admit that I'm intrigued by a blonde who visited half an hour ago. Owner of White's Tavern. First glass of wine is on the house for all officers injured at Guilford Courthouse." Fairfax leered. "What has she given *you* for free?"

Darkness coagulated in Michael's blood. Kate. Fairfax. Kate and Fairfax. No. Surely he was mistaken about that. He released a clenched jaw, knowing that Fairfax saw him do so. "You leave the rustics in this little town alone. And you ride out of this little town with Lord Cornwallis's army."

"I don't think so. I've broken my lower leg, and I'll be damned if I'll let the surgeon cut it off. I shall be recuperating in Wilmington awhile, Stoddard. And apparently, I've arrived just in time." He lifted the top sheet of paper and glanced at it. "Who is the Reverend Paul Greene?"

"He's a local rebel leader. And you don't need to be sticking your nose into such business."

"Well, he's quite a troublemaker, according to this report." He lowered the paper to the stack. "You've been here more than two months without rounding him up. Apparently I must show you how it's done."

"Go rot. There's room for only one criminal investigator in Wilmington—"

"You're so right." Fairfax shifted the blister of his glare to Spry. "And he doesn't need an assistant." He lolled his head back in the nest of pillows and laughed. "Ye gods, I'm so grateful you two visited. My leg doesn't hurt nearly as much as it did this morning."

He jerked his head upright to glare at Michael again. "Incidentally, I've been promoted." The color in his cheeks was vibrant, healthy. His eyes glowed like auroras. "I now outrank you. The next time you stop by and visit, Captain Fairfax will be in uniform."

And he'd expect more earnestness in Michael's greeting. The savage hammer of blood in Michael's ears urged him to throw himself forward and bury six inches of metal dagger in Fairfax's throat. Worth the noose, Fairfax's surprised expression as his lifeblood leaked all over the straw tick.

Fairfax grinned, as if hearing his thoughts. Michael's blood vessels nearly burst with the effort to halt the impulse. He corralled his breathing and made his voice quiet. "My promotion to the captaincy will come through in the summer. Check."

Fairfax's eyes widened. "What a surprise. Here I thought your pockets were empty. Well, then, congratulations." He leered again. "It sounds as though your captaincy will come through about the same time as my promotion to major. Checkmate." He sat straight and leaned forward with only a small flinch of pain. "Do you know why that will be checkmate, Stoddard? Because commoners almost never make it to the ranks of senior officers." Palms cradling the back of his head, he sank onto his pillows and studied the ceiling. "You may go now. Be a good fellow and have Stewart fetch me more tea."

When Michael reached the parlor doors, he plastered on a fake smile. In the foyer, he thanked Stewart and wished him a good evening without mentioning tea. On the porch, he wished the two infantrymen a good evening also. Only after he'd walked three houses away toward Market Street did he drop the smile.

At his side, Spry said, "I think we gave him a reason to keep his leg, sir."

Michael growled.

"If I'd been in your shoes, sir, I wouldn't have been able to restrain myself from pounding the snot out of him when he talked about Mrs. Duncan that way."

Michael growled again.

"How are we going to perform investigations with him here in Wilmington, sir? He'll constantly try to undercut us."

Michael had no answer, not even a growl. How the hell could Fairfax, confined to bed with a broken leg, have moved in on Michael's job in only two days? Had he moved in on Kate as well? Damn that son of a dog!

"I must admit that was a good bluff about the captaincy, sir."

"It wasn't a bluff. My promotion will be coming through in the summer or fall."

"What, now? Congratulations, sir! Although I wish there were a way you could advance to major, even if it meant you and I couldn't work together anymore. I think you deserve it."

Of course, there was a way for Michael to advance to major. He asked himself how much he deserved that promotion, and whether it was worth the trouble.

Spry headed for the barracks. Michael walked to White's, hoping to find Kate. The futility of his plan became apparent as soon as he rounded the corner onto Front Street in the late afternoon and spotted all the soldiers on the porch and in the street before the tavern. Nevertheless he pushed his way inside, where the din pummeled his temples.

He found an ale-spattered, sweaty Aunt Rachel distributing foamy tankards to a table of soldiers. All he could discern from her reply to his query about Kate was, "Not enough soup," and "Send her a note."

At the barracks, he retrieved stationery and writing implements from his trunk and composed a note. Should Kate's schedule permit her to meet him that night, he would be honored to have her company, and all she need do was send word to him at the barracks by eight. Michael sealed his note and sent it off with a message boy.

Ensign Chirpy tried to interest him in a game of chess. All those pawns, easily disposable. Michael declined.

The ensign left in search of a chess opponent. In his curtained-off corner of the barracks, Michael dug the three-page contract from the bottom of his trunk, read it, then hid it in his trunk. After a supper of beef stew, he returned to the barracks, lit a candle, read the contract again, and buried it in his trunk again.

Eight o'clock came and went, and there was no reply from Kate. Michael turned in for the night. Men on the other side of the canvas partition snored and mumbled and coughed in their sleep. The cot beneath Michael grew more rigid with each passing minute, creaking every time he shifted in search of comfort. His mind wouldn't let him rest.

He'd found Alexander Rouse and questioned him about the location of William Jones. Rouse denied knowing where to find Jones and opined that he'd fled the area after learning the fate of Captain Love. True, no one had seen Devil Bill since Love's execution. Perhaps he'd been scared off or cowed into submission. That would satisfy most commanders. But unless Michael managed to flush Jones from hiding in the next week or so, he anticipated a prickly meeting with Major Craig upon his return.

Why hadn't Kate responded to his message? Was she too busy, or had she allowed Fairfax to fascinate her? Kate had plenty of experience handling the louts who came through her tavern. But Fairfax knew how to charm and seduce. *Turned her head a time or two for ne'er-do-wells*, Enid had said of her. Angrily, Michael squirmed onto his other side.

Nick Spry was the son of a pirate. Christ Jesus! If Michael planned to retain his help in criminal investigation, it was imperative that he figure out how to cover himself. Especially with Fairfax in town.

Night ground on. A guard shift changed. Soldiers shuffled in and out of the barracks.

Had Kate and her brother terminated their whiskey business? Michael had given them fair warning. He shouldn't still be worried about them. But he was. Damn it all, why couldn't he stop hankering after Kate?

In memory, he kept hearing Helen Chiswell's words: *Fairfax will back you into a corner and force you to make decisions you may regret. He knows whether to offer a carrot or a stick. You'll do his bidding.*

When the first distant rooster announced the coming dawn, Michael rolled to a sitting position, feet on the floor. Given the reclusive nature of Mathias Hale and Adam Neville, he was certain that Claude Devereaux couldn't possibly return to Wilmington with his posse in less than three months. More likely it would be autumn before he heard from the assassin again. Fairfax, with his broken leg, would be in town for far too long for Michael, and Wilmington, to endure him, especially when he was circling the criminal investigator job that Michael had worked hard to cultivate.

He at last understood that he'd gone into his meeting with his nemesis the day before without any of the advantages he'd thought he possessed. There was only one kind of power that Fairfax respected, only one language he spoke. The language of senior military officers, and nobility, and their schemes.

Elbows on his knees, Michael hung his head, forehead braced in his palms. It was Tuesday the eleventh of April. He'd decided his course.

But not without a soft groan over the forfeit of another chunk of his soul.

***

The back door creaked open. Shadow from candlelight made pools of blackness out of Faisleigh's eye sockets. He smiled and murmured, "How good of you to stop by. Have you the contract?"

Michael slid it from his waistcoat and handed it to the older man. Faisleigh set down the candle on a table beside the door, unfolded the papers, and shuffled them until he found Michael's signature. He again smiled at Michael and shoved the folded contract inside his own waistcoat. He pitched softness into his voice. "Splendid. I shall make certain we get you a signed copy before you leave tonight. On the morrow, we shall discuss the process for reinstatement of your barony. But do come in now, and close the door behind you." After Michael had done so, Faisleigh picked up the candle, signaled for quiet, and gestured him to follow.

On the second floor, Faisleigh proceeded to one of the closed bedroom doors. An adjoining small table on which he set the candle held a book. There was a chair beside the table. He opened the door, waved Michael inside, then followed him and shut them in.

Her back to the door, Lydia, dressed only in her shift, sat at a desk writing, her golden hair a curly cascade down her back. She glanced over her shoulder, gasped at the sight of Michael, and righted the inkbottle before it tipped over. Then she rose in a blur of white lace and radiant smile and rushed past Michael to hug her husband, as if he'd just presented her with a yearling from the King's own stables.

Michael backed from them toward the desk a few steps. His gaze darted about in search of devices with Arabic and Indian names, but he saw none of them. He wasn't sure whether he felt disappointed or relieved by that.

Meanwhile, Faisleigh disentangled himself, tweaked Lydia's nose, and patted her bottom. He pivoted to Michael with a lewd grin and a voice just above a whisper, and he reached behind him for the door handle. "I shall be right outside." After stepping out of the bedroom, he waved the book at Michael and closed the door.

At least Faisleigh hadn't planned to join them.

Lydia's top teeth caught her lower lip. She padded to him, slid her arms loosely around his neck, and swept her tongue over her lower lip. "You weren't going to sign that contract. I know it. So what was it that made you change your mind?"

He said nothing. He strolled his gaze over her throat, shoulders, and breasts and opened the door he'd kept closed for a decade.

"Oh, I don't suppose it really matters." She dragged her nails down the front of his coat and worked at the top button, fingers in a hurry to command him. She'd always insisted on undressing him. "I'm far more curious to see how much you've learned in eleven years."

His gaze pinned hers. He seized her hands and marked the momentary widening of her eyes, the resistance in her arms, the upward tilt of her chin at being challenged. Then he brought one of her wrists to his lips and traced his lips across her palm to her fingers.

Her pupils dilated. Her shoulders relaxed. "Oh." Her breath grew choppy. "Oh, my. Yes."

Finis

Historical Afterword

HISTORY TEXTS AND fiction minimize the importance of the Southern colonies during the American War of Independence. Many scholars now believe that more Revolutionary War battles were fought in South Carolina than in any other colony, even New York. Of the wars North Americans have fought, the death toll from this war exceeds all except the Civil War in terms of percentage of the population. And yet our "revolution" was but one conflict in a ravenous world war.

From late January to mid-November 1781, Crown forces occupied the city of Wilmington, North Carolina. The daunting presence of the Eighty-Second Regiment nearly paralyzed movements of the Continental Army in North Carolina and prolonged the war in the Southern theater. Short on resources the entire occupation, Major James Henry Craig, the regiment's commander, resorted to unconventional strategies that bordered on insubordination, won the devotion of area loyalists and many neutrals (a feat Lord Cornwallis was never able to achieve), and enhanced his garrison's effectiveness.

Almost never do we hear of Craig's accomplishments. True, history is written by the victors. But also, the Eighty-Second's triumphs were bracketed and overshadowed by disasters that same year for Crown forces at Cowpens, South Carolina in January and Yorktown, Virginia in October. Had more British commanders adopted Craig's creative, fluid style of thinking, the outcome of the war might have been vastly different. An intriguing cerebral exercise for historians and those who write alternative history fiction.

Craig had been ordered to strategize fortification of a supply depot in Cross Creek (now Fayetteville, North Carolina), to assist the military initiatives of Lord Cornwallis in the backcountry. Early on, Craig realized the vulnerability of a supply train to Cross Creek, and thus the unsuitability of using the location as originally planned. Fearing that Cornwallis would enact a strategy that depended on replenishing his army's supplies in Cross Creek, Craig sent three messengers to the general to warn him about lack of supplies in Cross Creek. None of the messages reached Cornwallis. Suffering severe losses amidst his "victory" at the Battle of Guilford Courthouse 15 March 1781, Cornwallis's army limped on to Cross Creek, expecting supplies. Instead, the army was forced to march several days more to the only safe haven in North Carolina: Wilmington, and the Eighty-Second.

When Cornwallis arrived in Wilmington early during the second week of April 1781, Craig wasn't there to greet him. More than two weeks earlier, Craig had ridden north with a large party of dragoons and infantrymen on a multi-pronged mission. An informant passed along the location of Cornelius Harnett's hiding place. Harnett had been a member of the Continental Congress, the local Sons of Liberty, and the Council of Safety. Thus Crown forces considered him quite a prize to capture. Also, Craig realized that a visit from Cornwallis's army was likely, and he knew Wilmington's stores would never feed a second army, so he planned to supervise the drive of a herd of cattle back to Wilmington.

Harnett was captured, transported roughly back to Wilmington, and imprisoned in an outdoor pen. He died 28 April 1781, suffering from his treatment at the hands of the Eighty-Second as well as from smallpox. The herd of cattle arrived in Wilmington, too, and in due course, fed many a redcoat in town.

The precise date and location of "The Rouse House Massacre," also known as "The Massacre at Eight-Mile House," are unknown, but the incident occurred some time the first week of April 1781 at a tavern about eight miles northeast of Wilmington. The tavern owner, Alexander Rouse, was a patriot sympathizer, and militia captain James Love was an occasional patron. Love also partnered with William "Devil Bill" Jones in galloping their horses through Wilmington and firing weapons at people, mostly redcoats. Furthermore, Jones, Love, and a group of patriots had unsuccessfully plotted Craig's assassination. Craig therefore wanted Jones and Love dead. While he was rounding up cattle, word reached him of a gathering of patriots in Rouse's Tavern. Craig dispatched dragoons and infantrymen to Rouse's as well as to a tavern up the road owned by the Widow Collier. When Craig's men attacked, most patrons in Rouse's were in a drunken slumber and were killed inside. Captain Love fought his way out but was slain by a mulberry tree near the road. William Jones wasn't present at the incident and thus escaped. Witnesses afterward described pooled blood and spattered brains inside the tavern—and an "old woman" who huddled in the unlit fireplace with several children, all traumatized. Alexander Rouse was apparently so shocked by the incident that he relocated to Wilmington and accepted protection of the Eighty-Second.

When the Eighty-Second occupied Wilmington, William Hooper, one of North Carolina's signers of the Declaration of Independence, didn't have time to relocate his wife and family out of the area. He made the agonizing choice of leaving them behind in Wilmington so he could flee several days' travel away. During much of the Eighty-Second's occupation, Craig allowed Hooper's wife and family to live in Hooper's law office on Third Street. As for Craig's motivation for such lenient treatment, when he dealt harshly with other patriots like Cornelius Harnett, we can only speculate.

In 1781, neither Third Street nor Fourth Street in Wilmington had yet been laid out, although some buildings like that of Hooper's office existed on what eventually became Third Street. Because it can be difficult to visualize the strategic military importance of a town with so few streets, I've taken the liberty of granting "official" status upon Third Street and Fourth Street.

Colonial-era treasures in cities such as Boston and Philadelphia are well known, but few visitors to North Carolina realize that some houses and geographical features from the time of Craig's occupation remain intact in the historical district of Wilmington. A gem in the city's colonial crown is the house at Market and Third Streets. In April 1781, Lord Cornwallis headquartered there while resting his troops. The British general described it as "...the most considerable house in town." The Burgwin-Wright House has been beautifully restored and is open for tours.

Dramatis Personae

In order of appearance:

Michael Stoddard—officer of the King stationed in Wilmington, North Carolina. Lead criminal investigator for the Eighty-Second Regiment

William Jones (aka "Devil Bill")— miscreant, partner to James Love

James Love—miscreant and patriot militia officer, partner to William Jones

Alice Farrell—wife of tobacconist in Wilmington

Nick Spry—King's man, assistant investigator to Michael Stoddard

James Henry Craig—officer of the King, commander of the Eighty-Second Regiment

Helen Chiswell—owner of the house where Michael and Spry are billeted

Enid Jones—housekeeper for Helen Chiswell

Molly—laundress, wench, Spry's sweetheart

Ralph Gibson—farrier, business partner to Hiram Duke

Zeke Whistler—a lost boy

Elizabeth Duke—Hiram Duke's wife

Hiram Duke—farrier, business partner to Ralph Gibson

Clayton—British Army surgeon

Nigel de Manning—tutor to Geoffrey, Lord Wynndon in the household of Lady Faisleigh

Dorinda—lady's maid to Lady Faisleigh

Lady Faisleigh (aka Lydia)—mother to Geoffrey, Lord Wynndon

Felicia—housemaid to Lady Faisleigh

Rachel White (aka Aunt Rachel)—aunt to Kate Duncan and Kevin Marsh

Kevin Marsh—manager of White's Tavern

Kate Duncan (neé Marsh)—owner of White's Tavern

Ames—Lady Faisleigh's head coachman

Eve Whistler—scullery maid at Rouse's Tavern, mother to Zeke Whistler

Smedes—a wainwright, formerly a business partner to Harley Travis

Wigglesworth—King's man

Rowe—King's man, a dragoon

Anne Hooper—wife of William Hooper, signer of the Declaration of Independence

Adam Neville—scout, ranger, double spy

Harley Travis—coachmaker, wainwright, formerly a business partner to Smedes

Geoffrey, Lord Wynndon—the future seventeenth Earl of Faisleigh

David St. James—former lover of Helen Chiswell

Geoffrey, Lord Faisleigh—the sixteenth Earl of Faisleigh

Claude Devereaux—French assassin

Dunstan Fairfax—officer of the King, dragoon of the Seventeenth Light

Selected Bibliography

Dozens of websites, interviews with subject-matter experts, the following books and more:

Balderston, Marion and David Syrett, eds. *The Lost War: Letters from British Officers During the American Revolution.* New York: Horizon Press, 1975.

Bass, Robert D. *The Green Dragoon.* Columbia, South Carolina: Sandlapper Press, Inc., 1973.

Boatner, Mark M. III. *Encyclopedia of the American Revolution.* Mechanicsburg, Pennsylvania: Stackpole Books, 1994.

Butler, Lindley S. *North Carolina and the Coming of the Revolution, 1763–1776.* Zebulon, North Carolina: Theo. Davis Sons, Inc., 1976.

Butler, Lindley S. and Alan D. Watson, eds. *The North Carolina Experience.* Chapel Hill, North Carolina: The University of North Carolina Press, 1984.

Dunkerly, Robert M. *Redcoats on the River: Southeastern North Carolina in the Revolutionary War.* Wilmington, North Carolina: Dram Tree Books, 2008.

Gilgun, Beth. *Tidings from the Eighteenth Century.* Texarkana, Texas: Scurlock Publishing Co., Inc., 1993.

Hagist, Don N., ed. *A British Soldier's Story: Roger Lamb's Narrative of the American Revolution.* Baraboo, Wisconsin: Ballindalloch Press, 2004. ISBN1-893832-12-0

Massey, Gregory De Van. "The British Expedition to Wilmington, North Carolina, January–November 1781." Master's thesis, East Carolina

University, 1987.

Mayer, Holly A. *Belonging to the Army: Camp Followers and Community During the American Revolution*. Columbia, South Carolina: University of South Carolina Press, 1996.

McGeachy, John A. "Revolutionary Reminiscences from 'The Cape Fear Sketches.'" Essay for History 590, North Carolina State University, 2001.

Morrill, Dan L. *Southern Campaigns of the American Revolution*. Mount Pleasant, South Carolina: The Nautical & Aviation Publishing Company of America, Inc., 1993.

Peckham, Howard H. *The Toll of Independence: Engagements and Battle Casualties of the American Revolution*. Chicago: The University of Chicago Press, 1974.

Scotti, Anthony J. *Brutal Virtue: the Myth and Reality of Banastre Tarleton*. Bowie, Maryland: Heritage Books, Inc., 2002.

Schaw, Janet. *Journal of a Lady of Quality: Being the Narrative of a Journey from Scotland to the West Indies, North Carolina, and Portugal in the Years 1774 to 1776*. eds. Evangeline W. Andrews and Charles M. Andrews. New Haven: Yale University Press, 1921.

Tunis, Edwin. *Colonial Craftsmen and the Beginnings of American Industry*. Baltimore: The Johns Hopkins University Press, 1999.

Watson, Alan D. *Society in Colonial North Carolina*. Raleigh, North Carolina: North Carolina Division of Archives and History, 1996.

Watson, Alan D. *Wilmington, North Carolina, to 1861*. Jefferson, North Carolina: McFarland & Company, Inc., Publishers, 2003.

Watson, Alan D. Wilmington: *Port of North Carolina*. Columbia, South Carolina: University of South Carolina Press, 1992.

Discussion Questions for Book Clubs

1. What does author Suzanne Adair do to project an image of the Southern theater of the American Revolution in *A Hostage to Heritage*?

2. What did you learn about Revolutionary-era life that you didn't know before you read the novel?

3. What role does the historical setting play in *A Hostage to Heritage*? How does Suzanne Adair evoke a sense of place? What role does nature play?

4. In a thriller, the characters should be put in danger. What makes you worry about the fate of characters in *A Hostage to Heritage*?

5. For you, what is the most memorable scene in *A Hostage to Heritage*? Who is the most interesting character in the book? Why?

6. What is your reaction to the inclusion of real historical figures (book example: Anne Hooper) as characters in a work of fiction?

7. How would the use of modern forensics have changed the plot and outcome of *A Hostage to Heritage*?

8. Throughout history, nations and factions have used children in combat. Why do they do it? What circumstances make children consent to being involved in combat?

9. How does Michael Stoddard differ from your ideas of what redcoats were like during the Revolution? In what ways does having a redcoat as a hero challenge your beliefs or teachings? Why do you feel that way?

10. Why do you think that patriot townsfolk like Anne Hooper, wife of a Signer of the Declaration of Independence, would cooperate with redcoats during an occupation?

11. An eyewitness account of the historical "Rouse House Massacre" barely mentions the woman and children. In the fictionalization, why does Suzanne Adair personalize them?

12. How has Michael made himself vulnerable through his relationships with Kate Duncan and Nick Spry?

13. What was your reaction to the "deal" struck between Michael and Lord and Lady Faisleigh? If you'd been Michael, how would you have responded to their contract? Why?

14. Is justice served at the end of the story? Explain.

15. What do you think happens to the characters after the story ends?

Follow Michael Stoddard's journey as an investigator
in Book 4 of his exciting series

Killer Debt

A Michael Stoddard
American Revolution Mystery

by Suzanne Adair

A slain loyalist financier, a patriot synagogue, a desperate debtor. And Michael Stoddard, who was determined to see justice done.

July 1781. The American Revolution rages in North Carolina. Redcoat investigator Captain Michael Stoddard is given the high-profile, demanding job of guarding a signer of the Declaration of Independence on a diplomatic mission to Crown-occupied Wilmington. When a psychopathic fellow officer with his own agenda is assigned to investigate a financier's murder, Michael is furious. The officer's threats to impose fines on the owner of a tavern and link her brother to the financier's murder draw Michael into the case—to his own peril and that of innocent civilians. For neither killer nor victim are what they first seem.

Please turn the page to read the first chapter.

Chapter One

THE FILMY, GRAY quality of the smoke column rising to the southwest told Captain Michael Stoddard that they were too late. The residence was gutted. He and his patrol of six redcoats from the Eighty-Second Regiment could render no aid.

He'd seen far too much of arson's smudge upon the sky during his six months in North Carolina. Nevertheless, he pressed his mare toward the smoke through summer's swelter. A loyalist financier named Jasper Bellington owned the house and surrounding land. Bellington's business partner hadn't seen him since Friday, July twentieth, four days earlier. Tension knotted Michael's stomach. Had the loyalist and his three slaves perished in the inferno of his house?

Clear sky arced above the soldiers, a hot, hard awning of lapis. The road ribboned south through stands of long-leaf pines and live oaks, sand and shells sighing and crunching beneath horse hooves. Aside from the squawks of crows, the only other sounds keeping Michael and his men company were the ebb and swell of cicada-song in the brush, and the occasional dull clack of a leather-and-wood canteen lifted to the lips of a thirsty soldier.

A breeze blew the smell of sweaty horses away for a second. Michael, riding in front, got his first whiff of burned wood. He sat taller in the saddle, blinked sweat from his eyes, and spotted the entrance to Bellington's drive an eighth mile ahead. "There it is, lads. Come along." He urged his mare forward.

On the drive, trees shaded the men, and the sharp stench of charred wood blanketed them. Michael's gaze raked over the surrounding foliage for anything suspicious or dangerous. Rainwater from a thunderstorm two nights earlier had evaporated, and he spotted recent wheel ruts and hoof prints leading up the sandy track—potential evidence being obliterated by the passage of his patrol. He ordered his men off the drive, single-file behind him in the grass and low brush.

The smoking, blackened skeleton of Bellington's two-story house awaited them at the top of the drive, in a clearing ringed by singed trees. Heat oozed off the devastation. Whenever the breeze died, Michael heard the creak and shift of burned timber. Anyone trapped in the house after it was ablaze was surely dead.

Sweat dribbled from his scalp through his dark hair, down the sides of his face and into his neck stock. He removed his hat long enough to blot his forehead with a handkerchief, then signaled his men to dismount. For several seconds, everyone studied the ruin, and Michael sensed the men's apprehension over what they'd find.

Private Henshaw's voice was subdued. "Looks like the Reverend's work again, sir."

It did indeed. At the helm of a band of slippery, self-appointed dispensers of rebel "justice" was the Reverend Paul Greene, weapons smuggler and thorn in the Eighty-Second's side since January. In late May, he and his band began roaming the Cape Fear area, terrorizing the King's Friends, burning homes, and stealing slaves and other property.

Private Jackson cocked a fist on his hip. "Poor losers, every one of Greene's band."

Michael grunted and fanned away a cloud of gnats. "Desperate losers. All right, men, let's check those outbuildings and the stable over there for survivors."

With Henshaw watching the horses, Michael and the remaining soldiers fanned out, firearms loaded. By his order, the men avoided tromping through the crisscross of wheel ruts and hoof prints in the clearing. As he approached the stable, a horse from his party snorted. From the stable came a nervous whicker in response.

Michael and the two men nearest him, Ferguson and Wigglesworth, froze and studied each other. The same logic must be going through all their heads. Why would rebel arsonists leave a horse behind?

Was this some sort of trap?

Memory provided him with ghastly examples of the traps that rebels set and affirmed his caution. He motioned Ferguson and Wigglesworth forward with him and signed for the others to hold position. Heart thudding against his ribcage, he stepped to the hinge side of the right stable door and pressed his back to the outer wall. Ferguson sneaked to the hinges of the left door, with Wigglesworth just beyond him. All three held their firearms at half-cock and ready.

Michael rapped the door with his knuckles. "Hullo! Anyone in there?"

No human answered, but the horse rustled about and snorted once. "Hullo, we're from the Eighty-Second Regiment, here to help." No response. Seconds ticked by in Michael's waistcoat watch, in the creep of sweat down his back. "We're opening the door now." With the end of his fusil, he unlatched the right side of the door. It swayed ajar an inch or two with a soft squeak of hinges.

The wind shifted and blew the bitter, charred-wood stink over them, along with some ash. Wigglesworth and Ferguson fanned away the smoke, and Wigglesworth coughed. Michael motioned for Ferguson to push the door open with his musket, and the door yawned wide on its hinges. "No need to be alarmed. We're coming in now to help you." Before he could lose his nerve, Michael darted through the opening, fusil raised.

He expelled a pent-up breath and lowered his weapon. The only occupant of the stable was one nervous horse, a gelding tucked into a stall, his water pail empty. Wigglesworth entered behind him. He soothed the horse, backed him from the stall, and checked him over, then shrugged at Michael and shook his head. No sign of injury on the animal, but he looked thirsty.

From the droppings in the adjacent empty stall, another horse had been housed there as recently as a day ago. Why would rebels steal one horse and leave the other healthy beast behind?

He sent Ferguson to check the kitchen building for survivors and assigned Wigglesworth to water the gelding and ready him for transport back to Wilmington. Then he examined Bellington's two-wheeled gig. Sand clung to both wheels but crumbled off when he flicked it with a forefinger. The gig hadn't been driven in at least a day.

Was this the only vehicle to make those wheel tracks in the clearing and on the drive? Curious, Michael used the length of his booted foot to measure the distance between the gig's wheels. Outside the stable, two of his men held position across from him, awaiting his orders. "Search around the house," he called out before giving attention to the maze of wheel ruts, hoof prints, and shoe prints before him.

He walked out into the clearing, even though doing so muddled evidence. In addition to tracks from Bellington's gig, he recognized those of a four-wheeled vehicle. Not a wagon: the wheel ruts weren't thick enough. A passenger vehicle, then, perhaps a small chaise. The distance between the back wheels of the vehicle was almost a foot wider than the wheels of Bellington's gig. With a swirl of ruts, the chaise had halted before the house within the past two days. A man had exited on the left side and walked toward what had been the front door.

Michael cocked his head, gaze sweeping the trail of shoe prints up to the house. There was a round indentation in the sand to the outside of every right shoe print. Whoever Bellington's visitor had been, he walked with a slight limp in his left leg and used a cane but didn't lean heavily on it. From the length of his stride, Michael judged him of medium height, like himself.

"Mr. Stoddard—sir!" That was Jackson, at the rear of the house. The short soldier's voice quavered. "There's—there's someone inside!"

Michael's pulse kicked. He sprinted across the clearing for the back of the house. Rounding the corner, he huffed up to the soldier, who stood near a singed bench and several potted banana and citrus trees in the dirt behind the house. "Someone alive?"

"N-no, sir, it—it—" Jackson pointed into the charred timbers, his complexion greenish.

Michael faced the house. Over the stink of blistered beams, he got his first deep whiff of burned flesh. He coughed, grimaced, and swung his gaze back and forth before it probed deep into the tumble of timber and the wreck of books and furniture, into what had been the study. It lodged on the blackened, standing figure of a man.

No, not standing. The corpse was hanging—arms overhead, wrists apparently strapped together—from a beam. His shoes were flat on the burned floor. His head and crispy wig lolled forward, and to one side.

It was Bellington. Good gods. The clothing on his upper body was gone, and his chest—

Eyes bulging, Michael recoiled one step from the house. Horror and revulsion ground through him with a queasy grab at his gut. He closed his mouth on the smell, the taste, of violent death and incineration. The private staggered into the brush behind him and retched. Michael couldn't blame him.

Bellington's ribs protruded starkly, like some sort of roast. Before the house was set afire, and the man's body had burned, long slabs of flesh had been skinned off his torso. They'd since baked against his breeches. His murderer must have counted on arson obscuring how the victim had been tortured beforehand, flayed—

Flayed. His breathing shallow, Michael backed another step. Incredulous, he glared eastward, as if he could see across the Cape Fear River to Wilmington and the regiment. Outrage swelled in him and chased away his queasiness. Ye gods, this could not be so! But moments before in the clearing, he'd seen with his own eyes the evidence that a man with a left-leg limp and a cane had visited Bellington in the past day or so.

Maybe rebels hadn't murdered the financier and set his house ablaze. Maybe the true criminal was an officer and wore His Majesty's scarlet. Michael felt a sneer of determination peel his lip off his teeth. His breath hissed out, and he whispered, "Damn you, Fairfax!" It was long past time that Michael saw that devil hanged for indulging in his depravity, his *sport.*

Leaves and twigs exploded behind him with the discharge of a firearm, followed by Jackson's scream. From the front of the house, Henshaw hollered through the firearm's echoing report. With nowhere else to hide, Michael dove behind the potted orange trees, then sought better cover from the big-leafed banana trees beside them. The rotten-egg stink of black powder smoke rolled over him. Debris rained on the foliage not far away.

He could hear Jackson's ragged breathing somewhere out in the brush plus the running approach of soldiers through dead leaves. He turned his head and jutted his chin. "Stay back, men!" His own fear and hammering heartbeat hiked the pitch of his voice. "Take cover!" They fell back, around the side of the ruin.

Clearly this was an undesirable situation. Potted trees as a shield, heat from the house slowly simmering Michael's arse. Plus the color of his coat made a rebel marksman's job easy. Michael worked on calming the rabbit in his pulse and hoped his clothing wouldn't ignite. Fusil gripped in both hands, he peered between banana leaves. His gaze scoured the ground and lower trunks of trees. He spotted Jackson's musket lying on the ground.

Seconds thudded by. No more shots were fired. Where was the marksman? Where, for that matter, was Jackson? It sounded like the private had been hit. Had he lost consciousness?

"Mr. Stoddard, sir. Can you hear me?" Jackson's voice still quavered.

Michael squinted. "Yes, I can hear you, lad. Stay down. Are you hurt bad?"

"I—I think the ball skimmed my scalp, sir. Top of my head's bleeding. Hurts like the devil. A-and I think I'd be dead if I were a taller fellow."

Why hadn't the marksman fired again? Michael wasn't that difficult a target, and it sounded like Jackson wasn't, either. He stuck his hat on the end of his fusil's barrel and jiggled it to the side, beyond the banana leaves. Nobody shot at him.

Jackson's voice firmed. "While I was puking, sir, I tripped some kind of trap with a loaded pistol and a snare. Might you please help me down?"

Loaded pistol? Snare? "Help you *down*?" Fusil in hand, Michael rose, planted his hat on his head, and walked away from the potted trees and overly warm house.

From a sturdy sapling, Jackson hung upside down about five feet off the ground, one lower leg tangled in the rope of a snare. Blond hair on the top of his head was matted with blood. Nearby, a spring-gun—a lock, stock, and shortened barrel with a post—was mounted on a stump. Rope from both gun and snare lay mostly hidden in dead leaves.

The private made eye contact with Michael and wobbled out a salute. Michael propped his fist on his hip and heaved a sigh. "Ah, bloody hell."

End of Chapter One

Thank you for purchasing this book. Word-of-mouth is crucial to the success of any author. If you enjoyed the book, please post a review wherever your social media allow (Amazon, Goodreads, etc.). Even a brief review is appreciated.

Made in the USA
Columbia, SC
11 March 2022

57255095R00167